T0371001

THE HOUSE OF SEYMOUR

After an exciting career in journalism, on radio and television in England and Scotland, Joanna took to country life and writing historical fiction. Since publishing her debut novel, *The Agincourt Bride*, she has gone on to publish many more based on the rise of the Tudor dynasty, and has attracted an enthusiastic following of readers in Britain and around the world. *The House of Seymour* is her eighth novel.

Joanna lives in Wiltshire and is married with a large family and lots of grandchildren.

/joannahickson

BY THE SAME AUTHOR

The Agincourt Bride
The Tudor Bride
Red Rose, White Rose
First of the Tudors
The Tudor Crown
The Lady of the Ravens
The Queen's Lady

THE HOUSE OF SEYMOUR

JOANNA HICKSON

HarperCollins*Publishers*

HarperCollins*Publishers* Ltd
1 London Bridge Street
London SE1 9GF

www.harpercollins.co.uk

HarperCollins*Publishers*
Macken House, 39/40 Mayor Street Upper
Dublin 1, D01 C9W8, Ireland

First published by HarperCollins*Publishers* Ltd 2025
1

Detail from, and adaptation of: *Atlas of the Counties of England and Wales. Illustrator: Saxton, Christopher London, 1579 Source/Shelfmark: Maps.C.3.bb.5, 8 Map of Wiltshire. Image taken from Atlas of the Counties of England and Wales. Originally published/produced in 1579.* From the British Library archive / Bridgeman Images

Fleur-de-lys image: Shutterstock.com

A catalogue record for this book is available from the British Library.

ISBN: 978-0-00-854466-9

Set in Adobe Caslon Pro by HarperCollins*Publishers* India

Printed and bound in the UK using 100% Renewable Electricity at CPI Group (UK) Ltd

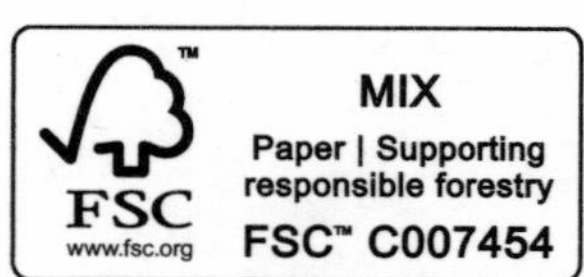

This book contains FSC™ certified paper and other controlled sources to ensure responsible forest management.

For more information visit: www.harpercollins.co.uk/green

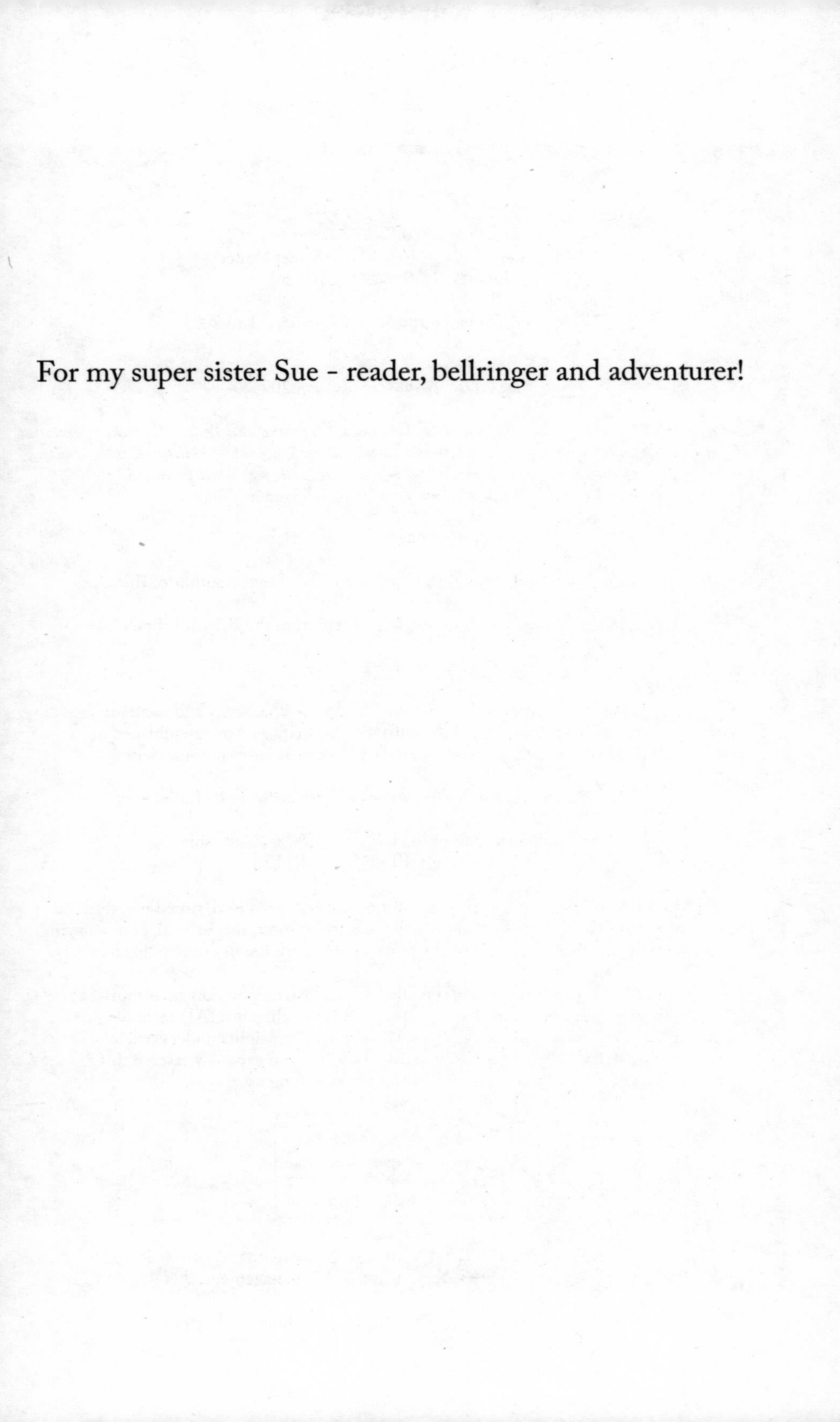

For my super sister Sue - reader, bellringer and adventurer!

Wraxhall
Slaugtenforde
West tetherton
Bromble
Whitleyhouse
Marsfelde
Coldaston
Colerne
Rowdon
Chipnhm
Stanley
Calne
Cumpton
Caterne
Coshm
Lekhm
Pewshm forest
Pinnels
Buckland
The shyre stones
Haselburye
Whethm
Calston
Dickridge
Bancaston
the Chapell of plaster
Box
Lacok
Hoddington
Spy
Atforde
Barthforde
Brumhm
Brumhm howse
Bathe
Wraxhall
Broughton Holt
Bagdon hill
Claverton
Munketon ferley
Witcomb
Chalfeld
Blakemore forest
Rowdon
the Deuyses
Combe
Stoke
Winsley
Staverton
Whaddon
Semmyngton
Luketon
Poulsall
Stert
Ashling
Stoke
Bradford
Frestforde
West wood
Helpton
Buckintn
Peterne wod
Peterne Werton
Crokwod
Henton
Iford
Trubridge
Keuyll
Steplaston
Vrcent
Farley cast
Winfeld
Maston
Estcot
Philips norton
N. Bradley
Eddington
Stok
Cheuerell magna
Cheuerell pua
Est Lauing
Wulverton
Rode
Broke
Bratton
Bayneton
Coulston
West Lauington
Lauerton
Westburye
Lullington
Beckinton
Vnder ye plaine
Salesburye
Dilton
Imber
Brackley
Costley
Vpton
Frome
Clay hill
Warmister
Norton
Hatsburye
Chilternes
Bisshop strau
Sutton mag.
Kunke
Selwood forest
Long leat
Tetherington
Vpton
Cedforde
Horningeshm
Deuerell long bridge
Hill deuerell
Cortington
Fisherton dela
Badhmpton
Charterhouse
Boyton
Sherinton
The fraye
Brixton deuerell
Stokton
Bapton
Maden bradley
Munkston deuerell
Wilye
Kingston deuerell
Pertwood
Chiklat
Chicklat ridge
Kilmanton
Over tefunt
The beacon
Berwick leonard
Chilmarke
Sturton
West knahill
Hyndon
Funthill epi
Funthill gifford
Nether tefunt
Mere
Est knahill
Tilbury
Fouant
Longlaine myll
Pen
Stoure flu
Esthatche
Sutton
Gillinghm forest
Sedgehill
Swaledyfe
Stoke
Warder castle
Austie
Broder
Occidens

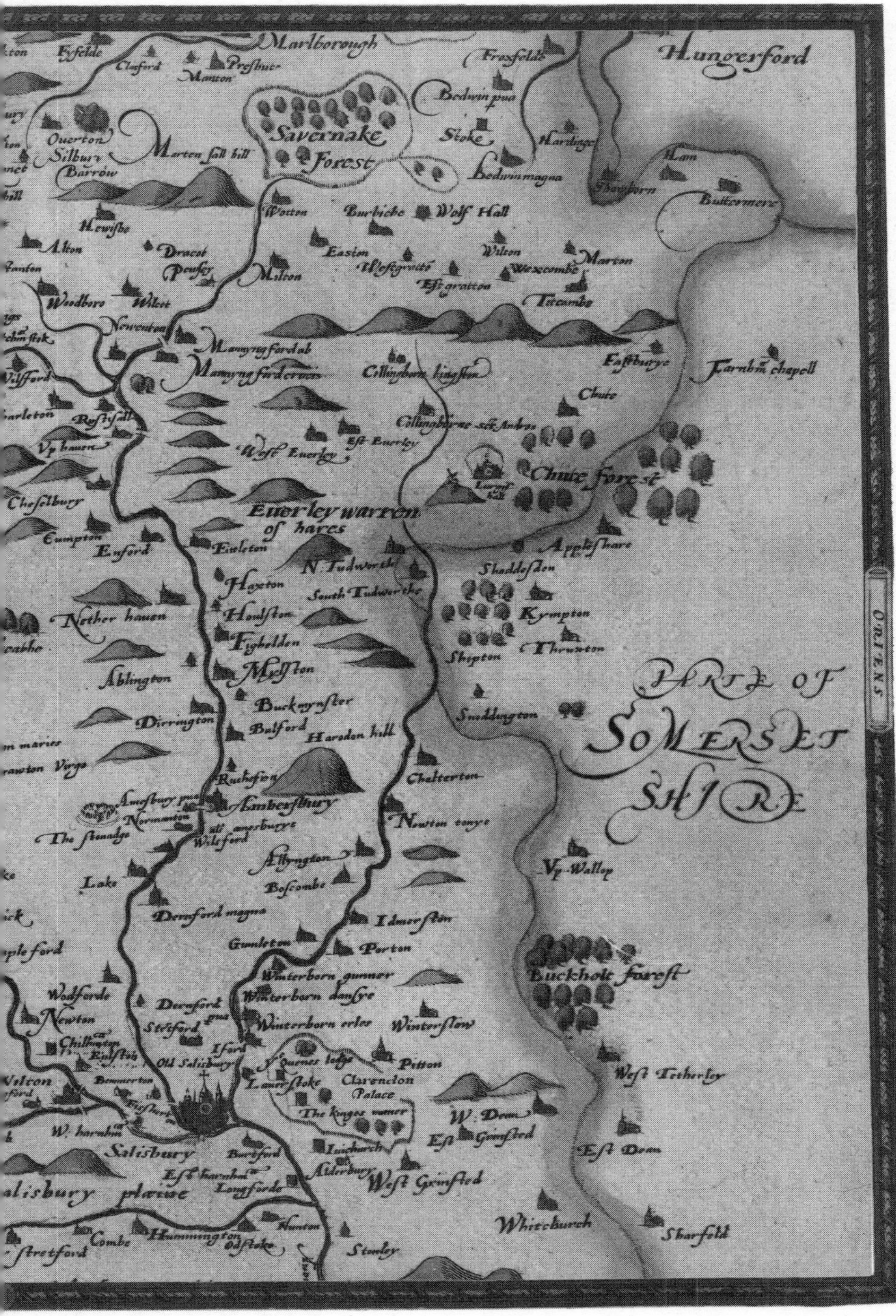

Marlborough
Hungerford
Frosfelde
Bedwin pua
Stoke
Harlinge
Bedwinmagna
Savernake Forest
Marten sall hill
Ouerton
Silbury Barrow
Clatford
Manton
Presbute
Eysfelde
Wotton
Burbiche
Wolf Hall
Easton
Wilton
Marton
Wexcombe
Titcombe
Est gratton
Hewishe
Alton
Woodboro
Wilcot
Milton
Newenton
Shalborn
Ham
Buttermere
Eastburye
Farnham chapell
Chute
Chute forest
Cillingborn kingston
Cillingborne sct Andros
West Euerley
Est Euerley
Euerley warren of hares
Chesselbury
Enford
Eisleton
N. Tudworthe
South Tudworthe
Applishare
Shaddesden
Kympton
Thruxton
Shipton
Haxton
Houlston
Fygholden
Nether hauen
Ablington
Buckmyster
Dirrington
Bulford
Harsden hill
Snoddington
Chelterton
Newton tonye
Amesbury
Ambersbury
Normanton
The stonadge
Wilsford
Lake
Allyngton
Boscombe
Demford magna
Idmerston
Gunleton
Porton
Winterborn gunner
Winterborn daunsye
Winterborn erles
Winterslow
Vp Wallop
Buckholt forest
ORIENS
PARTE OF SOMERSET SHIRE
Wodforde
Newton
Old Salisbury
Iford
Pitton
Clarendon Palace
The kinges maner
Laurerstoke
W. Dem
Est Grimsted
West Grimsted
West Tetherley
Est Dem
Salisbury
Burtford
Alderbury
Longforde
Salisbury plaine
W. harnham
Bemerton
Wilton
Combe
Hummington
Odstoke
Hunton
Standley
Whitchurch
Sharfold

DRAMATIS PERSONAE

Isabel Seymour – *(née Williams)*

Agnes Williams – *Isabel's mother*

Mark Williams – *Isabel's father and former Mayor of Bristol*

Robert Williams – *Isabel's younger brother*

(Sir) John Seymour – *son and heir to Sir Roger and Lady Maud Seymour*

Edmund Seymour – *John Seymour's younger cousin*

Johnnie – *baby son of Isabel and John Seymour*

Nan – *Johnnie's nurse*

Henry VI – *child king of England*

Humphrey, Duke of Gloucester – *Henry VI's Protector and younger brother of the late King Henry V (deceased)*

Eleanor Cobham – *Duke Humphrey's mistress*

Annie – *maid at Wolf Hall Manor House*

Sir William Esturmy – *(deceased) late Lord of Wolf Hall Manor and Warden of Savernake*

Maud Esturmy – *(deceased) Sir William's daughter and John Seymour's mother*

Editha – *Prioress of Easton Priory*

Jem Freeman – *Head Forester of Savernake*

Nat – *teenage poacher of Wolf Hall; later kitchen skivvy*

Col Carpenter – *his father, a Wolf Hall villein*

Matthew Henge – *farmer of Avebury, Wiltshire*

Nell – *Matthew's wife*

Jess – *Matthew and Nell's daughter, a shepherdess*

Star – *Jess's black sheepdog*

Addy (Adhelm) – *a failed apprentice and Jess's assistant*

Jankin – *a young archer*

Father Giles – *priest of the*

Church of St James in Avebury, Wiltshire

Queen Catherine – *the young king's French mother and Dowager Queen of Henry V*

Owen Tudor – *King Henry VI's minder, who later became Queen Catherine's steward and then, secretly, her husband*

Ham – *the Seymour cook*

Tobias – *called 'The Shepherd' in Avebury, who supervises the wool tithes*

Father Michael – *priest of the Church of St Mary at Easton Priory*

Magister Roger Bolingbroke – *priest, soothsayer and scholar*

PROLOGUE

Hampton Court Palace

Late September 1537

Towards the end of her pregnancy, the queen had been escorted with prayers and hymns into close confinement, accompanied by the ladies who would attend her until her precious child was born. She had chosen her favourite chamber in Hampton Court Palace, which overlooked a small courtyard leading to the main gate. To blot out the noise and bustle of the outside world, the walls and windows of the room were almost entirely hung with tapestries and curtains, but she had insisted that one window, overlooking the courtyard, should be left free of hangings so that she could see the remarkable timepiece that stood on the gatehouse arch.

It was an astronomical clock, which daily displayed all the different ways in which time could be measured and sounded by bells: the hour, the day, the month and the year, the phases of the moon and the signs of the zodiac – even the peak of high water at London Bridge. It was this last detail that caused Jane to look back on her life and to wonder, as the tides rose and receded, how her Seymour ancestors had weathered the ups and downs of their lives to bring her to her present state.

She recalled her childhood, spent tucked away with her sisters and younger brothers at Wolf Hall, the Seymours' Wiltshire manor, hidden in the midst of the Royal Forest of Savernake. From her teenage years she had been the butt of her brothers' jokes; teased for her quiet presence and her soft-spoken deference. 'Our little house mouse!' Edward, the eldest, had called her. 'The eternal spinster. No man's land.' But he had been wrong. Where Spanish Katherine had refused to follow the monarch's lead and proud Anne had broken the rules, she, Jane, had attracted a man's love with her gentle conformity and sweet smile – and that man was the eighth King Henry. What had happened since had brought fame and stature to her whole family. So now Edward was an earl and she, the timid mouse, had become Queen Jane.

Pressing the needle carefully in and out through the delicate linen she was embroidering, she felt a stirring in her belly, reassurance that the baby she carried was alive and growing. Time was moving swiftly on towards the birth, an event she contemplated with equal fear and anticipation. Fear for the child, because if it was not a boy there would be no rejoicing and the little girl would be merely another thorn in the king's side, while she herself would plummet in his estimation. But if a healthy boy were to be born he would be fêted and cherished and she would have the gratitude of the nation and the king.

Roused from this musing by an insistent knock on the chamber door, she heard an unfamiliar male voice addressing one of her ladies-in-waiting, asking for admission to enter, apparently unaware that men were not permitted into a lady's confinement.

After a brief exchange of words the door was closed and the lady-in-waiting crossed the room to the queen's side. 'The Garter King of Heralds wishes to show you the coat of arms that has been prepared for you, your grace. After the birth it is to be attached to the royal escutcheon. The king has approved an exceptional break of the rules of confinement so that you might see it.'

'Then I can make no objection,' Jane said. 'Let him come.'

When the Garter King entered the chamber he made a low bow, offering a roll of parchment tied with a tasselled gold cord. 'I bring to your majesty a new Seymour coat of arms, which, if you approve it, will be combined with the royal arms of England and France. May I have your grace's permission to reveal it for your inspection?'

Jane nodded. 'Yes, if you please; perhaps by the window where the light is best?' She handed her embroidery to one of her ladies and rose from her chair. 'I was not aware it was being prepared.'

'I think the king wished it to be a surprise, your grace,' said the Garter King, lifting his arm and releasing the cord.

The parchment unrolled in a burst of heraldic colours. As she moved forward to view it closely, Jane felt another kick from the child and smothered a smile. Perhaps she was not the only one eager to learn what family crests had carried the Seymours to their dizzy heights?

For several minutes she examined the coat of arms in silence. Six separate crests bearing a variety of images were gathered three on three within a shield.

Eventually she turned to the Garter King. 'I know the Seymour badge of course – the joined gold wings – and I recognise the king's personal symbols of lions and fleurs-de-lys, but could you please explain the other four?'

The Garter King bowed again. 'To honour your majesty and the female line in the Seymour family, his grace the king asked us to include the badges of the principal mothers of your house. The silver and blue pattern called vair represents the baronial fur of the Beauchamp family and your four-times great-grandmother

Cecelia of that honour; three red lions rampant denote Esturmy, and represent your ancestress Maud of that family, followed by the red and silver roses of the extraordinary Isabel Williams, who preserved the Seymour name so honourably through the wars of the last century. Finally, the three leopard heads of the Coker family introduce your great-grandmother, Elizabeth.'

Jane felt tears rise in her eyes and blinked them back. 'But my immediate grandmother is not included, nor my own remarkable mother; why is that?'

The Garter King blushed and cleared his throat. 'Your ancestors have been traced back four hundred years to their arrival from Normandy in support of our first great English monarch, William the Conqueror. King Henry wishes to establish that your son will have a mother who endows him with centuries of true English blood.' He continued apologetically. 'Commoners are not registered in the records of the College of Heralds, your grace.'

The queen took time to absorb this fact before responding. 'And will the Seymour coat of arms be added to the royal escutcheon if the babe is a girl?'

'I do not think the king has any doubt that your child will be a boy, your grace.'

Jane laid her hands on her very obvious belly and her response was couched in a tone of fierce determination. 'Yes, I believe the king has great faith in the Almighty. His children will grace the throne of England for many years to come.'

PART ONE

I

The City of Bristol

Shrove Tuesday 1424

'NO ONE TO CARRY it for you today, Mistress Williams?' The baker loaded the last small manchet loaf into the capacious basket the girl had handed over.

'Everyone is busy preparing for the Shrove Tuesday celebrations,' she replied with a smile. 'And it is only a short walk to our house.'

'Well, keep a tight fist on the handle. It's pancake day – the streets are full of thieves and beggars.'

'I'll do my best to avoid them, Master Baker.' She nodded and turned to make her way out of the bakery and into the busy thoroughfare.

It was approaching noon and people were pouring past the Wine Street shops, keen to get home for the pancake feasting. As she approached the City Cross a man suddenly appeared around its plinth and grabbed the handle of the girl's basket, pushing at her shoulder to try and release it. She yelled and tried to shove him off but, skinny though he was, he was also determined and abandoned her shoulder to haul on the arm that still clung determinedly to its precious load.

'Get off me!' Using both hands she jerked on the basket handle and pulled with all her strength. 'There's nothing valuable in here!' The parcels of loaves threatened to leap from their nest.

'In that case *let it go*!' He dug fingers tipped with blood from cracked and broken nails into her arm but she clung on stubbornly.

'No! I will not! You are making me bleed! Go away!'

'You heard what the lady said – get off her, you little runt!' A gloved hand proceeded to peel the filthy fingers away and twist the assailant's arm up his back. Feeling the basket free, the girl maintained her fierce grip and backed away, panting a little with shock. 'Are you all right?' her rescuer asked. 'You look rather pale. What is your name?'

She shook her head, indicating her assailant. 'I won't tell you that, not while he's still here.'

'Well, that's easily remedied.' Her champion hauled up on the hood of the would-be thief's jacket until his feet were almost off the ground, then kicked him hard in the rear end. 'Get lost, idiot! And don't try again!'

His kick sent the culprit flying and falling but he was up in an instant, yelling abuse and fleeing across the square to disappear into an alley. A ripple of applause rose from the small crowd that had witnessed the incident and the rescuer turned back to the victim, rubbing his gloved hands together with satisfaction. 'Well, that sorted him out. And how are you, mistress?'

The girl was frowning at the sleeve of her kirtle, which had been stained by the assailant's bloody fingers, but she still clung to the basket of loaves. 'I am unhurt, sir, thanks to you,' she said. 'But I could wish you had not kicked the boy so hard. He was clearly hungry and had he calmed down I might have given him a loaf from the basket.'

Her defender's brow furrowed, evidently non-plussed at not having his help applauded and not a little angry. 'Oh, forgive me for intervening, madam! Perhaps I should have let you lose the entire contents of your basket?'

She shook her head. 'No, but you might have removed one loaf and given it to him, as I would have done.'

'But then you could have accused me of theft, could you not?' His anger had barely abated but alongside his simmering temper, she was aware of his attention on her face and her figure, as his eyes appraised her, while allowing his hand to stray to the arm that held the basket. 'Will you at least tell me your name?'

She remained stubborn and backed off his grip. 'Perhaps, if you tell me yours first.' She began tidying the contents of the basket, avoiding the man's gaze.

It was his turn to shake his head. 'No, I'm not inclined to, since 'tis you who owe me favour.'

She pushed the basket up to her elbow and made a sketchy bob. 'Then good day, sir,' she said and walked away, just managing to catch his muttered response.

'Spoilt brat!'

In fact, the Williams family was not 'spoilt brat' rich, at least not in terms of silver and gold. Mark Williams preferred to put the money he earned as a merchant into buying property, mostly rented tenements and houses scattered around the city. His merchandising centred on the *Marie*, a barque which carried the sizeable flow of his cloth-exporting business across the Irish Sea to Dublin, and the *Trinity*, the ocean-going ship his father had bequeathed him and which he used primarily to import wine from Andalusia. Alongside other vintners, who mostly imported their wines from France, he had a big warehouse on the Avon dock, where his popular Sherish wine was stored in huge oak casks to mature, before being sold on in smaller barrels from his shop on the appropriately named Wine Street.

His daughter had only to pass the City Cross and the busy grain market to enter Corne Street, where her family lived. As she crossed the threshold of the handsome double-fronted house, her mother Agnes almost pounced upon her. 'Where have you been, Isabel? And what happened to your arm? Are you hurt?' She took the basket from her daughter and passed it to a hovering maid. 'Take this out to the kitchen, Maddie, and then go to the apothecary and fetch those remedies I ordered. They should be ready by now.'

Isabel shrugged off her cloak and hung it on a spare hook among other outdoor apparel, before following her mother down the passage to the hall – the large room where the family gathered and ate their meals. 'What remedies, Mother?' she demanded. 'Who is sick?'

'Your brother seems to have caught an ague. I expect it's nothing but it's wise to be careful. Now, why is there blood on your sleeve?' Agnes lifted the apparently wounded arm again.

Isabel shook her head, tossing the long strands of auburn curls that were not contained under her tight linen cap. 'It's not my blood, Ma. I think the idiot who tried to steal my basket tore a fingernail in the process.'

Agnes made a swift sign of the cross. 'Blessed Jesus! Did he hurt you?'

'Well, no – as you can see. And we still have all the manchet loaves. I had a bit of help from a passing stranger.'

'Oh! Who was he?'

Isabel rolled her eyes. 'I just told you – a stranger. And not an entirely nice one. I didn't like the way he kicked the would-be thief away.'

Her mother frowned. 'But I hope you thanked him, nonetheless?'

'Yes.' Isabel paused. 'Sort of. Anyway, how soon is dinner? I'm starving!'

'We have to wait for your father and he's meeting the Stamfords. I think we might be able finally to arrange your wedding. So you will be nice to Thomas, won't you?'

'Of course I will! I'm always nice to Tom. He can just be rather silly sometimes. Is Robert well enough to celebrate Shrove Tuesday? He and Tom are always teasing each other.'

'I don't know. Why don't you go and see how he is? He might cheer up a bit in your company.' Agnes immediately began to rearrange the table, which the servants had already laid.

'Yes, I will,' Isabel agreed. 'But I'll go and tidy up first.'

Isabel knew she was lucky to have a chamber to herself because most Bristol families had to share beds and rooms and even sleep under looms, if their parents were weavers. So she greatly appreciated the fact that her parents had managed to raise only two children, her mother having suffered injury bringing her son Robert into the world. And Isabel always understood that Robert was the most cosseted member of the family because he was the boy, who would inherit his father's business. She, two years older, was destined to make a suitably organised marriage with a childhood friend,

Thomas Stamford, the son of one of Bristol City's principal burgesses. His father owned even more property than hers and ran jewellery shops, one in the High Street and one on the famous old Bristowe bridge over the Avon River. Isabel accepted the marriage prospect willingly enough, as it meant she could continue her association with the 'Kalendaries', a group of priests and scholars who had established a library in All Saints Church at the foot of Corne Street. Hundreds of books were made available to any members of the public who had acquired the ability to read, and from an early age Isabel had discovered she had a talent for this, after taking lessons at the church, which her family attended.

Once she had washed her face and hands and taken off the stained kirtle, she donned her favourite gown of blue worsted and brushed her hair, before securing it with a circlet of white lace roses and setting out for her brother's chamber. The door was ajar and she pushed it open. 'Robert, are you awake?' she enquired softly of the shuttered room but received no reply. Crossing to the tester bed, she peered closely at the sleeping figure propped on the pillows, before laying her hand gently on his brow. The skin felt hot and dry. 'I think you need those remedies Maddie is fetching, brother,' she murmured. 'I'll hasten her up when she returns.'

Hearing voices of greeting coming from the front entrance she hurried to descend to the passage where her mother was welcoming the Stamford family. There was no opportunity to advise her mother of Robert's condition as kisses and baskets of cakes and sweetmeats were exchanged and Isabel undertook the task of dealing with the guests' outer garments. Among such old friends, there was a sense of cheerful anticipation, encouraged by the waft of roasted meat and buttery pancakes pervading the house, offering the promise of merry feasting before the solemn days of Lent laid claim to them.

'Where is Rob? Is he not joining us?' Thomas Stamford asked after kissing his intended's cheek.

Isabel's brow wrinkled. 'No, he's not well. Mother thinks it is an ague but I'm not sure, Tom. He's asleep right now and Maddie's gone to collect cures from the apothecary.'

'Oh, poor Rob. I'll go up and see him later. I've heard there is a malady spreading around the port. I hope it's not that.'

'Well, he hasn't been anywhere near the port as far as I know. Mother keeps a close eye on his whereabouts and she hasn't mentioned it.'

Thomas gave her a doubtful look. 'Is it possible to keep a close eye on a fourteen-year-old boy? From my own experience I doubt it. By the way, have you heard that our fathers have decided our wedding should take place at Easter next year?'

Isabel's eyes widened. 'No, I haven't heard that. Mother said it would be discussed today. I'm still only sixteen.'

'And I'm only seventeen, but we'd both be a year older by then. I think you'll find that it's pretty well fixed. Does that bother you? I can work on Father to change it if it does.'

'No, I'm not worried about marrying you at all, Tom.' She laid a reassuring hand on his arm and went onto tiptoe to kiss him again more eagerly. 'It's just that I'd like us to have a home of our own but I don't think they'll consider us ready for that by next year.'

'My parents assume you will come and live with us at first. There is a lot to learn about running a household, Izzy.'

'And I already know most of it. In another year I'll know it all. My mother will have seen to that and we want to have somewhere of our own, don't we?' She snatched a pastry from the platter of a passing servant and fed it to him with a giggle. 'We only need a small apartment with a fireplace and a feather bed, don't we?'

Her eyes teased him as Thomas brushed her lips with his and whispered, 'Your mother is frowning at us. When are we saying grace?'

2

Corne Street, Bristol

March 1424

MADDIE RETURNED WITH THE remedies just after grace was said and the first course of pancakes was delivered. Agnes excused herself and went to attend to her sick son, returning with a worried frown on her face.

'How is he, Mistress Williams?' young Thomas asked, reaching for his third honeyed pancake. 'May I go and see him?'

Agnes shook her head. 'Regretfully no, Tom. He has a fierce fever and it does not seem like a common ague. I think it may be a malady brought into the harbour by one of the foreign ships.'

'Oh, poor Rob! I thought there was something serious when I felt his forehead,' Isabel said.

Agnes gestured at her guests apologetically. 'I am sorry for bringing you into a house of sickness and will understand if you wish to leave.'

But the Stamfords demurred. 'You have prepared a feast for us and we have important matters to discuss about our children's future,' the head of the family declared. 'Let the celebrations continue!'

So, the union of the Stamford and Williams families was formally set for Easter the following year and Isabel and Thomas plighted their troth and exchanged the family rings produced by the two fathers. Before dark they all processed down Corne Street to church, to make confession and receive a blessing in preparation for the days of fasting ahead. Only Robert Williams remained unblessed, alone in his bed.

Two days later the priest was called to administer the last rites and Agnes, the usually steadfast and unflappable matron of the house, was in complete breakdown at her son's bedside. At the funeral, Master Stamford the jeweller asked whether the marriage between their children would still go ahead.

'Isabel is grieving bitterly now for her brother but by next year I'm sure she will be ready for a new life as Mistress Stamford,' Mark Williams assured him. However, before the end of Lent the loss of his only male heir had stirred his ambitions for his remaining child and he decided to invite one of his new wine customers to dinner.

'This man has placed a very significant order for Sherish wines,' he confided to his deeply mourning and indifferent wife. 'But more importantly, Agnes, I've discovered he is the heir to his vastly rich grandfather. Sir William Esturmy recently confirmed that the wardenship of a royal hunting forest and a substantial Wiltshire manor will go to John Seymour, whose mother is Esturmy's daughter. And, having lost his father only four years ago, while still under age, he only recently became the lord of a number of other manors in Somerset and Devon. He is truly a young man with a great future, who has already served as a Member of Parliament and is undoubtedly destined for a knighthood. His name is

John Seymour, he is only twenty-three and, most importantly, without a wife.'

Agnes lifted the lids of her constantly bloodshot eyes and heaved a sigh. 'But Isabel is promised to Thomas Stamford. They have exchanged rings and she loves him. She will not want to let him down.'

'She will when I tell her what I've just told you. Isabel is as worldly as any woman when it comes to her status.'

Agnes shook her head wearily. 'Even after seventeen years of marriage I'm not sure you understand women at all, sir, if that is how you regard them. But for that very reason I know you will not listen to me.'

Mark chose not to broach the subject of marriage to Isabel before he brought his new client to dine and was amazed to learn, when the two met, that John and Isabel were no strangers. After bowing over her hand, John looked up at his host and said, 'Your lovely daughter and I have met before, Master Williams, but in rather different circumstances, when we never actually learned each other's names. How pleasant to right that wrong in more agreeable surroundings.'

Mark's eyes widened as he turned to Isabel, seeking explanation. 'Izzy?'

'It was on Shrove Tuesday, Father, after I collected the bread. He saw off a would-be thief who tried to grab my basket. It was a kind act; I thanked him for it and we both went on our ways. No more than that. I told Mother.'

'Well, she had our son's illness on her mind and must have forgotten to tell me. But how fortuitous that you happened to come along, Master Seymour.'

'And how very sad that your son's illness proved fatal, sir.'

John Seymour made the sign of the cross. 'So recently as well. I feel honoured to be invited into your home at such a time.'

'Business cannot stop for long and we like to demonstrate to new customers the kind of dishes that go with our Spanish wines. Our cook is well acquainted with the appropriate flavours and they have become very popular in recent years. However, my wife has not yet felt able to face visitors and so Isabel volunteered to step in on this occasion.'

John Seymour made another bow in Isabel's direction. 'And I feel even more honoured as a result.'

With a faint smile she gestured towards the carefully laid table, gleaming with the family pewter, indicating the middle place set between three. 'Please make yourself comfortable, sir. Grace will be said after the wash bowl has been offered.' Taking the seat beside him, she beckoned to the servant waiting with the bowl and towel.

'I feel I should apologise for my churlishness on our last meeting,' John said as he dipped his fingers into the warm water and dried his hands. 'I was late for an important meeting. I hope there were no repercussions from your unfortunate encounter with the young scoundrel.'

'I think there were probably more for him than for me,' Isabel replied, carving a large loaf into three thick slices and using the tip of the knife to place one as a trencher in front of the visitor. 'He was so very skinny, was he not? Even starving, one might say.'

Mark Williams frowned and sought to change the subject as Maddie the maid placed a bowl of prawns and shellfish in front of the diners. 'This is one of my Spanish mother's recipes,' he said, nudging the spoon around for John to help himself. 'It uses one of our lighter wines as the basis for the sauce. There is a barrel of the wine among your purchases, Master Seymour, so you could get your cook to try it out.'

'Please feel free to call me John,' his guest urged as he spooned some of the hot food onto his trencher. 'I would like to encourage my Somerset cook to use seafood but my manors are all inland and we rely on freshwater fish for our fast days. This will be a treat for an inlander like me.'

'But you gave a Bristol street for your barrel delivery, John, so you must have property here as well, surely?'

'I do, yes, as of a few weeks ago. The tenement in the High Street was from an uncle's bequest and this week is my first opportunity to take possession. It has been a slow process because there were long-term tenants living in it and my agent only found them a replacement a few weeks ago.'

'I hope they are happily rehoused,' Isabel remarked, taking a spoonful from the bowl and passing it to her father. 'It must be sad to leave a home you have lived in for some time.'

John swallowed a mouthful and shrugged. 'It seemed preferable to leave that side of things to my agent. He had no problems to report.'

'Well, that's what agents are for, is it not?' Mark said cheerfully. 'A High Street tenement is a valuable asset. But I thought your bequest was to be from your grandfather, Sir William Esturmy?'

John cleared his throat. 'Yes, well, that broaches an unusual situation. There are two property bequests from two different sources but as yet only one of them has died. It is one of the advantages of being the eldest son among landed relatives who have produced no male heirs. English law states that the use of land and any properties on it can only be inherited by the eldest male relative, otherwise they revert to the ownership of the crown.'

Isabel made an astonished noise and quickly pressed her napkin to her mouth. Her father looked alarmed. 'Are you all right, Isabel? Here, have a drink.'

He pushed the jug of wine in her direction but she shook her head. 'I was just taken by surprise. I've never heard of that law, Master Seymour. Surely it means that women can never inherit land?'

John nodded hesitantly. 'I believe that widows of knights may inherit as long as they have underage sons but it becomes complicated if the widow outlives her sons. However, I am someone who is fortunate to benefit from two elderly knights with already married daughters.' He smiled broadly. 'And I hope you might call me John if it would please you to do so, Isabel. I very much wish us to be friends.'

Isabel's eyes dropped and her left hand rose to emphasise the betrothal ring on her finger. 'I do not think my intended husband would like that, sir, but thank you for the offer.'

John cast a glance at Mark, who blustered a little. 'They are both young yet. Nothing is final until the priest has blessed the union. Ah, here is the next course. The Spanish tend to eat small portions of different flavours, mixing the sweet with the sour and matching wines to complement each dish. That is why we deliver our wines in barrels, so that they can be tapped for small amounts while the rest remains untainted for future use.'

From then on John Seymour made conversation with his host but kept glancing away at Isabel, as if eager to engage her interest. She ate small amounts of each dish and kept the two men supplied with bread and wine but her father's remarks about her betrothal occupied her mind, especially when the visitor described the extent of his grandfather's bequest and his own intention, when it eventually came to him, to establish his main residence at the sinister-sounding Wolf Hall Manor. For a girl who had barely left the city walls, the very name raised the hairs on her neck and she cherished the fact that she had plighted her troth to a potential burgess of Bristol.

3

Henge Farm, Avebury, Wiltshire

March 1424

As spring warmed the air, sheep began to appear on the Marlborough Downs. Shepherds who had been struggling to keep their flocks fed in their folds during the cold months of winter, now hoped to let them flourish on fresh spring grass, gaining strength before giving birth to their lambs, whose fleeces would ultimately bring wealth to their owners.

The village of Avebury stood on a bend of the upper reaches of the lengthy River Kennet, where it turned east to cross the chalky Downs. It was a unique community, built among mysterious circles and avenues of giant stones, which appeared to have grown like pillars out of the ground. The subject of when, why and by whom they had been formed fiercely divided opinion. People born and living at close quarters with them tended to feel a great affection and respect for them, giving them names and believing in their ability to protect their flocks from harm. Others viewed them as just like any other feature of the landscape and incorporated the stones into their field hedges. One family had even used a giant monolith as the end wall of their farmhouse.

However, those who lived in the shadow of the village church saw themselves as Godfearers and held the stones in dread, believing them to be the work of the Devil. The sweeping plague of the previous century known as the Black Death had decimated the village population and was blamed on the evil influence of these mysterious and ominous monoliths. To celebrate the village's gradual recovery, the tithes gathered from the lucrative wool trade were being used to glorify the ancient church of St James, which had stood since before the Normans had conquered England. Long aisles had already been built on either side of the nave to make room for the newly flourishing community and work had begun on raising a tower at the west end, to be fitted with a ring of seven bells to keep the Devil at bay.

As if Satan wished to express his anger at this development, a violent storm raced in over the Downs during the ritual laying of the tower's foundation-stone. Lightning streaks illuminated the sky and some hit the earth with thunderous destruction, sending clergy and congregation racing for the church door, crying loudly for God to protect them from harm. Meanwhile rain lashed down, black clouds streamed low over the hills and sheep ran for cover, many ironically finding it in the lee of the great grey stones themselves.

One of these monoliths formed the wall of a longhouse, situated within the largest stone circle and listed in the Norman Conqueror's Domesday Book as '*Henge Farm, a property of two virgates*'. In the gloom of the storm a burly bearded man opened the farmhouse door and shouted into the maelstrom. 'Jess! Where are you? Jessie – come home!' Then he plunged out of the building waving his arms as if swimming through the almost horizontal rain and still yelling, 'Jessie, leave the sheep and come inside! The storm will soon pass and they have thick fleeces but you do not!'

After striding around the nearest stones, searching and calling behind each one, he gave up and returned, soaked and shivering, to the farmhouse. Inside, in the darkness of the closed shutters, his wife had waited anxiously, hoping to see their daughter enter with him.

'Could you not find her, Matt? She must be out there somewhere.' Pulling off his oiled coat, she went to hang it near the fire, the only source of light. 'She'll be sodden!'

Matthew leaned in as close as he dared to the flames. 'I thank the good Lord we were able to build a separate barn for the stock last year, so that they don't shelter in here as they used to. At least the house no longer reeks of wet sheep and we can keep a fire on the hearth. Jess must have herded the flock into the barn. It would be the sensible thing to do and she is sensible. But I wasn't going to walk all the way across to the causeway in order to find out. The storm will pass soon, Nell.'

His wife frowned, tipping her ear to the rattling shutters. 'It doesn't sound like it,' she muttered. 'You should never have encouraged Jess to take on the shepherding. It's too much for a girl of fifteen!'

'I didn't encourage her!' he snapped. 'As I've told you a dozen times, she wanted to do it. And she can. She's a natural shepherd. Better than most of the lads in the village.'

'Yes, that may be, but she's our only child. We should have hired a shepherd.' It was a regular marital argument and Matthew made no further comment. Nell bent to check the trivet over the fire. 'It's just as well I picked plenty of greens before the storm came,' she said. 'At least there's warm pottage to be eaten when it passes.'

Matthew turned from the fire, still shivering. 'I'd take some now,' he said.

Nell shook her head. 'No, we'll wait for Jess.'

Jess opened the wicket set in one of the Henge barn's huge double doors and quickly hauled in the pail she had left outside. In seconds it had filled with the rainwater streaming off the roof thatch. As she emptied it into the long water-trough, the sheep broke the huddle they were in and rushed to drink. Their fleeces had shed the rain which had skipped off the surface of their coats when the storm struck and she envied their thick, greasy protection. The homespun hooded tunic and canvas boots she wore herself were still saturated and her hands were shaking with the cold. She thought longingly of the fleece-lined jerkin she had left hanging from a hook by the farmhouse door and yearned for the hot pottage she knew her mother would have simmering on the hearth, fragrant with herbs and bacon.

'We'll go home soon, Star,' she promised her shaggy black sheepdog, which looked as forlorn as she felt herself. "Then we can warm up by the fire – what is it?'

Star had suddenly let out a bark and turned her gaze towards the barn door, then a loud hammering thoroughly alarmed both Jess and the sheep, which let out a chorus of bleats. With her heart beating at top speed, she found herself in two minds. Should she ignore the loud noise and shoot the big iron bolt on the main door, or take a risk and open the wicket? She wished it had a spy hole so that she could see who was there. Eventually, as the hammering continued, she shooed the sheep to the back of the barn, set Star to guard them and returned to the wicket. Taking a deep breath, she pulled it open. Filling the small doorway stood a hunched and hooded figure with a longbow slung over one shoulder.

Jess felt a rush of alarm, which quickly subsided when he brushed the hood back, revealing a youthful beardless face and a wet and weary grin. 'God bless you, mistress,' he said. 'May I take shelter?'

Jess stepped back and pulled the small door wide. It was the grin that had won her over and she returned it with a smile. 'How did you know there was anyone here?' she asked. 'The barn is usually only full of hay or sheep.'

His bow was clearly a treasured possession because the young man tucked it carefully under the header on the doorway before bending to step over the threshold himself. 'I think I was guided by angels,' he said, lowering the weapon off his shoulder and the dripping pack off his back. 'And I think I found one.'

'Hah!' Jess put her hands on her hips. 'They say the Devil comes with smiles and flattery!'

The lad sighed and leaned on his bow. 'But I'll wager he wouldn't have walked twenty miles to get here, only to be caught in the storm to end all storms.' He pulled his pack forward and sat down on it, clearly exhausted. 'Have you anything to eat? Those sheep seem to be enjoying the hay and I'm hungry enough to join them, but I don't like the look of your dog. Does he bite?'

At the far end of the barn, the flock had found the remains of the winter forage and the sheepdog was guarding them, occasionally sending the intruder a baleful glare.

'He's a she and she won't bite unless I tell her to. Her

name is Star.' Jess gestured reassuringly to the dog, which adopted a less threatening attitude. Then, turning over the empty water pail, she sat down on it beside her visitor. 'I'm afraid I haven't any food here. I'm waiting for the storm to die down before going to our farmhouse for supper. It's not far away and if you tell me your name and why you walked twenty miles to get here, I'll take you with me.'

After a pause he said, 'My name is Adhelm.' Then he raised his hand. 'And before you ask, a few hundred years ago a monk with that name was the abbot of a monastery in a place called Malmsbury, which is not too far from my home village. He travelled around a lot and preached sermons about God to ignorant heathens. Now he is my mother's favourite saint and I am her eldest son.' He gave Jess a pleading look. 'If I could, I'd change my name but I'm happy if people just call me Addy.'

She nodded. 'Addy it is, then. My name is Jessica, but I'm known as Jess.'

'And do I gather from your fleecy companions that you are a shepherdess?' He waved at the ewes and their canine guardian.

'A shepherd, yes,' she corrected him. 'A lot of men think women should not guard a flock but not my father. He's a farmer and these days sheep fleeces are the big money-makers, so he needs a shepherd and it's cheaper to have one in the family.'

'Don't you have any brothers?'

'No, nor sisters either.' She did not elaborate further. 'But that's enough about me. Why have you walked so far from home? Did they throw you out?'

Addy frowned, taken aback by her abrupt query. Then

he took a deep breath and nodded. 'Yes – more or less. My father has started running a new fulling mill on the stream that runs through our village. He wanted to make me his apprentice but on my first day I managed to badly damage the paddles. He took a staff to me in his anger and while she was salving my bruises, my mother suggested that I might do better working on the land. I've been practising archery and I really want to enlist as a soldier but she can't bear the idea. I think she just wants to separate me and my father. Her cousin farms here in Avebury. You may know him. His name is Matthew.'

4

Henge Farm

March 1424

Leaves and twigs lay scattered under the trees around the barn as Jess and Star herded the sheep outside but the sky had cleared, miraculously no trees lay felled by the storm and the last rays of sun were enough to light their way on the short walk to the causeway, which accessed the stone circle. The black dog was kept busy making sure that no ewe sneaked off to graze on the lush wet vegetation that grew along the bank of the surrounding ditch. Addy admired the way the sheepdog seemed able to read their minds and steer them back on the right path before they had taken more than a step or two out of line. When he made a move towards the ditch himself Star gave him the same treatment, warning him away with a deep insistent growl. Later he learned that the growth, newly sprung along its edge, hid a deep boggy mire, which the recent downpour had rendered more treacherous than ever.

When he had approached Avebury, at the end of his weary trek, the rain and the thick woods at the edge of the village had obscured the great stone circle and on reaching the causeway he gasped at the sudden revelation of it. The downpour had turned the upright stones almost black and the gathering dusk rendered them a fearful sight, dark and menacing as they spread away to each side, like a brigade of giants in battle formation. His bow was slung over his shoulder once more and Addy instinctively lifted his hand to check that it was there.

Although transfixed by the shadowy figures, he leapt when he heard Jess shouting, 'Addy! Can you help? Where are you?' He scanned the wide expanse of the circle in vain and it was only when Star came racing around one of the stones that he realised it formed the end of a building and along its foot one determined sheep was making a break for freedom. Dumping his pack, he raced to intercept, flinging himself over its back and wrapping his arms around its neck. There were a few moments of confusion as they fell to the ground together, before the ewe seemed suddenly to submit and lie still, upside down in his lap.

Jess was impressed. 'Oh, well done, Addy! We might make a shepherd of you yet!' She hooked her crook deftly around the sheep's neck and pulled it off him. 'I hope your bow isn't damaged.'

Addy scrambled to his feet and pulled the shaft off his shoulder, casting an anxious look down its length. With a sigh of relief he said, 'No damage, thank goodness!'

'Oh, good! Well, I'll just put this rebel back in the fold with her friends and then I'll take you to meet my parents. As you might have noticed, our farmhouse is built off the back of this stone. There's been a dwelling of some sort here for hundreds of years but ours is not quite so old! However, we call the ancient stone Grandfather, out of respect. No one knows how long it's been here!'

Addy looked around the rapidly darkening circle. 'I can't see any other houses though. Where is the rest of the village?'

Jess shrugged. 'Most people live near the river or down by the church.' She opened the gate into the sheepfold and Star chased the would-be runaway inside. Her companions were all huddled in one corner of the enclosure looking ready for sleep. 'Two other farmers share the grazing in the circle but none of the other villagers come up here very often. They're too frightened.'

'I can see why. The stones are fearsome!' Addy screwed up his face. 'Don't they frighten you, Jess?'

'No, not at all. I suppose I'm used to them and they've never done me any harm. Some say they mark the graves of giants and others that they were put there by the Devil.' Jess shrugged. 'Personally, I'm much more scared of the barrows out on the Downs. If the Devil is anywhere, that's where he'll be. But you must be cold and starving! I know I am and I'm sure I can smell supper seething on the fire.'

'What will you say to your parents?' Addy asked her, suddenly wary.

'I'll ask them why they never told me I had a cousin.' She gave him a cheeky smile. 'And if they say I haven't, then you've been lying and you're out on your ear! Come on.'

She waved her crook at him and ran off around the 'Grandfather', heading for the heavy wooden door halfway down the side of the farmhouse. Addy grabbed his pack and hurried after her but he hung back when he reached the door, hoping to hear what was said before he entered.

A female voice spoke first, frantic with relief. 'Thank God and His holy son you are here safe, Jessie! What a storm that was! We feared you might be hurt or even worse.'

Then a man's voice broke in. 'But I knew you'd be safe. Did you shelter in the barn?'

'I did, yes, Pa. And I had company.' Jess's voice rose in summons. 'Come in Addy, don't be shy.' Almost reluctantly Addy stepped over the threshold. Jess closed the door firmly behind him and turned back to face her parents. 'You never told me I had a cousin. This is Adhelm. He's come all the way from Castle Combe to look for work. He wants to be a farmer.'

Nell walked forward, looking wide-eyed at Addy. 'Adhelm? That is a saint's name, is it not? Surely a saint would not tell lies – but there is no Adhelm that I know of in our family.'

Addy turned to Matthew, who was frowning at him, saying nothing. 'If you are Matthew of Henge Farm, you had a cousin who ran away, did you not? Can you remember her name?'

'She was older than me and her mother died in the last weeks of the Black Death. I think she ran away with a man from another village. I remember my uncle's anger when the lord of the manor demanded a marriage fee for her absence and after that he wouldn't use her name. If he had to mention her, he called her the nithing, pretending she no longer existed. But my mother sometimes spoke of her as Meg.'

Addy nodded solemnly. 'We call my mother Maggie. They're both short for Margaret, aren't they?'

'You're not a freeman, are you?' Matthew kept a stern gaze on the boy, as if trying to read his thoughts. 'Won't your father have to pay manumission if you've left your village?' he demanded.

Addy nodded. 'Perhaps, I don't know. He's a fuller and runs one of the lord's fulling mills.'

Hearing her father's disquiet, Jess cut in. 'His father took a stick to him.' She glanced at Addy. 'You must have some bruises?'

He shrugged. 'A few, but that wasn't what he beat me for. It was because I'd been learning archery from a veteran of Agincourt.'

'What's wrong with that?' Matthew demanded. 'By royal decree all able men between sixteen and forty are required to practise archery every Sunday. I only stopped last year.'

'That was just it! My father didn't want to train me to work on the mill and then lose me to the French wars.'

'I can sympathise with that. Are you any good with a bow, boy? I see you've brought one with you.'

'I'm better with a bow than I am with a mill engine.' Addy risked a cheeky smile.

Matthew's expression remained stern. 'And how good would you be at farm work? The sheep are about to go onto the Downs and you'll be out in all weathers. Shepherding is hard work, as Jess will tell you.'

'But I could do with some help,' Jess said hastily. 'And Addy turned over a running sheep just before we came in this evening. I think he might make a shepherd.'

'All right then, if Jess backs you, you're in!' Without waiting for her response Matthew blew out his cheeks and thrust out his hand. 'She needs assistance and it would be good to have another man on the farm. Welcome to the Henge, Addy. Now Nell, for pity's sake dole out that pottage!'

5

Bristol

Easter 1424

After her brother's death Isabel took to spending long periods at All Saints Church, a short walk from her home, where she was welcomed by the Kalendaries, the group of clergy and laymen who tended the library of books kept there. It was not permitted to remove any volumes, and anyway most of them were too heavy to carry, but she found the quiet seclusion of their company, and the knowledge they dispensed, essential for settling the uneasiness that occupied her mind. Her mother had become a sad shadow of the wise and capable woman she had been before Robert's demise and no longer provided her daughter with the advice and support she had been accustomed to rely on, which left her bereft when her father announced his unexpected and unwelcome decision.

'I have cancelled the betrothal between you and Thomas Stamford, Isabel. The circumstances have changed and I no longer consider it to be in your best interests.'

He had found her in the long garden behind the Corne Street house, collecting herbs to add flavour to the braised rabbit being prepared for the midday meal, hoping it might encourage her mother to eat more than the few mouthfuls she had been consuming of late. His blunt announcement caused Isabel to drop the sieve in which she had been intending to wash her collection in the big water butt before delivering it to the cook. The time that it took her to pick up the herbs gave her a chance to bite back the loud wail that had been her first reaction.

Instead, she rose from her task and fixed him with a furious stare and a one-word response. 'No!'

Mark Williams met her stare with a scowl and an equally determined affirmative. 'Yes! I have better plans for my clever daughter, now my only child, and I demand that you hear me out.'

Isabel took a deep breath and began to walk slowly across the garden to the water butt. 'I will listen but do not expect me to break my vow to Tom.'

'You do not need to. It is already done and I have the ring back to exchange for the one you wear.' Mark's tone was imperative, almost jubilant.

She swung round, her face suffused with anger. 'You cannot do that, Father! We made our vows and I will not give up the one Tom gave me!' She thrust out the hand on which the betrothal ring was set. 'It has only to be blessed by a priest before God has joined us! I do not believe Tom would willingly have given up my ring.'

'No, he gave it to his father because he, like you, is under age. Both of you are legally bound to obey your fathers and Tom has done so, as I expect you to do. And when I tell you why I have done this you will thank me. Now, get rid of that sieve and let us talk this over sensibly inside.'

Mark took her spare arm at the elbow and went to steer

her into the house but she wrenched it away and stalked off ahead of him. 'I will deliver these herbs to the cook first and then I will obey your invitation but that may be as far as my obedience will go.'

'Do not try to cross me, Isabel, and don't keep me waiting.' Her father took care to make his voice sound implacable.

The room where he conducted his business was at the front of the house, where he met his customers and kept a sharp eye on the accounts and the progress of his merchant voyages. Mark was immensely proud of the fact that he had held the position of Bristol's Mayor for the previous year and had only recently and reluctantly given up the heavy gold chain to his successor, vowing to gain re-election in short time. The Mayor was more or less equivalent to royalty in Bristol and his lavishly fur-trimmed red gown of office took pride of place on a stand against one wall. It was no coincidence that he chose to wait beside it for Isabel to arrive.

She did not knock but opened the office door and stood silently under its carved architrave, framed like a portrait of the Madonna, clasping both hands over her breast so that the betrothal ring stood out prominently on the fourth finger of her left hand. It may have been coincidence that she wore a blue dress but the spiritual image was certainly not lost on her father, who had waited impatiently as what he considered increasingly unnecessary minutes passed.

'Even the Virgin Mary obeyed her father, Isabel,' he remarked dryly. 'And I worked hard to reach the highest rank in this city, so that my family would have the respect that went with it. Do you think I would have cancelled your betrothal if I did not believe you deserved the chance of an even more prestigious marriage – to a young man who is landed gentry in his own county and has been blessed with the chance to attain even greater wealth and status, and the prospect of royal connection and recognition. I would be considered a foolish and irresponsible father if I had turned down an offer for your hand from John Seymour.'

Isabel snatched at the door handle and closed it with barely controlled violence. Perhaps to give herself courage, she had taken the trouble to remove her cap and comb her auburn hair to let it fall like a silken wave from under a jewelled band. When she spoke, her voice cracked. 'But surely it would be a callous and unkind father who forced me to marry a man I do not like! Is that not also true?'

Mark swallowed a surge of impatience and his narrowed eyes were icy blue. 'It would be true if it were so but the truth is that you actually know very little of John Seymour and it is my opinion that you will quickly change that view when you do get to know him. And while you do, it may help you to know that he finds you a beautiful and suitable lady to grace any man's home.' Seeing her shrug he added, 'Those are his exact words, sincerely spoken.'

'I'd rather he appreciated my thoughts and intelligence than my suitability as a decorative object,' she retorted. 'The little I've seen of him leads me to consider him a man with little or no compassion. But I don't suppose you will be quoting that when you inform him that I refuse his offer.'

'No, I will not because you will not be refusing it. Whether you alter your opinion of him or not, I am expecting you to carefully consider your situation. There is no longer any future for you with the Stamford family and if you refuse this offer from John Seymour, you will lose your parents' love and respect. By hard work and good fortune, the Williams name has risen high in Bristol merchant society. Marrying our daughter to a young gentleman of such landed wealth and knightly potential will go a long way towards raising our family status even further, and even compensate somewhat for the loss of our son.'

Tears sprang into Isabel's eyes at the mention of her brother. 'I know I will never replace Robert in your estimation! And I think my mother will never recover from his loss.' The knuckles on her hands showed white as she clutched at the silver cross around her neck and lapsed into a long and sombre silence, which her father wisely chose not to interrupt. 'So, if she finds some comfort in my marriage to John Seymour then I realise I must agree to it and pray that you are right about his character.'

6

Bristol

20th May 1424

According to church law, Isabel Williams and John Seymour made their marriage vows in the porch of the Church of All Saints, Bristol, on the twentieth of May, witnessed in bright sunshine by a group of the Williamses' friends and merchant colleagues gathered on the steps. For it the bride's father wore his red mayoral gown, despite no longer occupying the position and thus defying the civic rule that it should only be worn by the incumbent Mayor.

Isabel's smooth complexion bore a solemn expression, as if the white roses on her headdress were uncomfortable and her gown of red satin too weighty. In contrast, her bare-headed bridegroom looked jubilant in his crimson doublet embroidered with the Seymour emblem of two golden wings joined together. He had obviously visited the barber's shop because his thick hair was neatly arranged on his neck and he was clean shaven, apart from a small pointed brown beard.

His relations had made the two-day journey from their Somerset holdings: his widowed mother Maud, John's two brothers Roger and William and a cousin called Edmund, who represented a Welsh branch of the Seymour family. The young men all sported dagged doublets in bright silks and provided enough wedding banter to keep the groom distracted while they waited at the church porch for the bride to arrive. Maud Seymour wore a lavishly fur-trimmed gown of bright blue silk, which rather outdid the dark-hued raiment of the bride's mother, who still fiercely maintained the spirit of mourning her son. As Isabel walked to the church between her parents, she noticed Tom Stamford hovering at the back of the crowd of well-wishers and felt her heart thump. She had not met with him since their broken betrothal and she had to swallow hard to hold back tears as the priest began the civic ceremony on the church porch. When the bridal party moved into the church for the Mass and blessing, she risked a brief glance back to the place where he had stood, but he was no longer there.

Many of the guests commented on the beauty of the bride but equally whispered among themselves about the pale delicacy of the bride's mother. So soon after her son's demise, Agnes Williams found no joy at her daughter's wedding feast, especially when the gregarious Seymour family filled her house with their boisterous and indiscreet banter. Isabel could detect her mother's relief when Maud Seymour declared her intention to take her leave the following day, insisting that her two bachelor sons escort her home as she was not feeling well. Meanwhile John had enticed his cousin Edmund to stay on to do him a favour, which he declared was a secret.

At the end of the day Master Seymour walked with his exhausted bride to his spacious tenement in the High Street, not quite drunk enough to fall asleep before bedding his virgin wife in their new nuptial bed. When at last she heard his even snoring, Isabel finally gave way to the tears she had been repressing throughout the day's proceedings.

Having finally fallen asleep, she woke next morning to find herself alone and enjoyed the treat of inspecting every corner of her new abode before John returned. After bidding farewell to his mother and brothers he had shared a jug of ale with his cousin at his local inn, which did not amuse Isabel, who had suffered too much of the smell of ale and wine and hoped her new husband would not turn out to be a drunkard. But when he took her arm and steered her to a nearby stable, she was delighted to be made acquainted with a dainty white mare.

'She is yours, Isabel,' John explained. 'I cannot imagine having a wife who does not ride but nor do I want to teach you myself because I am not patient enough. So, my cousin Edmund has agreed to stay on in Bristol for a while in order to teach you. You can't live in the country and not be able to ride.'

Isabel called the horse Snowflake and fell in love with her. As a city girl, born and bred and living close to a harbour, she knew more about ships than horses but one of John's stipulations was that she must be capable of sitting her horse at the trot before they could make the journey from Bristol to the Seymours' Somerset manors.

'We need to go there as soon as possible but I'm not going to put up with you riding pillion behind me on my new stallion,' he declared. 'And Atlas won't put up with it anyway, so the quicker you learn the better.'

She bit back the temptation to point out that she could read and write and keep a domestic account book, which she had been surprised to learn that he could not. And she proved a quick learner on her horse, with an instinctive feel for the mare's paces. Besides, she looked forward to her riding lessons with Edmund Seymour, who was of similar age as herself and more easy-going than his cousin.

John's plan to establish his new wife in his Somerset Honour by early May had to be abandoned when it transpired that she had quickly become pregnant and badly affected not just by morning sickness but by almost all-day vomiting. Having briefly enjoyed being mistress of her own home, she now had to hire a nurse who specified and cooked what food her patient might be able to keep down and firmly insisted on a pause in conjugal rights. This infuriated John, who took to spending much of his time at the local inn, which served food as well as ale, only returning to the High Street apartment to drink his own wine and sleep unwillingly alone. After a week he left for his Somerset manors, taking Edmund with him.

The nurse's name was Nan, a sturdy woman of middle age, who in due course advised her patient that riding would have to stop until the sickness ceased. Unwillingly Isabel obeyed her advice but walked with Snowflake every day and asked the groom to exercise her outside the city walls. The two Seymours returned to Bristol by September and John was mollified when Isabel's sickness eased in time for the move to the Seymour Honour of Hatch Beauchamp in September. 'My best gift will be having my wife in my bed again!' he crowed when she told him and presented her with a jewelled girdle. Isabel told herself that she must submit again to his rough couplings with Christian grace and prayed to get accustomed to it in time.

Her arrival at the Seymours' main seat was greeted enthusiastically by a gathering of tenants in the Great Hall and in January a healthy baby boy was born after a long and painful labour, studiously avoided by John, who arrived at the bedside to greet the child with ecstatic pride and immediately declare that he should be named John after him, according to Seymour tradition. With Roger Seymour standing as godfather, Isabel insisted the baby must have Robert as a second name in memory of her own brother and since she would not be attending the baptism herself and did not trust John to see to it, asked Edmund, who remained in the Hatch Beauchamp household, to ensure that the priest was advised of the fact.

'When will you have recovered enough to ride again, Isabel?' John enquired impatiently less than a fortnight later. 'It is more than time that you became familiar with our properties. The tenant villeins need to know there is a lady of their manor and a future lord. If they sniff the lack of an heir-apparent, they start thinking they can get away with all kinds of petty larceny.'

Isabel felt obliged to agree, with certain caveats. 'Of course I want to tour all your Somerset manors sir, but I need more than a couple of weeks before I will be able to ride Snowflake for any distance and we will need a covered wagon for Johnnie and Nan to come too!'

John forced a smile. 'Of course, Izzy. Anything for my son and heir!' He noticed her brows rise in indignation and added hastily, 'And of course for his beautiful mother!'

7

Henge Farm

March 1425

AFTER A FEW MONTHS, when the initial excitement of their family connection faded, Addy had begun to resent Jess treating him like a wayward pupil in a shepherding school, criticising every slip-up in handling and demanding that he learn the name of every ewe out on the Downs. Nevertheless, he did as she ordered and did the best he could because he felt he owed it to the Henge family, who had been kind and treated him so well. Also, apart from the messier matters involved in tending sheep, he quite enjoyed taking them out on the Downs with Jess when she wasn't in a bossy mood. In fact, although he kept his feelings fiercely to himself, he knew he was growing disturbingly fond of his pretty cousin with her plait of golden hair. He also found himself becoming ridiculously fond of one or two of the sheep. One day in spring, on their return from the Avebury Down, when she had finished counting the ewes into the fold, he reckoned that one of his favourites was missing.

'We're one short,' he told Jess casually. 'Did you notice?'

She frowned, keen to get inside the farmhouse for supper.

'No, we aren't. You do the count again if you don't trust mine but I think you'll find I'm right.'

'It might be better if you did it,' Addy pointed out, 'since I've already noted the absence. And it's Curly that's missing, by the way.'

'No, it's not. I'm sure I saw her. You do another count if you like but I'm hungry and Star and I are going in for supper. Don't be too long about it though. I smell pigeon pie so I think Mother has raided the dovecot.' Jess made for the back entrance into the farmhouse, closely followed by her faithful hound.

Addy shrugged and made his way back through the outer gate that led into the stone circle, taking his pack with him. Curly was the escapee sheep he had managed to catch on his arrival at Henge Farm so he felt a curious affinity with her. While he was watching her sisters enter the fold and listening to Jess do the numbers, from the corner of his eye he was sure he had spotted her slipping off in the direction of her favourite hideaway, a hole behind one of the great stones close to the farmhouse. Now, when he found her there and chided her, she returned his gaze with pleading eyes, as if to say, 'Don't tell anyone!' Because she was busy birthing her lamb.

He knew he should probably tell Jess straight away but she was enjoying a well-earned meal and having watched numerous lambs being born out on the Downs, he reckoned this was an opportunity to show her that he was capable of overseeing a birth himself. So, when Curly produced her progeny with no sign of trouble, he was ready with a stalk of long grass plucked from the edge of the circle ditch, to clear the lamb's nose and receive a welcome sneeze as satisfactory evidence of life.

Just to ensure all was well, he stood back and waited for the ewe to begin the necessary maternal removal of the birth juices but she showed no interest in this essential task, appearing to settle into the effort of delivery all over again. This worried Addy because Jess had told him that Wiltshire Horn sheep only ever gave birth to one lamb each spring. Just to make certain he grabbed another handful of long grass and leaned into Curly's hideout to make a quick examination, while also wiping down the slimy little lamb as best he could. When he saw an unmistakeable hoof protruding from the birth passage, he decided it was time to call on some help.

Jess's mood had mellowed when Addy approached the kitchen trestle, where she and her parents were enjoying their supper. 'Have some of Mother's pigeon pie, Addy,' she suggested. 'It is delicious! Did you check the count all right?'

'I think my piece of pie might have to wait, Jess. Can you come with me right now? One of the sheep needs your help.'

Jess stood up, anxiety suddenly written all over her face. 'Which ewe is it? What's the matter with her?'

'Just come with me and you'll see.' Addy didn't want to reveal the disagreement over the count to her parents, so when she made a step towards the rear exit, from where the fold was reached, he called her back. 'No, we'll go the front way. It will be quicker. Bring Star and your crook.'

As Star joined them from her place by the fire, he made for the door that led to the stone circle and Jess followed, barefoot because her boots were at the other door. Once outside he began to explain. 'I didn't want to tell you in front of your parents but Curly did escape the count and she's down in her favourite retreat behind one of the stones. But

Jess, she's already birthed a lamb and it looks like she's about to have another.'

'A second lamb? Are you sure? That's never happened before!' Jess was now almost running. 'Which stone is it?'

'The first one after the grandfather stone. Jesu, it's getting dark. We should have brought a lamp. I could see a foot but I'm hoping she will have birthed the whole lamb by now.'

'Not if the other foot got stuck!' Jess increased her pace, panting as the stone in question loomed out of the growing gloom. 'Oh Curly – you've always been naughty!'

When they reached the ewe's hideaway, she clearly was in trouble and her first lamb also looked weak and shivery. Jess flung herself down beside the hole and reached to see if she could pull the visible leg any further out but the effort only caused the ewe to bleat feebly.

Jess held out her hand. 'We need to get her out of this hole, Addy. Can I have your jerkin? If we can tuck it under her we might be able to heave her out together.'

Reluctantly Addy removed the required apparel and spread out the sleeves. Then he lay down and fed one of them under the prone sheep, which Jess just managed to lift. After she scrambled from the hole, together they hauled the distressed animal out onto the level ground and Jess immediately knelt and pushed back the protruding leg.

'We need two legs to pull on, so I'm going to see if I can find the other one and pull them out together. Can you look after the other lamb, Addy, and try and rub some strength into it? If the twin is alive, they'll both need to suckle quickly.'

Addy nodded and turned away as Jess pushed up the sleeve of her smock and thrust her hand up to the elbow into the birth canal, ignoring the noisy protest from the sheep.

'Luckily I have small paws,' she reassured the indignant ewe and suddenly gave a soft whoop of delight as her hand closed over two small hooves. 'Now come on, Curly – just a few pushes and your mystery lamb will be with us!'

In the event it was more Jess's pulling than Curly's pushing that brought the twin lambs together and they were both breathing and suckling by the time the moon had risen and Matt and Nell had left the farmhouse to come and see what all the excitement was about.

When they'd heard the whole story, Addy experienced a first real sense of Henge Farm family approval. Matt not only gave gruff praise for the evening's endeavours but also revealed that during his last visit to the local alehouse Addy's name had cropped up. 'Bates, who marshals the Sunday archery sessions, reckons you're the village's best shot, Addy,' he remarked. 'If there's a Wiltshire muster for the French wars, I'm afraid we might lose you.'

'He's too young surely, Father!' There was a sharp note of anxiety in Jess's protest.

'No, he's not, Jess. How old are you, young man? And don't lie to me!'

Addy bit his lip, then took a deep breath. 'I know, I should have told you but I thought you'd realise from my beard. I'm seventeen next month.'

8

The Road to Easton Priory, Wiltshire

April 1425

'CAN'T YOU KEEP UP, Izzy?' There was a distinct note of irritation in John Seymour's voice as he rode back down the dusty road to urge his dawdling wife on. 'I have to get there before the funeral!'

Not inclined to hurry, Isabel was enjoying the delicate greens of the spring countryside as they rode along the banks of the River Frome, bordering the counties of Somerset and Wiltshire. To emphasise her mood, she drew rein and slowed her mare to a halt. 'We're going as fast as we can! Snowflake doesn't have the long stride of your Atlas. Anyway, they won't bury Sir William without his heir being present, or they wouldn't have sent a messenger.'

That messenger had made a hasty journey to the Seymour seat of Hatch Beauchamp in order to advise John of his uncle's demise and his own accession to the wardenship of the Royal Forest of Savernake. He was now guiding them to take swift legal possession of the attached manor of Wolf Hall. However, he had slowed down to come back and endorse Isabel's remark. 'The lady is right, sir, the ceremony will not take place without you and it will be several more days before the coffin reaches the burial site. Funeral processions move slowly.'

Apart from his urgent desire to take possession of his new property, John Seymour also did not take kindly to being lectured by a hired hand. 'I do not need you to tell me that, sirrah! Just you attend to the apparently necessary sumpter and I will handle my wife's unnecessary excuses.'

The sumpter horse was carrying clothes, mostly formal apparel to wear to the funeral of Sir William Esturmy, which was due to take place at the Priory Church of St Mary at Easton, a mile or so from Wolf Hall Manor. It could be expected to attract many of Wiltshire's worthiest citizens and, despite John's protests that a sumpter horse would slow them down, Isabel had managed to persuade him that appearing covered in the dust of the road would not make a good impression on their first venture among the county's gentry. She had also wanted to take young Johnnie Seymour with them but this time his father severely drew the line. The Seymour heir was at an age when noisy outbursts of pleasure or pain were uncontrollable and John organised that the child and the faithful Nan should travel separately and more slowly in a covered wagon, along with a selection of Hatch Beauchamp servants, under the mounted command of young Edmund Seymour and a security guard.

Recently the baby had ceased to want the comfort of the breast and since her milk had consequently dried up Isabel had no reason to claim the necessity of keeping her son at her side, a situation she regretted from motherly attachment but also because she was certain that breast-feeding would be preventing her conceiving another child. She had sought other methods of avoiding conception supplied by a wisewoman friend of Nan's - such as various uses of dried weasel testicles and even the womb of an infertile goat but was recently certain that none of them had worked. Various changes in her body and mood gave her reason to fear another bout of maternal sickness followed by birthing misery and at seventeen she felt she had more exciting things to spend her time on, like learning how to run a big country manor and discover the secrets of the surrounding forest.

First however there was the tedious process of attending the funeral of an old man she had never met.

Sir William's obsequies took place in the Priory Church of St Mary, the resting place of all the Esturmy Wardens of Savernake since the Norman Conquest. As expected at the passing of a renowned knight, the nave was crowded to overflowing and the Seymours found themselves objects of much interest and speculation. But before the murmuring could become too loud, it was overwhelmed by a sudden blast of sound that echoed around the church and a muscular man in a leaf-green tunic and colourfully embroidered baldric moved slowly down the central aisle, holding an extremely long, flared brass instrument to his lips. Blowing the Great Esturmy Hunting Horn required powerful lungs and, since the reign of King John, had been traditionally blown whenever the sovereign entered the Royal Forest. On this occasion however it was sounding farewell to the last Esturmy to hold the office of Warden, while behind its mournful message moved eight strong men, shouldering the casket in which he lay.

Processing after them came a column of clerics: the Bishop of Salisbury and representative clergy from the parishes and religious houses of Savernake, each wearing their finest ecclesiastical robes. But walking directly behind the bishop was a woman in plain white, wearing a nun's wimple and barbe with a red and blue cross sewn on her scapular. Amazed to see a woman processing among such a grand company of priests, Isabel made a mental note to find out who she was and what the cross represented.

After the coffin was safely placed on the waiting catafalque and the trumpet fell quiet, the Bishop of Salisbury began the lengthy Latin prayers for the dead, succeeded by each of his lesser clergy – a long and drawn-out process which inevitably had the standing congregation shifting on their feet. Then, while a choir sang a requiem, the bearers lowered the heavy lead-lined coffin down into the dark depths beneath the church and the vault was closed, with more psalms and prayers as the priests followed the choir down the aisle to the exit. In the ensuing silence the hushed congregation made its way out into the churchyard where servers began to mingle among them, offering cups of warm mulled wine which, in the chill spring wind, John Seymour eagerly accepted. Isabel however refused and instead scanned the crowd for the lady in white.

She knew that Easton Priory had been founded to provide hostel shelter to pilgrims making their way on foot to Southampton to take ship for the continent of Europe. Making offerings at the shrines of famous saints promised Christians heavenly indulgence against sins committed in their earthly lives and Isabel's Spanish father had inspired her with stories of the shrines he had visited as a young man, on his journey to England from southern Spain. As she mused on this memory, she spotted the nun who had led the procession of clergy wearing the red and blue cross and, murmuring an excuse, quickly navigated the gravestones to cover the short distance between them.

The lady in white smiled a welcome. 'God's greeting, Mistress Seymour. You are the new Warden's wife, are you not? I noticed you in the chancel. Welcome to our church. I am Editha, Prioress of Easton.' She gestured to the man who stood beside her. 'Have you met my Lord Hungerford?'

The baron made her a courtier's bow. 'I would certainly remember if we had met. Welcome to Wiltshire, mistress.'

Isabel bobbed a curtsy. 'Thank you, my lord. It is kind of you to attend Sir William's interment. I hope you have not had to travel far.'

He made a dismissive gesture. 'I would not miss my friend Esturmy's obsequies, and besides I always enjoy a ride across Salisbury Plain. The fresh air clears my head.'

'Which must be full of matters of national importance, my lord Treasurer!' John Seymour had moved up beside Isabel and made a bow. 'Allow me to introduce myself. John Seymour, the new Warden of Savernake Forest. I hope my wife is not disturbing the train of those fresh thoughts.' Isabel frowned and looked away, irritated by what she considered a demeaning remark, and noticed that an armed guard wearing the baron's sickle badge had moved up behind John with his hand on his poniard, as he made his bow to the wealthy Treasurer.

'Your beautiful wife could only delight with her presence, sir,' said the baron, irritably waving his fierce-looking bodyguard away. 'Allow me to offer my condolences on the death of your grandfather, Master Seymour. He was well known and respected in several counties. It must be an honour for such a young man to follow in his footsteps. Are you fully informed of the duties and privileges?'

'Not entirely, no sir, but I only took over the manor yesterday and have yet to ride the forest boundaries. I have a Head Forester, however, who is itching to give me copious information.'

At this point the Prioress moved to Isabel's side. 'I would very much like to show you something of our work here, Mistress Seymour. Shall we leave the gentlemen to their business?'

Being a merchant's daughter, Isabel knew business and religion had held equal importance in her family and she feared that unless she was privy to John's conversation, she would learn little of its content. However, meeting Prioress Editha was also of great interest to her, so she resigned herself to accepting her offer with a smile and a nod. The nun led her nimbly through the gravestones towards the Priory House, an elegant stone building that stood opposite the church on the pilgrims' road.

'I will not keep you long, Mistress Seymour,' she said as they entered the house, 'but I wanted to take this opportunity to begin the relationship I hope we may establish with the new Warden, and I often find it best to achieve good neighbourliness through the distaff side.'

'Mm,' Isabel responded with an appreciative noise. 'Woman to woman often works best,' she agreed. 'And being a Prioress is an unusual position for a woman, is it not? I have never met one before. Nor have I met a Trinitarian. I am eager to learn about your calling.'

Editha fingered the red and blue cross at her breast, as if to reassure herself that it was still there. 'We are few and far between but Trinitarians are a mixed calling and the nuns among us are often better at handling troubled pilgrims, especially male ones. Also, we have subtler ways of persuading wealthy people to give generously to our principal cause.'

'And what may that cause be, my lady?' Isabel said, sounding genuinely curious.

'I wonder if you have any idea of how many heathen raids are made on towns and villages along the northern coast of the Mediterranean Sea? And how many Christian youths and soldiers are held to ransom and used as slaves while captive? We Trinitarians are dedicated to raising money and using it to buy their freedom and bring them back to Christian shores.'

'Actually, my father was born on the coast of southern Spain where young Christian men were in constant danger of being carried off in pirate raids by Muslims. When he was still in his teens, he only just escaped one and was encouraged by his elderly father to take ship to the north for safety. He ended up in the port of Bristol but he never told me about the enslavements. That sounds terrible.'

'Yes, it is, and as well as providing food and shelter to passing pilgrims here at Easton we make sure to tell them of their Christian duty to make an offering to our Trinitarian relief fund.' Editha frowned. 'I am very interested to hear more of your life, Isabel, but I'd like to have more time. Would it be possible for you to come to the Priory again, when we are not restricted by obligations in the churchyard?'

Isabel nodded enthusiastically. 'I would be honoured to make a longer visit, perhaps in a day or so when I think my husband has plans to ride the boundaries of Savernake.' She gave her hostess a meaningful glance. 'It will give me some time to make decisions of my own. There is much to organise in the Wolf Hall household.'

Editha took her young visitor's hand. 'I can imagine that but I would be delighted to welcome you to join me at dinner after Sext on any day soon. And now perhaps we should make our way back to the churchyard and our various duties.'

'Where the Devil have you been, Isabel?' John Seymour was red-faced and tight-lipped when he pounced on his wife as soon as she returned from Prioress Editha. The churchyard was still full of Wiltshire dignitaries enjoying the mulled wine and John had consumed more than his fair share. 'When we're among people of rank I expect you to remain at my side, not wander off pursuing your own interests. The Lord Treasurer was offended by your disappearance and I was obliged to make your apologies!'

'The Prioress kindly took me to her house for a necessary reason and you were deep in conversation with Lord Hungerford at that moment. I was only minutes with her!'

'What would the Prioress want with you anyway?'

Isabel tossed her head. 'I haven't found out yet but I intend to. Can we go back to Wolf Hall now? Where are the horses?'

9

Wolf Hall Manor and Easton Priory

30th April 1425

TWO DAYS LATER, SHORTLY after dawn, Isabel watched John and Edward Seymour ride out through the gate of Wolf Hall Manor and felt her heart lift. They were going to meet Jem Freeman, the Head Forester of Savernake, carrying saddlebags of food and drink, ready to make their initial venture deep into the woods, and she took a grateful breath, free to do as she liked, without interruption.

Her first inclination was to turn around and look in detail at the mansion she now called home. Despite her original alarm at the manor's name, in the few days she had spent at Wolf Hall, she found herself growing increasingly fond of it. It was a long, rambling building and, being set within a forest, inevitably had a main frame of wood. Huge trunks of stripped oak pushed upwards to the thatched roof, supporting lime-painted sections of wattle and daub. Isabel had seen many houses of this kind in her home city but while Bristol's buildings were crammed together into streets, this country manor was a rather more spacious structure with a stone-built hooded hearth and chimney on the long north side and a bank of shuttered windows on the south.

The ground floor was mainly given over to the hall, the focus of business and family life, but at its east end a wooden stair built against the wall gave access to first-floor chambers partitioned under the roof beams. Behind the service screen at the west end of the hall a passage led across the width of the house to front and back entrances and, beyond that, to two cross-wings housing a pantry and a dairy and the Warden's office, which held a ladder stair up to the solar and the manor lord's bedchamber.

It was of concern to Isabel that the outside of the mansion looked as if it was suffering from neglect; parts of the roof thatch were slipping and the white lime covering the daub was tending to flake but when she had pointed this out to John and suggested some basic repairs would soon make things right, he just grunted and retorted pompously, 'It's not worth it because I intend to build a new mansion anyway!' She could not find any logic in this but made no further response, knowing he was bound to dismiss her opinion. At such times she knew that Tom Stamford would never have treated a woman so dismissively and wondered wistfully what lucky girl had acquired his love and companionship.

Still enjoying her sense of freedom, Isabel set off to the stable block at the back of the rear courtyard and found one of the lads already grooming Snowflake, ready for the ride she planned to make to Easton Priory.

'You'll need a groom to escort you, mistress,' he suggested but she shook her head and told him just to have the mare ready soon. As she walked through the hall to take the stair up to visit her son, she mused that at least she had achieved one successful element of her marriage, who would probably be still asleep in one of the upper chambers alongside Nan's truckle bed. Little Johnnie grumbled at being wakened at first but when he saw his mother he gave her one of his gummy smiles and gurgled as Nan changed his napkin before handing him over for Isabel to give him his cow's milk.

While she hugged him on her shoulder to pat up a burp, she tried unsuccessfully to dismiss the wish that she could cuddle up with her little son every night and avoid the bed in the master chamber at the other end of the house. She bore John's frequent couplings with patience but no pleasure. He ignored any attempt she might make to suggest more affectionate and comfortable pairings and there were many times when she wondered if love-making with Tom Stamford, who had shown her obvious affection, would have been more pleasurable. She was more or less certain now that there was another child on the way but as yet she had not told John. It had become quite clear to her that his needs took precedence over her wellbeing, or her own pleasure.

Having ridden to Easton for the funeral, she was familiar with the route, but in her leisure this time she chose to take a detour off the path to visit a flowering glade that had caught her eye. Clumps of primroses and cowslips flaunted their bright yellow petals around a spring which gurgled merrily out of the ground. Tree canopies clustered overhead dappling the sunshine and birdsong filled the air with music. The city girl in Isabel dismounted and led Snowflake to drink from the spring, while she absorbed the pleasure the forest gave her and the relief of not hearing John's impatient cries of 'don't dither, Izzy!'

At the village of Easton, she rode slowly past the villeins' simple cots and the pilgrim hostel, taking in its sprawling barn-like structure and the simplicity of its planked wooden walls and humble outside benches, where several pilgrims were taking the sun and acknowledged her passing by. The thatch-roofed Priory with its various outbuildings was situated further along the well-trodden road and the Church of St Mary, with its stone-built belltower and extensive churchyard, occupied a walled area on the opposite side. Behind it the villeins' ridge fields sprawled out to the source of the River Avon at the foot of Easton Hill. It was a peaceful scene except for the occasional shout from a group of boys in the field, who were throwing stones to scare the birds off the newly sown seeds.

Uncertain where she might leave her horse, Isabel dismounted and led her up to the Priory entrance door. When she used the knocker, a face appeared behind a spy hole and asked her name.

The response surprised her. 'You are expected at the Prioress's house, madam. I will send someone to take your horse.'

'How did you know I was coming?' Isabel asked, when she had been admitted to the house.

The Prioress smiled. 'I did not know but I had warned the porter nun to expect you at Sext on any day. I had great faith that you would come soon because I have a proposition to make.' As she spoke the bell began to ring for the noon call to prayer and the Prioress had even installed a second prie-dieu so they could both kneel to honour the sixth hour before taking their seats for dinner.

The meal was served by a postulant nun and adhered strictly to the Lent rule of bread, fish and wine, and once finished was quickly cleared so that the Benedictine rule of silence during meals could be abandoned and they could settle down to discuss Editha's proposition.

'I have not brought you here in order to convert you to our devotion to the Holy Trinity, Isabel,' she began with a smile. 'But I'm sure you are aware of the wars that constantly flare around the Holy Land and draw young Christian warriors away from our shores to fight for our faith. But perhaps you are not aware that many of them who are captured by the infidels are dragged into enslavement on their captors' properties and sent in chains to work in their fields in fearful heat and dreadful conditions. The mission of the Trinitarians is to rescue them and bring them back into the arms of Christ and our particular mission as nuns is to raise the funds which finance these rescues and allow brave monks to bargain with their Muslim captors for their release. I'm pleased to say that we have great success, both in raising the funds and gaining many releases.'

Isabel's brow creased in concern. 'Is that not dangerous work though, my lady? Bargaining with heathen non-believers surely cannot be easy?'

'Our members trust in God and are blessed with much skill at the task. But of course I would not involve you in that side of our work. When I learned that the new Warden's wife was young, intelligent and beautiful, I immediately hoped that I might be able to interest her in joining me in a fundraising endeavour that involves the Dowager Queen.'

'Queen Catherine? The Boy King's mother?' Isabel could not hide her excitement.

The Prioress nodded. 'Yes, I thought that might surprise you. But I have a connection with one of her ladies-in-waiting and it was she who told me that her mistress had learned of the plight of these captured French and English soldiers and expressed great concern. My friend suggested I might explain the Trinitarian rescue missions to the queen and perhaps raise some royal interest. Of course I agreed but first I needed to consult my superiors to ask if they would approve of me making a royal approach. All this was some weeks ago and I have recently received permission to proceed. But I can't travel to Windsor on my own and I also cannot imagine any of my sisters here at Easton making such a journey. Some are too old and others are not used to riding as you and I are, so you are my best hope. Besides, I believe a young lady like you would be well received at the royal court and meeting the queen might be a valuable introduction for you.'

Isabel could feel the excitement building in her chest, a fluttering sensation which she could not control. The thought of visiting Windsor Castle, the focal point of English power for hundreds of years, was almost overwhelming, and just to step into the presence of the reputedly beautiful French mother of the young King Henry the Sixth would be glorious. Then reality brought her abruptly down to earth. One thing she knew for certain about her husband was his determination to achieve royal court hunting patronage at Savernake Forest and she feared that even making a brief contact with royalty before John Seymour had achieved his own ambition to do so would be stamped on with a heavy boot. And yet she could not bring herself to abandon all possibility.

'I would be honoured indeed to accompany you in such an endeavour, my lady. And I believe my father would be thrilled if I was to play even a small part in achieving the release of one Christian slave of the infidel. As a boy he was nearly captured from his Spanish home by infidel pirates and fled to England as a result.'

'So, you are half Spanish and married to an Englishman,' the nun remarked. 'And do you have children?'

'Yes, a boy called John after his father.'

A smile lit the Prioress's face. 'Then you have already fulfilled his greatest desire. Congratulations! Every landed gentleman requires a son and heir, does he not?'

Isabel was pondering how she could explain the difficulty she might have in persuading her husband to agree to her making the journey to Windsor when her hostess rose from her chair to end the meeting. 'I pray our efforts will bring some comfort and purpose to Queen Catherine.' The Prioress lowered her voice. 'At court, with my Lord Gloucester as Regent and Eleanor Cobham now apparently his permanent mistress, she is becoming isolated and losing influence over her royal son.'

Isabel didn't have time to think more about this comment before the Prioress said briskly, 'Now I must let you go. I have business to discuss with the Pilgrim Sister and I'm sure you need to get back to that young son of yours. We must meet again soon, Isabel. I will keep you in touch with the Windsor expedition.'

10

Wolf Hall

30th April 1425

Towards the end of their day-long exploration of the southern section of the hunting forest, the trio of Wolf Hall riders had come upon a youth bearing a hare he had obviously caught in a trap. The sun was setting and he must have relied on there being no Foresters about at twilight, so he was swinging along one of the pathways whistling under his breath, with his prey tied to the belt of his tunic. He did not hear Jem, the Head Forester, moving up quietly behind him, his horse's hooves silent on the soft earth, and he did not turn and run until it was too late to throw himself into the undergrowth. In seconds he was scooped up by his belt and hanging over the horse's neck, screeching in angry protest.

Despite being upside down, the young poacher kept on yelling but the Forester maintained a firm hold on the belt around his waist, while guiding his horse with the other hand. 'I know who you are, Nat,' he said, 'and I know what you've stolen, to say nothing of trespassing on the king's property. You'll not get away with it.'

'My family has a licence!' the boy insisted.

'A liar as well as a thief.' Jem jerked on the belt. 'I know you and I know your father. His name is Col and he's the Wolf Hall carpenter. No villeins are licensed to take game in the forest. You thought to take advantage of the old lord's death, but there's already a new lord at the manor house and he's riding right behind us. He'll judge what's to be done with a sneak thief who set an illegal trap. Now shut up and start praying that he's not going to send you to the Marlborough Castle dungeon.'

The boy did not stop complaining but began trying to fiddle about with his belt buckle, causing Jem to haul him up by his hood so that he began to choke. 'Don't you dare try and throw down that hare, you lying villain! That hare is evidence and it comes with us – all the way to Wolf Hall!'

As the sun set over the paved courtyard between the manor house and the stables, two of the grooms set about building a fire on the Forester's orders. Jem waited until John and Edmund had ridden in and dismounted before lowering the damp and dishevelled poacher off his horse's withers into the head lad's keeping. Nat had stopped yelling his innocence and was revealed as a sad and rather puny boy, who made several attempts to escape the hand that held his belt, before hanging his head and refusing to speak at all when John asked his name. One of the stable lads was sent for a rope and then there was more angry and increasingly terrified swearing when the agile Forester managed to avoid some desperate kicking, while the boy's hands were bound together behind his back before he was dragged to the stable wall and tied to a hitching ring. After dodging several more increasingly feeble kicks, Jem managed to remove the belt that held the dead hare and hand it to John.

'Here is the evidence, Warden. The culprit's name is Nat and he's the son of Col the carpenter, one of your villeins. You witnessed the crime and you are the judge. What is the verdict?'

The two Seymours exchanged glances. Edmund frowned and gave a negative shake of his head, causing his cousin to scowl and make a dismissive wave of his hand. 'A new Warden needs to make his intentions clear,' John told him, and turned to approach the accused youth, stopping just short of kicking distance to hold the dead hare up before him. 'All game in Savernake Forest belongs to the king. Illegal poaching of any kind will not be tolerated.'

The boy turned his head, refusing eye contact as John Seymour continued. 'By rights such a crime should be heard before the Swain Moot, but that will not sit for another three months and I do not wish to commit such a skinny young offender to that long in the Marlborough Castle lock-up. He might never emerge alive. So, as lord of the manor, I choose to reduce the sentence to a shorter and more suitable punishment.' For a brief moment a look of hope crossed the poacher's face until John turned to the Forester, who was now standing beside the fire holding a thin metal poker with a cypher on its tip. John nodded approval, eyes blazing as he evidently relished the thought of making his first mark as Warden. 'To ensure that no one forgets the Savernake rules again, we'll put an S on his cheek. Shove the iron in the fire, Forester.'

Seeing no reason to hesitate, Jem obeyed the order as an anguished yell from the prisoner was overridden by an even louder scream of fury from the back door of the manor house.

'No-o-o!' Isabel Seymour came running into the firelight, carrying young Johnnie. 'You cannot do that! He'll be scarred forever. What kind of a life will a branded villein have?' Confronting her husband, she held the baby up to him, just as he had held the hare up before the offender. 'Imagine if someone did that to your son!'

John Seymour's face suffused with anger. He dropped the hare and grabbed the child from her. Thinking it all a game, little Johnnie gurgled happily as his father lifted him high and declared to the growing gathering of stable workers, 'My son John will be Warden after me. He will uphold the law, just as I do not break it like this piece of shit!' He gave the cowering poacher a kick on his bare shin and turned to the Forester. 'Do it, Jem! Johnnie can watch.'

Isabel shrieked, 'How dare you?' and leapt to grab at the baby's wrap but missed. 'Give him back to me. He should not see this!'

'You should not have brought him out here then, madam.' John turned away, keeping his son well out of her reach, while Jem carried the red-hot brand from the fire to the stable wall and signalled one of the grooms to hold the prisoner still. Then he grabbed him by the hair, shoved the right side of his head against the bricks and jammed the red-hot brand onto his left cheek. Even though it was held in place for only a few seconds and Isabel's ear-piercing shriek smothered the sound of Nat's agonised scream, the smell of burning flesh was pungent. As Jem walked back to the fire the young culprit slumped against the wall shuddering, all protest succumbing to utter shock. For a brief moment the scream made even the Warden jump and lower the baby down from his precarious height.

Isabel instantly snatched the child from him. 'That was unforgivable!' she snarled, her face wrinkling with disgust. 'That boy can be no more than twelve years old and you have scarred him for life. I will bear you no more children if this is how you treat them!' She was fighting back tears.

John's nostrils flared. 'Do not dare to threaten me, madam! Breeding is a woman's only purpose – I assure you that you will have no choice.'

'I will take the veil!' she declared, clutching the baby to her breast so tightly that he gave a yell of protest.

John Seymour shook his head. 'Not without my permission, which I assure you I will not give.' Then he turned towards the nearby fire. 'You know where Nat lives, Forester. Take him to his mother and tell her why her son is branded a thief.' Then he picked up the abandoned hare and headed for the manor house. 'This should not be allowed to go to waste. It will make a good dinner.'

Isabel made comforting noises to her baby son, her eyes wide with fury and brimming with tears. Edmund came forward to put a sympathetic arm around them both. 'I want you to know that I do not condone this tyrannical act,' he said. 'And I feel sure that my cousin will come to regret it.'

Isabel sniffed loudly, forcing back the tears and taking some comfort from his embrace. 'Yes, he will. He certainly need not think he will sleep in my bed again,' she declared furiously. 'Because I intend to raise the ladder stair behind me tonight and every other night. Only women servants will be admitted to the upper floor.'

Edmund's brow creased in an expression of surprise. 'I don't advise that, Isabel. You will drive John into some whore's arms, or else he'll become morose and angry and take it out on you when you inevitably emerge from your sanctuary. It won't work.'

A stubborn look spread over her face and she wriggled out of his embrace. 'We'll see, won't we? If he promises never to order another branding, I might consider changing my mind. You can tell him that.'

II

Wolf Hall

2nd May 1425

'THE TORCHES HAVE BEEN lit, madam, and I have your supper.' It was Nan, calling from below the ladder stair.

Isabel crept out of the chamber and closed the door, taking care not to wake little Johnnie, whom she had just got to sleep. She tugged the ladder over to the gap in the floor. 'Are you alone, Nan?' she called quietly.

'Yes, madam, and the dish is hot.' There was an anxious note in the nurse's voice.

The ladder slid slowly down from the upper floor, its feet settling on the reed matting of the hall below. Nan hitched up her skirt and began to climb the steps, carrying the meal in a basket in one hand and clinging on with the other as she ascended. Performing this duty alarmed her and she prayed that her stubborn mistress would soon give the situation up. Carrying Johnnie up to the solar had been bad enough but at least he wasn't piping hot!

As soon as it appeared Isabel took the basket from her. 'Bless you, Nan. Has Master Edmund come in for supper yet?'

Nan gratefully eased herself off the ladder. 'No, ma'am.

He and Master John were giving orders to the stable lads. I heard something about riding to Salisbury tomorrow.'

'Aha!' Isabel crowed. 'I might be able to come down when they've left, then.'

Any abandonment of her mistress staying up the wretched ladder came as music to the nurse's ears. 'Yes, ma'am, it looks like it.'

At this point Edmund appeared at the ladder's foot. 'Are you pulling this in, Izzy, or can I come up?' he asked. 'John is grumbling about supper to the cook and he wants me to get some smart apparel from his clothes chest.'

'Come up then!' Isabel called as Nan hurried away to help the young maid, who was too often the butt of John Seymour's wrath. 'Poor Annie tries but it really is time we hired a proper cook.'

Edmund appeared through the opening. 'Well, don't let John have anything to do with that,' he remarked. 'He'd hire some pretty milk maid who knows more about flirting than frying.'

Isabel nodded. 'You know him so well.' She watched Edmund step off the ladder. 'Why does he want to go to Salisbury?'

'Apparently the Duke of Gloucester has come to Clarendon Palace and John thinks he'll be able to have a chat with him. Gloucester is all but king of England though and I'll be amazed if we get past the park gate.'

'Oh, are you going too? I was thinking we might go to the market in Marlborough. I'm hoping to find a cook in the hiring queue.'

'Good luck with that. I'm afraid I am under orders. One of the grooms will escort you though.'

'No, I'll just go on my own. It's not that far.'

'It's eight miles. There might be outlaws.'

She gave a hollow laugh. 'I'm sure John would be delighted if I was abducted by outlaws! It will be his bad luck if I'm not.'

Edmund's response was ambiguous. 'He won't admit it but he misses your company – and not just in bed. I should not let him catch me up here because he already complains that you and I converse too much together. But I've been told to get his formal apparel to put in his saddlebags. Could you give me a hand? Nan would not know what to choose, would she?' He grinned.

'I will help you but we mustn't disturb Johnnie. I've just got him to sleep.' Now that John was not coming to the marital bed Isabel had taken to sleeping with little Johnnie.

Together they hurriedly collected John's best doublet and hose and a pair of fashionable long-toed shoes. 'He would need these for a meeting with the duke but I'd wager a groat he won't get near him,' Edmund whispered, gathering up the collected clothing and footwear. 'Close the door after me, Izzy. I'm in trouble if he hears us talking together.'

Unfortunately, when he returned to the ladder, he saw his cousin standing puce-faced at the bottom.

'What in the name of hell were you doing up there that took you so long, Edmund!' he demanded furiously. 'Where's Izzy?'

His cousin shrugged and stepped onto the top rung. 'In her chamber which she locked after me,' he said, throwing the clothes and shoes he'd collected down to his cousin. 'We can hardly appear at Clarendon Palace in sweaty tunics and mud-spattered boots.' He reached the bottom of the ladder and frowned at John. 'What is the problem, John?'

'She must have let the ladder down for you!'

'No. I didn't have to ask her because Nan was coming down anyway and left it for me. Jesu – what are you doing!' John was already three rungs up the ladder before Edmund grabbed the hem of his riding tunic and stopped him. 'There's no point in going up there now. I heard her shoot the bolt.'

'I only want to talk to her.' John stepped down reluctantly, still red in the face. 'She's got to see sense!'

'Isabel knows we're riding to Salisbury tomorrow. So, if I were you I'd wait until we return. Things might have calmed down by then.'

Edmund hardly had time to finish the sentence before his cousin landed a heavy punch in his stomach, making him stagger backwards, 'Ugh!'

'Don't ever tell me what to do, Ed! And don't you go near my wife again!' John's face suffused with anger and he glowered at his cousin. 'You'll be on the road out of Wolf Hall if you do. Go and tell Annie we're ready for supper. The cook is ill and she's useless in the kitchen so I doubt anything will be fit to eat.'

Still gasping, Edmund retreated hurriedly, arms wrapped around his middle, in shock and humiliation at John's outburst. It was a couple of minutes before he could breathe evenly enough to convey John's message and when he got to the kitchen, he was assailed by a smell of burning meat. 'What happened?' he coughed, waving his arms. 'Has something died?'

Annie shook her head and wiped her eyes with a kitchen

cloth. 'No, Master Edmund. I'm afraid I left some bacon too long on the griddle.'

Edmund peered more closely at the maid's face. 'You've been crying, haven't you? Did Master John shout at you, too?'

She nodded, head down to avoid his gaze. 'He said I was a waste of space and threatened to throw me out. He won't, will he?'

'Well, if he does, I'll be coming with you, Annie. He's just threatened me with the same thing. He's angry with the world because his wife won't speak to him – or do anything else with him for that matter.' Edmund tried to sound more reassuring than he felt. 'Now, let me have a look at that bacon. Surely some of it is worth saving.'

Even from the outside kitchen they could hear the sound of John hammering on the door of the solar. Then, behind that noise the sound of little Johnnie yelling, having been roused from his deep sleep. There was nothing from Isabel, who kept a defiant silence, refusing to respond to John's loud calls for her to open the door.

Edmund exchanged alarmed glances with the little maid. 'I think we need a new cook, Annie. One who doesn't get ill. If Master John does not get regular and well-cooked meals, he becomes impossible to live with.'

12

The Long Barrow, Silbury Down

3rd May 1425

'ROUND THEM UP, STAR! Go!' A glance up at the sky had inspired Jess's urgent order to her sheepdog, which she followed with a shout to her assistant. 'Run, Addy! We must get to shelter. Move the ewes on fast!'

Addy had been taking an opportunity to strengthen his pulling arm by flexing the string of his longbow as he walked. But hearing the alarm in her voice he instantly set the bow over his shoulder and quickened his stride, racing to urge a straying ewe away from the patch of spring clover she had stopped to graze.

Before noticing the storm clouds, Jess, Addy and the sheep had followed the River Kennet from Avebury to the foot of Silbury Hill, where they had begun moving the flock further south, up the long slope of Silbury Down, which had meant crossing the ancient paving of a Roman road. Addy had been amazed by its condition. 'I learned that the Romans left England hundreds of years ago but this looks like it was built yesterday! Where does it go?'

Jess shrugged. 'I'm not sure. I don't think you'd have used it coming from Castle Combe and it's too narrow for the big ox wagons. But if you're walking or riding, I've heard that it's still the quickest way to get from Bath to Marlborough.'

Addy had turned to look back at the way the road followed the river, which flowed directly east towards the morning sun. But the sun wasn't visible, blocked from view by a bank of threatening black clouds. 'Holy Jesus!' he exclaimed. 'That doesn't look friendly. We're going to get very wet!'

'Not if we get to the barrow on time. It has a cave entrance. Run!'

Ahead of them, at the top of the Down, a long hump rose from the ground, which Jess knew to be one of numerous barrows that dotted the slopes and heights of these stark uplands. But while she had no fear of the stone circle where she lived, these particular stones formed the entrance to a mysterious long barrow which had a demonic reputation, and although the chamber behind them would provide essential shelter from the approaching storm, the whole structure filled her with deep apprehension.

However, it was not the first time the sheep had been herded under these particular stones and the two shepherds and the dog had no trouble steering them under the rough portico, formed by several more giant stones laid vertically and horizontally above them to form a cavern. In the innumerable years since the barrow was built, a carpet of shrubs and moss had settled on its roof and along the entire length of the mound, closing over the cracks and forming the entrance space into a dark but relatively watertight mausoleum. Terrified by the noise of the approaching storm, the sheep were more than willing to squeeze through its narrow opening, set at one side, and once inside they immediately crowded together and lay down, gradually filling the chamber with their distinctive smell, as the black clouds burst directly above them and sheets of rain began to fall.

There were fifty ewes in the flock Jess's father had entrusted to his daughter and she was proud that she had so far managed not to lose one of them to flood, fire or infection. With the lambing season fast approaching she was hoping the small herd would double in size and by November their fleeces would earn top money from the thriving local cloth industry. She knew that had she not got the sheep to shelter before the storm hit, one lightning strike could have ruined that profit.

In the dark she heard rather than saw Addy moving among the ewes and calling out, 'Where are you, Jess? I can't find you.'

She chuckled with relief. 'I have no idea where I am but I know what I'm going to do, and that is take a lesson from the sheep and catch up on some sleep. I recommend it.'

'I don't know how you'll get to sleep with all the noise of the storm. It's worse than the one you once rescued me from. Do they usually happen so often in this part of the world?' Addy's voice was still trembling from the last violent blast of thunder, which had sounded as if it must shake even the huge stones around them. Stones which had stood for countless years.

'I expect it will only last for a couple of hours. Take a tip from the sheep. They're used to resisting everything nature can throw at them. Ah, there you are.' She felt a booted foot make contact with her shin and shifted it away. 'You can share my ewe if you like, she's very comfortable and doesn't seem to mind being used as a mattress.'

'It's all right,' he said and stretched out his hand, grateful to feel the grainy texture of stone under his fingers. 'I seem to have found a wall. Hopefully it will protect my bow.'

Jess sighed. 'You and that bow! When will you use it for something useful, like bringing down a rabbit or a hare? Then we could make a fire and have a decent meal instead of just cheese and apples!'

'You're only saying that because we're in the dark and I can't see to prod you with it,' Addy protested. 'You know you don't like to see animals killed.'

'I don't mind eating them though, especially roasted over a good hot fire. Will you do that for me one day?'

'I'll think about it,' he teased, already realising there wasn't much he wouldn't do for her. But there was another desire that would not leave him alone and the storm had agitated his need to satisfy it. In the dark and infused with guilt, he felt in his pack for something he had brought with him from Avebury; something he had kept hidden from Jess.

Despite proving to be quite good at the various skills needed to work with the sheep and growing disturbingly fond of Jess, he still yearned for what he imagined to be the comradery of a band of archers firing at the enemy. In the deep gloom of the barrow chamber, he laid his bow down against the base of one of the great stones and folded his fingers reassuringly around the flint and the small candle lantern he had concealed in his pack. He had no idea how, but he felt that these three items were the tools that might steer his future.

For what seemed like hours Addy lay wide awake, envying the snoring coming from both Jess and the dog, which from the sound of it, he enviously imagined, was curled up somewhere very close to her mistress. As the hours passed, he heard the storm gradually ease and cease to batter the great stones at the front of the barrow and this change in the exterior racket encouraged him to make a move. So as not to disturb the sleepers he felt carefully around him and gathered up his backpack and bow, then, hunched over to avoid hitting his head, he felt his way around the stone walls in what he estimated was the direction from which he had entered. But the sheep had been shifting about and his sense of direction must have become muddled, so that instead of finding the narrow exit gap in the stones, he found himself making his way from the relative gloom of the entrance chamber into the pitch darkness of a low-roofed tunnel and his heart began to beat faster.

Jess had told him about the Avebury villagers' belief that the barrows had been built by the Devil's henchmen and that they were the way Satan lured people to everlasting punishment for their sins in the flames of hell. He had covered his ears and told her to stop, but the damage had been done and the images she conjured had never left him. To add to his mounting panic, in the darkness he ran his hands over the scratchy walls of the tunnel and found that the stones were warm, as if they stood at the edge of a fiery furnace. Terrified of what he might have come across and forcing himself to swallow his dread, he eased off his pack and felt inside for the flint and lantern, casting in its depths for the scrap of fabric he had packed which might catch a spark and provide the flame that would light the candle. After several fruitless attempts at raising a spark, he finally achieved blessed light and was amazed to find that he was facing not a pile of bones but the entrance to a weed-encrusted passage that appeared, from the amount of wild vegetation it housed, to have not been used for many years. 'Someone made another access,' he whispered to himself. Carefully shielding the flickering flame from the sudden breeze, he leaned to peer more closely at the tunnel's structure. Then the flame died.

13

The Long Barrow, Silbury Down

4th May 1425

JESS WOKE WITH A start, an apparently wet cloth wiping her cheek. It was Star, urging her awake. The chamber, which had seemed such a boon during the storm, was now a stinking prison, the air fetid with the smell of sheep's breath and excrement. Blinking in the gloom faintly illuminating the chamber, she raised her head and noticed that there were only a few sheep left and no sign of Addy or Star. She gave a sigh of relief and hauled herself to her feet, assuming that they must be taking care of the missing ewes. Jess made for the exit, reckoning that the sheepdog was at last showing some appreciation of her new assistant and helping him to keep an eye on the rest of the flock.

Stretching and yawning, she grabbed her crook and pack and made for the narrow exit, now easily discernible by the morning light creeping through. The remaining sheep followed behind at her call. Half-blinded at first by the unaccustomed glare, she blinked with surprise at the sight of the rest of the flock, spread about and grazing the damp grass on the slope of the Down, with Star now sitting sentinel, like a canine queen, up on the crest. But there was no sign of Addy.

Dropping her pack against the largest entrance stone, she strode further up the hill, wondering if perhaps Addy had gone to chase a wandering ewe back to the rest of the flock and Star had failed to assist him. She called the dog to her side. 'Where's Addy, girl? Did he go searching somewhere?' Star cocked her head, as if listening intently, but there was no further helpful sign from her. 'He must be here somewhere.'

From the hilltop the view south was panoramic, stretching away across miles of empty grassland to an extraordinary escarpment and ditch, which carved its way like an ocean wave across the lower slope of the next line of hills. Shepherds on the Downs called this feature the Wansdyke and spread the notion that it been built by slaves during the Dark Ages as a boundary against invasion from the north. This tale from legend sprang to Jess's mind as her eyes swept the valley, but she could see no sign of any stray sheep or of Addy and had to quash another burst of anxiety about his absence. Of course he must be somewhere near, she told herself, he couldn't just disappear.

She fought the idea of his disappearance as she returned to the barrow and sent Star out to round up her ewes, so that she could make a headcount. Whatever happened, she did not want to risk any absences from her flock. Besides, she hoped that by the time the sheep were counted, Addy would saunter back from wherever he had gone and receive the sharp end of her tongue for wandering off.

She did not know whether his pack and bow were also missing, because in the gloom and stench of the chamber she hadn't bothered to search it before she left. Now she was assuming that he would have taken them with him but her niggling worry made her think that she should check. When with relief she had made a successful headcount of the ewes, she gave an order to Star to guard them and gritted her teeth to make a return to the dark and fetid chamber. Once back inside, she wished fervently that she had some form of light, because although a few rays penetrated the narrow entrance, they did not stray much further than a few yards. Being determined to establish that there was no evidence of Addy left inside, she screwed up her courage and felt her way around the side wall.

Although she had taken shelter in the barrow before, it had only been for short periods during flash thunderstorms. Never had she ventured in further than a few yards or been tempted to explore deeper. Local folklore suggested that the length of the barrow had been closed off many years ago by frightened parishioners, heeding the devilish warnings of their priests, so it was an unwelcome surprise when her careful blind exploration suddenly revealed a gap in the wall, indicating the presence of an open passage, presumably leading into the ancient burial chambers. And at this point she decided that she could leave her sheep alone with Star no longer. If Addy had ventured into the pitch-dark passage and become lost and confused it would need light and help to rescue him. A vivid mental image of the church painting, showing the flaming result of Satan's march into hell, drove her to turn around and feel her way back as fast as possible towards the light of day.

Once outside, Jess drew in great gulps of fresh air as she cast her gaze over the sight of a well-ordered flock grazing quietly under the eagle eye of Star watching for any sheep that might start wandering too far. She also took in the scene with disappointment, having held a last hope of spotting Addy somewhere, perhaps at a distance, sending his precious arrows to plunge into a handy knoll. But there was no Addy and no bow and arrows. She collected her own pack and crook, called Star to round up the flock and looked up at the eastern sky. Clouds were gathering to block the sun but there was no sign of rain. If they set out now, they could be back at the farm by dinnertime, but however would she explain Addy's absence?

'What do you mean, Addy's gone missing?' Jess's father echoed her own anguished announcement when she found him in one of the Henge field strips, hoeing around a ridge of onion shoots. 'Don't you know where he went?'

'No. I never saw him go.' Jess went on to describe their evening race to the long barrow to avoid the storm. 'We were settled in the entrance chamber behind the stones, sheep and all, and Addy was there too. But when I woke at dawn the storm was over and he was gone. I don't know where he went or why. He has just disappeared.'

'But were all the sheep there? You didn't lose any ewes, did you, girl?' Farmer Matt was all concern for his prize investment.

Offended, Jess snapped back. 'No, there are no ewes missing – just a member of the family! And I am really worried about him. I cannot believe he would have left me without a word. I'm frightened that he might have gone exploring down the barrow passage and got lost – or something worse. Perhaps the Devil does send his imps to haunt the barrows as the priest says. I called out for him but there was no answer and it's pitch black down there. Addy might just be terrified and waiting to be rescued. Please will you come up the Silbury Down with me? We can take a torch or lantern and at least make sure he's not there.'

Matt looked churlish. 'If you called for him, Jess, he'd surely have answered if he'd been there.'

'He could have panicked and hit his head. The passage is lined with stones. He might have been knocked out cold when I called.'

Her father sighed and reluctantly shouldered his hoe. 'Oh, very well. We'll take a light up the Silbury Down but we'd better hurry. It'll be dark soon.'

The flock of sheep was folded and dusk was falling by the time they reached the long barrow and lit the lantern they had brought with them. Star set a nervy tone for the search by refusing to re-enter the front chamber, settling instead for sitting guard at the narrow slit between the massive stones that gave reluctant admittance to the two uneasy humans.

'I'm surprised none of the ewes got stuck squeezing through here,' Matt grumbled as he extracted himself from their grasp. 'Especially as they're all in lamb.'

'Well, I'm glad none of them birthed here,' Jess said. 'It wouldn't have augured well for the newborn, starting life in a dark hole. Hold the lantern higher, Father – I want to check there are no signs that Addy has been through here since we left.'

For the first time she was able properly to see the place where she had slept the previous night and her eyes widened in shock. Not only was there still a pungent smell of sheep but the floor was dotted with mounds of droppings, which were already crawling with flies. But crucially she was also able to see into the dark passage that led between the burial chambers, revealing a muddle of bones spilling out from several collapsed entrances.

Matt moved towards it, holding the lantern more closely. 'It looks like these escaped the Devil's imps, only to be disturbed by human hands,' he growled, a gruff catch in his voice. 'But I won't be able to get down that tunnel, Jess. It's too low for me to bend that far. If you want to check the whole thing, you'll have to go yourself. But are you sure you want to?'

Jess looked stricken. 'What if I find him unconscious, or even dead? I wouldn't be able to carry him out on my own!'

Matt shook his head. 'No, you wouldn't, but I very much doubt you will find him at all. However, if you do, we would have to think about getting help from the village. If you don't feel you can go down the passage alone, I understand completely and we'll just have to assume that he left somehow without letting you know.'

Jess put her head in her hands in desperate cogitation. She couldn't bear to think that Addy might be lying alone at the tunnel's end or even that the Devil might have led him into eternal fire to atone for his sins. Surely he had not lived long enough to commit sins sufficiently heinous or numerous to deserve that fate? But if none of this applied, where was he and how had he disappeared?

After a long pause she lifted her head, jutted her chin determinedly and held out her hand. 'Give me the lantern, Father, I'm going in.'

Matt gazed at her fiercely, before nodding and handing it over. 'But wait a moment, Jess.' He plunged his hand into the pocket of his farmer's smock and pulled out a full spindle. 'Tie the loose end to your wrist and let the thread trail behind you. I hope it's long enough to reach the end of the passage and when you do, give it a jerk – once for finding Addy and twice for finding nothing. Now go! I'll be here at this end, praying for you.'

14

Clarendon Palace, Salisbury

5th May 1425

AT THE END OF their ride to Salisbury, John and Edmund Seymour stabled their horses, enjoyed a meal, and slept with their saddlebags in an attic dormitory on truckle beds, only to wake with sore heads and an argument about whether they would manage to gain entrance to Clarendon Palace. John was remarkably sanguine about it and after eating a healthy breakfast and handing over a silver groat for the hospitality, tucked his weighty money purse into the front of his long-sleeved doublet and donned his fashionable chaperon hat. 'Let us make a stroll around the city before we collect the horses,' he suggested. 'The barman told me last night that when the court is in residence the Pale Gate to the palace is busy in the morning with carts supplying food and drink. So it will be better to try our luck in the afternoon.'

Edmund shrugged. 'In that case I'd like to make a tour of the cathedral. I'm told it is spectacular and in the Chapter House you can see a copy of the two-hundred-year-old document which declares that no one is above the law, even the king who signed it.'

'That was King John, who managed to get much of it

changed, I'm told.' His cousin shot him a wicked smile. 'Us Johns don't take kindly to being told what to do!'

'Sometimes you have to though,' Edmund retorted. 'Wait until you come face to face with the Duke of Gloucester, if you ever do!'

Remarkably John's optimism about gaining entry to Clarendon Palace proved well founded, even though it lightened the money purse on his belt considerably. He managed to argue his way through the Pale Gate and, after a half-mile ride up the hill and over the drawbridge into the palace precinct, John's clinking purse and persuasive tongue even acquired them accommodation for the night and admission to the Great Hall, but only at places well down the trestle and when they finally made their way there, the evening supper service was over and the wine jugs were empty.

Choosing to ignore the steward's order not to wander from their place, John left the bench and set off up the hall to confront one of the few servers still available.

'We were delayed by the steward in his office. We need supper lower down the hall. All the dishes and wine jugs there are empty.'

The server drew himself up, like a fighter preparing for battle. 'Service has ended. There will now be music and dancing.'

'A man cannot live by music and dancing.' John's voice rose well above the general chatter. 'I have paid for hospitality and I'm sure the duke would not like to hear that two of his guests had gone to bed hungry. What is your name?'

'I am a servant of the crown. I am not obliged to give you my name, sir!' The man's tone rose defiantly.

'What is the trouble here, Paul?' A distinctive female voice spoke from behind John. 'Is there some delay in the entertainment?'

Blood rushed to the server's face. 'No, madam. This gentleman was asking for preferential treatment and I was endeavouring to explain why it was not possible.'

John hastily turned and bowed to the lady, a striking figure with a pale and beautiful face, a melodious voice and dressed in a cornflower blue satin, her throat lavishly garnered with pearls. Although briefly lost for words, he managed to express his dissatisfaction without rancour. 'I assure you, my lady, that I was requesting no more than is due. We have paid for overnight hospitality and now it seems there is no supper available.'

The lady's deep green eyes rounded in exaggerated astonishment. 'I have never known the Clarendon kitchen to run out of food. Can this really be true, Paul? I must inform the duke!'

'That won't be necessary, madam. I was on my way to ask the cook if an exception could be made.' The server made a swift and deep bow and strode away towards the service screen. The lady watched him go before turning and surprising John with a slow wink and an unexpected observation. 'The servers like to think they rule the roost in here. Now, tell me your name.'

'It is John; John Seymour of Wolf Hall.' He made a flourishing bow. 'And may I be permitted to know yours?'

A rippling laugh swam up from her throat, like a blackbird's song. 'You must be the only one here who doesn't know it, John. I am Eleanor; Eleanor Cobham.'

John felt his cheeks burn, feeling suddenly at a

disadvantage, realising that he had failed to recognise the Duke of Gloucester's influential long-standing mistress, especially as his cousin wandered up just in time to hear the name spoken. Edmund immediately made the low, courtly bow his dance master had taught him and said, 'Humble greetings, Mistress Cobham. I am John's cousin, Edmund Seymour. The reports of your beauty and grace have been sorely understated, it is an honour to meet you.'

Eleanor gazed at the handsome young man, eyeing him from head to toe, like a hawk eyeing its prey. 'To call it an honour may be premature, Master Edmund, but I thank you for your compliments anyway.'

She turned and gathered up her skirts, indicating an imminent departure, but John made another hasty bow, raising his smoothest voice and offering his widest smile to her departing back. 'I have important matters regarding a royal hunting park to place before his grace, my lady. I wonder if you might consider raising my case with his lordship?'

There was a soft rustle of silk as the skirts were lowered again and Eleanor turned back, her expression no longer so agreeable. 'A week ago, there would have been no hope of that,' she retorted. But then she appeared to be mulling his request. 'However, the duke has made a good recovery from his recent illness and actually intends to lead tomorrow's hunt, if the weather is fine. If you have come mounted, you might find an opportunity to broach your matter then, Master Seymour. Good luck to you and good evening.'

As they watched her swiftly make her way back to the high table a young page appeared from the service screen carrying a large dish in one hand and a wine jug in the other. Edmund almost pounced on him. 'Are those for the Seymours by any chance?' When the page nodded, he relieved him of the jug and added, 'Let us find a good place to consume them. Follow me.'

15

Savernake Forest and Wolf Hall

5th May 1425

FOLLOWING THE MOUNTED RULE she had been taught and which John never obeyed, Isabel rode the last mile to Wolf Hall at a walk but found it very tempting to break into a trot because the rain, which had started as a drizzle, suddenly became more intense. However, had she sped up she would not have noticed the shadowy figure flitting between the forest trees, where they grew close to the road, spreading their branches overhead as if they might soon meet up with their cousins on the other side. She had been hearing morning Mass at the Easton Priory church and visiting Prioress Editha, in case she had any news about their Windsor visit, but she had not. Now she urged her horse off the road and into the path of the mysterious skulker.

'Woah there, stranger, what are you doing here, apart from getting very wet?'

As she got closer, Isabel saw that he was a youth and was prepared for him to run for the trees but to her surprise he stopped and made her a sketchy sort of bow, as if he wanted to make a good impression. 'Until I saw you, milady, I was lost but now I'm hoping you might be able to help me find my way.'

For some reason the young man reminded her of Tom Stamford, and whereas she might have been wary of an unknown stray from the woods, she felt sympathy instead. 'Perhaps I can. If you walk beside my horse, I'll take you to my kitchen and you can dry off. What is your name?'

He was already nodding in response to her offer. 'My name is Jankin and I thank you.'

Isabel took note of the young man's pack as she urged her horse down to a slower walk. 'You have a heavy load, Jankin. Savernake Forest is very easy to become lost in. You must be tired.'

'I did get some sleep under a bush last night.'

'That was brave of you. I'd be frightened in the forest at night. There are wolves in there, you know.'

The youth looked rather shocked. 'Are there? No, I did not know. I was trying to catch up with a troop of soldiers. I thought they might be recruiting. But I must have missed them.'

'There are some in the vicinity. I heard they were camping at the castle in Marlborough. Did you go there?'

Jankin looked up at her in surprise. 'No. I just came over the Downs and got lost. I must have missed the town.'

She was frowning now, wondering if he was homeless. 'Have you had anything to eat?'

'I'm all right.' He sounded defensive. 'I don't want to be a nuisance.'

Isabel detected a hint of panic in the lad's voice. 'All right. No more questions. The street of houses up ahead is the Wolf Hall Manor village and the house is on the other side of that wall. Look out for any loose geese; they can be aggressive.'

Once the village had been navigated and the gate opened and shut, Isabel handed her horse over to one of the grooms and ushered Jankin past the bread oven and into the kitchen. The ever-present cauldron of pottage was simmering on a trivet by the fire, sending up wafts of fragrant steam. Isabel watched his eyes rivet on the pot and thought she could almost hear his mouth watering.

'Why don't you drop your pack and sit by the fire to warm up?' she suggested. 'Annie here will give you some hot pottage. Meanwhile I have a baby to feed in the house and I'll find you some dry clothes.' She turned to the maid of all tasks. 'Keep an eye on him, Annie, and give him a bowl of pottage. I want him to be here when I get back. Make sure he is.'

A handy hook in the passage took her wet cloak and she gave silent thanks to the Lord that her husband was still away and could not argue with her wish to help the unknown youth who had emerged from the forest. Something had stirred a memory of the skinny-looking thief who had tried to steal her basket of bread in the days before her brother had died. The remorse she had felt about the way John had kicked him away like a bag of offal had returned to stir her charitable nature but her instincts about Jankin told her he could be trusted.

Annie was not so certain. She ladled a helping of pottage into a wooden bowl and placed it on the central table. 'Don't you think to take any advantage of my mistress, boy,' she warned, whipping a wooden spoon from a pot and banging it down nearby. 'She has a heart that is too kind and I'll use that spoon in some painful places if you try any funny business.'

Jankin left his warm perch on the fireside stool and moved to the table. He picked up the bowl in both hands and raised it to his lips, making a slurping noise as he eagerly sucked the pottage down his throat. 'Good heavens!' Annie exclaimed, watching the speed with which the pottage was consumed. 'Anyone would think you haven't eaten for a week! Here, hand me the bowl, I'll get you some more.'

By the time Isabel returned, bringing some of Edmund's work clothes, Annie and Jankin were both sitting at the kitchen table kneading bread dough as if they'd been friends for years. Annie stood up, looking rather sheepish. 'I made him wash his hands, ma'am,' she said.

Isabel's eyebrows rose. 'So I should hope,' she said, laying the bundle of clothes on the other end of the table and gesturing at a curtained corner where the cook slept, only now there wasn't a cook anymore because he had been sent back to Hatch Beauchamp on John Seymour's orders. 'You can take these over there, Jankin, and put them on. They're my husband's young cousin's and I think they should fit.'

Jankin rose and went to pick up the bundle. 'Won't he miss them, ma'am?'

She smiled and shook her head. 'No. He's gone to Salisbury and won't be back for a day or two. We'll wash and dry the clothes you're wearing now and you can put them on again tomorrow. He'll never know.'

While Jankin was occupied behind the curtain Annie confided quietly in Isabel. 'The lad told me he'd heard there was a recruiting patrol somewhere hereabouts and he wants to find it. He looks a bit young to me but he wants to enlist as an archer.'

'Yes, I know where he was headed but has he said where he comes from?' Isabel asked, frowning. 'He doesn't look very old. Not much beard growth. Do his parents know what he's up to, I wonder?'

'When I asked him that he just shook his head and said the recruiting sergeant wouldn't bother about his age when he saw how good a shot he was.'

Isabel rolled her eyes. 'Ha! He doesn't hide his light under a bushel, does he? I'm tempted to call him out on that.'

The rain stopped in the afternoon and Isabel decided to take her forest wanderer at his word. 'If you really are a good archer, Jankin,' she said, 'I'll take you to Marlborough Castle tomorrow to see if the recruiting party are still there and you can show them your skills. It's market day anyway and I need to hire some kitchen staff to help Annie. She's run off her feet.'

Jankin frowned. 'I have no doubt about my skill with a bow but unfortunately my own broke when I tried to shoot a squirrel in the forest.'

'Don't worry about that, you can use one of my husband's. He has several and he won't know.' Isabel smiled. 'Unless you break it, of course.'

The youngster's eyes grew wide. 'I am quite strong, because I've done a lot of practice.'

'Well, we'll risk it, shall we? Come into the house and choose which one you want to use.'

After Jankin had made his selection and impressed Isabel with the quiver of arrows he took from his pack, they made their way to where a rough target had been set up behind the stables. 'Master Seymour has marked a few distances, so you can take your pick and work backwards if you like,' Isabel suggested.

Jankin narrowed his eyes and studied the distant pegs. 'I'll just try the bow first,' he said, pulling on the bowstring. 'I'm not sure how fast it will fire.'

Isabel nodded and stepped back a few paces. 'Take your time.'

At first the arrows flew erratically but after a few shots Jankin got the feel of the bow and sent one straight into the central ring. He gave Isabel a sudden grin and tipped the bow upwards. The next arrow buried its head in the trunk of an ash tree ten yards behind the target.

16

The Clarendon Hunt

6th May 1425

JOHN SEYMOUR WAS IN a glum mood as he and Edmund set off to find the hunt. They had missed the early start due to sleeping too long in their narrow but surprisingly comfortable rope-slung bed. By making enquiries with one of the dog handlers they learned that the hunt had set off for the gate that led to the Winchester Road and the vast eastern spread of the Clarendon Forest. 'They could be anywhere in there,' John complained. 'We'll never find them.'

'Of course we will,' Edmund said. 'When we hear the horns, we follow the sound. I bet there are hundreds of beasts in there. They won't have had to go far to find big game.'

His assumption proved correct and once through the next Pale Gate it was easy for them to follow the disturbed ground caused by the hunt, and after only a few minutes they heard the sound of the horn and the thundering hooves of chasing horses. When they caught up, they were surprised to find that rather than a stag, the prey was a large boar, which had already turned at bay in a brake of brambles growing against a rock wall at the foot of a steep crag. Among the fierce mastiffs sent in to hold the boar at bay, there was already a casualty. Having fallen foul of its sharp tusks, a dog's body lay motionless in a bloody heap under the boar's cleft feet. It was also evident that one of the duke's knights had already been chosen to make the kill and was advancing slowly and deliberately with his spear held aloft. Hampered by the furiously snarling dogs who had changed their attention to the corpse of their own kind, the knight made a desperate thrust but failed to hit a vital spot and the spear remained waving ineffectively from the boar's thick neck.

Slipping as he stumbled backwards from the gory scene, the knight nearly lost his balance entirely and was subjected to a tirade of laughter and mocking comments from the unsympathetic knights and nobles gathered around the duke, who shouted his own abuse from the saddle. 'God's blood! What a farce! No boar's head for you, Sir Francis! Not for that feeble thrust! Now – who's going to take up the challenge and make the kill?'

There was no immediate surge of enthusiasm for the task among the jeering followers; at least not until John Seymour suddenly hurled himself from his horse, threw the reins at Edmund and stepped forward through the mounted ranks. 'I will make the kill, if it please your grace,' he yelled, attracting astonished exclamations from the crowd.

The Duke of Gloucester glared down at him, brows knitted. 'I don't believe I know you, sir.' He glanced around the startled company. 'Does anyone recognise this man? And if not, why is he here?'

There were puzzled looks and disapproving grunts but no immediate reactions until a female voice rose above the continuing yelps of the mastiffs and the growls of the boar. 'Yes, I know him, your grace. I met him in the Great Hall yesterday evening. His name is John Seymour.'

It was Eleanor Cobham, sitting pillion behind a groom, whose horse stood close to that of her lover's. The duke's dark brows lifted in surprise and murmurs of disapproval burst from the mounted followers but her lover shrugged and smiled at his mistress before turning to glance back down at John. 'Well, if my lady knows you that's good enough for me, John Seymour. The task is yours.' He waved a regal hand in the direction of the growling boar and its surrounding host of snarling canines. 'But as I see you have no spear, so your task will be twice as difficult. You must retrieve the one in the boar's neck and use it more efficiently than Sir Francis did.'

John made a bow. 'Thank you, your grace,' he said. 'And if I succeed, I beg the honour of an hour of your time to make a proposal to you.'

The duke cast a swift glance back at his mistress, one eyebrow raised in enquiry, and received a nod. 'Very well,' he said. 'Now be quick and show us your skill with a spear, Master Seymour, lest we lose another mastiff!'

Edmund had never seen his cousin wield a spear and had no idea whether he was risking his life or making a clever move. However, fearing that John's fervent desire to find royal backing for his new venture at Wolf Hall might have led him into a desperate fool's errand, he edged his way around the gathered mass of horses to find a clear view of the boar and of his cousin, standing on the edge of the trampled baying theatre, already weighing up his plan of approach.

'Why hasn't the fool at least got his poniard in his left hand?' Edmund muttered to himself, drawing his own blade from the short scabbard on his belt. But then he realised that John had another plan in mind altogether, when he saw him swiftly duck under the boar's raised head and drag the dead mastiff out from under its feet. Being busy fighting off two attacking mastiffs at his shoulder, the boar had stamped his foot and tossed his head, releasing the body and allowing John to haul the bloody corpse far enough away, making a target more tempting for the other hounds, who had been starved for days to make them ferocious. Within moments they became more interested in tearing flesh from the dead member of their pack, rather than risking life and limb attacking the boar, and John was able to make a grab for the spear without fear of being tripped up.

By now, the watching crowd were yelling their support and urging John on with shouts of 'Kill, kill!', which he obligingly did, using both hands to thrust the sharp point of the spear under the tusker's front leg and into the heart of the beast. The boar began to shudder, its head drooping and legs shaking as its killer pulled the weapon free and stepped hurriedly back, while the mighty creature sank to the ground with a loud thud, blood spurting from the open wound. The dog handlers rushed in to collar the mastiffs, still snarling and fighting over their former kennel-mate, and John walked slowly back across the trampled killing-field to raise the spear to the Duke of Gloucester.

'The boar is yours, your grace!' he declared triumphantly. 'A feast to celebrate your recovered health! I think I have avoided spoiling the haunch.'

The duke raised his hand in salute, his bearded face

creased in a wide smile. 'A fine and cunning kill, John Seymour! And the boar's head is yours. Were your hands not bloody, I would offer you mine, but I have not forgotten my agreement to hear your proposal. My chamberlain will arrange a meeting.'

17

Church of St James, Avebury

6th May 1425

THE FIRST SIGHT THAT met Jess's eyes when she entered the church was the newly painted mural above the chancel arch. The faded fresco had been recently refreshed, and under the sunlight beaming through the high clerestory windows, its writhing line of figures stood out as a frightful warning of purgatory. Men and women in shredded garments of blood red, bruise purple and poisonous yellow lurched or crawled on crippled limbs, while ahead of them reared bright orange flames and behind pranced the Devil's imps, leaping and grinning with prodding forks in hand, urging them on into an eternally burning purgatory. Jess closed her eyes and turned her back as tears blurred her vision. She only forced them open when she heard the village priest emerge from the sacristy. He was carrying an altar cloth: white linen embellished with a colourfully embroidered image of Christ on the cross, the wounds on his head and body dripping with blood.

'God give you good day, my child,' Father Giles said, pausing beside the ancient stone font, proudly displaying its carving of two venomous wyverns with dripping jaws, twisted tails and clawed feet, appearing to attack an alarmed cleric. From her childhood Jess had always wondered why innocent newborn babies should be plunged into a bowl that was supported by such fearful images. However, the priest appeared unaware of the Christian turmoil displayed all around him. 'You look haunted, mistress. How can I ease your suffering?'

Dragging her gaze from the font, Jess uttered the first thing in her mind. 'Tell me that the Devil does not send his imps and dragons to force sinners down a burning road to hell!'

The priest shook his head. 'I cannot tell you that, my child, because it is true that he does, and they do. We who live here in Avebury must be fully aware of death's inevitability, when we are surrounded by so much pagan profanity.' He gestured up to the mural above his head. 'The painting on the wall reminds us to pray constantly to God to protect us from the Devil's malevolence and hell's eternal flames.'

Indignation forced Jess's voice to a new height. 'Does Satan's evil will extend to raising a storm to force a young shepherd to seek shelter in a pagan barrow, then sending his imps to carry the lad away to hellfire?'

The priest's response was pitiless. 'I have heard of such mysterious disappearances but they invariably indicate the failure of the person concerned to fulfil his duty to the Lord our God.' In the pause while Jess shook her head and gulped, Father Giles reached for her hand. 'Will you come and make confession, my child? It will restore your faith and settle your mind.'

Jess tore her hand from his grasp, turning her face from his suddenly lascivious gaze. 'I have nothing to confess, Father! I must go!' As she ran back down the aisle towards the south door of the church, she could sense the priest's lewd expression following her departure and prayed that her encounter had not stirred a hornet's nest.

Hurrying back through the village, she noticed a group of village women gathered around a strange man. Visitors were rare in Avebury because outsiders shunned the stone circles and avoided the people who lived so close to what was generally thought to be their malign influence. Force of habit made Jess pull the hood of her shepherd's smock over her forehead and increase the speed of her walk. She had made her visit to the church early in the morning in order to light a candle and offer a prayer for Addy and had already fled from the priest with his terrifying confirmation of the Devil's works ringing in her ears. All she wanted now was to get back to her dog and her sheep and escape to the peace and familiarity of the Downs.

However, when she reached the Henge farmhouse and made straight for the sheepfold at the back, she found her father already there. 'Ah, Jess, at last! Where have you been?' Without waiting for an answer, he pointed to a ewe that was standing alone in a corner of the fold, away from the rest of the flock. 'I think we have another lambing on the way there. Take a look.'

Grateful to find a distraction from her morbid thoughts of Addy, she climbed over the fold gate and headed straight for the straining ewe, collecting an excited welcome from Star on the way. 'Steady, girl,' she admonished the dog. 'You mustn't frighten the sheep mother.'

Matt wandered across to join her, watching with approval as she made her inspection of the ewe. 'Well, you're right, Father, she's definitely on the way but I don't think she'll deliver it for a while yet. I'm sure she'd rather do so out on the Downs rather than cooped up in the fold anyway, so I think I'll take them out when I've got my things packed.'

'A man came here half an hour ago,' Matt said suddenly. 'Said he was Addy's father.'

The blood drained from Jess's face. 'What did you tell him?'

Her father shrugged. 'I told him the truth. Addy tried shepherding but obviously didn't like it because he took off without a word. I said I didn't know where he'd gone and I wasn't impressed because he'd left me in the lurch. In fact, he didn't seem surprised about his son's departure. Said that he'd probably get a message from him when he got settled somewhere.'

'You didn't mention the long barrow at all?'

'No, why should I? He didn't look very pleased but he didn't argue. Then he grinned at me and added, "It'll be one less mouth to feed."'

Jess was amazed and offended on Addy's behalf. 'Is that all? Doesn't he care?'

'It seems not. Nor did he want to hang around. I offered him hospitality but he turned it down.'

'Poor Addy. He said that he and his father didn't get on but what will his mother think? She was the one who sent him to us.'

'He didn't mention her.'

'Surely, she'll want to know what's happened to her son? Don't you want to know, Father?'

Matt shrugged again. 'Not greatly, Jess, if I'm honest. Either he's a foolhardy young man who will regret leaving us or he's stumbled on an opportunity he just can't resist. Now, are you taking the sheep out or not? I have work to do too, you know.'

18

Clarendon Palace

6th May 1425

WITH UNUSUAL INTEREST THE Duke of Gloucester watched John Seymour make the dipped knee and low extended bow reserved for the young King's Protector. 'Good evening, Master Seymour,' he said. 'That courtesy made me understand what gave you the idea of reaching under the boar to collect the carcass of the murdered mastiff. And throwing it to distract the others was a brave master stroke. All in all, it was a neat and cunning kill. I congratulate you!'

John straightened up. 'Thank you, your grace. I'm only sorry that I missed the first chase and failed to witness your own kill, which I understand was swift and clean.'

'Yes, I appreciate a tidy execution. The resulting cuisine is always more tender.' The duke strolled across the audience chamber to two cushioned chairs set either side of a carved chimney piece surrounding a hearth where a fire was lit. His cream fur-trimmed silk doublet and purple long-toed shoes were the height of fashion. 'Take a seat and tell me about this proposal you mentioned. It had better be a good one.'

Somewhat bemused by being offered a seat at all, John

settled on the edge of the other chair and cleared his throat nervously. 'I think I can promise you that, your grace. It concerns the Royal Savernake Forest, which I believe you have had cause to deal with before, in your capacity as Keeper of the King's Forests south of the Trent.'

A deep frown creased the duke's brow. 'Yes indeed, although it was the Warden I had issues with, rather than the forest itself. I was obliged to suspend his term of office because he was neglecting his obligation to the king's larder and failing to enforce the forest laws. If I remember rightly his name is Sir William Esturmy and while I was away in the Low Countries, he managed to persuade the Privy Council to reinstate him in his post. Aside from causing me some annoyance, I have since had little time or inclination to take up the case again. Why? What is your connection to Savernake?'

John took a deep breath. 'No doubt your grace's recent illness has made you unaware that Sir William Esturmy died towards the end of March. As I assume you know, the wardenship of the Forest of Savernake was made a hereditary post by the great Conqueror and since Sir William was without male heirs the honour has fallen directly to me, as his eldest grandson. With it also comes the manor of Wolf Hall, which lies in the middle of the forest and . . .'

The duke sat up straight and raised his hand to bring his guest to an abrupt halt. 'I visited Wolf Hall after I had taken over the Savernake wardenship and I remember an unimpressive manor with an unimposing manor house, situated somewhere in the vicinity of Marlborough Castle. It had very little to recommend it.'

John felt his spirits sink into his boots. This was not the

way he had hoped the audience would go. But he took a deep breath and rallied for another effort. 'I agree, your grace, that Sir William allowed the place to deteriorate somewhat in his later years but that is why I seek your help. For one thing, surrounding that unimpressive manor there is a forest with twice the hunting territory available here at Clarendon and it contains probably three times the number of deer and boar, as well as two packs of wolves . . .'

Duke Humphrey suddenly raised a hand and leaned abruptly forward, bringing John to a sudden halt. 'Wolves? Are there truly wolves in Savernake? Why was I not informed of this?' His tone had changed from bored to indignant. 'I have been given to understand that wolves had been almost entirely wiped out in England, with only a few dens still to be found in the Marches and, I believe, in the forests of Lancashire. Are you sure of this, Master Seymour? Have you actually seen one?'

John hastened to take advantage of this sudden eager interest. 'My father used to tell me that they would herd deer into certain parts of the forest to feed the wolves so that they didn't eat the people, but I thought he was teasing me. Now my Head Forester tells me it is unwise to disturb the packs in spring because the bitches are breeding. Needless to say, I am anxious to visit their territory as soon as possible. Perhaps when we venture into that part of Savernake you would be interested in joining us? Not to hunt them just yet, because the pups will still be suckling, but if it would be of interest . . .'

The duke broke in eagerly. 'Yes, John! You can definitely count me in for that!' The sudden use of his Christian name raised the new Warden's hopes. 'But give me good warning of when it will be, because I am often tied down by Privy

Council meetings and so on.' He leaned further forward in his chair. 'And now that you have dangled this tempting prospect before me, what was the real reason for requesting this meeting?'

John risked a bold leap. 'I am hoping for your advice regarding the best use of Savernake's attractions, sir. The forest is on direct routes to Clarendon from London, Windsor and Winchester; ideally situated for you and the king's courtiers to break their journeys and enjoy the benefits of unmatched hunting. Being at the very centre of the best chases, Wolf Hall would be perfectly placed to welcome such illustrious guests, were it not for the inadequacy of the accommodation. So, it is my aim to build new and luxurious facilities to attract them. Would you and your court make use of such an attraction?'

Humphrey stroked his beard thoughtfully before revealing his thoughts. 'First of all, John, you have to consider your own risks. Don't forget that although you are the lord of Wolf Hall and its manor, you do not own the forest. You may be the hereditary Warden but the forest belongs to the king. So, you could invest in an expensive hunting development, only to find that the king takes the forest for himself and closes it to everyone else.'

'But how likely is that, your grace? It has never happened so far.'

'In fact, it has,' the duke responded. 'King John claimed it for himself, until the barons of Magna Carta repudiated his claim and he was obliged to hand it back. But the more important consideration is finance. Do you have the money to risk on such a project?'

There was no skirting around the main reason for seeking

the meeting with the duke now. John swallowed hard and launched into his proposal. 'Yes and no, my lord. Wolf Hall is not presently providing great revenue but my other manors provide a good income. It will not be enough to cover all the cost of the improvements I envisage and for the remainder I was hoping for a loan from the Exchequer, considering the service I have already rendered as Member of Parliament for Ludgershall and expect to do so again.'

This last remark earned a loud and explosive laugh from the duke. 'Aha! Now we reach the true reason for your presence here at Clarendon! There is hardly a member of the king's court who does not want a loan from the Exchequer but, as you know, I do not hold the office of Treasurer. The present Treasurer, Lord Hungerford, holds property quite close to yours I believe. Why do you not take your proposal straight to him?'

John was ready for this suggestion. 'Yes, I have every intention of doing so, your grace, but I am certain that a word in my favour from you would definitely tip the balance.'

The duke burst out laughing again. 'You want me to be your referee on a loan to build a mansion on your crumbling manor? I have to say that you do not lack audacity, John Seymour! For in reality, I hardly know you, so why should I trust you?'

'You cannot, my lord, but I give you my sworn promise that I am your most trustworthy subject. Also, I have the thing you want most ardently – the means to acquire your wolf-skin.' He knew that this rather flippant remark was made at the risk of offending a man who virtually ruled England and could have him clapped in irons if he so chose – and yet it seemed a risk worth taking.

Duke Humphrey leaned back in his chair and drummed his fingers on both the armrests, submitting John to a minute-long stare from his cold blue Plantagenet eyes. Then his fingers ceased drumming with a decisive thump. 'You have mistaken the thing I want most ardently, John, but I will achieve that without your help. However, if you organise me a wolf hunt and I acquire the wolf-skin I also desire, I will stand surety on a loan from the Exchequer towards your new hunting lodge. But my presence at any wolf hunt must remain a secret between us; and if word should get out, I will blacken your name from London to Ludgershall! If it does not, I will consider us friends, patronise your new premises and bring the court to Wolf Hall. I may even consider a knighthood. But do not count on it.'

John's face suffused as he leapt from his chair to kneel at the feet of his seated host. 'A wolf-skin shall be yours, your grace, and the source shall never be revealed; that I can promise. And before that, a visit to Wolf Hall Manor will be organised at your convenience, to scrutinise the wolves of Savernake. May I kiss your hand to seal the deal, my lord?'

The duke slid his right hand off the chair-arm and watched John make the accepted gesture of fidelity. His expression remained fierce. 'That makes you my liegeman, John Seymour, and believe me, I will hold you to all aspects of allegiance and loyalty.'

John looked up into the cold eyes above him and felt the hairs on his arm rise under the silk of his court doublet.

19

Clarendon Palace

6th May 1425

WHILE JOHN WAS PLEDGING his heart and sword to the Duke of Gloucester, Edmund Seymour was enjoying the music in the Great Hall, where the trestles were cleared away and the minstrels had descended from their gallery to provide a sequence of merry tunes for popular dances. He had hung back from taking part, even though the steps he was observing were all those he had been taught in the dance classes his mother had insisted he should attend.

He could almost hear her voice saying, 'You are a younger son of a younger son, Edmund. Looks will go a certain way towards attracting well-dowered young ladies but the addition of light feet on the dance floor will often clinch a good marriage settlement.' The memory made him smile.

'I wonder what you find so amusing, Master Seymour?'

The voice was familiar but he still felt a slight shock when he turned to find Eleanor Cobham standing beside him in another stunning gown of deep marigold. He made a swift bow. 'I was recalling the dance classes of my youth, my lady, and my mother's insistence that I attend them.'

'You are still a youth, Master Seymour, and your mother

was, or is, a wise woman. There is nothing worse than finding oneself obliged to take the floor with a clumsy partner who treads on one's skirts.' She made a gesture towards the minstrels, who had ended one dance and were preparing for the next. 'I should like to sample the success of your mother's advice. Will you dance with me?'

Still blushing at her comment on his youth, he made another deep bow and took her offered hand to lead her into the circle forming for the Almain, much to his relief because it was a dance he knew to be fairly slow, with steps that were easy to remember. It also gave some opportunity for conversation, as they set off around the big circle that the dance demanded.

Eleanor lost no time in starting the conversation. 'As you are here, I take it you were not included in the duke's invitation to meet your cousin, Master Seymour? Do you know anything about the proposal he is making?'

'It seemed like more of a summons than an invitation,' Edmund said, as they made the first turn within the ring, adding when they set off on the circle again, 'I believe I know what John wants to discuss but I would be breaking a confidence to tell you.'

His partner nodded, beginning a sequence of slow skipping steps forward. 'Perhaps we will be able to judge whether he was successful or not by his mood when he returns. Meanwhile I propose that we liven up this dance by doubling the paces and speeding up the turns. What do you think?'

Edmund had no time to respond before, without waiting for his agreement, she was true to her word and increased the speed of the steps, nearly bumping into the couple ahead of them. However, the change was quickly adopted by the rest of the dancers and the minstrels were obliged to follow by livening up the beat, with the result that those watching from the sidelines started to clap to the new rhythm and the dancers began to stamp and call out and the whole hall echoed to shouts of gaiety and glee. After a dozen whirls around the circle had been completed and the dance finally slowed to a halt, there was much clapping and laughter, mostly aimed at Eleanor and her partner, who were cheered and praised for enlivening the evening.

Onto the dais and into all this merriment strode Duke Humphrey, closely followed by John Seymour. The duke stopped at the top of the dais stair and held out his arms to Eleanor, who immediately lifted her skirts to climb to his side. 'You have been stirring up the minstrels again, I gather,' he said, kissing her cheek, then pointing at the man she had just left. 'And who is your handsome partner in crime this time?'

His mistress lifted their linked hands to her lips and kissed his fingers. 'Well, it would have been you, my lord, had you been here. But Edmund Seymour made a very able alternative.'

'Hah!' Gloucester turned to the man behind him. 'Another Seymour! Anything to do with you, John?'

John's brow knitted as he stared, blank-faced, down at Edmund. 'I could disown him if you order me to, your grace. But if not, yes, he is my cousin – my young cousin – who has yet to learn his place in society.' His tone and expression had flattened with irritation.

Eleanor Cobham came to the rescue. 'Edmund Seymour does not deserve the ire of either of you. It was I who asked him to partner me because he looked like a man who might be light of foot, as indeed he is.' Her gaze swept over the rest of the dancers gathered on the floor of the hall. Meanwhile Eleanor and the duke descended the dais steps together and formed the lead pair for a Basse dance as John took his cousin's arm and led him off to one of the window embrasures at the side of the hall where the stone benches gave some privacy.

As murmurs and nods of agreement spread around the room, Edmund grinned up at his cousin, his shoulders shaking with mirthful relief but his mind tinged with fear that his prancing with the duke's mistress might have scuppered John's plans for Wolf Hall.

'You want to be careful not to appear too friendly with the duke's mistress, Ed,' John began sotto voce. 'Duke Humphrey is not a man to be crossed.'

Edmund sent him an enquiring look. 'Was it not a good session, then?'

John made a horizontal wave of his hand. 'So-so. At least he's agreed to pay a visit to Wolf Hall. He wants to come and see the wolves when we visit their den. But he doesn't want the dens made public. I'm a bit worried that he'll demand sole access to them.'

'So, he won't be bringing the court to Savernake, or supplying any funds towards a new mansion?'

'As far as that's concerned, nothing is certain. He advised me to approach Lord Hungerford for a loan from the Exchequer – said he'd put in a good word for me.'

'And will you? Make an approach, I mean?'

'I'll probably try but I fear a dismissal. Anyway, we have no reason to stay on at Clarendon anymore. We'll make an early start in the morning and have a good breakfast at a tavern before we ride. So don't go celebrating your conquest of the Protector's mistress with too much of Humphrey's Spanish Sherish.'

Edmund had been watching the duke and his lady as they followed the steps of the Basse dance. 'He's trodden on her toes twice and her skirt once,' he told John. 'The smile never left her face.'

John's face cracked. 'She's definitely aiming to become a duchess then,' he murmured. 'She is a brave woman.'

20

Marlborough, Wiltshire

6th May 1425

ISABEL AND JANKIN WALKED under the gate arch at Marlborough Castle to the sound of hammering in the bailey and the sight of military flags and banners being lowered from the battlements. The Wiltshire recruiting party was clearly moving out.

Like a bee seeking pollen, Jankin rapidly identified the commanding officer, walking out of the only tent still standing, and immediately turned to Isabel with an apologetic expression on his face. 'I'll leave you here then, milady. It looks as if I'm only just in time.'

Isabel experienced a twinge of regret. She had grown rather fond of her surprise guest. She felt sure there was no question of him not being enlisted when, young though he was, he could send an arrow much further than anyone else at the manor. There was a lump in her throat as he said farewell and marched off towards the recruiting officer's lonely tent. 'If they don't take you on there's always work for you at Wolf Hall,' she called after him.

It made him turn and laugh, shaking his head. She couldn't tell if he was dismissing the very idea of him not being accepted or simply mocking any notion of working in a domestic kitchen.

She had left Annie out in the market and went to search for her among the gathering of men and women seeking employment. Having failed to secure any suitable kitchen servants from the tenant families at Wolf Hall, Isabel had decided this was the only other way to seek a cook and a skivvy and release Annie to work at what she was better at, housekeeping. A steward was also needed to run the household and keep the accounts but John had made it clear that this was to be his choice. One that still had not been made, much to Isabel's additional irritation, since it was she who had to read the tallies and make entries in the books, a task she found tedious.

After the next hour or so questioning the individuals Annie had picked out from the crowd of would-be domestic servants, Isabel was pleased to find that among them was a burly chef called Ham, whose arms and hands looked as if they might make short work of a pig's carcass. Her enquiries drew from him the welcome fact that he had recently managed to purchase his manumission, allowing him to leave his home manor, and was looking for work as a freeman elsewhere. Further questioning revealed that the newly married lady of that manor had wanted to be rid of him because she disapproved of his loose observation of fast days. Ham had the rotund figure frequently seen among chefs and butchers, which did not offend Isabel, who was satisfied that one such would be well able to handle the heavy iron pans and cauldrons in a busy kitchen. He confessed that he had never found time to marry and as a single man would be amenable to being accommodated within the kitchen building, as long as he had a bed to keep him off the floor.

'And the use of a terrier to catch the rats and mice, my lady,' he stipulated with a straight face. 'I like to keep the vermin out.'

Isabel's brows rose at this stipulation, being unaware that there might be a problem of that kind at Wolf Hall. 'I'm glad to hear that, Ham, and I think the head huntsman might be able to supply what you need,' she said faintly. 'There are all kinds of dogs in his kennels.'

Satisfied with this arrangement, Isabel had just settled matters with the rotund chef, when her attention was drawn to the sound of marching feet moving through the market. A column of men wearing red and white striped jackets were scattering the shoppers as they passed up the market hill, making for the old Roman road out of Marlborough. Isabel had to run through the crowd to see if she could catch sight of Jankin among them and there he was, waving at her from the back of the company, a big grin on his face. Behind the marching men plodded a line of pack horses laden with large panniers of supplies and after that a capacious cart full of longbows and quivers of arrows. Clearly Jankin had made the grade.

On a sudden whim, Isabel ran up to the column, getting as close to Jankin as she could. 'Shall I send word to your parents to tell them where you are?' she yelled over the stamping feet.

Jankin's face coloured a dark red and he shook his head violently, averting his eyes. 'No!' he shouted, making violent gestures with his fist to dismiss her and her idea. The man marching beside him snorted with laughter and the line marched on, leaving Isabel angry and embarrassed. She slowly wended her way back through the crowd, frowning at the sniggers of derision.

'Like a pretty boy soldier, do you, whore?' Isabel felt a surge of pain and indignation as a heavy hand clamped on her arm from behind.

At that moment a deep and furious voice growled at her side, 'Leave her alone, hogo, or there'll be atterclaps!' and an even mightier fist wrapped itself around the attacker's wrist.

It was Ham, infuriated at the thought of injury to his newly acquired mistress. Isabel had no idea what his outburst in the local dialect meant but it seemed to have the desired effect on her assailant, whose grip dropped instantly. The brawny chef immediately grabbed him, pushed the man's arm up his back and marched him away through the crowd, before hurling him to the ground in a convenient space and advising him to take his 'hogo' with him and 'leave my lady alone!'

When he returned to Isabel's side he said gently, 'Bobbish now, madam?'

Still round-eyed at her rescuer's actions, Isabel nodded, having little clue what he meant. 'Yes, thank you, Ham,' she said. 'And if it isn't too rude, would you tell me what you said to the man?'

'Ah, there's no reason why a lady like yourself would use such language, ma'am. I beg your pardon but that's the way we have to talk to the riffraff around here sometimes. I just called him a "bad smell" and threatened "consequences".'

Isabel laughed. 'Well, I congratulate you on your restraint, Ham! And thank you for your timely action. I know who to call on for protection in future!'

Ham gave a rare smile, showing a rather gappy set of teeth. 'Always at your service, ma'am.'

21

The Haunch of Venison, Salisbury

6th May 1425

APPROPRIATELY THE FIRST INN the Seymours encountered as they entered the Salisbury marketplace on their way home was the Haunch of Venison, a tall, black-beamed, thatch-roofed hostelry that looked popular, with a steady stream of Salisbury citizens passing through the open door, even early in the morning. Around the back the stables looked clean and well-tended, enough at least to prompt them to hand the reins over to one of the grooms.

'What's the taproom like?' John enquired. 'Is the ale drinkable?'

'Best ale in Salisbury, sir,' the lad replied with his hand out just far enough to receive the coin John slipped into his fingers. 'And, like the stables, the whores are clean.'

The Seymour grin appeared instantly. 'I'll hold you to that, boy!'

Which brought a deep frown to Edmund's visage as he hauled the saddlebags from his horse's back before the lad led it away. 'What did you mean by that, John?'

'Just what I said. I'll hold him to his word, should I choose to test it.'

'And will you?'

The frown transferred to John's face. 'What do you think, boy? My wife has barred me from her bed and shows no sign of relenting. If temptation beckons, I can be no angel!'

The taproom was crowded with men filling their stomachs before their day's toil, perhaps in the still incomplete Salisbury cathedral precinct, or on the market stalls, or the looms in the many weaving lofts that were turning the city into a thriving centre of the cloth industry. The arrival of two booted and spurred horsemen attracted little interest as the Seymours made their way to the racks of ale barrels behind the bar.

'We've put our horses in your stable and we're looking to break our fast,' John announced to the burly man guarding the barrels. 'I hope you're able to accommodate us?'

The tap-man pursed his lips through the bushy beard that framed his plump face.

'A girl will bring the ale and take your order for food.' His gaze swept the busy room. 'You might have to share a table but it'll get quieter soon, when they start going to work. I could keep your bags under the racks while you eat if you wish. No one tries to steal from the Big Barrel!' One fist hit his prominent chest.

'I can well believe it! Edmund, give the man our bags.' The bulging saddlebags were handed over.

The big man turned from his task. 'I'll send a girl with your ale.'

They sat opposite each other at one end of a long table, nodding at the group of four men occupying the other end. Within a minute a girl in a brown dress, white cap and a coarse linen apron arrived with the jug of ale and two mugs. 'Big Barrel said you wanted to order food,' she said, placing them on the table. 'There's fish stew or onion pie with greens.'

'We're sticking to Lenten fare then,' John remarked. 'Pity.'

'Rules of the house, sir. Come back Sunday if you want the haunch of venison.' There was the hint of a smile in her voice as she continued, 'That's the house special.'

'Do you cook it yourself, mistress?' he persisted.

She made a derisive noise. 'Cook wouldn't let a woman near his kitchen. Will you have the fish or the pie?'

Edmund broke in. 'I'll have the fish. And some bread to mop up the juice. I take it the fish is fresh?'

'Swam up the Avon this morning, sir. And what is your choice?' This last was aimed at John, who was flipping a silver groat between his fingers.

'I think I'll toss for it,' he said. 'Heads for the pie and tails for the wench.'

For a second or two she stared at him, frowning, then gave a brief nod. 'Toss it,' she said. It spun from his hand and landed head up on the table. 'It'll be the pie then.' She scooped the coin swiftly into her apron pocket before swirling away.

Edmund blew air. 'She's off with your groat and you're well out of pocket, John!' he exclaimed.

His cousin shrugged. 'We'll see. We need to eat anyway. Pour the ale, Ed.'

They clinked tankards before taking long draughts of the contents. Within minutes the same girl returned with their order and placed two pence on the table. 'Your change, sir,' she said.

She had an inflection in her voice that John couldn't

place. 'Keep it and bring us some wine, if you please. Have you some good Gascon red? Oh, and have you a name?'

She cocked an eyebrow but ignored his second question. 'Two tuns of good Gascon wine arrived in Southampton only last week on a ship from Bordeaux and a hogshead found its way to us yesterday. I'll bring some but it's not cheap. A farthing per jug and the jugs are not large.'

'Take back the two pence, bring two jugs and keep the change for yourself. But only if you tell me your name and come and sit with us. We are bored with each other's company, are we not, Ed?'

'If you say so,' muttered Edmund. He had already started eating his stew.

The barmaid gathered up the two pence. 'I'll bring the wine.'

Edmund lifted his head from his bowl and watched her walk away. 'I can't think why you're interested, John. She's not much of a looker and she won't have anything remarkable to say. I thought you were wanting to mix with the nobility, not with a half-wit serving wench.'

'She may be a skivvy but she's not a half-wit, Ed, and there can be more fun in a working girl.'

'There are probably more interesting folk among the customers,' he retorted.

John cut a slice out of his pie. 'Well, if you don't want to stick around don't let me stop you finding other company. Most of it looks pretty rough in here though.'

'It's you that's choosing to mix with rough company, if you ask me.'

'I didn't ask you. Just mind your own business.'

Edmund slid off the end of his bench. 'And you remember that we're on the way home.' By the time the barmaid put in another appearance he had started a conversation with the two men who remained at the other end of the table.

Two small jugs of wine and a pair of horn mugs had appeared in front of John. 'I see your friend has left you,' the girl observed, sliding into the abandoned seat.

John pushed his own empty trencher away and reached for one of the jugs. He poured wine into the mugs and pushed one across the table. 'He's not a friend, he's my cousin – my young and stupid cousin.'

'But a good-looking one.' She gave him a cheeky grin as she lifted her mug.

Having clinked and drunk, John raised an eyebrow and commented, 'Looks aren't everything. This is good wine though, as you promised.'

'I didn't promise to give you the benefit of my company though, did I? But as you can see, the taproom has cleared a lot and Mister Big is in a good mood. One of the other girls can cover my tables.'

'I haven't noticed any other girls.'

'What do you mean? Four of us have been running around like squirrels – oh! I see, you're flattering me. Thank you but you don't need to. I know I'm not the youngest or prettiest . . .'

He cut in, putting down his mug and placing his elbows on the table to lean closer. 'You are the most interesting.'

Her brow puckered. 'I thought for a moment you had intended to ask me "how much for sex?", but for some reason you changed your mind.'

John slammed the flat of his hand on the tabletop. 'Ha! You're a clairvoyant, are you? A mind reader?' He turned his hand over to offer the palm. 'Will you read it for me?'

Her responding laugh was warm. 'I like you, John, but I can't read minds. Sometimes I wish I could!' She drained the other mug and set it down. 'No, I just like working in a taproom. I meet interesting people.'

He gave her fingers an affirmative squeeze. 'So do I.'

She snatched her hand away. 'Don't bother to flatter me again, John Seymour! See – I already know your name because I recognised the badge on your saddlebags: two gold wings joined together.'

'And you know it's the Seymour badge!' John rolled his eyes. 'I told Edmund you were the brains in this place. He called you "a half-wit serving wench".'

'Did he indeed? What a rude youth – but so good-looking!' Turning her head to glance up the table at Edmund, their eyes met and she pressed her finger into her temple and made a screwing motion. He flicked a finger at his nose in reply. 'I don't think he likes me,' she said, smothering a laugh. 'What a pity.' She gathered the wine jugs and mugs and stood up. 'Thanks for the drink, John. I must get back to work now.'

'You've frightened her off!' Edmund called from the other end of the table. 'Not your type after all, John?'

'Oh, I wouldn't say that.'

'What is her name then?'

'That's for another day.' He stood up. 'Come on – time we left.'

22

Wolf Hall

7th May 1425

JOHN AND EDMUND STOPPED only once to rest and water the horses and covered their thirty-mile journey to Wolf Hall Manor in good time, arriving just before sunset. The stable lads had settled the horses and only one of them was still on duty but quickly dealt with the tack, handing the saddlebags to Edmund to carry to the house. John had wandered across the yard, intrigued to see the door to the kitchen closed and smoke rising from the chimney. When he opened the door, he was even more surprised to hear a loud and irritated voice yelling, 'Shut that door!'

'Who are you, may I ask?' With his hand on his sword hilt John aimed the question at the big man who had turned from the hearth with a large wooden spoon in his hand and a somewhat stained apron covering his rotund frame.

'Who would you guess? I'm Ham, the new cook, and I haven't time for interruptions. My lady wants her supper.'

John flicked his hand across his chest in the sign of the cross and lifted his face to the smoke-stained beams. 'Glory be to God!' he declared. 'At last, we have a cook! Welcome to Wolf Hall, Ham. I am John Seymour, lord of this manor, and I too want my supper. I hope there is plenty of . . .' He paused. 'What are you cooking?'

Edmund appeared behind John, and Ham made an awkward bow to both men. 'Welcome home, sirs. It is Saturday but if you don't mind stretching the Lenten rules by a few hours you can have some of the chicken stew I'm cooking for Sunday's dinner. There should be plenty and I can make something else for tomorrow.'

John nodded. 'That's a good idea, Ham. We've been riding hard all day so we'll pray for divine forgiveness and eat your stew. Just give us time to wash off the dust of the road and greet the family.' He gestured at Edmund. 'This is my cousin Edmund, who also lives here. So, you'll have three of us at table.' He turned for the door, waving his hand and calling over his shoulder, 'And make sure you save some for yourself! Good to have you here.'

They found Isabel with young Johnnie on her lap, sitting by the fire in the hall. 'Oh, you're home!' Isabel rose to exclaim, patting her baby boy onto her shoulder. 'We didn't expect you until tomorrow.'

'We couldn't wait!' John planted an enthusiastic kiss on his son's flaxen hair. 'What are you doing up, young man?' he asked the baby. 'Is your mother leading you astray with her Arthurian legends?'

Isabel held up the book and protested, 'It is my Book of Hours! Johnnie loves the pictures of saints and angels.'

'Oh. I didn't know you had one.' John, narrow-eyed, watched Edmund greet Isabel with a kiss on the cheek, then tweak Johnnie's nose in greeting, making the child sneeze. 'I'm not sure he likes that, Ed,' he said.

When the men had stood back Isabel couldn't wait to

reveal her news. 'We have a cook, John. A real chef, who can butcher meat, as well as make subtleties. His name is Ham.'

'Yes, I know. I found him in the kitchen. He certainly looks the part.'

'You approve, then? I wasn't sure you would.'

'I'll wait until I've tasted his food but it certainly smelled good and we're starving hungry.'

Isabel's face dropped. 'But there won't be enough! He thought there was only me for supper, and Nan and Annie of course – and himself.'

John shook his head. 'He seems very resourceful, your Ham, and I think we'll all be fed. Where did you find him?'

'In the Marlborough market. He'd left his home manor because the new lady didn't like him. He even paid his manumission, so he must have made some money from his cooking.'

John took her by surprise when he suddenly leaned in and kissed her lips, sending her hand to her mouth and a frown to her brow. 'I think he'll be a great asset,' he said. Then he drew back and added, 'I hope I can get up to our chamber now because I would like a quick change of clothes and I don't want to let Ham's delicious-smelling meal go cold. Is that going to be possible?'

Having made up her mind not to become beguiled by her husband's sudden pleasantries, Isabel turned to Edmund. 'Would you mind fetching what he needs, Ed? Nan will let the ladder down for you.' She laid stress on the 'you' with a sideways glance at John. 'She is busy making the cot up with clean linen and I'm just about to put Johnnie to bed.'

John's eyes narrowed with anger, but Isabel stared him

out. 'Nothing has changed here, John,' she said. 'Except the arrival of Ham, so be grateful for that, as I am.'

There was a heavy silence, then Edmund spoke up. 'Just tell me what you want, John, and then we can make ourselves fit for the table and Johnnie can go to bed. I'll go and call Nan out to manage the ladder.'

'No, I'll call her.' Isabel walked towards the wooden arch that led through the hall screen but John stepped into it before she could get there.

'I managed to get a meeting with the Protector,' he said with pride. 'He is coming to Savernake later in the spring. He wants to hunt the wolves.'

Isabel stopped in front of him. 'Congratulations.' Her tone was cold. 'Now, if you'll excuse me . . .' As if on cue, Johnnie gave a big yawn. 'Your son wants his bed. Tell Ham I'll have my supper up the ladder. He can put it in a basket and Annie will bring it.'

23

Easton Priory and Wolf Hall

Mid-May 1425

After returning from Clarendon Palace John and Edmund continued to make daily excursions with the Head Forester, to familiarise themselves with the tracks and pathways. This gave Isabel freedom to make regular visits to Easton Priory, where she attended Mass and found pleasure and sometimes inspiration speaking with the pilgrims. Importantly, she was also able to keep in touch with Prioress Editha regarding the proposed excursion to Windsor Castle and on her third visit she learned that a courier had arrived with a letter bearing a royal seal.

'It comes from Joanna Belknap, the Dowager Queen's lady-in-waiting I told you about,' Editha said, handing it to Isabel to read, which she did with growing excitement.

Greetings to my good friend Editha, Prioress of Easton.

Having told Queen Catherine about the efforts made by your Trinitarian Order to raise money to ransom enslaved Christian soldiers, I am tasked by her grace to invite you to visit her at Windsor Castle to reveal more about the brave and serious work of the Order's monks and nuns. But she urges you to come soon, as the Royal Council has recently ruled that since the king will be six this year he should only be attended by squires and educated by priests, male tutors and knights. His new governor, the Earl of Warwick, believes women weaken young boys' minds and so an Act has been passed in Parliament that the king's mother and her female household should leave Windsor and take up residence at Hertford Castle, which would mean a longer journey for you. Signed with good wishes, Joanna Belknap, Lady-in-Waiting.

'Why should the Dowager Queen be parted from her son?' Isabel cried. 'Surely that is cruel – for both of them.'

'It does seem unkind, certainly,' agreed Editha. 'But the Earl of Warwick was a favourite of the king's father and I'm told he made a solemn oath at the fifth Henry's deathbed to make a knight of his infant son. He has obviously decided now that it's time to begin that process, so he has returned from fighting in France to make good his promise.'

'But surely that should not include sending away his mother!' Isabel was still incensed. 'A prince needs to understand right and wrong before he learns to fight and rule.'

Disapproval gathered on the Prioress's face. 'Well, I think we should avoid making any statements like that in the Dowager Queen's presence,' she said. 'We are not going all the way to Windsor to criticise the Earl of Warwick or the Royal Council. We are going to encourage Queen Catherine to make a generous donation to the Trinitarian cause. And as Lady Belknap says, we need to leave quite soon.'

Isabel blushed bright red and lowered her gaze, nodding in silent agreement. She now realised that if she were to join the Prioress on her important mission, she would have to find some way to persuade her unpredictable husband that it was a good idea. Either that or hope that he might be making a journey somewhere himself. Riding back to Wolf Hall she kept Snowflake at a slow pace, her mind busy with plans for the much longer journey she might make to Windsor and a niggling worry that John might spoil the whole plan that she and Editha had made to depart the following day. By the time she reached her destination she had made two decisions. Firstly, that she would not bother the Prioress with her own fears about whether she would be able to make the journey at all and secondly that she would not tell her husband where she was going.

That afternoon she took two saddlebags up to the solar before pulling up the ladder stair. Then she set about choosing suitable clothes to wear in the Dowager Queen's court, hoping that her wardrobe could supply apparel subtle enough to provide a personable appearance, without being attractive to thieves on the road and pickpockets in the inns on the way. Sensibly she realised that the Prioress's head-veil and wimple might well deter most bandits, but their protection might not stretch to her secular companion.

She had just completed her packing and was considering whether to venture down the ladder and go and find Nan and little Johnnie, when Edmund called up to the solar unexpectedly. 'Can I come up, Izzy? John's not here.'

Isabel was surprised but also relieved. Perhaps now she could have supper in the hall instead of sitting on the clothes chest. 'Wait, I'm coming down, Ed,' she called and heaved the ladder over the hatchway.

'This has really got to stop!' was Edmund's exasperated welcome as she reached the bottom.

'Tell that to your cousin,' she retorted. 'Where has he gone anyway?'

'He didn't favour me with that information, just said he'd be away for a couple of days and rode off in a southerly direction. If I were to make a guess, I'd say he was heading back to Salisbury.'

'He'll be lucky to get there before dark, won't he? Even on the sprightly Atlas!' They were walking through the passage and into the hall, heading for one of the cushioned window seats with a view over the brow of the hill down to the Bedwyn Brook.

Edmund shrugged. 'There's a full moon tonight. Look – it's already on the rise. I just hope he doesn't overwork Atlas.'

'I doubt that will happen,' Isabel said. 'He loves that stallion more than his son!'

As they sat down to talk Nan walked slowly down the eastern stair from the upper rooms, carrying baby Johnnie.

Isabel stood up, moved swiftly to meet them and swept him from the nurse's arms for a hug and a kiss.

'I'll leave him with you then, madam,' Nan said.

'Oh yes,' Isabel agreed, as Nan hurried off through the service arch. 'I wonder what there will be for your supper, Johnnie? Mother's milk as usual I expect ha ha! But actually, I've arranged for the Reeve's wife to nurse you for a few days while I go to Windsor. You'll like her, I'm sure you will.'

'Windsor? Why?' Edmund's eyes grew wide. 'When are you going there, and who with?'

Isabel sighed regretfully. 'I shouldn't have said that because I don't want John to know. You mustn't say anything until I've left but I'm going to Windsor Castle with the Prioress of Easton. She's been invited to the Dowager Queen's court to tell her about the Trinitarian Order's mission to ransom captured Christian soldiers. Editha is hoping to secure a royal donation to the cause and I don't want John to know. He'll probably be jealous and lock me up or something. Which would be ironic when I'm locking myself away anyway! I don't think he'll be able to stomach me going to Windsor Castle before he's ever been himself. So now I am going to have to rely on you to keep my secret, Edmund.'

'When are you going? If you're not back before he returns, he'll be out of his mind and I will have to tell him.'

'We are leaving tomorrow. It was only decided this morning and I don't know how long it will take us to get there and back. The Prioress says to pack for at least three days – possibly four or five.' Her wide eyes and lips offered Edmund an excited smile. 'Oh Ed, don't look so worried! Young Johnnie has you and Nan and the Reeve's wife to look after him and I'll be all right with the Prioress!'

'How do you know?' Edmund almost shouted. 'Have you ever travelled any distance without a retinue? There are thick forests hiding bands of thugs. You have no escort and no idea how to avoid them!'

'But we'll be dressed like nuns and have no money to give them, so they won't bother us. Anyway, we'll stick to the busy roads.'

'Hmm.' Edmund chose not to make any reference to Isabel's lovely face and soft hands – enough to attract a lecherous bandit. 'Is it worth it though, Izzy?' he almost pleaded. 'Why don't you just send a few gold coins via the Marlborough royal couriers?'

Isabel shook her head, sending him a look of incredulity, as if he had no idea of the purpose of the journey. 'No, Edmund, I can't. The effort of the journey means as much to me as the ransom money does for the poor enslaved soldiers.'

24

Henge Farm

Mid-May 1425

Now that the ewes were beginning to lamb in earnest, Jess didn't like to stray too far from the farmhouse. Her father had made it clear that responsibility for the lambing was entirely hers but she knew that if something went badly wrong, she could always call on his help, as long as she kept the sheep close by. There was plenty of shelter behind the mysterious stones in the Great Circle and spring grass for the ewes and new lambs in the water meadows along the River Kennet. All the Avebury shepherds tended a sturdy breed of sheep known as the Wiltshire Horn, so called because on most other breeds only the rams grew horns but out on the Downs the Wiltshire ewe's unusual growths provided good weapons against foxes and badgers and handy handles for when they needed restraining for shearing.

As she watched over the first births, taking short sleeps when she could, Addy weighed heavily on Jess's mind. She cursed him often for not being there to help her but there were also times when she simply missed his company and berated him out loud. 'Wherever you are, Addy, I hope you're as tired and weary as I am and not living it up doing some cosy, inside job!' Then she would remember the Devil's imps and the hellish flames on the church wall and regret her reproaches. The bones and smells of the ancient barrow still lingered in her mind and she would often send up silent prayers that Addy's corpse did not lie untended in the darkness of the passage, while his soul burned in torment.

She worried that the priest might have spread the word about her visit to the church and her rapid departure when he offered her what she considered a dubious confession and so she was pleased that as time passed the Godfearers' dread of the massive stones still continued to deter them from coming to the Great Circle. But then, at precisely the wrong moment, the one person she most dreaded encountering made his unwanted appearance.

When she had first taken up shepherding her father had arranged for her to learn the ropes from a man known as The Shepherd. His given name was Tobias and Jess knew that he was hand in glove with Father Giles on Sundays and holy days but spent the rest of his time out on the Downs keeping a close count of the herds, to ensure that the correct tithes were paid from the money their fleeces and carcasses provided each year. Woe betide any farmer who tried to hide a fleece or a lamb from The Shepherd's eagle eye.

However, this was not the reason Jess feared him and did her best to avoid him. During her lessons in sheep management, she had disliked the hungry way he eyed her, as if she was a juicy plum. She did her best to keep her distance but in the last lesson she attended, he had demonstrated how to make an internal examination of the sheep's birth canal.

'You'll never be a shepherd if you can't help a pregnant ewe in distress,' he told her and insisted she copy him by bending down to locate the correct opening and push her hand and wrist into it. That was when she felt him lift her skirt and push his own hand up between her legs.

Incensed, and careless of the ewe's bleated objections, she had ripped her hand free and leapt to her feet, turning in fury on her molester and slapping his bearded face, leaving a trail of sticky fluid behind. As she backed off, she shook out her rucked smock and snarled her disgust. 'I knew you were a lecher! That's the last time I'll allow myself to be alone with you! I've a mind to tell the priest what you just did.'

The Shepherd merely laughed. 'Oh, I wouldn't do that,' he said. 'He's the biggest gossip in the village. And before you run away, I'll just confirm that you have passed the test. I don't wish to see you again.' For the latter part of this pronouncement, he had to raise his voice, because his pupil was already striding out of earshot. At the time, Jess had pondered whether to tell her father of the incident but in the end decided against it, thinking it might persuade him to drop the whole idea of letting her herd the sheep. Since then, and until she suddenly saw him approaching the Henge, she had managed to avoid Tobias. Now she wished fervently that her father might appear.

'How many in your herd?' The Shepherd asked brusquely. 'I have it listed at fifty ewes but it looks smaller than that.'

Jess wished she could just ignore him but realised that he was an official doing his job and a refusal might bring repercussions. 'I've had fifteen successful births and there are thirty-five still to come. The ewes with lambs are in the water meadow.' On the spur of the moment, she decided not to tell him of the second lamb Curly had surprisingly produced, in case he drew conclusions of Satanic interference.

'Any still births?' Being illiterate, Tobias was using tallies to keep a note of numbers and carried them in bundles in a satchel slung over his shoulder. Father Giles would translate their information into a tithe log, which would be checked when the fleeces owed to the church were stored in the tithe barn.

'No, and I'm not expecting any.'

'There are quite a few in the village. Some ailment, it seems. You're wise to keep yours separate.'

'I always keep separate.'

'I hear you lost your assistant. You could do with him now.' There was an odd expression on Tobias's face. 'Seems strange that he just disappeared.'

'I don't need him,' Jess said and turned her back to walk towards the Henge farmhouse. To her relief she saw her father appear out of the front door and increased her pace.

'His pa came here, you know.' The Shepherd shouted to make her hear. 'He must be missing him. It can't be easy losing a son.'

Farmer Matt took up the exchange and increased his pace. 'Haven't you got other flocks to bother, Tobias?' he called. 'Jess needs her dinner.' When father and daughter met, they turned and quickened their pace towards the open farmhouse door.

Before it closed behind them Tobias managed a last tirade. 'The whole village thinks it fiendish! They believe the Devil took him. It won't go away.'

Jess gazed at the bowl of pottage her mother placed

before her and felt nausea clutch her stomach. She looked up at her father who was already spooning his portion into his mouth. 'Is it true, Pa?' she asked. 'Do they say he was stolen by the Devil?'

Matt paused with the next mouthful halfway to his mouth. 'Ask your mother,' he said, before gulping it down.

Nell brought her own bowl to the table and sat down. 'The priest says you need to go to confession, Jess. You haven't been for weeks and people whisper that it's because you've been communing with the Devil.'

'And what do you believe, Mother?' Jess asked. 'Do you think the same?'

'Of course not!' Nell was emphatic. 'But you should take confession. You haven't even attended church lately, Jess, and that is bound to make people suspicious.'

'Don't you tell them I'm lambing, Ma? None of the shepherds are attending church at present.'

'That's just it, Jess. The working men are excused but women are bound to attend, even if they bring their spindles with them. Father Giles says we are weak and easily tempted by Satan.' Nell had lowered her head, avoiding eye contact with her daughter.

'And you believe him, do you?' Jess shoved her bowl away and soup splashed over onto the table. 'You think I have met the Devil and led Addy astray!'

'You slept in the long barrow, Jess! The Devil's imps could have come to you while you were asleep.' Nell's bowl was also being ignored now.

'But if they did, why did they take Addy and not me?'

'I don't know, Jess!' Nell's voice cracked. 'Perhaps they

took him because he wasn't asleep and he saw them. Maybe you were lucky.'

'Lucky! How can you call me lucky?' Jess pushed back her stool and stood up. 'You tell me that the village thinks I'm a witch! You do know what happens to witches, don't you? They get drowned on the dunking stool. Is that what you want for me, Mother?'

'No, Jess!' Nell was red-faced and tearful. 'I just want you to go to confession and stop shepherding. It is against God's will!'

Matt suddenly banged on the table with his spoon. 'That's enough, woman!' he bellowed. 'You've been listening to that damned priest and he's turned your head. Jess is an excellent shepherd and the angels love shepherds! Addy just decided to leave because he disliked putting his hand up a ewe's backside! It isn't every man's idea of a way of life. He was too embarrassed to confess it and ran away without telling us and now Jess is taking the blame.'

Jess walked to where he sat at the end of the table in his farmer's chair. 'Thank you, Pa. At least you are on my side. But I'm still frightened because although Ma is right about telling me to take confession, I can't go to Father Giles. I'm sorry, Ma, I know that you do but I just don't trust him. And please don't feel bound to include that fact in your next confession, because I will never forgive you if you do.'

'But wherever will you take confession if you don't go to Father Giles?' Nell wrung her hands in her anxiety for her daughter's soul.

Jess moved to her mother's side, stirred by her obvious love and concern but still fearing her clear belief in the priest's obedience to the secrecy of the confessional. 'I don't know, Ma. I've heard there is a well-liked priest who serves the nuns and pilgrims at the Easton Priory. When all the lambs are born, I might go there.'

Nell's brow furrowed and she turned to her husband. 'Matthew, have you heard of this priest – this place? Is it far away? Surely she can't go by herself!'

Matt put down his spoon and scratched his head. 'I helped to herd some sheep there a couple of years ago – a bequest from a dead landowner. It's on the eastern edge of Savernake Forest, on the Pilgrims' Way. I suppose if I could find another shepherd to look after our sheep I could go with her.'

Jess stamped her foot. 'I don't need an escort! And I know the way.'

25

Queen Catherine's Court, Windsor Castle

17th May 1425

'I WAS HORRIFIED WHEN I learned that our brave Christian knights, captured in battle by infidels, are made slaves and set to work in the fields in heathen lands! It is truly terrible.'

The Dowager Queen's English was fluent but her accent still betrayed her French birth. 'I consider it remarkable, Prioress, that the monks of your Order risk their lives to travel to such dangerous places and negotiate ransoms with the infidels.'

Editha had been offered a cushioned seat at the foot of the raised chair in which the king's mother sat, while Isabel shared a stool among the queen's ladies-in-waiting and tried not to grimace at the pain it caused her after days in the saddle.

The Prioress reassured the queen. 'They are brave indeed, your grace, but they put their faith and trust in the Trinity to keep them safe. What is more I believe it is thankfully rare that any brother fails to return from his travels and only on a very few occasions do they fail to bring their unfortunate warriors with them. We believe they are protected by prayer and the generosity of our donors, whose great benevolence provides them with ransoms that are impossible for the infidel to resist.'

'It is certainly a cause that I find I cannot resist . . .' Queen Catherine began her response but was distracted by a disturbance at the entrance to the receiving room, where an indignant chamberlain was attempting to announce an unruly visitor.

'Stand aside, you ignorant fool! I am the young king's Protector and have urgent business with his grace's mother!'

The Dowager Queen's ladies sprang to their feet as a man in a mud-splashed royal-blue tunic and black turban hat strode into the room, leaving muddy footprints on the woven reed matting.

Queen Catherine remained surprisingly calm and firmly seated. 'I think you might have wiped your feet before you ventured into my presence, Humphrey,' she said. 'What is the cause of this unwelcome interruption? Can you not see that I am entertaining an important guest?'

Duke Humphrey glared at the Prioress, who had politely stood up, recognising the arrival of a royal prince. 'Any church matters will have to wait and your nun here will have to leave,' he snapped, turning then to gaze around the room, 'along with all these other ladies. I need to speak with you privately.'

'What is so urgent that you have lost all sense of decorum, my lord? If my guest and my ladies are to leave it will be at my request, not yours. So, if you have something to tell me I suggest you do so now and quickly, so that we may continue our meeting.'

A sarcastic smile curled on the duke's lips. 'Very well, but be warned that you will not like what I have to say and will definitely wish you had dismissed your attendants, especially the nun.' He turned his gaze on the Prioress, who raised a sardonic eyebrow under her wimple and sat down again.

At the same time the queen gestured to her ladies and Isabel to take their seats once more. 'There – the floor is yours, my lord,' she said. 'But not for long. We are looking forward to a visit from the king.'

The duke stepped back a few paces to ensure that his voice would reach everyone in the room. 'You would not wish your young son to hear what I have to say, madame, I can assure you of that. Perhaps here in Windsor you are unaware that word is out in London concerning the dubious way you are rearing his grace the king. How there were rude japes and jests at the Twelfth Night feast in January and on Shrove Tuesday you were to be seen dancing closely with the Earl of Mortain, feeding each other from the same trencher and sharing the same wine cup. There has been widespread gossip in the inns and taverns about you having forced the young king to watch naked tumblers and bawdy jesters for Mortain's entertainment and wantonly removed your widow's weeds to expose your hair and throat.'

Here he paused and pompously swept an arm to indicate the beautiful pearl and diamond necklace, which the queen was wearing around her smooth throat that day. After the Royal Council had declared the imminent separation of the royal households, Catherine had elected to put away the widow's weeds and black wimple and barbe she had worn ever since the death of King Henry the Fifth three years before, and brought out her fashionable robes and decorative headgear, like the jewelled silver mesh nets which held her golden hair that day.

During the duke's theatrical speech, Catherine's shoulders had begun to shake with laughter and she raised an imperial hand to intervene. 'Really, my lord, you have quoted scandalously unreliable sources – the kind of London gambling and drinking dens your brother, my beloved husband, frequented as a young man, before he saw the light. However, I believe you have been ill and may not have heard that I am considering an offer of marriage from Edmund Beaufort, Count of Mortain, now that the Royal Council has unwisely handed the king's education over to the Earl of Warwick's retainers. I wonder how long it will be before they discover that my son has the making of an intellectual, who will rule by persuasion rather than bullying power, unlike some members of the present Council.'

Before she could finish the duke had broken into raucous laughter. 'Ha, ha! It is you who are sadly out of touch, madame! At my request the Parliament has already passed an Act preventing the Dowager Queen of England from marrying any man at all, especially one who is a Beaufort and known to be illegally desirous of the throne. Mortain has learned of this Act and the fact that any marriage foolishly undertaken with the Queen Dowager will be punished by the confiscation of all the groom's titles and property. That is why Mortain will be returning to his French properties next week and looking for another bride.' He made a pause to let this information sink in, before adding with a jubilant smile, 'And why there will be no second husband for you, madame; not as long as I am the king's Protector.'

Along with her lady-in-waiting companions, Isabel

was visibly shocked by this smug announcement and she could see that it had seriously upset the Dowager Queen, although she was fighting to keep the evidence from her face. Catherine de Valois was only twenty-six and doubtless cherished the idea of a second marriage and more children, but this blunt announcement had just shattered the hope of sisters and brothers for her lonely little king.

She took a deep breath and stood up. 'Well, my lord duke, if that is all you came here to say then you may take your leave.'

The duke tugged his beard and appeared to ponder. 'There is just one more thing. When you are embroidering your hundredth smock in Hertford Castle and regretting your dreary single life, the beautiful young woman whom you recently refused to appoint as a lady-in-waiting will be enjoying court life here at Windsor and the company of our delightful young king.'

At this obvious reference to Humphrey's mistress Eleanor Cobham, whom he had once before failed to wriggle into the Dowager Queen's entourage, Catherine's bright blue eyes became angry slits, which focused fiercely on the duke's and actually caused him to shift his gaze. Her voice became iron hard. 'Not, I think, if your sadly neglected spouse, the Countess of Hainault, has anything to do with it. You should see to your own disastrous family life, my lord duke, and I will handle mine. Now, save the chamberlain a task if you please and close the door behind you.'

Silence from the room's occupants accompanied the duke's abrupt about-turn and stamping march across the room, where the door still stood open. It was slammed shut with a reverberating crash that made everybody jump and

Joanna Belknap ran across the floor to her mistress, whose face had turned sheet-white. Editha had already noticed her pallor and stood up to ask if she was feeling faint. Isabel rose from her stool in alarm, hesitating whether to make the same trip across the room, as the queen sank slowly back into her chair on her lady-in-waiting's arm.

'I think we should continue our discussion later, Prioress,' she said with a faint smile. 'Belknap will show you something of the castle and arrange a place for you at supper. I hope to see you there.'

Editha nodded and backed away. 'Thank you, your grace. I trust you feel better very soon.'

Isabel made a curtsy to the unheeding queen and prepared to follow the Prioress towards the exit but they were halted by a commotion at the door and the chamberlain announcing the arrival of King Henry and his squires, who stood back as he almost ran to greet the queen. 'I met the Duke of Gloucester on the way here, my lady!' The child king bent a swift knee before her chair then kissed her hand, looking concerned. 'He seemed cross and said you were weeping but I can see now that you are not.'

Catherine gave a soft laugh and bowed down to kiss his cheek. 'I am much happier to see you, Henry, than to converse with Gloucester, who has nothing to say that is worth hearing. These ladies are much more interesting.' She beckoned to the Prioress and Isabel. 'They raise funds to send brave monks to ransom and rescue Christian prisoners of war from their infidel captors. Do you not think that a marvellous venture?'

King Henry turned his attention politely to the two visitors. 'Yes, I do,' he said with a nod. 'And I would give money to the brave monks who do it, if my Treasurer would let me. I will pray for them though.'

Prioress Editha smiled and thanked him profusely and the queen tucked her arm around the boy's shoulders. 'Good. And I will give something in your name, Henry. Now let us go to my solar and you can tell me what you have been doing with your new tutors.' With a brief gesture she signalled Joanna Belknap to look after her guests and drew her son towards the privy door to her apartments. Two of his squires followed discreetly.

The lady-in-waiting and the Prioress shared a sympathetic smile. 'She sees so little of her son these days,' Joanna confided, 'and she will see even less after she leaves for Hertford. But I'm sure she will meet you both again at supper. Meanwhile let me show you something of Windsor Castle. Have you the energy after your long ride?'

Prioress Editha sent Isabel an enquiring glance and smiled at her eager nod. 'Yes, it will be good to stretch our legs and I've heard so much about the chapel here and the boys' choir.'

'We'll go there first, then. They might be rehearsing and they do make a beautiful sound.'

26

Wolf Hall

20th May 1425

JOHN SEYMOUR PACED THE hall floor like a caged animal, punching one closed fist into the palm of his other hand and muttering expletives, watched with rolling eyes and a shaking head by his cousin. 'For the love of Jesus, the woman has not returned!' I swear I will kill her when she does!' Why the hell did you let her go, Edmund? I left you in charge here.'

'I cannot recall you doing so, but anyway she would not have listened. I am hardly qualified to issue orders to your wife, am I?'

John stopped pacing and squared up to his cousin. 'That is a pathetic excuse! Any man is entitled to issue orders to a woman! You should have locked her in the room she is so keen to keep me out of!'

Edmund exhaled noisily. 'Calm down, John. Perhaps you should worry that she may have come to harm on the journey back – or even on the way out, which would be terrible to think. But all being well, she will be back soon. And if she has spent time with the king's mother you should be proud that the Seymour name is heard at her court. Ahh!'

He crouched over his ribs where John had just landed one of his heavy punches. 'The Seymour name is mine, you fool! Not for some stupid female to play around with. Women are not made knights for service to the monarchy, are they? No – and that's because they do not belong at court! I just hope to God she has not encountered Duke Humphrey and ruined my efforts to retain his interest!'

Edmund coughed and staggered towards the service arch, breathless and unable to speak. Eager to leave his cousin to get over his tantrum, he made his way out into the back yard and paused to force some air into his lungs. At the same time Ham, the cook, emerged from the kitchen and approached him with a concerned frown.

'Are you not well, Master Edmund? You look pale, if I may say so.'

Edmund tried to straighten up and took another gulp of air. 'I'll be all right, Ham. I just had a fight with Master John, which I lost.' He tried to smile but achieved a grimace. 'If you could rustle up some soothing concoction that would calm him down that might be very helpful. I am going to take a ride to get over it.'

Not wishing to take the horses into Easton Priory in a sweat, the Prioress and Isabel had used the last few miles of their return journey to remind themselves of the highlights of their visit to Windsor Castle. Editha had particularly enjoyed her face-to-face conversations with Queen Catherine, delighted on the second day, at a more private meeting with her grace, to have received the promise of a substantial donation to the Trinitarian cause.

'The extraordinary thing on that occasion was the queen's

obvious reliance on her new Head of Household, Owen Tudor,' the Prioress recalled. 'I'm sure it cannot be often that so much royal faith has been placed in a commoner, especially a Welshman.'

'She does seem to rely on his opinion, not being prepared to put a sum on her donation until he returned from his trip to Hertford Castle,' Isabel agreed. 'She spoke about him in such glowing terms, I'm sorry we did not meet him.'

'Well, I'm sorry we shall probably not be able to meet with the Dowager again, since she leaves so soon for Hertford,' Editha said. 'I must hope that her generosity will run to making regular donations without personal reminders.'

'Perhaps you can write to Owen Tudor. He seems to hold the purse strings and have her ear, so you might keep contact through him?'

'Yes, that is a good idea. And he might keep a tighter rein on communications. I fear the queen's correspondence would be subject to too much interference.'

Isabel nodded sagely. 'Ah yes, of course.' She turned in the saddle to see how closely their royal escort was riding; a guard ordered by the Protector, apparently out of concern for their safety on the return journey, which had seemed to her suspicious, considering the attitude he had displayed towards women. She was worried that any guard appointed by Duke Humphrey might already have inspected the content of their saddlebags.

Editha seemed more concerned about Isabel's welfare. 'Are you worried about your welcome back at Wolf Hall? From your confidences I gather your husband is not aware of you coming with me to Windsor. Some men might punish their wives for doing such a thing without permission.'

Isabel shrugged. 'He shouts a lot but so far that is all. And he had better not get fierce physically when I get back because I am expecting his next child, which he does not yet know.'

Editha made a brief grimace. 'It doesn't show, so you'd better tell him if he threatens violence. From my experience of male pilgrims, one of the most common reasons for them walking barefoot to visit a saint's tomb is to beg holy indulgence for violently maltreating their wives and daughters.'

'And do you believe they will receive it?'

The Prioress frowned. 'You might ask that of the pilgrims themselves. They should not be making the journey if they do not truly believe it will be to their soul's advantage in the hereafter.'

'That would explain why so many more men than women tread the pilgrim way then,' Isabel remarked.

'And why those women who do so are almost invariably widows,' Editha concluded, adding with a rueful smile, 'or repentant brothelkeepers. They're the females who have the money to buy indulgences, from fleecing their customers. It is a wild world we live in, Isabel.'

'But you are sheltered from it at the Priory, surely?'

'It may seem that way but you would be surprised at how much trouble and strife come to our doors. I hope you will continue to visit us frequently to offer the pilgrims the benefit of your youth and sympathy. And to bring me your friendship too of course! You have come like a ray of sunshine into my life.'

Minutes later, as they rode past the Easton Hostel, they saw a horse and rider turn into the Priory messuage. 'That looks like Edmund Seymour!' Isabel exclaimed. 'What is he doing here?'

'I think perhaps he is looking for you,' Editha said. 'Sent by a furious husband maybe?'

'Well, at least you can send Gloucester's so-called guard home,' Isabel suggested. 'It looks like I'll have an escort.'

'I am so glad I caught you before you got to Wolf Hall, Izzy,' Edmund confided once she had completed her farewells to the Prioress. 'Otherwise, you might have ridden straight into a maelstrom. Because John is beside himself with fury! I'm still sore from the punch in the belly he threw earlier today.'

'Dear God! When will he learn to keep his temper, Ed? He'll never earn himself a knighthood if he continues to behave like a child. I suppose he's cross that I went to court and met King Henry and the Dowager Queen before he did?'

Edmund made a negative shake of the head. 'No, I think it's more that you left Wolf Hall without his permission. I know he went off to Salisbury without telling you – but that's not the point with him.'

'What did he do in Salisbury, has he told you?'

'No, but I can guess. He said he'd be a couple of days but he only returned yesterday, looking pretty pleased with himself, I must say.'

'And what do you think pleased him, Edmund? Or do I need to ask?'

The young man raised his shoulders in a non-committal shrug. 'It is probably better if you don't, Izzy. Let's just go home and see what happens, shall we?'

*

The ladder stair leading up to the manor lord's chamber was in place in the hall and John Seymour was poring over piles of tallies on the long table, his face screwed into an expression of agonised frustration. Edmund was glad he had opted to enter first because as soon as he made an appearance a handful of tallies flew past his left ear and clattered onto the floor.

'About time you put in an appearance again, cousin!' John exclaimed. 'Where the hell have you been? And did that useless wife of mine go off to Windsor with the key to our chamber in her pocket? I can't even get to the clothes chest to find a clean pair of hose!' He stood up and stalked around the table, the deep creases of anger in his brow causing Edmund to take a few steps back, almost knocking over Isabel, who dodged around him before addressing her husband.

'If you had looked in the solar you would have seen a clean set of clothing laid out there for you, John. I assumed you'd need a change when you returned from Salisbury. I know I need one now after my journey from Windsor.'

She was heading for the stair as she spoke but John shoved Edmund out of the way and grabbed her by the sleeve of her riding jerkin. 'Not so fast, madam!' he yelled, his face only inches from hers. 'How dare you disappear off to Windsor without telling me? And Duke Humphrey was going to meet the Dowager Queen when he left Clarendon Palace. I suppose you made yourself known to him without telling me as well?'

She stepped back from his sour breath and said quietly, 'I did see the duke, yes. However, I do not remember you telling me that you were going to Salisbury, sir, so I could not tell you of my intention to visit Windsor. But perhaps we could compare our trips over supper? Personally, I am very hungry.' She turned to mount the ladder stair and was completely unprepared for the savage push John gave her, which cannoned her forward into the hard wooden steps.

'Don't turn your back on me, woman!' he shouted. 'I asked you a question.'

'Jesu, John!' Edmund bounded around his cousin to catch Isabel as her knees buckled under her. 'What did you do that for? The poor girl is pregnant!'

There was a long pause as his words sank into John's fevered mind. 'Pregnant? How? She's been locking herself up there for weeks!'

Pale-faced, Isabel hauled herself around to face him, leaned back against the steps and clasped her hands over her stomach. Her voice came in jerks. 'This is not a Wolf Hall baby, John. It was sired at Hatch Beauchamp and will be born before Christmas – if it survives! But be it alive or dead, boy or girl, it is yours.'

27

Avebury

22nd May 1425

THE CHURCH OF ST James at Avebury was crowded with Godfearers, their rosy faces lit by the precious wax candles and their moods lifted by the sharp smell of incense wafting from censers swung by young acolytes in white robes. To please her mother Jess had folded her sheep at Henge Farm, risking the arrival of the last few lambs occurring safely without her attendance, in order to accompany her parents to the celebration of the new tower. Feeling strange in her best dress of pale natural linen and hampered by the full skirts that almost touched the ground, she pulled her spinster's veil and circlet low over her forehead and hoped that no one would recognise her as the girl who usually dressed in working smocks and shepherd's boots.

They had purposely stood in the nave at the back of the church and all went well through the Mass, the incomprehensible reading from the bible in Latin and the usual long and ranting sermon from Father Giles. However, when it came to taking communion at the chancel steps, Jess recognised one of the acolytes distributing the blessed communion wafers. They had played in the street together when they were youngsters. Unfortunately, when he reached her in the line, he recognised her and, screwing up his face, instantly spat on the wafer before placing it on her tongue. Nauseated by the thought of swallowing it, Jess waited for him to pass on to the next communicant before putting her hand to her mouth to swiftly remove the wafer. Her mother was standing behind her and frowned fiercely as she noticed her slip it up the tight sleeve of her kirtle but Jess ignored her obvious disapproval. As she walked back up the aisle, she could still taste the acolyte's foul spit and had to put a hand to her mouth as she nearly vomited.

Outside the church Nell and Matt waited to greet their friends but, ignoring her mother's beckoning gesture, Jess headed straight up the hill towards the Great Circle, eager to get back to her sheep. As she sped along, hoping she had avoided the rest of the villagers, she felt a sharp thud on her back and a stone clattered down to the ground behind her. Risking a rearward glance, she saw a group of three youths following in her wake and occasionally bending to pick up missiles from the stony road. She increased her speed as another stone caught her on the shoulder and a series of taunts followed.

'Running to meet Satan are you – Jess the Shepherdess?' 'Spreading your legs for the Devil?' 'Going to lie with Lucifer?'

The sneering stress in the loud shouts made her realise that the youth she had recognised in the church must have gathered a pair of like-minded louts, all intent on persecuting the one-time playmate who was now considered the village witch. This was far from being a childish prank and they were gaining on her, hampered as she was by her long skirt.

Terrified, and determined to outrun them, she hoisted it up and increased her speed, hoping to reach the Henge Farm house before they caught up with her. Handfuls of stones were flying as she veered off the track towards the causeway and one caught her on the side of her forehead, drawing blood from her eyebrow, which began to hamper her vision.

'Got you, witch!' She felt her veil tugged from the circlet that secured it to her hair as one of the pursuers grabbed her loose locks, painfully pulling strands from her head as he did so and bringing her to a halt. That was when she began to scream loudly and kick out at his shins, but she didn't have her heavy shepherd's boots on and against those of her assailant her light slippers were of little use. He was quickly joined by the two other bullies, who began spitting in her face and shouting further abuse.

'Satan won't help you now, witch!'

'And he won't save you when they tie you on the dunking stool!'

'Why wait for the dunking stool?' snarled the largest of the assailants. 'We can toss her over the rail, into the ditch. Satan will never find her there!'

The causeway was fitted with wooden fences on either side and Jess managed to hook her arm around one of the top rails and hang on. She had no wish to be tipped over into the deep ditch that surrounded the circle and was full of stagnant water and village offal that was hidden from above by a thick growth of stinging nettles. She also kept up her loud screaming, hoping her father might have left the church.

'Wait! We need to look for witch-marks first,' another voice growled threateningly, grabbing at her skirt. 'Satan puts them on their cunts, doesn't he? Spread her legs and let's have a look.'

Despite Jess's screams and kicks her skirts were thrown over her head and although she writhed against the rough tugging she still clung to the wooden rail for dear life. As a result, she felt her legs being pulled apart and sickeningly, fingers beginning to explore her private parts. 'You will swing for this!' she bawled, spitting out the cloth of her kirtle, which now hung over her head. 'And then you'll rot in hell!'

Suddenly sensing that the three assailants were totally distracted by their crude searches she let go of the rail, shoved the skirts back over their heads and, throwing all niceties to the wind, sent a stream of urine over the groping hands. Taking advantage of their horrified confusion, she then pulled her skirts down and made a break for the circle, leaving the bullies cursing and swearing and making sounds of disgust, too full of self-concern to immediately renew the chase. So she got a good head start, racing away towards the farmhouse.

Then, as she ran, she heard the blessed voice of her father bellowing at the top of his voice at the three assailants, 'I see you, you filthy buggers, and you'll all be in the Moot Court before you can clean your evil fingers! I saw what you were doing to my daughter and God will surely punish you for it, but before that you'll be in the stocks for a good long time. Now begone back to the church and ask Lord Jesus' forgiveness for besmirching his blessing! And while you're there, take a good look at the painting on the chancel screen to see what happens to ugly sinners like you!'

Jess stopped and turned to see the three youths who had assaulted her giving the farmer a wide berth as they scampered away, casting furtive glances behind to make sure he wasn't following them. She felt blood still dripping from the wound on her temple and staggered over to lean against the comforting strength of a friendly stone, as her father hurried to her side.

'Poor Jess! Those hogo stinkers need stringing up! Your mother should never have made you come to church. It was a big mistake.'

'Well, at least I now know how I stand in the village, Pa,' she said in a shaky voice. 'Those filthy perverts were all apprentice shepherds. I knew them and they knew me. But that didn't stop them hurling stones at me and threatening me with the dunking stool. I'm cursed by the Devil without ever having encountered him. Whatever can I do now?'

Matthew put his arm around her shoulders and pulled her close. 'Come on, girl, let's get you home and clean up that wound. Your mother will be back soon and we can talk about it.'

'I'm so glad she didn't witness it, Pa. It would justify all her warnings against me becoming a shepherd.'

Her father's brow furrowed. 'Well, perhaps it wasn't such a good idea after all, Jess. Those three young criminals might only be an early warning.'

'I hope Ma comes back from church soon,' Jess said when they had gained the safety of the Henge farmhouse. 'And the thugs don't start shouting filth at her, just for being my mother! Perhaps you shouldn't have left her in the village on her own.' She put her hand up to her forehead to see if the wound was still bleeding, found that it was and went to her mother's rag-bag to find something to bandage it with. 'The first thing I'm going to do is change from this stupid dress. I'd have outrun those thugs if I hadn't been wearing it and had my boots on. If she doesn't come soon, you'll have to tie this for me. I don't want to get blood all over my best clothes.'

Right on cue Nell walked through the front door, took one look at Jess and broke into cries of horror. 'What have you been doing, girl? You look as if you've been in a fight.'

By now Jess was sitting in her father's chair, her face as pale as cream.

'Well, she certainly put up a good one!' Matt exclaimed. 'And it was three against one.'

'What do you mean?' Nell began to fuss around her daughter and Jess was grateful to feel a cool hand on her brow and then a cold cloth pressed against the wound. 'Now, are you going to tell me what happened?'

Jess shut her eyes and shook her head carefully. 'Pa will tell you,' she said.

To Jess's relief, Matt left out the groping element of the story but the chase and the throwing of stones at her daughter had Nell red-faced with anger. 'Who were these boys?' she demanded. 'Do you know them, Matt? Will you report all this to the Reeve? They should be punished!'

Matt shrugged. 'Of course, I should report it but I'm not sure how much the Moot Court will help. You know yourself, Nell, that most of the village might well excuse the boys. Because, like them, they truly believe Jess is a witch. There is a real risk of her being publicly accused of consorting with the Devil and the boys being praised for exposing her sin.'

'What!' Jess leapt to her feet and the bloody cloth fell to the floor. 'Don't say that, Pa! Before this I'd never so much as thought of the Devil, let alone consorted with him or his beastly imps!' She made the sign of the cross. 'Why should I even be a suspect?'

'You shouldn't be, of course, Jess,' Matthew agreed. 'But something is going wrong in this village. Gossip is spreading about your visit to the long barrow on Silbury Down and perhaps the time has come for you to make that journey to Easton Priory. And I will come with you.'

'No, Pa, you can't. There's the farm and the sheep and lambs to think about. And you can't leave Ma alone here when there might be danger. I'll walk to Easton by myself. I look like a boy in my smock and boots anyway and I'll tuck my hair under my hat. If anyone asks me, I'll pretend I'm hunting for lost sheep or going to a new shepherding job. And I'll take my crook and Star with me. She'll keep nosy folk away. We'll be all right.'

Nell was indignant. 'But you don't know the way, Jess! And it's not right that you should have to leave. This is your home!'

'It's not my home if I'm not wanted here. Maybe it will be again, especially if Addy comes back. But meanwhile all I can do is make myself scarce. It is the only way.'

28

Wolf Hall

23rd May 1425

ISABEL HAD SPENT DAYS closeted in her bedchamber behind a locked door – secured once again from the inside. She spent the time crying, eating the food Nan brought her and hugging what she hoped was still a living being tucked in her womb. When she finally felt the baby kick she felt a huge surge of relief, left her bed, donned her best houppelande and rode Snowflake in silence beside John Seymour's Atlas to the church at Great Bedwyn. On the way back John spoke to her for the first time since the incident at the ladder stair.

'I prayed for the child you say you carry, Isabel; prayed that he would not have come to harm, either from your long ride to Windsor or the collision with the stair.'

There was a long pause before she responded. 'There were four errors in that sentence, John. One, I am definitely carrying a child; two, it is just as likely to be a "she" as a "he"; three, there was no danger from my ride to Windsor; and four, what you call a "collision" with the stair, I call a deliberate push from a wicked brute.'

John remained silent for a long period and Isabel thought

he might be building up for a burst of anger but when he eventually spoke it was clear that he had been collecting his thoughts. 'I expect you think I spent my time in Salisbury wenching and whoring and I admit I was not entirely celibate but I was careful because I hoped to return to Wolf Hall and make peace with you. Finding you absent and not knowing where you had gone was a shock, Isabel. Why did you do it?'

Isabel kept her eyes fixed on Snowflake's ears. 'The opportunity arose very suddenly and when Edmund told me you had ridden off without explanation, I thought I might as well do the same. Could you have resisted the offer of a visit to Windsor Castle and a meeting with the king's mother, I wonder? I think not. I told Edmund where I was going and who with, so you did find out when you came home. Anyway, it doesn't sound like you spent much time thinking about me while you were in Salisbury.'

'I went there primarily to try and find us a steward and I think I have.'

'You mean you killed two birds with one stone.' Isabel gave him a sidelong look. 'Don't tell me you found him in a brothel!'

John's brow creased in what she thought was anger but was surprised when he laughed. 'Actually, it is a woman?'

It was Isabel's turn to laugh, but her laugh had a hollow sound. 'I do not believe it! Only you could try and bring your slut into the house disguised as a steward!' The road was clear and she clapped her heels into Snowflake's sides, setting the mare into a canter and leaving a cloud of dust. 'I'll be back for Ham's dinner!' she shouted over her shoulder.

Edmund had been keeping his distance, aware that

the couple ahead were actually speaking to each other for a change, but when he saw Isabel disappear at a canter, he trotted his gelding up to Atlas's side. 'I thought the war was over, John, but I see I was wrong.'

'She is not yet twenty, Ed, and when we married, I thought she would be a dutiful wife – but now I sometimes think I married a witch! She simply doesn't understand a woman's place.'

'Not your idea of it anyway,' Edmund said. 'But you'll have to give her some credit for being lively and beautiful! You would hate to have a boring wife who wouldn't say boo to a goose!'

John gave his cousin a withering look. 'Sometimes you say the stupidest things, Ed. She doesn't have to be beautiful and lively – just docile and available and preferably not too clever. Isabel gets up my nose and I can't stand the way she expects perfection from me – it's never going to happen!'

Edmund gave him a shake of the head. 'Poor John! Never mind, Ham is roasting that haunch of venison you brought up from Salisbury. We can have a rare dinner today!'

John's face suffused and he punched his cousin's arm. 'God preserve us! You're part of the trouble, Ed! You're a man – get off her side or you'll have to go!'

Meanwhile Isabel's sudden burst of speed had partly been because she wanted to discover how Nat, the young poacher, was faring after receiving his agonising branding. She left her mare with a stable lad and set out to walk the short distance to the Wolf Hall village. Once there she set about finding the cot belonging to the boy's family and took a guess that it would be the most well-tended, since his father was the village carpenter. As she stopped in front of one that looked the most likely, she began to realise that there was surprisingly little evidence of life in the village, except for a few wandering geese and chickens and three young girls playing in the back yard of the cot before her. And yet Sunday was always a holiday for the villeins.

Taking a deep breath to steady her sudden nerves, she tapped on the door. It felt like a long wait before she heard a bolt drawn back and an invisible female's voice spoke through the inches-wide gap that opened. 'Who is it? What do you want?'

'It is Isabel Seymour – from the manor house. I'd like to speak to Nat, if that is possible.'

'No, it' s not. Go away please!'

The fact that she said 'please' encouraged Isabel to persevere. 'I have been away or I would have come sooner. I'd like to know if Nat is all right. Is his wound healing? Does he need any help?'

The heavy wooden door was suddenly pulled back on its hinges until it graunched halfway open on some small obstacle. 'No, I'm not all right. Nor will I ever be. Look!' Nat's face appeared around the door and Isabel blinked at the still raw S on his cheek, surrounded by blackened and flaking skin. She felt her stomach clench and make the baby kick and she must have gone pale because the boy called out, 'Ma! The lady looks funny. Come and see!'

The first face reappeared to inspect the visitor and then pulled the door noisily back over a loose entrance stone. 'I'm Col's wife, mistress. You'd better come in.'

The cot was similar to the rest of the village homes, one square, gloomy room with a central hearth and various items of furniture of different sizes and uses. The hearth was always alight for cooking and warmth and smoke from the fire filtered out through the thatch.

Col's wife pulled the only armchair out from a corner and offered it to Isabel. 'Sit here, milady. Ye look faint.'

Isabel sank gratefully into the chair. 'Thank you. I really came to see how Nat is. Is his wound healing? It still looks raw.'

Nat had been hovering in the background but leapt in at this point. 'Pa wants me to wear a bandage but Ma says I should leave it to heal in the air. It still hurts like hell, especially when I stir the pottage near the fire.'

'He doesn't have to do that,' his mother chimed in. 'One of the girls can do it.'

'But I like doing it, Ma! I want to be a cook.' The boy's face screwed up with enthusiasm, then he turned abruptly away to hide the pain the action gave him.

'I saw the girls playing in the back yard,' Isabel said. 'Is that all your family, or are there more? I'm sorry, I don't know your name?'

This was enquired of her hostess but Nat jumped in. 'It's Liz and my brothers are with my father at the meeting in the corn barn.'

'Shush, Nat!' Liz muttered. 'The lady doesn't need to know that.'

Isabel tucked the matter away but pursued the boy's earlier enthusiasm. 'Well, if you're interested in cooking, Nat, you should meet our new cook. I could ask him to come and see you if you're not going out yet and perhaps there might be work for you in the manor kitchen when you're healed.'

'His father wants Nat to be apprenticed to him, as a

carpenter,' Liz began but was immediately interrupted by her son's eager response.

'But I'd rather be a cook, milady! So yes, send him over if he'll come.'

Feeling stronger, Isabel stood up. 'Well, I can only ask him but meanwhile, you look after that injury, Nat, and, if I may, I'll come back in a few days and take another look at it and I'll let you know about Ham the cook. Now I won't keep you any longer from that delicious-smelling pottage.'

Liz nodded vigorously. 'Yes, it would be best if you left before Col comes back,' she said.

Isabel pondered this final remark as she hurried back to the manor house and decided not to tell John about it yet, if at all. Anyway, she had a feeling the meeting in the grain barn would make itself felt one day.

29

Easton Priory

27th May 1425

THE EASTON HOSTEL WAS unusual in that it was run by nuns instead of monks. Nevertheless, it provided the same service and facilities that the pilgrims would encounter at hostels all along their trek: a bed of straw in a sometimes-crowded dormitory, fresh water to drink and wash in, a hot evening meal and a breakfast of bread and milk. Wealthy pilgrims sometimes tried to buy special favours – a more comfortable bed or a jug of wine – but the Trinitarian rules did not allow it.

'True pilgrims do not waste money on wine and feathers,' the Prioress would chide any enquirer. 'And the Order does not provide luxuries. All offerings go towards ransoming Christians from the infidels. So, if you wish to spend more of your money you are welcome to add it to our donation coffer.'

As well as preaching to the local villagers and vendors, the resident priest, Father Michael, also attended to the spiritual needs of the nuns and occasionally heard confession from pilgrims, some of whom had suffered ghostly visitations of the Devil as a 'black dog' on the isolated road that ran across the Marlborough Downs. Few pilgrims were wealthy enough to carry letters of credit to refresh their purses on their journey and so were obliged to carry sufficient coin to pay for their food and accommodation, which attracted thieves, especially to those travelling solo through lonely landscapes. A dog was a good deterrent, especially if it looked fierce. However, as tales of the Devil's double were well known, none of the pilgrims' dogs were black, so when Isabel was in the hostel yard, filling jugs of water from the well, she was surprised that a slight figure in a shepherd's smock and brimmed hat, who walked in carrying a crook, was closely followed by a black dog.

'I'm afraid you've arrived too late for breakfast and too early for dinner,' she said, greeting the stranger with a welcoming smile to disguise her misgivings. 'And the nuns are in chapel for Terce. But there's always something in the kitchen if you're hungry. Are you a pilgrim? Have you walked far?' Still trying to judge whether the new arrival was male or female, Isabel realised that her curiosity must have showed because the visitor pulled the hat off and a thick plait of fair hair tumbled down her back.

'I am a shepherd,' Jess said quietly, her eyes swivelling to detect any chance of being overseen or heard. 'I've walked over the Downs during the night in order to meet with your priest because I've heard he is a kind and wise man.'

'Father Michael? Well, he's not here at present but he'll be along soon. And yes, he has a reputation for being kind and sympathetic. Would you like to wait for him in the church or are you hungry and thirsty and in need of sustenance? My name is Isabel. May I ask yours?'

'Yes, it is Jessica, but people call me Jess. And my dog is

called Star – she's a sheepdog.' The animal gave a brief wag of her tail on hearing her name. 'I brought her with me for protection.'

Isabel nodded. 'It's a good idea, especially if you've been walking alone on the Downs. But a black dog could be a problem. The locals and most of the pilgrims believe the Devil appears as a black dog sometimes. Did you have any trouble on your walk?'

'No. I'm used to being out on the Downs with my flock, and Star is well known around my village. We've never had any problem about her being taken for the Devil.'

'Good. Well, if you follow me to the kitchen, we'll find some bread and milk but I'm afraid Star will have to wait outside. Or I can bring it out to you if you don't want to leave her.'

'Yes, thank you, that would be kind. I don't like to leave her in a strange place. Will she be allowed in the church when the priest comes?'

'Father Michael is very easy-going. I don't think he'll mind unless he's actually saying Mass.'

'Perhaps Star and I could wait here?' Jess asked, indicating a nearby bench.

'Of course, you must be weary; I won't be long.'

While Jess was waiting, a group of pilgrims emerged from the hostel and she swiftly jammed on her hat, hiding the long plait and pulling the brim over her forehead. Then she put a steadying hand on Star's neck because the dog's hackles had risen at the sound of the pilgrims' voices.

Then suddenly one of the female pilgrims stopped dead and let out a scream, making the sign of the cross. 'It is the Devil!'

The whole band of pilgrims came to a sudden halt, all of them staring wide-eyed and open-mouthed at Jess and Star. Jess was equally shocked, unable to think how to react, especially when one of the male pilgrims suddenly pulled out a poniard.

'The dog is the Devil,' he declared, advancing on the pair. 'The lad may not realise.'

Jess forced herself to respond, still fiercely holding Star's scruff. 'No, she's a sheepdog! But she will protect me so please *stop*!'

However, the man kept moving forward, causing Star to tear herself from Jess's grip and leap towards him, snarling. In panic the would-be assailant took a step backwards and tripped over a stone in the path. He might have fallen on the knife as he did so, had it not been for the fact that Star had tried to catch it as it spun from his hand and fell a yard away from its owner.

Jess rushed forward. 'Come here, Star! Heel!' In her haste to catch the dog, her hat fell off and her plaited hair was revealed, but she also realised that there was blood around Star's mouth. 'Clever girl!' she whispered, hastily reaching for her hat and picking up the knife as she did so.

Meanwhile the man was struggling to his feet cursing loudly, as Isabel appeared from the kitchen carrying a bowl of bread and a mug of milk. She ran to place the food on the bench and, with an angry frown, took the poniard from Jess. 'It is his knife!' Jess said hurriedly, indicating the pilgrim owner.

Isabel confronted the knife's owner. 'No blades allowed in the hostel! This should have been left with the Prioress for safekeeping. Are you hurt?'

The man looked down at his hose, dusty but undamaged. Again, he made the sign of the cross. 'It seems not, thanks be to God. But I still fear the presence of a Devil dog in a holy place.'

'It is not a Devil dog. It is a sheepdog and as much one of God's creatures as you are.' Isabel turned to Jess, who was gently inspecting Star's mouth. 'I should take the food to the church, Jess, and wait for Father Michael. He won't be long now.'

Jess nodded. 'But I need to wash Star's mouth. It is bleeding where the blade must have nicked her.'

'Take her to the church and I'll come with water and a cloth as soon as I can.'

'That is not a shepherd, it's a girl!' The female pilgrim had noticed the telltale plait. 'And she's dressed in men's clothing, against God's holy rule!'

'Go to the church now, Jess,' Isabel muttered more insistently. 'Shut the door and take shelter in the chancel!'

30

The Church of St Mary, Easton Priory

27th May 1425

FATHER MICHAEL ENTERED THE Priory Church to find Jess and Star sitting on the chancel steps. Drops of bloody saliva had gathered on the marble at their feet.

'Has there been an accident?' asked the priest, hurrying forward.

Jess stood up hastily. 'It will stop bleeding when the kind lady brings a cloth. I'm sorry about the mess, Father.'

The priest shook his head. 'I don't think it will stain. Poor dog, how did he come by such a wound?'

'One of the pilgrims thought she was the Devil in disguise and came at her with a knife. But he tripped and fell and my dog picked the blade off the ground where it fell, but it cut her mouth.'

'Ah. So, she is a bitch and a clever one at that.' Father Michael went to move closer but Star let out a growl and he stopped short. 'Pray tell me, what is her master's name?'

'I am not her *master*,' Jess revealed. 'I am her mistress and a shepherd and she is my best friend.' She removed her hat and let the plait loose once more. 'One of the pilgrims said my wearing a shepherd's smock is against God's holy rule. Is that really so, Father?'

The priest seemed unconcerned. 'Perhaps. It might depend on the length of the smock. But when you mentioned a kind lady, would that be Mistress Seymour? She often comes to the hostel and is very helpful.'

'She told me her name is Isabel. She's coming to the church soon with something to treat the dog's wound.'

'I see. Well, now it only remains for me to discover your name and purpose, daughter. Why have you come here today to the Church of St Mary?'

'I have come for you, Father. My name is Jess.'

Just as she spoke the church door opened again and Isabel came in carrying a bowl of water and some soft cloths. She walked carefully up the nave so as not to spill the water. 'God be with you this morning, Father Michael,' she said. 'I see you have met Jess.'

'And also with you, daughter,' returned the priest. 'Yes, and I have met Star, the snatcher of the blade. I take it those are for her?' He indicated the bowl and cloths. 'Have you waved the dog's would-be assassin away now?'

Isabel placed the items carefully down on the marble steps. 'I have, and he was not a bad man. He meant well, thinking misguidedly that he was protecting all of us from evil.' She put out her hand and stroked the dog's head.

There was a gasp from Jess. 'I have never seen her allow anyone except me to do that. She must be aware of needing your care.'

Isabel smiled. 'I'll look after her if you like, while you go to the confessional. I take it Jess has told you how far she and Star have walked to receive your absolution, Father?'

'No, Mistress Seymour, but I don't want to know where she comes from or how far she walked. As you know confession is entirely between the priest and the confessional. So, I think it best if we go there straight away and leave you to your happy relationship with the dog.' He beckoned to Jess. 'Come daughter, follow me.'

Jess released Star to Isabel, who immediately began gently to wipe the blood from the dog's mouth without any apparent objection from the patient. Jess patted her and whispered something in her ear before hurrying to follow the priest. She had rehearsed everything she wanted to confess during her long walk, but as she entered the dark interior of the confessional, she feared she wouldn't remember half of it. On the other side of the mesh grille, she could hear the priest intoning a Latin prayer, which of course she could not understand, so she settled on the kneeler and waited.

On the chancel steps Isabel carefully removed all trace of the dried blood from the fur on Star's mouth, surprised at how much trust the dog seemed to have in her, allowing her to pull the lips back without any protest. 'I think I know how to stop the bleeding, Star,' she said, as if expecting the dog to understand. 'I'll tear a strip off this soft cloth I brought with me, roll it into a sausage shape and press it between your gum and your lip. But you must let it stay there for a while until the bleeding ceases.'

Star's head remained completely still with her head on Isabel's lap, as if she had understood everything, or perhaps she was just exhausted from the long trek to Easton and grateful for the chance to rest while her kind nurse rolled up the muslin and gently pushed it into position.

Meanwhile in the confessional, after an extended

silence while she gathered her thoughts, Jess began the mysterious and sad story of Addy's disappearance from the long barrow and the unfortunate reaction of the village Godfearers. She also explained why, during the last few months, she had been unable to go to confession because she did not trust the priest to whom she would have to confess.

'And I am sure it was he who spread gossip about me around the village, Father, declaring that I had been communing with the Devil and was responsible for the disappearance of my fellow shepherd from one of the long barrows on the Downs,' she concluded. 'I have had to flee from my home for fear of being declared a witch.'

'But you have not told me why this man might want to discredit you, Jess. Had you offended him in some way perhaps?'

'Oh no, Father! Quite the opposite in fact.' Jess's voice rose in indignation. 'It was him and his acolytes who dishonoured me in ways I cannot for shame describe.'

She heard Father Michael clear his throat, as if he needed time to absorb her revelations. Eventually he said, 'Do not feel obliged to do so, but tell me if you will how old you are, Jess.'

'I will be seventeen in a few weeks.'

'You are young – for a shepherd I mean. Hardly yet a woman and working out on the Downs among all the other male shepherds. Were you not frightened?'

'Not of the shepherds. They may be thought hard and uncouth men but they are gentle with their ewes and kind to all creatures, including me. While I was training at the age of thirteen, one of them even gave me Star as a puppy, when one of his sheepdogs birthed a litter. As well as how to round up the ewes, he advised that I should teach her to defend me, which I did. That's why I was so surprised that she took so easily to Isabel.'

'I can tell you that Isabel Seymour is a lovely lady. She hates violence of any kind. Animals tend to understand this. But now please tell me about your religious duties, Jess. Do you pray regularly and attend church every Sunday as God and the law demand?' The priest spoke gently but firmly.

Jess felt the blood rise in her cheeks and was glad the cleric could not see her. 'Like most of the shepherds I don't attend Sunday services between Easter and Michaelmas, Father, because shepherds are exempt due to their need to care for their flocks out on the Downs. But I do say my prayers.'

'What prayers do you say, daughter? And how often?'

'I only know the Lord's Prayer and Ave Maria and of course the shepherd's psalm. All the other prayers are in Latin and I don't understand them.' Jess felt more and more inadequate as she answered the priest's questions.

'Well, daughter, I believe you are diligent in your work and truthful in your answers and so I will grant you absolution from whatever small sins you have committed. But there is no doubt that you have been neglecting your duty to God, which makes you very vulnerable to the Devil's wiles. So, I advise you not to return to your village, where his influences are evidently greatly present. Which means you should not return to your work as a shepherd either, because the Devil and his imps are known to haunt vacant places like the Downs and especially the barrows. Those you should avoid at all costs. The Virgin Mary particularly protects young women of your age, so I want you to seek her help by reciting the Ave Maria twelve times on waking and before sleep. Will you promise to do this?'

'Yes, Father,' Jess murmured, 'but where am I to live if I cannot return to my family, where I belong?'

'I will consult with the Prioress about giving you shelter for a while. And perhaps Mistress Seymour might be looking to expand her household. They have only recently settled at Wolf Hall.'

'But I cannot abandon Star, Father! Would the Prioress and the lady allow me to keep my dog at my side?'

'I don't know,' the priest admitted. 'But whatever you do, do not neglect your duty to the Holy Mother in heaven. Can you count?

He could not see the fierce frown that creased her brow. 'Of course I can count! I could hardly have shepherded a flock of sheep out on the Downs if I could not count them every day.'

'Ah yes, good! Then find twelve smooth stones and keep them in your pocket. Use them to count your Aves and do not go near any barrows. Then I think you will be safe and even happy again by the Virgin's Feast Day in August. May God bless you, my child, and please consider wearing a dress.' She heard the smile in his voice. 'Now go in peace and comfort your dog, for whom you have much to thank.'

31

Wolf Hall

28th May 1425

THE DUKE OF GLOUCESTER's note came out of the blue on the day before John and Edmund Seymour had intended to make their own expedition to the wolves' den. It was not a missive to be ignored.

> *To the Warden of Savernake Forest from the Protector.*
>
> *I am staying briefly at Marlborough Castle and wish to inspect that aspect of the forest to which you recently drew my attention. I will be at Wolf Hall Manor soon after dawn tomorrow. One squire and my lady will accompany me. She would welcome your wife's company.*

John passed the note to Edmund. 'I thought he wanted to keep this wolf hunt a secret and now he brings his mistress! Is her presence in his bed not enough?'

Edmund quickly perused the note. 'Your real problem is not his lady but your own,' he said. 'Will Isabel agree to come? You haven't managed to get that chamber door opened yet.'

'This would be a good opportunity though, would it not?' John shot Edmund a wicked glance. 'Jem the Forester says wolves don't attack humans but they might have a go at a hellcat!'

Edmund's brow crumpled into a frown. 'That isn't funny, cousin! Besides, I know that Izzy was intending to take in that shepherd girl she's been talking about. She mentioned going to Easton to collect her tomorrow, while we're in the forest.'

'Well, the shepherdess will have to wait, Ed. I'm relying on you to make sure my wife rides out with the Protector's hussy, if that's what he wants. There is a lot resting on this outing.'

'Then you tell Ham to get making some tempting savouries and sweetmeats to take in the saddlebags and I'll work on Izzy.'

Isabel was to be found in the rose garden, where she was letting young Johnnie enjoy some fresh air, carrying him along the grass paths between the newly flowering bushes.

Edmund entered the garden and swept him out of her arms. 'Johnnie's quite an armful now, isn't he?'

'That's why I bring him here. The spring is putting flesh on his baby limbs!' She watched the baby give a happy gurgle. 'But what brings you out here, Ed?'

'Royalty, I'm afraid.' He pulled the Protector's note from his doublet sleeve and handed it to her. 'Your presence is required – at very short notice, I should add.'

Isabel scanned the note and looked up, with a deep frown. 'I take it this "lady" is the Eleanor you danced with at Clarendon Palace? I'd wager it is you she wants as a companion rather than me. Besides, I want to bring the shepherdess here tomorrow.' She handed back the note.

Edmund tucked it away and returned the baby to his mother. 'John really needs to impress the duke on this expedition, Izzy,' he began. 'He would truly appreciate your presence and you are the lady of the manor. It's in both your interests to appear together. Couldn't you collect the shepherdess the next day?'

'I suppose it wouldn't make much difference.' Isabel gave him a sharp glance. 'No one is going to harm the wolves, are they? I can't bear the idea of seeing a beautiful creature murdered.'

He shook his head emphatically. 'No! It is purely a chance to see and admire them, because wolves are very rare these days. It would be foolish to spread the news that there are any in Savernake because most of the bailiwicks would vote to kill them off.'

'Or else Duke Humphrey wants them all to himself? For one big blood-bath hunt!'

Edmund gave a nervous laugh. 'He's hardly going to want a blood-bath with two ladies in the party, is he?'

'From what I've seen and heard of him I wouldn't be surprised,' Isabel responded. 'But if my presence prevents it, I'll play hostess to his paramour. I haven't forgiven John for branding the boy Nat though, so he need not think I have!'

32

The Wolves' Den, Savernake Forest

29th May 1425

NOT WISHING TO BE outshone by Eleanor Cobham of glamorous reputation, Isabel had donned her best brown riding habit and cream chaperon hat for the excursion to the wolf den. Apparel that was nevertheless completely eclipsed by the duke's mistress who, paying no heed to accepted hunting attire, arrived sporting a bright pink kirtle and full-skirted maroon jacket, with a large and expensive ostrich feather on her black hat, pinned with a large diamond brooch.

'No wolf is going to miss that outfit in a greenwood,' Edmund murmured to Isabel as he helped her mount up to greet her visitor.

'I see that we both favour grey mares,' Eleanor observed a few moments later as she inspected Isabel's trappings, while delicately consuming a sweetmeat selected from the tray offered by a lackey in Seymour livery. 'They make us stand out from the parade of bays and chestnuts sported by the men, do they not?'

'I'm afraid I spend most of my time riding my horse to and from the pilgrim hostel at Easton, only a mile or so down the road,' Isabel confessed, ignoring the question. 'I leave the forest business to my husband. But I am keen to see the wolves at their den. I believe they are beautiful animals. Have you ever seen one in the wild?'

Eleanor shook her head. 'No, but I have seen a few wolf-skin hearthrugs in my time and I believe their pelts make wonderfully warm fur-lined houppelandes for winter. My lord Humphrey covets one of them, I believe.'

'Oh.' Isabel swallowed hard and managed to murmur a faint acknowledgement of what was to her a dreadful revelation, before Jem Freeman, the Head Forester, blew a blast on his horn and called the small troop to order. 'The light is good enough to set out now, ladies and gentlemen, so two abreast if you please and servants at the back.'

'Do we ride all the way, Forester, or must we do some of it on foot? I only ask for the ladies who may not have the right footwear for muddy paths.' It was the well-booted duke who spoke, mounted on the tallest steed – a handsome chestnut stallion, which ensured that John, on his beloved Atlas, would ride a couple of head-inches below the Protector.

'I am wearing perfectly good boots,' declared Eleanor, lifting her skirt and displaying a well-turned ankle shod in bright red leather. As Isabel silently offered a polished black boot for inspection, she suddenly found herself longing to see those scarlet boots smothered in dark brown Savernake mud.

After nearly an hour navigating a long series of wide tracks, well-trodden by human and animal footprints, the party turned off onto a narrow pathway, which ended in a glade enclosing a huge elm tree.

'We'll leave the horses here and continue on foot,' Jem

said, dismounting at the edge of the clearing, where the elm appeared to have discouraged any other tall vegetation from growing too close. 'We call elm trees "widowers" here because they shed their big branches without any warning and have been known to kill who-or-whatever is beneath them.'

'I've never heard that said of elm trees, Forester,' Duke Humphrey declared as he dismounted and handed the reins to his hovering squire. 'Are you sure it's not an old wives' tale?'

'Well, I've helped to dig someone out from under one such branch, your grace, but I wasn't able to ask him if he heard it fall.'

John finished hitching Atlas to a sturdy holly bush, well out of the big tree's reach. 'So, as we're going on foot we have to look out for elms, as well as wolves, do we?'

Jem grinned, leading Eleanor's horse to what looked like a suitably low beech branch. 'Yes, sir, but luckily there aren't many other elms in this part of Savernake and I know where they are.'

Eleanor strolled across the clearing towards the duke, collecting mud and fallen leaves on her red boots, which she then picked off with a fastidious expression and began flicking them at the duke, who turned to see where they came from. 'You didn't tell me there would be wet leaves and mud, my lord,' she complained.

He flicked a leaf off his polished leather jacket and turned to the Forester, asking testily, 'Are we anywhere near the den now, sirrah, or should we pause for some refreshment?'

This question came more as an order than a suggestion and the two lackeys in charge of the panniers hastened to open them and arrange more pies and sweetmeats on platters.

Ham's skills in the kitchen provided the ideal comfort for frayed royal tempers, washed down with horn mugs of John's precious Sherish wine, and in due course Eleanor's mood warmed enough to engage Isabel in conversation.

'This wine is delicious! Aren't you going to indulge or does it not agree with you?' The question was laced with faint censure as she took another sip.

Isabel lowered her voice to reply, as if she might reveal a close secret. 'It is not me that the wine disagrees with but the babe I am feeding. His nurse tells me it makes its presence felt – or smelt might be a better word.'

'Oh! You have a child already!' It was more of a muted exclamation than a question. 'How I envy you! I have always wanted children but so far God has not granted me that honour. Is this your first?'

'Yes. Or should I say, the first we have, but actually John has little to do with him – apart from being the father of course.'

'How lucky you are! I pray constantly for a child without success. The duke has two by early affairs in his life but I seem not to be blessed. Perhaps if we married, God might be gracious . . .' She fell suddenly silent, as if sensing an interruption, even though her back was turned.

Without realising, the two women had lowered their voices and the men seemed to sense intrigue. Duke Humphrey strolled across to join them and John Seymour and the Forester clearly felt obliged to follow.

'What are you two gossiping about?' the duke demanded.

'Just speculating whether we will actually see any wolves today,' his mistress replied in a teasing tone.

Jem hastened to reassure her. 'The wolves in this part of

the woods have favourite feeding stations, where they drag their prey, so we'll visit them as we go. And if they're not visible there we'll approach the den which is not far away now. We should be safe if we don't go too near, because when their bellies are full the wolves get sleepy and lie down for a nap. I hope to find a well-fed and snoring pack for you to observe and assess and the mud will let us make a silent arrival and retreat.'

'Aren't there sometimes single wolves in the forest who have been evicted from the den?' the duke asked. 'Might they not be a danger if we come across them as we go?'

Jem nodded. 'Yes, your grace, I know of at least five around here and they're the ones to hunt when the season opens. Which reminds me, if we're going to hunt them, we will need trained wolfhounds.'

John grimaced. 'As I am told by our head huntsman. He says if he can't get some from Wales, he may have to go to Ireland for them.'

'Ah, an Irish wolfhound is a beautiful animal!' Eleanor exclaimed. 'My father had one for years and it would hunt anything! And yet when I was a young girl, I could curl up with it by the fire.'

Jem looked impressed. 'Then you were braver than me, madam.'

'Well, brave or foolhardy! I promise not to try it with any wolves or wolfhounds in Savernake!'

Unfortunately, the tour of the feeding sites proved unrewarding. There were plenty of chewed bones but no sign of wolves. 'We'll go to the den then,' said Jem. 'We'll have to be careful not to make ourselves too obvious. They'll know we're there but as long as we keep still and quiet they'll be undisturbed. I'll tell you now that there should be eight adult wolves, including the pair who are the parents of this spring's brood. The pups will be about five weeks old by now but probably not yet venturing out.'

After a short walk, the party quietly took their viewpoint under the lower branches of a venerable oak tree, situated a score of yards away from the gathering of wolves sprawled under a similar tree, where the roots were exposed to form the entrance to the nursery, the pups invisible, well below ground as expected. Six adult wolves lay in various forms of lassitude, while sunlight gleamed through spring-green oak leaves over their variegated fur coats of grey, black and brown, as the canopy above them fluttered and waved in the breeze. However, two guardian wolves sat upright at either end of the resting group, alert to any hint of danger. It was one of this pair that slowly approached halfway to the second oak and sat down again to examine the group of intrusive humans through deep amber eyes.

'I thought you said wolves weren't interested in humans, Jem?' John's whispered response was laced with a mixture of irony and alarm. 'This one looks mighty interested to me.'

The Forester replied in an undertone. 'I've had them walk all around me at a certain distance without any problem, sir. If you are fearful we can leave quietly but at this moment his grace appears to be fascinated by the coat of the other guardian wolf. It is a very handsome straw colour but he is a juvenile – not yet quite the age and stage required, I think.'

'It is too young!' Isabel's loud reaction made the nearest guardian's hackles rise.

Duke Humphrey responded resoundingly. 'On the contrary, Mistress Seymour, it is the perfect target and I hope to return whenever it reaches maturity and claim the pelt for myself.' Without any sign of fear, he stretched his cramped limbs and marched away from the den, calling over his shoulder, 'A very satisfactory exercise, Seymour. Now, we must make haste! My lady and I have an appointment in Marlborough with the High Sheriff of Wiltshire this evening.'

'Go for him, young wolf!' Isabel whispered under her breath. 'Now is your chance!'

'Humphrey survived the battle of Agincourt,' muttered Eleanor unexpectedly. 'Nothing kills him.'

33

Wolf Hall

29th May 1425

After the visit to the wolves' den, the Seymours arrived back at Wolf Hall Manor at sundown, having parted with the royal contingent where the old Roman road forked to Marlborough. John was delighted with the result of the day's events and declared that Jem the Head Forester should have one silver groat as a reward for his excellent guidance and another for keeping an eagle eye in future on the straw-coloured wolf.

'And Izzy, the duke has invited us to join his next gathering at the mansion on the Thames he inherited from his brother Thomas of Clarence. There have been some major improvements there and he now calls it Bella Court. I've heard that the entertainment he put on there last year was stupendous. Definitely an excuse for a new doublet for me and a new gown for you.'

Isabel made no response to this revelation but John seemed not to notice and continued to report the highlights of royal life described by his benefactor during their Savernake sortie. But he did not have much more time to gloat because when they turned into the rutted road that led to the Wolf Hall village it became obvious that smoke was swirling lazily up from the manor messuage, wafting across a blood-red sunset.

'Something's burning!' the Forester exclaimed and clapped his heels to his mount, sending clods of wet earth flying.

'I think it's a barn thatch!' John yelled, following suit, while Isabel thanked the Lord that the village street appeared deserted. Edmund and the two retainers trotted more slowly, demonstrating more care for children and poultry.

The manor gates were standing open and the horsemen all cantered straight past the stable buildings and on to the second yard, where it became clear that the roof of the big granary barn was the source of the smoke. However, by luck and thanks to the previous night's rain, the straw had not burst into flames but smoke was curling over the big entrance porch, licking the top of the great barn doors.

Bringing Atlas to a sliding stop, John cast his gaze around the yard, which was suspiciously empty. 'Where is everyone?' he shouted furiously. 'Why is no one tackling the fire?'

'Perhaps because they were responsible for setting it?' suggested Jem. 'There's been a lot of villein meetings lately, according to the Reeve.'

'Well, why didn't he tell me?' John was red-faced with anger.

'Maybe because you were not here.' It was Edmund who spoke. 'But right now it looks like we're going to have to tackle this task ourselves, not sit around here discussing it. We need buckets of water and a long ladder!'

While the men stabled the horses and collected the necessary items needed for fire-fighting, Isabel stabled Snowflake herself before making her way to the manor house, stopping first at the kitchen where Ham was busy preparing a meal, unaware of the potential drama that had been playing out on his doorstep.

Isabel made her way straight to her bedroom and as she removed the mud-splattered riding outfit she had worn to the wolves' den, she recalled the visit she had made to Nat's home and the warning she had gathered from Liz about the villeins' meeting in the tithe barn – a smaller building sited further away from the manor house and the granary; a warning she had not conveyed to John. She opened the chamber shutter that overlooked the barn and the farmyard and realised that the wind would have blown the smoke away from the house and had anyway now become a mild drift, due to the dousing it was receiving from the first men up the ladder.

On climbing to the bedchamber, she had neither drawn up the ladder stair nor locked the door and she immediately regretted these omissions as her heart lurched the moment she heard John's voice close behind her and his hands feeling her breasts through the front of the smock she had stripped down to.

'Aha – at last a chance to touch this child you say we are expecting – and indeed there he is!' His murmured words came close to her ear and one hand busied with his hose while the other felt the slight bump on her belly. She froze and her skin shivered into goosebumps as she felt his manhood hardening against her hip but she found herself unable to protest or deny him, being intensely aware of the futility when the house was empty and the men all otherwise involved.

'I'm sure the babe won't object if we play around him a little, will he, Izzy?' John's voice was a low whisper as he pulled up the fine linen of her smock, pulled her around and pushed her back against the open shutter.

She mouthed a faint 'No!' as he forced her legs apart but he responded with a faint but hoarse 'Yes!' as he pushed into her. 'Just relax. We are man and wife, remember? We have an obligation to pleasure each other and I'm sure the babe won't be bothered.'

Far from being as certain as he was about the safety of the baby, she shut her eyes, clenched her fists and forced herself to submit calmly through the ensuing minutes, knowing that he was within his marital rights and that she had no way of refusing him without causing possible danger to the baby. When he made a long final thrust with a satisfied sigh and pulled away, she pushed him off with a two-handed shove and a gargoyle stare and immediately turned her back. Making her way to a small coffer, she brought out one of Johnnie's napkins and bent over to wipe herself, ostentatiously staring narrow-eyed at John as she did so, as if to say, 'I am wiping you off as a coward and a rapist.'

He finished adjusting his clothes and blew her a kiss. 'I'm sure you have been missing our couplings, Izzy. We must do it again soon. We need to make up for lost time,' he said, leaving the room with an apparently careless wave.

'If you have harmed the baby I will kill you,' she muttered under her breath and pulled a clean shift over her head.

34

Easton Priory and Wolf Hall

30th May 1425

JESS FELT DESPERATELY LONELY lying with Star in the straw. The Prioress had asked her not to take her dog into the hostel or anywhere near the passing pilgrims. She had been invited to use one of the empty stables in the yard behind the Prioress's house as a kennel, so she had chosen to use it as her own accommodation as well. After making her confession she had hoped the distress she felt at being labelled a witch might have lifted but Father Michael's demands and the Prioress's stipulation about hiding Star had only served to further stir her sense of isolation. When the lovely lady called Isabel had left to go home, she'd said she would come back the next day but she had not, which added to Jess's misery.

'We are not wanted anywhere, Star,' she whispered to her dog as they shared their bed of straw in the stable for the second night. 'I have made my confession; I might as well go home tomorrow and take whatever fate throws at me. We'll walk the Downs in daylight because the priest said the Devil's black dogs only appear at night.'

When she finally fell asleep her dreams were not of the

Devil and his imps, nor of the fiendishly dark barrow, but remarkably of Addy. However, he was not in the farmhouse or even on the Downs with the sheep; he was somewhere she did not recognise, an unknown and ragged landscape, full of the sound of guns blaring and men shouting and the swish of arrows overhead. Fear filled her mind and she wanted to run away, but something made her stay and she knew that it was Addy. He was in danger, or was about to be, and she tried to read his mind. Suddenly there was a loud bang and he yelled someone's name and ran off into a cloud of smoke. She was woken by a wet tongue on her face – Star! Thrashing about in the straw, she must have woken the dog.

At Wolf Hall, Isabel had also tossed and turned late into the night, wondering whether she should leave the ladder stair down and admit John back to his marital bed. She did not relish the notion but she also greatly disliked the idea that he had visited brothels during his time in Salisbury, which made his rough coupling with her after the visit to the wolf den of great concern. She knew nothing of bawdyhouses and was uncertain whether they might cause harm to her or to the infant she was carrying. But while she despised her husband's treatment of the boy Nat, she began to worry that her continued denial of his marital rights might have brought injury to her unborn child. Her thoughts turned to prayers and concluded by promising to try once more to obey the Church's rules on marital obligation.

'But I beg you, Holy Mary, to urge John to do the same and to stay away from bawdyhouses,' she added, before finally nodding off to sleep.

It was not a long and refreshing sleep however, and before

dawn she had dressed and made her way to Snowflake's stable. On the way she popped her head into the kitchen, where the industrious Ham seemed never to go to bed and always had a selection of enticing dainties and wafers available. As the sun rose, he was busy making honey cakes for breakfast. 'Can you give me some in a basket, Ham?' she asked. 'Oh yes, and have you managed to show young Nat around the kitchen? What did you think of him?'

Ham's head tilted to one side; his fleshy lips pursed in thought. 'He'll do as a skivvy,' he said with a nod. 'If his father lets him come.'

'From what I know of Col he'll be glad not to have to look at that awful wound every day. I hope it doesn't worry you. Will you house him somewhere in the back here? He shouldn't take up much room. Maybe his father might make him a cot bed.'

The cook shook his head. 'Beds don't feature in villeins' houses, ma'am. A pile of rushes will be luxury to him.'

Isabel recalled the sight of her brother lying in the four-poster that had been his deathbed at about the same age as Nat. 'Very well, Ham, you are king of the kitchen. How long before he can start?'

'Any time now. He can't wait to get out of the family home. Says his father can't look at him.' He popped the last sweetmeat into a woven willow basket. 'Who are these for?' he asked.

'The Prioress at Easton but I expect she'll share them around. I'm bringing a girl back with me from the Priory. She's been a shepherdess but it seems to have gone sour on her.'

'What will she do here, milady?'

'It depends, Ham. I don't know how long she'll stay so I might just get her to help Annie in the house to start with.'

He looked relieved. 'Good idea, ma'am. I was worried you might leave Annie with me as well as young Nat! She'll never make a cook! But she's a nice girl and a good housekeeper.'

Jess and Star left Easton at daybreak, not even waiting for the Prioress to emerge from her house to attend Prime and receive thanks for her hospitality. Her vivid dreams of Addy and Isabel Seymour's failure to come back on the previous day had upset her badly and she felt a desperate need to get out onto the Downs and take refuge in her family home, whatever the consequences. She hurried through Easton village without making eye contact with anyone, although quite a number of people were up and about: men and boys heading for the fields, girls carrying buckets of fresh water from a local spring or loading spindles for their mothers, who were digging in their back gardens, collecting spring vegetables for the dinnertime pottage. In sympathy with her mistress, Star stayed faithfully at Jess's heel, deterring any approach from inquisitive children, who backed away from her dark-eyed stare. Once outside the village they came upon a fork in the road and both horse and dog stood uncertainly, while Jess tried to recall which path she had come from on her journey from Avebury.

Isabel rode through the busy Easton village enquiring every few minutes after a girl with a black dog. When she reached the fork, she drew rein. There was no one in sight to ask the question again. She knew the right-hand road carried another route to Wolf Hall but reckoned Jess wouldn't know that, and as trees lined it profusely, indicating Savernake Forest, she concluded that a shepherd was more likely to take the open road on the left, which offered a distant view of the Downs. Taking a deep breath, she urged her horse onto the path that looked less trodden. The grey mare instantly broke into a trot, as if she at least was confident that they were on the right track. Isabel smiled and gave her a pat on the neck. 'All right, Snowflake, you sniff her out!'

The mare only slackened her pace when the pathway took a sharp turn to the left and she lowered her nose towards the ground, as if she had picked up a familiar scent. Ahead the terrain began to rise and after some time they encountered a small stream that crossed the track at speed, servicing a mill wheel. 'Where there's a mill there's a miller,' Isabel told Snowflake as they neared a small house from which a man was emerging. Before it a hock-high ford formed a crossing and the mare splashed on steadily through it.

'Greetings, Mr Miller! I am following a friend. Have you by any chance seen a young shepherd with a black dog?'

Snowflake was pawing the ground, irritated by the noise of the wheel and the tight hold Isabel had on her reins, so she at least was relieved when the miller nodded, waved a hand up the nearby hill and shouted above the noise of the mill wheel, 'They're up there somewhere, heading for the Wansdyke!' In the distance there stood a single sarsen stone on top of the first of a gradually climbing row of peaks. 'They stopped for a drink from the stream and she said she was heading for Avebury.'

Avebury! Isabel frowned deeply. That was where Jess had been fleeing from. So why was she heading back there now?

'Thank you!' Raising a hand in acknowledgement, she gave the mare her head. 'Go on then! Fetch them, Snowflake!' she urged and the horse broke into an enthusiastic canter.

They were resting in the sunshine, their backs to the stone on the first hill, and Isabel leapt off her horse to express her delight. 'We found you, Jess! Thank God!'

Jess gazed up at Isabel and tears welled in her eyes, but Star instantly leapt forward to greet her.

'Hello, Star! How is your wounded mouth? Don't knock me over! And Jess, don't cry!' Isabel knelt down beside the emotional girl. 'Is it because I didn't come yesterday? I am so sorry. My husband insisted that I ride out with someone very important and there was no way to let you know. I expected you would wait at least until today and I came to Easton as soon as I could this morning, but you'd already left.'

'I thought you must have changed your mind.' Jess sniffed and wiped her nose on her hand. 'I was so grateful that you had been kind to me and then the head nun told me that I must keep Star away from the pilgrims and suggested she be shut in one of the stables. I didn't know what to do so I just slept two nights with her there and when I woke this morning, I decided I'd go back to the Downs and seek work with the shepherds. I know a number of them who might give me work.'

'Oh!' Isabel sighed. 'The miller told me you were heading for Avebury. I wouldn't blame you if you didn't want to join our household. It's not the most comfortable in the county but there is a warm hearth for Star to sleep at and you can join her there if you like. We'll find plenty for you to do. You haven't met my little Johnnie. He's only a baby, but soon he'll need someone young to look after him when his nurse takes over my next baby. Could you teach Star to play with him perhaps?'

'You're pregnant again?' Jess became more animated. 'My sheep are lambing at the moment and Star and I miss their leaps and bleats. She would be a perfect guard dog for a little boy.'

'Then you must both come to Wolf Hall! By the way, we also have a great cook called Ham, who makes lovely meals for us and his sweetmeats are delicious.' She leapt suddenly to her feet. 'Oh! I was so keen to find you that I forgot to give some of his cakes to the Prioress. Are you hungry? Shall we have one now?' She opened the saddlebag on patient Snowflake's withers and pulled out a bundle. 'They're a bit squashed but they'll still taste wonderful. Here, help yourself!'

She offered the open bag to Jess, who stood up to plunge in her hand. 'I am starving, my lady!' she admitted, sinking her teeth into a rather battered honey cake. Her eyes grew round with awe as she chewed and when she had swallowed, she stared at Isabel as if the world was spinning. 'That is angel food, ma'am! I have never tasted anything so sweet!'

Isabel laughed and watched her take another bite. 'Have you never tasted honey, Jess? Well, we don't have honey cakes every day but those were made for an important person. However, if they persuade you to join us at Wolf Hall, they will have done good service. Have another!'

35

Wolf Hall

End of May 1425

'DAMN THE MAN!' JOHN Seymour flung down a recent letter delivered by courier and reached for his goblet of wine. He took a hefty gulp and announced to the crowded dinner table, 'Duke Humphrey wants to come hunting! Only he wants to come on the feast of John the Baptist and this time he's coming to take prey!'

'Not wolves already?' Isabel was horrified. She had managed to make dinnertime with a few minutes to spare, having brought Jess into the hall just in time to introduce her to the rest of the household, except John, who had been too distracted by the royal command to make anything but a grunt in reaction to her arrival.

Edmund picked up the royal missive and swiftly perused its contents. 'No wolves, Izzy,' he reassured her. 'And it's only the duke and his courtiers coming to hawk game birds for the feast of St John and chase venison for the larder. But that's awkward financially.' He turned his gaze to John. 'Isn't it, cousin?'

'Yes. Tomorrow is the last day of May and being officially a holiday I'll have to pay the villeins extra to take enough people from the fields to raise the maypole and set fuel for fires, to say nothing of providing food and ale. And now we'll have to do it all again in June! But that time there will be a royal retinue demanding the best food and drink. However at least he's not bringing his doxy, so you're off the hook, Isabel. It will be men only.'

'Well, that's a relief,' Isabel acknowledged. 'And so, tomorrow's celebrations can be a rehearsal for the duke's. But presumably he'll be paying us for the pleasure and not expecting us to meet the cost?'

'Hm.' John made a face. 'I wouldn't rely on it.' But at least he gave Isabel a wry smile, rather than an angry snort.

Isabel was amazed at the speed with which the Wolf Hall garden was almost transformed into a pleasure palace. The coloured ribbons on the painted maypoles in the rose garden were the first attraction and then the music of the village band, scratchy though it was, as the children immediately gathered to practise their dances. Rusty though the band was, it provided a sense of fun and laughter which kept their fathers happily building fire pits for the next day's stag roasts.

All of them were smiling at the thought of the promised extra farthings and the jugs of ale on the following day and there was no mention of the failure of the fire at the big barn a few days before.

John and Edmund went together to the tithe barn to see what might be done to make it possible for a banquet hall after the St John's Day hunt. 'Is there anything we could do about the smell of damp reeds in there?' John asked Isabel when she brought Johnnie out to view the activities.

'I sent Annie and Jess into the woods to gather spring flowers, so we can test if they will smother the smell,' Isabel said. 'They should be back any time now.'

'Those two seem to be getting on rather well together, I noticed.'

'Yes, but Jess is worried about Star going into the kennel with the hunting pack, like the head kennelman suggested. She says the pack won't accept her. Couldn't we allow the dog into the hall at night? She loves sleeping near the hearth and she'd be a good guard dog if anyone thought about trying to raid the strongboxes.'

'Where does Jess sleep?'

'She and Annie put pallets down by the hall hearth. But I'm not sure it's safe for them to be lying loose about the house.'

'Why not? Servants have always slept around the fires.' John paused and looked enquiringly at his wife. 'Incidentally, I noticed that the ladder stair was left down last night. Was that intentional or an oversight?'

Isabel fell back to avoid his gaze. Her cheeks were flushed. 'It was down all day. I thought you hadn't noticed. You didn't say anything.'

'I was too busy planning the duke's hunting party and anyway, I thought you'd just forgotten to raise it for once. Did you leave the chamber door unlocked as well?'

'Yes, but you didn't notice that either.'

There was a triumphant note in John's voice. 'Well, I've noticed it now and I'll be there tonight, wife. Do not lock the door!'

They had reached the tithe barn and paused in the wide-open entrance. Isabel tossed her head and strode through the barn doorway. ‘Oh, this smells lovely already. Move out the haystacks and it will make a fine banqueting hall!’

Jess and Annie were sitting together on one of the haystacks making garlands on ribbons. Isabel hoped they hadn’t heard the nature of the conversation outside the tent. She didn’t like the idea of a reconciliation between the lord and lady of the manor being the subject of bawdy laughter among the household.

‘Those flowers are beautiful, girls!’ she declared. ‘Are they for the village?’

‘Yes,’ Annie reassured her. ‘We picked them in the woods for the village wives. We’re making coronets for their children. Everyone is in a good mood with the sunshine and the prospect of the May Day revels tomorrow.’

‘Do they know about the Duke of Gloucester coming to hunt at the feast of St John?’ Isabel asked.

Jess nodded. ‘Oh yes, the lord told the Reeve and he seemed quite excited! One of the men asked if there would be extra ale. I think he reckoned on some of it coming his way!’

‘Huh! He’s hopeful!’

‘I looked in on the kitchen early this morning,’ Annie said, ‘There were feathers flying around everywhere.’

Isabel laughed. ‘Ham will be in his element.’

When she was out of earshot Annie raised an eyebrow and remarked to Jess, ‘The mistress seems more cheerful than of late. I wonder what has buttered her bread?’

That night, when supper was over and the night-candles were lit, John filled two precious glasses with Sherish wine and handed one to Isabel, blatantly ignoring Edmund who still sat at the supper table. 'I hope this might celebrate a change in our mutual regard.'

There was a moment of hesitation on Isabel's part, which must have alerted Edmund to the solemness of the occasion, for he pushed back his chair and stood up with a knowing smile aimed directly at her. 'I can sense when three is a crowd and wish you both a goodnight.'

As he made his way up the east stairway to his chamber, he heard two delicate glasses being carefully clinked and two married people, who had not shared a bed for many weeks, make silent vows to try again. When they made their way to their bedchamber, the baby had been taken to Nan's care and the ladder stair was firmly raised to cut off any disturbance.

'May I unlace your gown?' In the lord's chamber, John was rapidly down to his shirt but Isabel had taken her time, waiting for help to perform that task on the back of the loose houppelande dress she preferred, both for comfort and to disguise her pregnancy.

'Well, if you do not, I shall have to sleep in it,' she said. 'The choice is yours.'

He smiled roguishly. 'I knew that as soon as you dismissed the servants.' He began the unlacing, planting a swift kiss on her neck before the process started. 'Where are they, by the way?' His fingers got to work with swift precision.

'In the solar and yes, I do trust Edmund.' She emphasised his cousin's name. 'And you have obviously done this task much too often, though I don't recall ever with me!'

John chuckled as the loosened lacing allowed the houppelande to drop to the floor. 'Some annoying maid always got in the way.' He moved swiftly around her until they were face to face and placed his hands on her shift, where her nipples immediately hardened and his eyes spoke his need to hers.

Isabel surprised herself by matching his desire, pressing her lips to his again and again and pulling him over to the bed. The shift and shirt were soon abandoned and John discovered a fiery passion in his young wife that he had not felt before. After they lay, satiated, in each other's arms, they had only to slip between the sheets for their eyelids to droop and their minds to slip into dreamland. 'We have a busy day tomorrow, Izzy,' were John's last words as sleep overwhelmed him.

36

John the Baptist Day

24th June 1425

IN EARLY-MORNING SPRING SUNLIGHT the sound of lute and shawm heralded the arrival of the duke's cavalcade as it made its approach to Wolf Hall. Despite the hour, it brought the villagers out of their cots to stand alongside the rutted road that ran up to the manor wall, where the sturdy iron gate stood open in welcome and the whole household waited to greet their royal visitor.

As the leading horse moved through the gate, John and Isabel made hasty genuflections beside the two sturdy flagpoles standing sentinel on either side of the entrance, displaying the Seymour standards. A sudden breeze stirred the banners and startled the leading horse, and the young boy sitting in a pommel seat in front of the rider gave a surprised shriek that turned to nervous laughter. 'The horse jumped, Uncle!' the little lad cried. 'I might have fallen!'

'No, you're safe with me, Harry,' Duke Humphrey assured him, his arm firmly around the boy's waist. 'I would not let you fall. And we are here now anyway. This is Wolf Hall.'

John and Isabel exchanged amazed glances, swallowing their surprise at the unexpected arrival of the young king, before John stepped hastily forward. 'And you are very welcome, your grace. We are honoured to receive you. May I lift you down from your uncle's horse?'

A man wearing half-armour moved around from behind the duke's horse and spoke with a deep, lilting voice. 'I will attend his grace if you please, sir.' He reached up to lift the boy down from his seat and smiled at him fondly. 'Your lady mother told me to take special care of you, did she not, your grace?'

Safe on the ground, the little king smiled and nodded. 'Yes, she did, Owen.' Then he turned to John and added politely, 'Thank you for the offer, sir, but we must do as my mother says. She is the queen.'

John bowed again. 'Then indeed we must, your grace. May I present my wife, Isabel, and somewhere behind us with his nurse is our son Johnnie, who is a few years younger than you.'

Isabel repeated her curtsy, trying to forget that it favoured the man who had crowed over splitting the young king from his mother. 'Much too young to play with you I'm afraid, your grace,' she said with a smile aimed directly at the royal child.

Duke Humphrey dismounted and approached John. 'I am sure your wife won't mind, Seymour, if we leave the king and his guards here while we make the chase. I thought it would do him good to see some of the forest but obviously a wild hunt among men is too dangerous for a boy of three. Maybe next year, eh, Harry?'

Realising that the duke had no intention of actually asking her if she minded, Isabel said nothing and dropped another demure curtsy, relieved that he showed no sign of having noticed her among the ladies in Queen Catherine's audience chamber earlier in the year.

John bowed in agreement. 'Indeed, my lord. There are refreshments ready for you now while the horses are rested.'

The duke clapped him on the shoulder. 'I remember your cook's sweetmeats, John. Bring them on!'

John nodded. 'My cousin Edmund will be hunting with us if you agree, my lord. And Jem, the Head Forester, who perhaps you remember, is already out with the lymers seeking suitable prey.'

'Excellent,' said the duke. 'We need him and his men, don't we? And the greyhounds and mastiffs! Let Savernake display its best sport, eh? Now, lead me to the wine and wafers, Seymour, and then – to the hunt!'

37

The Tithe Barn

24th June 1425

THE LITTLE KING'S ENTOURAGE decided to take over the big field of ploughed strips to play their games, to the concern of the villeins who were worried for the safety of the late spring vegetables and had to cross their fingers and hope that they didn't trample them. 'At least they're keeping the birds off the new seed,' the Reeve pointed out. Most men of the tenant families had gathered in the garden, building the fires they intended to leap over in the early evening as part of the ritual revels of St John the Baptist's Day. The women and children had been gathering bunches of wild herbs to burn on the fires, in order to drive away the Devil's demons. On the longest day of the year they believed that such rituals would bring prosperity and blessings to the manor.

Meanwhile the duke's cavalcade rode away over the Bedwyn ford, waved off by the little king, who was now wandering among the newly planted field strips with the handsome Owen, firing arrows to frighten the crows and guarded by a posse of strategically posted soldiers. With Star on guard under the top table in the decorated tithe barn, the two young household maids were clearing the trestles after the hunters' refreshments and laying down fresh linen and napkins ready for when they returned.

'It's a pity the duke liked those gorgeous honey cakes so much,' Jess complained. 'I could live on them and he didn't leave us any!'

'I didn't take to the Protector,' Annie remarked in an undertone. 'He makes it very obvious that he thinks women should be seen and not heard. But the king's minder Owen is another matter, don't you think? He is handsome and very polite and his voice is smooth as silk. No wonder the queen likes him.'

'How do you know that, Annie?' Jess was wide-eyed now. 'I didn't even know we had a queen until today. The king is too young to be married, surely.'

Walking into the barn with a pile of napkins, Isabel heard Jess's last remark and laughed. 'Of course he is. Queen Catherine is his mother. And she was married to the last king, Henry, the Fifth I think it was, but he died when his son was only nine months old. She is French and as well as being king of England, he is also king of France, poor little thing.'

'How can he be poor if he's the king of two countries? I don't understand.'

'Well, you don't really need to, Jess, unless you marry a soldier and then you might learn why we are at war with France, even though he is their king too. I certainly don't know the answer.' Isabel handed her a pile of linen. 'Meanwhile start setting out the fresh napkins. There will be a mountain of laundry after this visit!'

From under the main trestle, concealed by the voluminous

cloth, Star gave a warning growl. 'Quiet, Star!' ordered Jess. 'All is well.'

But for Jess all was not well. Isabel's remarks about war with France had vividly recalled a memory of her smoke-filled dream, with the terrifying noise of guns and the cries of injured soldiers. She had experienced several returns of this nightmare since its first occurrence and each time it grew more vivid and apparently more frighteningly connected with Addy.

In the manor garden the sun gradually dipped towards the None bell with no sign of the returning hunters and the menfolk were standing with brimming mugs of ale beside as yet unlit fires, grumbling about the lateness of their dinner. Meanwhile the Wolf Hall children had tired of practising leaping the unlit fires and had instead invented tag races, becoming noisier and more uncontrollable by the hour. The adults drank more ale and began clamouring for the promised dinner but Ham refused to deliver it before the duke arrived back from the forest.

Only the little king was served fish blancmange in the tithe barn, brought to the table by Nat, the kitchen scullion, watched by Nan and little Johnnie. The nurse and the king's minder held a stilted conversation over the fruit and flowers decorating the cloth of the trestle.

Nan smiled blithely at Owen as she revealed that, 'Johnnie is still too young for fish, even in a blancmange.'

'So I see.' The Welshman smiled back at the nurse. 'He looks very healthy though. Living in a forest must suit him.'

'He was a wedding baby,' revealed Nan proudly. 'Such children are sturdy.'

'How interesting.' Owen removed the scarcely touched bowl of blancmange from the king and offered him a ripe pear. 'This looks much better, your grace,' he said. 'I think his grace might prefer to wait for the banquet,' he informed the nurse.

As if disapproving with the rejection of the fishy offering, the baby began to cry and Nan hurriedly decided to depart.

'She did not ask my permission to leave,' remarked the young king solemnly.

At the far end of the barn in front of a rear open door, Isabel and Jess were using the evening daylight to finish the festoons, while outside in the manor garden the older boys were practising leaping over an unlit fire and Nat, the kitchen skivvy, was at last attending a large pre-roasted bullock carcass, turning it on a spit to ready it for the banquet and poking red heat out of the white-hot charcoal. A few yards away his father Col was downing his sixth mug of ale, casting angry looks at the ruddy S scar on his son's cheek and holding forth about how much he hated the Warden of Savernake. One by one the others grew bored with his moaning and moved further away, tossing aggravated remarks over their shoulders about having heard it all a dozen times before. As the Reeve left, exasperated, he shouted, 'Jesu Col, just stop bothering us and give Seymour a taste of your rage!'

'I will – you'll see!' the agitated man yelled and banged his empty mug down on a trestle.

This bitter exchange carried to Nat's ears and, still holding his hot poker, he walked over to confront his red-faced father. 'I like my new job, Pa, and the Seymours have been good to me – specially the lady. So don't you go and do anything to spoil my pitch!'

'Bah! Get out of my way!' His drunk and irate father grabbed the red-hot poker from his son and shoved him off his feet, then headed in long strides towards the wide-open doors of the tithe barn.

38

The Hunters' Return

24th June 1425

THE CAVALCADE OF HORSES splashed through the Bedwyn Brook, sending sparkling drops over everyone but the two guards leading it. 'If you want to attract noble customers you can add a good stone bridge to your list of improvements, John!' Duke Humphrey shouted, shaking off the shower as best he could. 'Your pot of gold is shrinking rapidly!'

'Nothing that can't be solved by having friends in high places, your grace!' Their horses scrambled up the opposite bank side by side and set off on the track, which led uphill alongside the Wolf Hall field strips.

'Well, don't include me in that group.' A wicked smile split the duke's face. 'I'm still paying for renovating the Thameside house my Uncle Thomas of Exeter left me in his will.'

'Luckily my esteemed neighbour Lord Hungerford is now Chancellor of the Exchequer and he is always looking to invest the country's wealth in reliable ventures, my lord.' John jerked his reins as his mount tripped on a stone when they neared the top of the rise. Then before the duke could respond to this remark he frowned fiercely and added,

'Jesu did you hear that noise? It's coming from the manor. Something's going on! Guard – make speed!'

Suddenly a high-pitched scream could be heard echoing down the hill towards them.

'Holy Mother! The king!' yelled Humphrey, spurring his horse past the surprised guards. 'Out of my way!'

The rest of the rise was covered at a gallop and the cavalcade thundered towards the tithe barn around the back of the manor house. When they reached it both men flung themselves from their horses and ran.

The sight that confronted them was chaotic. The two guards who had been on duty outside had not noticed the poker held close to his leg in Col's hand as he entered the barn, and had not immediately sensed trouble, assuming he was one of the servants coming to move furniture or collect dirty dishes. He had passed through the entrance without hinderance and quickly scanned the other occupants. The sight of the young king gave him a jolt. Here was a situation his ale-addled mind had not expected and when he saw Owen bend to whisper in the boy's ear and push him down under the table he began to panic. Having seen and heard the nurse leave with the indignantly yelling Johnnie, he had expected to find the Warden's wife and her servant alone in the barn. He'd caught sight of them working in their corner but he had not bargained for an armed soldier in a cuirass advancing around the table, pulling a poniard from the sheath on his belt.

'Stop right there!' Owen ordered in a resounding voice. 'Who are you?'

But Col's drunken instinct was to keep to his plan and, having noticed the open door behind the two women in the corner, he swerved swiftly in that direction, putting the table between him and the Welshman. However, he had not reckoned with the snarling black dog, which suddenly emerged from behind the floor-length cloth covering the ladies' table. Star leapt at him, sinking her teeth firmly into the hem of his dark blue tunic, but he pushed on, dragging the dog behind him and leaping up onto the table straight at Isabel, who screamed in terror. Star fell away and Jess caught her by the collar, dodging out of the attacker's advance.

Colin achieved one swing of the red-hot poker, which grazed across Isabel's cheek before becoming entangled in her delicate veiled headdress, which caught alight, scorching the skin on her temple and burning her ear and cheek, before falling to the floor. Isabel's screams dissolved into terrified gasps of pain and fear and her attacker lurched through the open door behind her shouting, 'See whether Seymour likes looking at a scarred face every day!' he yelled, tripping suddenly over his own feet.

Before he could get up and run, a poniard was at his throat and Owen hauled him to his feet by the scarf attached to his capuchin hat, kicking the cooling poker away as he did so. 'What in the name of Holy Jesus did you think you were doing?' he asked, tightening his grip on the scarf so that his prisoner's face began to turn purple as he fought for breath and could make no reply. 'You have badly injured your mistress!'

Isabel stood up, pressing her hand to her facial injuries, then gasping at the sight of the blood and burned skin on her hand. Hearing her shocked whimpers of pain, Jess ushered her dog back under the table and ran to her aid, horrified by the damage done. 'No, don't touch your face,' she warned but Isabel stared at her, pushing her away.

'It hurts!' she cried, pulling at what was left of the veil, which was now tangled into her frizzled hair.

'But you don't want to make it worse,' Jess urged, handing her a clean napkin. 'Here, hold this over it. You are bleeding.' But Isabel just stood, wide-eyed and open-mouthed, letting the napkin droop in her hand, while the blood ran slowly through the disaster on her face.

At this point Nat entered the barn and ran across the floor to throw himself at her feet. 'What has my pa done? Aah!' His face screwed up in anguish as he spotted the bloody fluids seeping from the blackened skin, which stretched from her earlobe to above her temple, where frizzled strands of hair still smouldered. Speechless, he pressed his hands together as if in prayer but he could find no words and simply turned and ran outside again.

The little king had emerged from under the table and moved towards Isabel but was stopped by John Seymour and the Duke of Gloucester, who had rushed into the barn together and came to a panting halt. Duke Humphrey knelt down before the small boy and took his hand.

'What has happened, Henry? There was terrible screaming. Are you hurt?'

The king said nothing, still shaken by his brief glimpse of Isabel's face. He shook his head in horror and pointed over the duke's shoulder, causing the two men to adjust their gaze. John turned around to see Isabel with a bloody napkin in her hand and one side of her face an appalling mess, streaked with tears and blackened skin. He ran to the table. 'What has happened? Jesu, Isabel! You are wounded!'

He instinctively turned his gaze away, unable to look at the carnage done to his wife's cheek and ear. 'Who did this?'

Owen hauled the choking Colin forward to the duke, still holding him tight by the scarf of his hat, with the poniard at his throat. 'Here is the culprit, my lord. His grace was not the target, the poor lady was.'

Colin made a series of unintelligible gobbling sounds and King Henry said, 'Owen pushed me under the table, Uncle. I am not hurt but the lady is.' Then he pointed at the Welshman's struggling prisoner. 'And I do not think that man will live much longer if Master Tudor does not let go of his throat.'

Owen abruptly released the scarf and quickly hauled his prisoner's arm up his back, still showing him the poniard. 'Just keep your mouth shut,' he ordered. 'We've heard enough of your squalling.'

John had instantly realised the seriousness of Isabel's condition but kept his gaze averted. She was still shaking with shock but was now holding the napkin firmly over the damaged side of her face. 'Isabel must seek some attention for her wound,' he said, turning to Jess and lowering his voice. 'Take her to our bedchamber and ask Johnnie's nurse to look at it. She should have some idea of what treatment is needed. I must stay here until the dinner is over and the king and the duke set out for Marlborough. I cannot leave them unattended.'

Isabel turned her head to look at him, slowly and with obvious discomfort. By now her left eye was half-closed and drooping, lashes missing. 'This was aimed at you, John,' she said. 'For you to suffer what Colin suffers when he looks at his son's scar.' Her voice cracked and tears began to flow, forming rivulets through the bloody damage to her cheek. 'Remember this when you see the end result, because it will be your fault.' Slowly she held out her shaking hand for Jess's support. 'Take me by the back way, Jess. We don't want to spoil the duke's dinner.'

PART TWO

39

Easton Priory

Beginning of October 1425

More and more, as Isabel watched the passing pilgrims taking their early steps in search of indulgence and remission of their sins, she grew torn about her own hope for heavenly clemency. She felt she must have failed to deserve God's indulgence and He had shown His displeasure by destroying her good looks. Convinced of this holy denial, she doubted whether she would ever be entitled to receive God's approval, even if she had no idea how she might have offended Him.

Three months after the red-hot poker ruined her face, as she walked in the cloister with Jess, she knew that her baby was at last on the way. A chill wind blew loose leaves swirling over the flagstones as she clutched at her swollen belly and heaved a sigh. 'I think the baby is coming,' she said.

Since the dreadful wounding at Wolf Hall, Jess the one-time shepherdess had become Isabel's personal maid, companion and almost her only friend. 'Shall I alert the infirmarian, ma'am?'

'Not yet. It may just be a warning stab. And I also doubt she'll be much help when it comes to a birthing. There can't be many – if any – births in a nunnery! Let us finish our circuit.'

Jess nodded. 'I think it's better to be upright as long as possible, to help the baby to drop. My sheep always stood up until the last minute.'

'Are you calling me a ewe, Jess?' Isabel said indignantly.

'Of course not, ma'am. It's nature. Just the same for everything. Autumn leaves fall to the ground, we fall down when we're tired and all offspring fall to earth before they manage to stand up.'

'Hmm. Well, I intend to have this baby in a bed, thank you very much.'

'Did you have Johnnie in a bed?'

Isabel's brow furrowed. 'Do you know, I cannot remember. Ahh!' Again, she clutched her belly and spoke through the pain. 'I think I had better find that bed. The second time it might all happen more quickly.'

Jess made a suggestion. 'Or perhaps you might walk in the garden on the grass, until your waters break. It will save soaked bedsheets.'

Her mistress drew the line. 'Perhaps you haven't noticed that it happens to be raining! No – just help me to my chamber and then tell the Prioress.'

'Should we not inform the baby's father?'

'Why would we do that?' Isabel had increased her pace. 'Anyway, he's probably away somewhere hiring builders for his new hunting lodge. Anything to get away from a wife with only half a face.' Her tone had become icy.

After the fateful Baptist Day dinner and the exciting leaping of the bonfires by those men brave enough to do it, the Duke of Gloucester and King Henry had left for

Marlborough Castle and John Seymour had made his way up the ladder stair to find his wife still very shocked and tearful. He had no idea how to deal with what he considered a hysterical woman who had only the previous night been a beauty in his arms. He stood at the end of the bed, tongue-tied and unable to look her in the face. Eventually he simply turned and left, without a word of comfort or encouragement for the shocked and bandaged woman who was his wife.

The day after the terrible incident, with Edmund's help Isabel had managed to ride slowly to Easton Priory and Prioress Editha had immediately taken her into her own house. After the infirmarian had treated the burns and she had slightly recovered from the shock, Editha had offered her a nun's wimple to hide much of the damage to her face but even when the scars had stopped seeping and developed healing crusts, she did not return to Wolf Hall and took it as an insult that John had not even tried to persuade her to do so. In fact, he had only come to visit her once, three days after the dreadful event when her injury was at its most painful. His presence had resulted in a blazing row, because he had continued to avoid her gaze and given her no words of comfort or offers of help. When she became disturbed and began to cry, he had turned his back and berated her in angry bursts of displeasure. The weeks of reconciliation, which had seemed so promising in the days before the dreadful wounding, had very obviously completely vanished from the very moment John had seen her in the tithe barn and registered the ruination of Isabel's lovely face. Over the following days she came to realise that his view of their marriage had always been entirely based on her use as a bed companion, a provider of Seymour offspring and, most importantly, a beautiful face. She knew without a doubt that he would now avoid her completely and be looking elsewhere for what he considered his 'due comforts'.

The Priory became Isabel's sanctuary, a place where all the inmates except the pilgrims went about their business wearing wimples and veils which hid their hair, their ears, and much of their cheeks. Once her wounds healed, she learned that people did not tend to stare at women in wimples and, in order to face the world, she had taken to doing the same, hiding as much as she could of her still-livid scars. Assuming she would change her mind in due course and go back to her husband and family, Prioress Editha had allowed her to wear the headdress but not the white robe and red and blue badge of the Trinitarian Order. Instead, she had her high-waisted houppelande gowns and loose mantles brought from Wolf Hall, along with her oiled heuque and hooded cloak for inclement weather. Meanwhile Jess had persuaded Father Michael to keep her dog Star in the walled garden of his priest's house, so that she could be near her mistress and on the long summer evenings the two young women and the dog took walks together out on the Downs. Luckily, although the scars were ugly, they had not damaged Isabel's eyesight, so she was still able to ride out regularly at a gentle pace on Snowflake, until her growing belly made it too uncomfortable. Then Edmund Seymour had offered to ride the mare for her exercise, at the same time remaining a frequent visitor, keeping Isabel up to date with news from Wolf Hall.

Eventually, on the second day of October, as the birth pains came more frequently and were increasing in strength, she began to call on St Margaret to ease her travail and Jess became worried about the slow progress. The infirmarian, having never given birth herself or, as a life member of a convent, ever witnessed one, only succeeded in upsetting Isabel by constantly calling on the Almighty and expressing her own fears for the outcome.

'Jess, please tell her to go away!' Isabel begged. 'You have birthed more lambs than she has ever eaten. You can help me more than anyone.' So, the nun was ejected and Jess mopped her mistress's sweat-dampened brow and, when Isabel became too weary to speak, prayed to St Margaret for her.

By coincidence, or possibly intuition, Edmund Seymour chose to pay an afternoon visit and because of the tense situation the Prioress decided to allow him into Isabel's bedroom. There was no need for him to ask how she was, because the anguished cries that echoed down the narrow stairway spoke for themselves.

He flung himself down beside the bed. 'May the Lord bless you, Izzy!' he cried. 'What can I do for you?'

Isabel took a breath and a brief moment of respite to grab his hand and squeeze it. 'Jess thinks the baby is upside down, Ed. She wants to pull it out but she is frightened she won't be strong enough. Can you . . .' But the next contraction took her breath away before she managed to draw enough strength to scream once more in pain.

It was then that Edmund noticed a figure at the end of the bed, disguised under a sheet tented over Isabel's knees. 'How can I help, Jess?' he asked the half-hidden girl.

Jess emerged, her face shining with sweat and her hands gleaming with birth fluids. 'I have managed to bring one leg down but the other one is stuck.' She looked at Edmund's hands and shook her head. 'Your hands are too big but if you could find me a cord, I might be able to tie it around the one that is stuck and pull it free.' Seeing his shocked expression, and thinking twice about telling him of her success with her sheep in the past, she lowered her voice to whisper in his ear. 'I think it's the only hope. It may damage Isabel but if we don't do it the baby will die and so might she.'

'Is it shepherding that tells you this?' Edmund asked, raising his voice over Isabel's groans. 'And do I have to remind you that Isabel is not a sheep? Why is there no midwife here?'

'Because my mistress insisted that I would be just as good and I don't want to let her down!' Jess's tone was defiant. 'Come on! We're wasting time and it's not on our side. Please find that cord, Master Edmund! Ask the Prioress!'

40

Wolf Hall

3rd October 1425

Edmund rode the two miles from Easton to Wolf Hall in less than half an hour, riding fast to beat the dusk but also to clear his head and make sense of the previous hour's proceedings. Even so, when he finally reined-in to pass through Wolf Hall village, his mind was still haunted by the sight of Isabel's bleached-white face and the memory of the life-or-death task Jess had been obliged to perform. Relieved to hand his mount over to one of the stable lads with the briefest of greetings, he strode towards the manor house, which was still shrouded in wooden scaffolding but bearing no sign of the pargeters who, earlier in the day, had been in the process of adorning the freshly white-washed walls of the newly extended and reroofed residence with numerous plaster models of trees and forest animals.

The footprint of the manor house had changed considerably but the central passage remained the same. However, the room to his right, which had once been the household dairy, had been given a hearth and chimney and become the business chamber and treasury, its sturdy three-plank door boasting a formidable lock and key. Edmund took a deep breath and rapped on the middle plank.

'Is that you, Edmund? Come in, damn you. Where have you been?' It was the voice of his cousin John.

Edmund pushed the door open and entered. 'I went to the Priory.'

As usual, this induced a deep scowl on his cousin's brow. 'Whatever for? There's no welcome to be had there.'

In the corner, behind the desk at which John sat, a polished wooden staircase now climbed to a new and expansive principal bedchamber.

'That depends on who you are,' Edmund said calmly, knowing these words would further enrage John.

'What does the bitch want now?' he growled. 'She always calls on you to hear her complaints.'

Edmund sighed and bit his lip. 'Actually, she wanted to give you a present.'

'Ha! Probably an adder in a box! Anyway, where is it?'

'Oh no, it isn't an adder. It is a daughter. Earlier this afternoon she gave birth to a baby girl called Margaret. I thought you'd like to know. That is why I have galloped all the way from Easton.'

There was a period of fraught silence, except for the tapping of John's fingernails on the surface of his work table as he stared silently at Edmund for a long minute. 'Have you seen her?' he asked finally. 'What does the baby look like?'

Edmund paused before replying, trying to decide if he should tell John just how near both mother and child had been to their heavenly rest. 'Small and very fragile. She was taken to the church for immediate baptism, just in case. In the absence of anyone else, the Prioress was her godmother and I stood as godfather.'

John's face suffused with anger. 'How dare you! It was not your business, or hers, to do any such thing! It is the parents that choose the godparents!'

Edmund shrugged. 'Well, the priest was willing to accept me and in view of the circumstances it was just as well, because the poor little mite is only clinging to life and could have died unshriven. Surely you would not have had an innocent soul refused entry into heaven?'

'I would not have known about it at all if it had not been for your interference! Why can you not stop sticking your nose into my family affairs, Edmund?'

'I only went there to exercise Isabel's horse but the Prioress asked me to visit her because she was in labour and there was a problem.' Edmund risked the rough end of his cousin's tongue. 'You really should go yourself if you don't want others interfering.'

John shuddered, avoiding eye contact. 'I don't want to see Isabel,' he said.

'Are you sure?' There was a significant pause. 'It is possible it could be your last chance to see her alive.' Edmund slipped that in to see whether John would show any reaction.

'What the hell d'you mean?'

'I mean that both mother and child nearly died in the process and would have done, if it hadn't been for the birthing skills of the shepherdess. Even so Isabel is badly torn and the babe has a twisted foot.'

'I don't want to hear the grisly details!' John slammed both hands down heavily on his desk and stood up. 'Damn the shepherd girl! Why didn't she leave things well alone?'

Edmund banged his fist on the other side of the desk. 'I can't believe you said that! You would have lost them both.'

'Yes, I would! But as it is, it seems I am still landed with a damaged wife, who obviously wishes she was a nun and now presents me with a crippled daughter!' John strode around his desk. 'So, no thanks for bringing me that news, Ed. Now – I am going to find some supper and a jug of strong Sherish wine and then soon you and I are going to Salisbury to meet a master mason about building the new hunting lodge.'

'Oh. Do you really need me? I want to keep a check on Isabel, even if you don't.'

John's brow furrowed deeper. 'That's exactly what I forbid you to do! She is my wife, Ed, not yours – you need to remember that, if you want to take responsibility for Hatch Beauchamp and the Somerset Honour on your majority!'

For a few moments Edmund paused to consider these words. The Honour John referred to was the management of six Somerset manors – a considerable part of the Seymour estate which, since the deaths of John's parents, was being overseen by a temporary steward. Having recognised Edmund's business ability, John saw the financial advantage of keeping their organisation in the family, once his cousin had reached the legal age of twenty-one. As a younger son of his own Welsh family, Edmund realised the value of John's offer.

'Well, I suppose she has the Prioress and the shepherdess to care for her at least,' he said reluctantly. 'But I'm coming back from Salisbury as soon as the master mason has been met. You're on your own after that!'

John shrugged. 'I don't think I will be, if Alice accepts my offer,' he said smugly.

Edmund expelled air with exasperation. 'I have no wish to have anything to do with your sordid intentions with the barmaid!'

41

Easton Priory

5th October 1425

After her traumatic childbirth, Isabel did not return to full consciousness for nearly two days, giving Jess a serious problem about feeding the baby. From her time as a shepherd, she knew that when women in the village had trouble providing enough breastmilk for their newborn children, they often sent members of their family to seek ewe's milk as a substitute. But October to March was no time for lambs to be born, therefore no ewe's milk.

'You have missed the lambing season,' she complained to her unconscious mistress. 'So where am I meant to find milk for your little girl? We have no wet-nurse and since the great disease, cow's milk is not considered safe for newborn babies.'

In her desperation she decided to consult Father Michael, who turned out to be a fount of local knowledge. 'What you need is goat's milk, Jess,' he told her. 'And there is one farm nearby that spurns sheep and keeps goats instead. If you take a walk along the Avon River, after about two miles you will come to a village called Milton and the farmer's name is Peter, whom I happen to know keeps a herd of them and there are always at least one or two of his goats in milk. He takes their milk to market in Pewsey every day but you don't have to go that far. In fact, if you go now, he will be back from the market. Just mention I sent you and he'll sell you some straight from the udder!'

'Oh, that is marvellous, Father. I know many people rely on ewe's milk in these circumstances but I never thought of goats! Do you think their milk is safe? I hope it wouldn't be for long but actually I don't think I have any other choice.'

'Let's hope so then,' said the priest. 'I will pay a visit to Mistress Seymour and pray for her.'

'Thank you, Father. She needs all the help she can get. If the baby cries while you're there please pick her up and comfort her. I'll go to Farmer Peter straight away and I'll be as quick as I can.'

Jess and Star took the riverside path to Milton, where the obliging Farmer Peter quickly supplied a life-saving skin of strange-smelling milk.

'It comes straight from the udder,' he advised. 'Add to it the same amount of spring water and let it cool enough for the babe to suck. Do you have a feeding spoon? No? I will lend you one of my wife's. She had feeding problems sometimes too and the goat's milk was a great supplement.'

When he returned from the farmhouse with a small horn spoon he said kindly, 'That milk should be enough for a couple of days. Keep it cool but not cold and I hope the mother will have recovered enough to provide for her baby by then. If not come back for more. Return the skin and spoon when you can.' He pointed at Star who had sat calmly at Jess's feet. 'That is a lovely dog. She is well trained. Does she herd flocks?'

Jess nodded. 'Flocks of sheep, yes. She is not familiar with goats.'

'It's a pity she's black. I could use another dog but not a black one; not in these parts.'

'Well, that is good, because she's not for sale. How much do I owe you, Master Peter?'

The farmer smiled. 'That is hardly quarter of an udder-full. There is no charge for a sick lady and a starving baby. I just hope it solves your problem, and that your mistress wakes soon. Hurry back to her now.'

When she stopped at the spring where the Avon rose, Jess realised she should have brought a spare container to bring water from it but she managed to add some directly to the contents of the milk skin.

When she reached the Priory, she found Prioress Editha in Isabel's chamber, trying in vain to console the tiny girl's wailing. 'Father Michael had to leave at the Sext bell,' she explained. 'Did you find some milk?'

Jess was emptying the contents of her pack. 'Yes, now I just have to work out how to feed little Margaret without choking her. The farmer gave me a horn spoon but I didn't like to say that it would be too big for little Margaret's mouth.'

'How about dipping the corner of a clean napkin in the milk and seeing if she can suck it?' Editha suggested. 'If you take her from me, I'll go and fetch one.'

The Prioress made a swift return with the napkin. 'And a note has been left addressed to your mistress. I'll leave it on the table.'

After a messy half hour much milk had disappeared from the dipped napkin, some of it down the front of Jess's kirtle but most of it, with gentle persuasion, down the baby's throat. It was enough to cause little Margaret's eyes to droop and close and she was tucked into the basket crib in which her big brother Johnnie had first slept. Jess took the remaining goat's milk down to a cool corner of the Priory's dairy and returned to Isabel's chamber in utter exhaustion, to curl up at the end of the bed and fall straight to sleep.

However, her whirling mind did not allow her peace. Back came the noisy, haunting dreams of men in battle, wielding swords and spears, mounted and on foot, some of course armed with longbows. In her dream Jess scanned the lines of archers for a glimpse of Addy but under their domed helmets and protective neck and cheek plates it was impossible to tell one from another. Every time one man was hit and fell to the ground, her heart seemed to leap in her chest. When she woke, she could barely raise her head and her eyes were full of tears.

'Why did you leave me for that, Addy?' she demanded out loud. 'How could such a field of fire win your heart, over the glorious sweep of the Downs in spring? I will never understand.'

'Have you been dreaming, Jess? You've been crying out in your sleep.' It was Isabel, finally emerged from unconsciousness. 'What has happened? Where is my baby?'

Jess struggled to clear her head and clambered off the bed. 'She's here, in the cot, asleep. Do you want me to wake her?'

Isabel turned her head, her eyes fixed on the child that lay in the cot beside her, before turning her head to cry out, 'No, no! Not if she's alive and breathing. Oh, Jess – I can remember such fear and pain and now here you are, telling me I have a baby girl and all is well! How can I ever thank you?'

'You are thanking me now, just by being alive!' Jess felt tears filling her eyes and wiped her hands impatiently across them, anxious not to worry Isabel about her own frailty or that of her tiny daughter. 'The baby has taken some goat's milk because I thought it might be some time before your own milk will flow. What should I get you to eat and drink to make it happen?'

'Oh, goat's milk is said to be of great nourishment, but did I not tell you that I had arranged a wet-nurse? She is a farmer's wife who lives just outside Easton village. The infirmarian knows her. And you were crying out for someone called Addy, Jess. Who is he?' As she spoke her voice weakened and faltered and her eyelids drooped again.

Jess reached for the patient's damp forehead and was glad not to have to answer the question.

42

The Haunch of Venison

Mid-October 1425

'MY FATHER'S GOING HOME tomorrow so he'd like to meet with you now if that's convenient.' Alice was collecting the mugs and trenchers from the two Seymours as she spoke. 'You're invited for cakes and wine with him in his chamber at the back of the tavern. I'll come and accompany you when I've taken these to the scullery.'

'Does the invitation include both of us?' John sounded genuinely grateful and Edmund looked irritated, angry that the master mason had not been available to meet them when planned so that he could return to Wolf Hall. Now he feared that the entire visit was a setup to take him away from the situation at the Priory.

'Of course. I'll be back in a few minutes.'

When she returned Alice had removed the apron she wore over her russet work dress and replaced her maid's cap with a green silk veil and circlet, which revealed her dark brown hair. 'You look quite businesslike now, Alice,' John observed.

He received a smile for his remark. 'Father likes to pretend

I don't work in the tavern.' She placed a hand on his arm. 'You may escort me, Master Seymour.'

As they closed the rear door of the taproom behind them and turned down a covered walkway, Alice turned to ask their unwilling companion, 'What will you do when you reach your majority, Master Edmund? Will your brother endow you with one of his many manors?'

Edmund was not prepared to discuss Seymour estate business with a woman he regarded as a taproom floozy. 'Who knows, mistress. He has very grandiose plans for his own future, so by the time I reach twenty-one we will all probably be bankrupt.'

Alice raised an eyebrow and turned to her escort. 'And how are these plans going, Master John? Have you built the steward's quarters yet?'

He grinned and looked down at her enquiring face. 'Not personally of course, but yes, we are just waiting for the tiles to come for the new roof. No more noises from mice running in the thatch.'

'That is good to hear.' Alice stopped at a door where a shiny clapper on the polished woodwork invited a tap for admittance.

A handsome man of middle age stood inside, wearing a fashionable grey doublet. 'Welcome, young sirs, won't you please come in? I have heard a great deal about you!' His voice was warm and there was a slight lilt to his speech.

John made a careful bow. 'Thank you, sir. It is kind of you to invite us.'

Edmund moved forward to briefly echo his thanks and their host replied, 'You must call me Brian. I am Irish, you see.' As if to emphasise the point a shaggy grey hound rose from its cosy position on a wolf-skin before a blazing fire and wandered up to John, sniffing his thigh and nudging it with his nose as if to say, 'Have you got something for me?' 'Boru, that is very rude!' Brian scolded. 'He's an Irish hound, you see, and has no manners.'

'He is a wolfhound, is he not?' John dared to stroke the dog's gleaming head and was rewarded with a lick on the hand. 'He is certainly very friendly.'

'Not to wolves he's not!' laughed Brian. 'Although he is past hunting now. That's why I've made him my guard dog. Now look, Alice arranged some delicious cakes and some wine just come in from Bordeaux, so let us sit around the fire and talk about her.' He cast a smile at his daughter and she narrowed her eyes at him as they all settled into chairs around a low table.

Brian plunged straight in by asking an awkward question of John. 'Alice told me you have a wife, John. Why have you not brought her to Salisbury?'

John replied briskly, having anticipated the subject. 'Our daughter was born quite recently. It was not an easy birth and my wife is not yet churched.'

'I am sorry to hear that. I hope she is being well looked after. Does your daughter have a name yet? Has she been baptised?'

John flashed a fierce glance at Edmund, willing him to keep his mouth shut, before turning back to Brian. 'Yes, but it was done very quickly, just in case. Her name is Margaret.'

'Ah yes, for St Margaret, the patron of difficult births. A good choice.'

There was an awkward silence as John appeared unable to respond to this remark.

Edmund broke in to ease the conversation, leaning past Alice to change the subject. 'I gather you are familiar with the mason we have come to meet, Master Weaver. Can you tell us more about him?'

'Yes, of course. His name is Martin Burford and his father is seized of the land adjoining my farm outside Salisbury. But there are three sons and as Martin is the youngest he was sent off at an early age to be articled to a local builder. He is now a fully fledged builder himself and established as a mason. I think you will like him and he would do good work for you.' He turned to John. 'But of course it depends on when his present job at the cathedral is completed. When are you hoping to start work on your development?'

John moved easily onto solid ground. 'As soon as we have acquired the necessary hunting lodge to attract the Duke of Gloucester and the royal court to pursue their sport in Savernake Forest. When they come to hunt, the duke wants accommodation within the forest and I have promised him to provide luxurious lodgings if he brings me paying patrons.'

Brian looked puzzled. 'That sounds like a good arrangement but if you have gained his acquaintance, might you not be better to serve the duke in the royal court with a view to advancing your personal fame and fortune?'

John nodded. 'You're right, and I will. But Duke Humphrey is mostly a man of letters, who is spending all his own fame and gold on establishing a centre of learning in a magnificent palace he owns close to London on the River Thames. So, I intend to be the courtier who holds the job of providing his personal hunting and relaxation in Savernake Forest. Let the lawyers and magisters make fame and fortune with their words, I intend to make them by providing the duke and his court with action and enjoyment.'

'And so, you're handing the serious post of steward of your household to my daughter,' Brian mused with a frown. 'Female stewards are non-existent in Ireland. Are there many English women holding down such a position?'

'I don't know, sir, but there are many wives of landed gentlemen who perform a steward's role without holding the title. I think it is merely a matter of having the right aptitude and education, not a matter of whether you are male or female.'

The Irishman considered this before asking, 'Your own wife does not have this aptitude, I take it?'

John paused before replying. 'She is well educated but also very devout. She spends a lot of time in helping pilgrims at the nearby Priory hostel.'

'So now you wish to deprive me of my daughter's company and skills to the advantage of your household, Master Seymour. Is that your best intention? Or is there some other agenda?'

His gaze swerved from John to Alice, who immediately returned a deep frown and responded rather crossly. 'What kind of a question is that, Father? Master Seymour is our guest and there is no cause to imply anything other than a business arrangement – one which my luck in receiving a suitable education would let me fulfil.'

Brian studied John's face with deep concern. 'Alice was a baby when we came from Ireland to take advantage of the demand for weavers in the Salisbury cloth industry and the cloth merchants tempted us over by providing a school for the weavers' children, which Alice was lucky to attend.

We made good money, my wife and I, enough to acquire a farm, which had been abandoned due to the Black Death. Once that was thriving again, thanks to my wife's farming skills, I gave up weaving and bought this tavern. Sadly, I lost my wife to a late surge of the pestilence and will be selling the farm but Alice and I have come a long way since, here at the Haunch of Venison. However, I am prepared to see her spread her wings and take a job she really wants to do, as long as I know she will be safe.'

John hastened to try and mollify Brian's reservations. 'I appreciate your concern for your daughter, sir, and if she joins our household, you are very welcome to visit her at any time. As soon as work is begun on the hunting lodge, I expect to be frequently absent, attending to my duties as a member of the next Parliament and monitoring activities at my other manors, so she will have considerable responsibility. But there will always be trusted guards left at Wolf Hall for the household's protection.'

Alice cut in to address John directly. 'And being now of age, I have made my decision to come to Wolf Hall anyway, whatever my dear father says.'

Brian threw up his hands. 'Just like your mother! So be it – you will be a steward and I will be a proud old man!' He lifted his cup of wine. 'Let us drink to that!'

43

Easton Priory

12th October 1425

Isabel kept the two men waiting on their arrival at the Prioress's house, telling the sub-Prioress to say that she was being bathed, although in fact she was still trying to get her tiny baby to take the nipple, fearful that Margaret might never thrive without her mother's milk. She did not wish to do this in front of two men.

As she gently pushed her breast to the seeking mouth of the small marvel that had endured such a traumatic birth, she wondered for the hundredth time how they had both survived it. Knowing how many women and their babies died in such fearful circumstances, her feelings flitted between gratitude for the godsend of Jess's shepherding experience and Edmund's unexpected arrival and the sinful wish that neither had ever been there, so that she and her child might have lost the battle but found their heavenly rest.

Over the past months, ever since the disastrous St John the Baptist's Day party, Isabel Seymour had grown more and more depressed and indignant, not just because her husband had failed to come and see his new daughter but mostly because he had never accepted the scars which had destroyed her face and she knew he never would. Ever since the incident in the Wolf Hall garden he had not looked directly at her and when she eventually succeeded in begging him to do so, he found a mirror and held it up for her to look at the ruin of her own face. It had been a traumatic moment for the woman who had relished the knowledge that she could easily attract the admiration of men. Right at the point when there had been a chance of leading a fulfilled life as a lady of the manor, she had felt the earth deny her the chance. How could she ever now be a wife, tied to a man who could not bear to look at her and who, as a result, was bound to seek his needs and affections elsewhere?

She felt there was nothing she could do but turn for comfort to the Trinitarian nuns and embrace their belief in the love of God and the teachings of Jesus Christ. However, she knew that it would not be long before the Prioress would expect her to leave the Priory guest house and either take her vows and a cell with the nuns or return to her loveless home and hapless children. Only Jess, with her own demons to fight, and Father Michael's Masses and confessionals were of any solace to her. Even the little creature who was still refusing her breast could not improve her mood.

When Jess returned from taking Star for her usual morning walk up the hill behind the pilgrims' hostel, she was immediately accosted by John Seymour, waiting with Edmund in the entrance hall of the Prioress's house. He demanded testily that she tell her mistress he would not wait much longer to see his daughter. 'I gather the child is crippled and I have a right to see how badly she is damaged!

If my wife does not wish to see me you can bring the babe down here.'

Seeing Jess's brow pucker with anger, Edmund was quick to intervene. 'I'm sure my cousin would like to thank you for assisting his wife with the birth but as you can imagine, he is anxious for the future of his daughter, who is after all unable to care for herself.'

Jess nodded acknowledgement of this but was also keen to remind both the men of Isabel's frailty. 'My mistress is in a very poor state. She is worried for the baby and I am worried for both of them. Neither have recovered from the birth and the baby is not feeding well. I will ask my mistress what she wishes me to do.'

With that she turned her back and hurried up the stair to the private quarters, leaving John puce with fury. 'That girl is without manners! And I am not thanking you for thanking her, Ed! What she should have done was find a midwife!'

'There was no time, John!' Edmund exclaimed. 'You were not there! Nothing about the arrival of this poor child was good. Her very existence is a miracle. I told you.'

John began to pace the floor, striding to the foot of the stair as if he would make a desperate rush for the top, then turning on his heel and striding back towards the iron-studded exit door where he stopped abruptly and turned. 'What in God's name should I do, Ed? I am completely at a loss! Will they live? Will they die? Should I stay, should I go? There seems no point in being here!'

Edmund put both hands on his cousin's shoulders and pushed him firmly to where a bench stood against the wall, astonished that John allowed him to do so and expecting one of his wicked punches. 'You should sit down and wait, John,' he said. 'Jess will bring news as soon as she can.'

Jess did bring the baby down for John to see but little Margaret was crying and he could hardly bear to look at her. Under the warm stole she was wrapped in it was impossible to detect the injured limb and even when Edmund managed to unwrap it, tight swaddling had been applied in an attempt to straighten it against the good leg. For one brief moment John touched the little girl's cheek, but rapidly withdrew his hand, as if he feared she might disintegrate.

When Jess took her back up the stair John shrugged. 'There is no chance that poor little thing will survive,' he said to Edmund. 'I'm going back to Wolf Hall.'

'Why not go to the church, John?' Edmund suggested. 'Father Michael will probably be there and might offer consolation.'

John shook his head and pulled the door open. 'I shouldn't have come here and I won't come again.'

It was late afternoon before Isabel sent a message to say that she would receive the Seymour brothers and when Edmund came alone, she showed no surprise. 'I knew he would not come,' she said.

'He is a coward,' Edmund said flatly.

She shook her head. 'No, he is right. I am of no use to him now.'

'I dispute that but your little girl is his little girl and he has to recognise her. He cannot pretend that she doesn't exist!' Edmund was adamant. 'I will force him to do so.'

Isabel sighed. 'You are a good man, Edmund Seymour. And I will always be in your debt. But although I am married to your cousin, I can no longer claim a link with him because he will never even look at me.'

Edmund reached out and stroked the wimple she was wearing, where it hid the ugly scar. 'I told you; he is a fool. And so far, he has been a lucky one but if he's lost you, then now I think his luck has changed.'

She shook her head. 'It is too late. Only the day before the incident I was thinking we might have come to some sort of understanding. He seemed quite different – even happy! But now I don't think it would have lasted. I see now that I have to make my own peace with myself and accept the appearance God has given me – and which he will never accept.'

44

Wolf Hall

11th November 1425

FOR SEVERAL DAYS JOHN shut himself in his new office, working on architectural ideas for the Wolf Hall hunting lodge and counting the entries in his ledgers to see what was financially possible. He only emerged when hunger and other bodily needs made their demands. If Edmund happened to encounter him somewhere in the building, he stopped to listen to what his cousin had to say but made no responses. It was as if he was waiting for something to bring him to life and, after a week, that something happened.

Following his employer's instructions, one of his new house guards, a retired soldier implausibly called Sparrow, harnessed a sturdy workhorse into the shafts of a wagon and set off for Salisbury, where he loaded the back with Alice's belongings. Sharing the driving seat, they set off at dawn and made the trip from Salisbury to Wolf Hall in a day.

'However did you manage that?' Edmund asked when the cart trundled into the stable yard as dusk fell. 'You can't have stopped at all!'

'Oh yes we did,' Alice assured him, swinging down from

the high seat with youthful agility, despite her long skirts. 'Sparrow wouldn't overwork the horse so it was rested, fed and watered twice. Luckily, it's been a sunny autumn day and we sang songs nearly all the way up the river and over the Downs, didn't we, Sparrow? His were marching ballads and mine were Irish ditties.'

Edmund looked at Sparrow in amazement and received a nod and a wide grin in response. 'Well, I'm glad you enjoyed each other's company,' he said. 'Let me carry some bags.'

Sparrow shook his head. 'I'll do that, sir. You show Mistress Weaver into the house.'

'Get one of the grooms to help you then, Sparrow.'

'Where is Master John?' Alice asked as they walked towards the manor house. 'And how are Isabel and the new baby?'

'That's quite a story, which you might need strong drink to hear. John is in his office, which he has hardly left. Shall we do the room first?'

Alice gave him a troubled stare. 'Oh, I see. Yes, then, let's do the accommodation.'

A curved stairway now led up from a corner of the Great Hall into the upper-floor solar and the new east wing. It was wide enough for two people to climb at once and for furniture and chests to be carried up to the chambers.

'You have a bedchamber on this floor but there is also a small workplace leading off the service screen on the ground floor, close to the cellars and food stores. That way you can keep one eye on all the goods that come in and out of the manor house and the other eye on the servants at the same time. That is to be your job as steward, as I understand it.' Edmund looked at Alice for confirmation.

She sent him a long look and a sigh. 'And I thought I was just coming to make the books balance.'

He returned the look with a nod. 'That too, I imagine. It's not an easy job. And you haven't got an easy master.'

'Yes, where is the lord of the manor? I thought he'd have heard us by now.'

Edmund shrugged. 'Perhaps your arrival might cheer him up but I wouldn't count on it. He's been shut away in his apartment for a week now.'

'That doesn't sound like him. What has caused it?'

'It sounds terrible to say but it may be because his wife hasn't died.'

'What!' Alice came to an abrupt halt before the top stair. 'I thought the beautiful Isabel was still in confinement at Easton Priory.'

'Yes, she is but she is no longer the beautiful Isabel. Didn't he tell you of the awful injury she suffered at the hands of a demented villein at the last John the Baptist celebrations?' Edmund paused as she shook her head. 'Well, it has caused an apparently permanent rift between them. So much so that he has said he will not visit her in her confinement and has made no effort to acknowledge the child. It is not a happy situation, Mistress Weaver.'

'Great heavens! You have never called me "Mistress Weaver" before! Are we not friends? I thought we were. If you must use "mistress" please add Alice after it, if you would.'

He gave her a sideways look and a smile. 'Then I will answer to Master Edmund.' At the top of the stair, he stopped at the first door in a newly built corridor. 'This is your bedchamber, close to the stairway.' He opened the door.

'I'm afraid the room is not ready for you because we were not expecting you so soon but that can quickly be rectified.'

Alice walked in and crossed to the window, where the shutters were closed. She opened one, shivered and shut it again. 'Well, the view is nice but the wind is sharp. I doubt the window will be opened much in the winter. But at least there is a bedstead and I have my own bedding in the cart. Once Sparrow has brought up my belongings I will have this cosy in no time.'

'Good.' Edmund smiled. 'Now I'll take you down to show you the buttery before Sparrow starts blocking the stairway with your chattels. Then we can try drawing the wolf from his lair.'

'I caught a tempting smell from the kitchen as we passed. Supper might do the trick,' she suggested as they descended, meeting a stack of boxes and bundles already at the foot of the stairs.

'Unless he's taking it in his office.' Edmund made a path through the baggage and took Alice's hand to help her step over it, just as John made an appearance through the passage entrance.

At the sight of the two he exploded. 'What the hell do you think you're doing, Edmund? I told everyone that when Mistress Weaver arrived, I was to be informed immediately but instead I find you both hand in hand and descending from the guest apartments! How long has this been going on?'

Edmund grew red-faced, which did not pacify John at all, but Alice withdrew her hand from his, thanked him graciously for the assistance and turned her attention to the equally red-faced John. 'I'm flattered that you wanted to greet me first, Master John, but apparently you have shut yourself away for days, so it's hardly surprising you were not aware that Sparrow and I had arrived. Luckily Master Edmund was in the stable yard and has shown me my sleeping quarters. And before you jump to any more conclusions the bedstead had no ropes and no pillows. And right now, I'm hoping that this splendid new wing contains a garderobe because I could certainly use one.'

John's expression creased with distaste. 'Carry on, Edmund,' he said tartly. 'Your kind of task I think.'

Alice caught Edmund's eye and smiled as Annie entered the hall from the passage with a tray of supper dishes. 'I see my saviour!' she said, waving to the maid. 'A female friend in need, who might show me the way to a privy!'

John's expression was a mixture of horror and admiration.

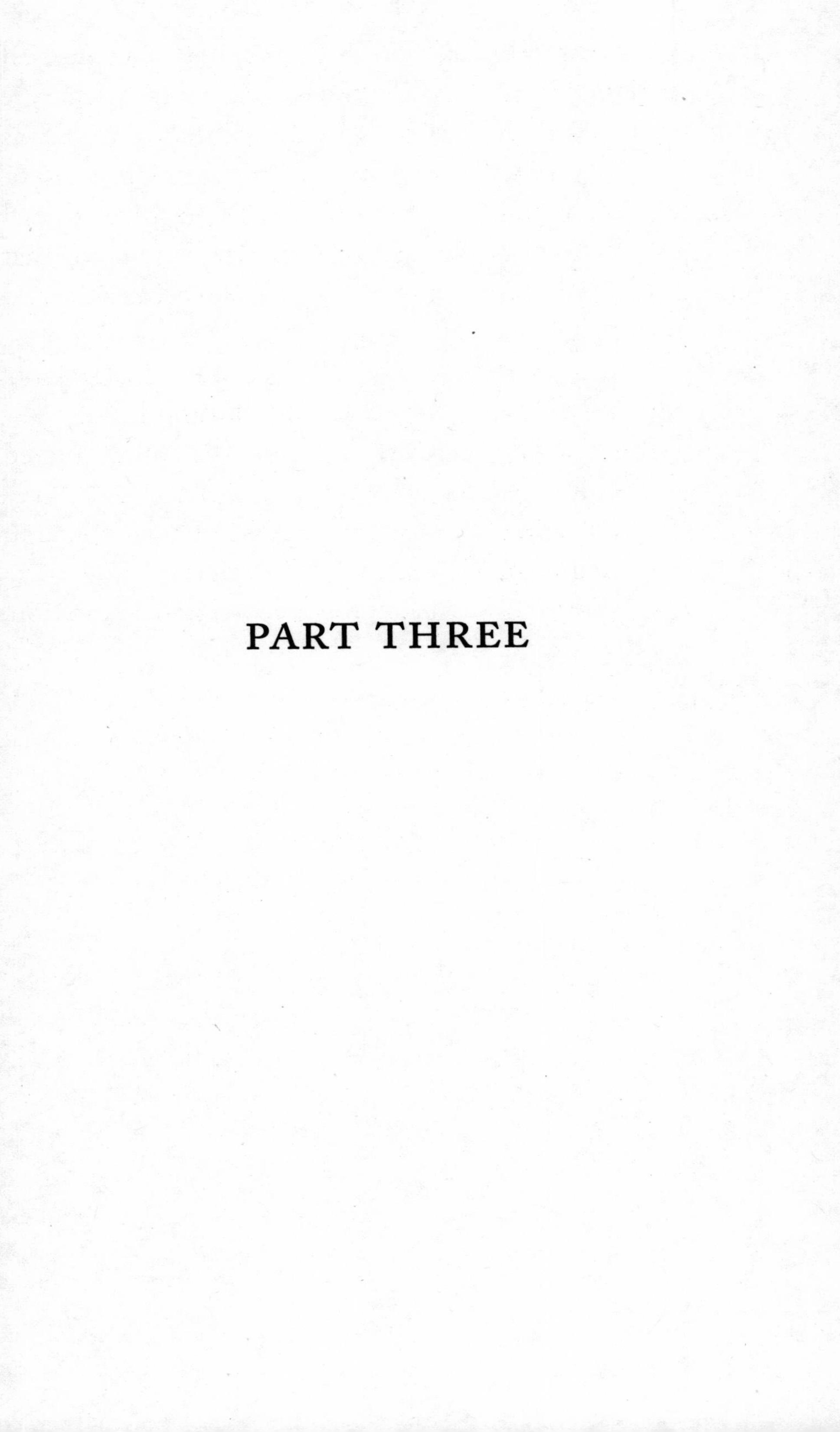

PART THREE

45

Bella Court Palace, Greenwich

Twelfth Night 1428

JOHN SEYMOUR'S FIRST SIGHT of the Duke of Gloucester's newly refurbished palace of Bella Court was from the stern of the Thames ferryboat he had hired in London. But before making the trip downriver he had spent two days in the city purchasing new clothes, in order to ensure he was suitably attired at the duke's Twelfth Night celebrations. He had only received the invitation in late November, on his return to Wolf Hall from the second of his autumn tours of the Seymour manors with Alice, ostensibly to check on his bailiffs, although what they thought of the unusual business arrangement went unrecorded.

After the Christmas and New Year festivities were over at Wolf Hall, there had hardly been time to gather his belongings and make the three-day journey to the city, where he found lodgings and toured the shops of the tailors of Threadneedle Street. Now he hoped the result would suffice in the glamorous halls of Duke Humphrey's recently upgraded palace.

The Twelfth Night invitation had informed John of the changed status of the lady who had helped him attain an audience with the Royal Protector at Clarendon Palace three years before, because it had come, rather pointedly, from 'The Duke and Duchess of Gloucester'. In secret, and only days after Duke Humphrey had received news that his regrettable marriage to the Countess of Hainault had been declared invalid by the Pope, he had married Eleanor Cobham. John had only needed one night in the taproom of his Cheapside Inn to learn that this union did not chime well with the average Londoner and had sensibly decided that this was a subject best avoided, if possible, in the new duchess's company.

A short time after arriving in his chamber at Bella Court, a page knocked on his chamber door to deliver a summons to the Protector's apartments. Having only had time to shake out the blue fur-trimmed gown he had chosen as his court apparel and arrange the folds of his new turban hat, he bade the page wait while he made himself respectable before following him down numerous passageways to the Protector's private abode. When the duty chamberlain knocked for entry and received permission, to John's surprise he found Duke Humphrey installed on the cushioned seat of a recessed window overlooking the Thames, reading a book.

Feeling strangely awkward making a court bow to a man whose legs were sprawled upon seat cushions, nevertheless he made it a flourishing one. 'Greetings, your grace. And thank you for inviting me to share the amusements of Twelfth Night.'

Humphrey set down his book and swung his legs to the floor. 'The meeting of the Royal Council has been postponed, John, and I am free to share my time with friends rather than colleagues. I was sorry to find in your acceptance note that your wife would not be with you. It is some time since our visit to the wolves' den, when I believe she was enceinte. Is she not well?'

John chose to dissemble. 'She had a very difficult birth, my lord, and both she and the child are still suffering the after-effects. I am not sure either of them will ever entirely recover. But may I congratulate you on your marriage, my lord. I look forward to renewing my acquaintance with the duchess. I trust she is thriving in her new status.'

'You will shortly see for yourself, Master Seymour. But first I called you here so that we can discuss my abiding desire to hunt the Savernake wolf pack. I hope my interest remains a secret between us. I do not want every member of the Royal Council seeking their own wolf-skin rugs. That would ruin its pleasure for us and doubtless wipe out your wolf dens in months.'

John gave him an emphatic nod. 'I assure you, my lord, that only the trees of the forest know that you covet a wolf-skin.'

'And the beautiful sand-coloured animal still thrives, I trust?'

'The pick of the bunch, sir, but equally please do not reveal to anyone that you have him particularly in your sights.' John emphasised his words with a finger to his lips. 'When is it that you envisage coming to hunt?'

'Well, not until you have completed your hunting lodge, John. I want to bring my wife and take her hunting with me as well, so we need comfortable accommodation and delicious food – haunch of venison and roast heron's breast every night! Oh – and mountains of those delicious honey cakes your cook makes. Can you guarantee those by next autumn?'

John took a deep breath and opened his mouth to suggest that bringing Duchess Eleanor might jeopardise the secrecy of the dens but before he could make his point the door opened to admit the new duchess herself, strikingly glamorous in a shimmering gold silk houppelande gown and fashionable butterfly headdress. He had to swallow his response and make a suitably reverential bow while she crossed straight to the duke, who swept her into an eager embrace.

'You come at a perfect time, Eleanor!' Humphrey was keen to reveal. 'Master Seymour is about to confirm the booking for our wolf hunt.'

They both turned expectant eyes on John, who abandoned the idea of making any restrictions and nodded decisively. 'All being well, before next Christmas, your graces! We will fix a date to suit you and it will be an event to remember!'

Duke Humphrey chuckled. 'Splendid John! Please follow us to the Great Hall for the first banquet of the season! We cannot serve wolf flesh, of course, but I ordered venison for the main dish. I confess that it comes from my own deer herd in the new park here at Greenwich.'

On hearing this John spent the first hour of the banquet wondering whether the Greenwich deer herd would mean that wolves would be the only attraction for the duke at Wolf Hall. However, to his surprise, when the music and dancing started it was not long before Duchess Eleanor came to claim him for a turn around the floor. At the end of the dance, she thanked him but added an afterthought. 'I look forward to dancing with your cousin Edmund when we come to Wolf Hall, Master John. He is a superb dancer, is he not?'

John made a big effort to respond agreeably but couldn't resist a back swipe. 'Yes, he has dainty footwork, my lady, but little skill with a sword I'm afraid.'

The duchess tilted her head enquiringly. 'Well, I certainly recall your dexterity with a spear on the hunting field, Master Seymour! And it was that which brought you here, was it not?' She accepted his offered hand to lead her back to the dais, where her husband was regarding them with one eyebrow raised. 'What weapon will you find with which to impress the duke next time, I wonder?'

'There are many to choose from, my lady.' John spoke as she withdrew her hand and made her way up the short steps of the dais, leaving him conscious that he would not be invited to join the newly wedded ducal couple, seated as they were in two chairs that subtly resembled royal thrones and guarded by attendants bearing fierce-looking halberds. He wondered whether such protection was due to the many violent objections he had heard in London's alehouses, expressing anger over the duke's marriage to his paramour. He puzzled as he turned to mingle with the other invited courtiers, whether Eleanor Cobham might live to regret her determination to acquire royal state.

The following day dawned as brisk and bright as the last had been and, still feeling a little wine-hazy from the previous evening's over-indulgence, John put on his hunting boots ready for a morning walk, ruminating on the people he had encountered at Bella Court and making mental notes of those he might consider approaching to seek financial support for the Savernake relaunch. The company had been distinguished and lively and he did not expect to meet any of them at an early hour at the breakfast table – nor did he, but a page brought him a note, hand-written by Duke Humphrey, inviting him to come to the new viewing tower at the top of the highest hill on the river bank at noon.

Having broken his fast, he set off to walk along the Thames pathway and as he passed through gaps in the riverside trees, he caught glimpses of the deer herd, of which he had learned with some anxiety and, after some time, the impressive new viewing tower. The sun, gradually climbing higher in the sky, turned his attention to tackling the steep hill upon which the tower stood and the nearer he got, the easier it was to see that three people stood behind the crenelations on the roof. He had counted five floors and so, when he found the entrance door open, he thought it prudent to take a brief rest before tackling the steep spiral stair. When he finally stepped through the door at the top, he saw that a stranger in clerical clothing was there with the duke and duchess, standing around a table bearing several impressive books and intriguing instruments.

'Aha, John!' the duke called across the flagstones. 'Come and meet my intellectual friend, Magister Roger Bolingbroke. He who regularly visits my growing library and consults the stars on various aspects of my life.'

John obeyed by walking briskly across the roof space and halting within reasonable bowing distance. 'A very good morning to your graces and to your distinguished companion. I imagine we all feel nearer to God at this lofty height?' His tone was one of enquiry, puzzled as he was by the unexpected presence of the cleric.

'We three share an interest in the almighty celestial and its power over us all, as you say, John. And, as well as being an Oxford priest, Bolingbroke has a reputation as a reader of palms and stars and is a teacher of great standing. So, Magister Bolingbroke – now that Master Seymour is here as a witness – please tell us the results of your investigations regarding the future of our beloved nephew, the king?'

His reply was brief and his expression matter-of-fact. 'I did not need the moon or the stars for this task, your grace. At his stage and age, my recent interpretation of signs and omens on the hands of the little king give me every indication that he will live a good and eventful life.'

Duke Humphrey rolled his eyes as if this was the last thing he wanted to hear. 'Come now Roger, you can do better than that. No one is assured of a perfect existence. Surely your astrology gives you evidence of dips and highs along the way? And now that the Earl of Warwick has taken over as his tutor, I need to know whether my own influence on the king will dwindle. What do the stars predict for Warwick, for instance?'

The magister rubbed his hands together and produced a thin smile. 'You did not require me to read the earl's horoscope, your grace, but my studies of Greek philosophy tell me that if you have influenced a child before he is seven, then he is yours forever. So, as Warwick has not made much impression on him yet, as the young king is just seven, I can predict that there will be little the earl can do about it. The boy is your acolyte.'

Humphrey grunted. 'Hmm. What do you think, Eleanor?'

His duchess nodded. 'As I have always assured you, my lord, there is no need to question his majesty's high regard for you. At least not until he marries and that will not be for some time, I imagine. Perhaps we should rather ask Magister Bolingbroke to concentrate on what the future might have in store for us, now that we are married? Is not that why he is here?'

'Yes, but all in good time. It is the king's attitudes that concern me most because I have just received an order from France, from my brother the Duke of Bedford, which I am to pass on to the Royal Council.' The duke's demanding glare swept around the gathering before he continued. 'Now that Dauphin Charles has managed to get himself spuriously capped King of France in Rheims Cathedral, which I am told is where French kings have been traditionally crowned, Duke John wants to demonstrate the futility of that event by having King Henry of England fulfil the promise made to his father on his deathbed: namely that the French crown be placed on the head of England's king in the cathedral of Notre Dame in Paris. But before that takes place the boy must be crowned and consecrated with the holy oil in Westminster Abbey, a deed that will invest a great deal of power and influence in those young hands. I wish to ensure that my influence will continue to be needed and heeded.'

Roger Bolingbroke bowed solemnly. 'I have no doubt it will be, your grace, but may I suggest that my next task should be to consult your horoscope and the king's together, to let you know how they blend in the future.'

The duke's brow wrinkled fiercely. 'That is no longer very easy to arrange, since Warwick took over. Would the stars not indicate how wearing not just one crown but two might affect the young king's attitude towards our wars with the French, for instance? At present he publicly deplores the number of English dead and injured on the battlefields and wants to bring the fighting to an end! What would your clairvoyance reveal of his opinion of that, I wonder? At present I fear my brother, King Henry the Fifth, will be turning in his grave!' He held up a stern fist and turned to John. 'What are your thoughts, Seymour? You have a young son. How will you steer his thinking as he grows older?'

This sudden change of direction took his guest by surprise but he instinctively knew what kind of reply was wanted. 'Well, as you know, my lord, I am a staunch supporter of the Lancastrian belief that France and England should be united under one king, as the fifth Henry, your royal brother, fought so hard to achieve. I will make sure that my son feels the same and has the aim and attitude to serve a like-minded monarch.'

Humphrey nodded vigorously. 'Just so, John, but sadly my little nephew has not been taught the importance of this and worries more about the number of dead and injured soldiers. The Earl of Warwick does not seem to have succeeded in tackling this weakness in the mind of his young charge, more's the pity!'

Duchess Eleanor chose to intervene at this moment, having waited with furrowed brow for her turn to speak. 'So now perhaps we can at last turn your skills to our own concerns, Master Bolingbroke? Otherwise, I shall be obliged to consult my own personal wisewoman on the matter in hand.'

'And who and what may that be, your grace?' Bolingbroke put the question in a dismissive tone, laying a mocking stress on his way of addressing the new duchess.

Eleanor ignored the scholar's curled lip and produced a

cold smile. 'No one you would know, being of the wrong sex I'm afraid, Magister. However, I would consider it good manners if, when you finally reveal the results of your astrological investigations, you address them to both of us and not merely to the duke, as has been the case in the past.'

Bolingbroke turned his gaze to the duke for endorsement of this request and received an impatient nod. 'As my lady asks, Roger,' Humphrey snapped.

Eleanor's cheeks dimpled at her minor victory and raised an eyebrow at John, who felt obliged to offer a twisted smile, feeling uncomfortably out of place in what was clearly an awkward matrimonial friction. 'I am sure your wife would understand, Master Seymour,' she said.

46

Wolf Hall

Mid-April 1428

At Wolf Hall, the manor-house garden had now disappeared under piles of red bricks and the tents of the masons working on the rapidly growing guest tower. The sloping field which it would overlook had been ploughed and seeded for meadowland, replacing the ragged arable strips where the villeins' crops had once been raised and providing a tempting view over the luscious spring-green spread of Savernake Forest. Beyond the flowing waters of the Bedwyn Brook the trees stretched as far as the eye could see and a brick-built bridge already spanned the stream's width, where once a ford had made the crossing unreliable. A gravel drive now led off a newly laid track from the Marlborough Road, giving direct access to the new tower and the manor house.

John Seymour had just arrived back from another trip to his Somerset manors and was admiring the progress made on the tower since he'd left. 'Your men work impressively quickly, Master Martin,' he said as they stood together beside the first growing tower. 'They've been remarkably swift in their efforts so far and I hope they can keep it up. I really need this building finished by November.'

The mason sucked his teeth. 'I can't promise, Master Seymour. It really depends on the weather. We've been lucky that it's been kind to us so far.'

'Well, tell the men there will be an extra groat at the end of each week if they meet your targets, Martin.'

Martin nodded. 'As the tower rises higher it becomes more dangerous work, so the extra coin will be well received, Master Seymour. Thank you.'

Months had passed since Isabel had returned to Wolf Hall but she had never found any sign of an amnesty with her husband while he still could not tolerate the scars that had ruined her face. The separated couple occupied opposite ends of the extended house and when John was in residence, they avoided each other completely. Isabel never made an appearance at the daily meals if he was there, taking hers in the rooms she shared in the new wing with her children and their nursemaids, and John avoided using the eastern wing completely, occupying only the manor lord's quarters at the west end above his business office.

Entering through the front door, he put his head around the passage door to the Great Hall, saw Annie performing her daily task of laying the cloth for dinner and withdrew. He had already told Ham the cook of his arrival and knew that there would be a place for him at the table. Realising that dinner would not be long, he turned across the passage and entered his office, surprising Alice, who jumped as she was poring over one of his ledgers.

She hurriedly closed the book. 'Oh! I knew you were back but I saw you inspecting the building work on the tower. Martin's doing a good job, isn't he?'

'Yes, but what are you doing in my office?' He walked

around the big table he'd installed and gave her a swift, but ardent, kiss on the lips. 'Are you checking the figures without me?'

'But of course I am. I'm your steward, remember? It is up to me to make the books balance.'

'And what shocking details have you discovered?'

'I was going to discuss it with you anyway.' She opened the ledger again, finding the page she'd closed. 'There's a new entry here that registers five hundred pounds from Lord Hungerford's bailiff. It's written in your scrawl so you must have entered it on your arrival, before you went to speak to Martin. The ink would have been wet so you left the ledger open, so of course I read it. What have you sold?'

'Nothing. I have borrowed five hundred pounds against one of my other manors in Devon in case the tower builds overrun.'

'Is that why you went off to Devon without me? I knew there was some secret reason. Which manor have you jeopardised?'

'There is no jeopardy, Alice! This is merely insurance against losing the Duke of Gloucester's wolf hunt due to bad weather. Now, Annie's laying the table for dinner so let's go and eat.'

'Fine, but I still think you should have consulted me about it. Seeing such a large entry in the ledger was a big shock, especially as in your absence I usually discuss large entries with Isabel and I know Hatch Beauchamp is the only manor we have worth five hundred pounds. It is the Honour of your Somerset holdings. We wouldn't want to lose that to Hungerford!'

'I was going to tell you. I just hadn't got round to it. And

Hatch isn't affected! By the way, how much have you seen of Isabel while I've been away? I've just seen her come back from the Priory.'

Alice frowned. 'While you were away Isabel joined us at meals but she still won't come if you're here. It's a pity because we both get on really well and I enjoy her company.'

John closed the door he had just opened. 'Do you think she knows about us?' he asked, lowering his voice.

'Of course she does. Well, I'm pretty sure she does, but she won't talk about it, certainly not with me. I think she probably lays it all at Father Michael's feet in the confessional and of course he can't discuss it with anyone.'

'What about the shepherdess? Does she know about us?'

Alice became irritated. 'I don't know. Could we talk about something else? If the staff know about us, they don't say anything to me either. I hope that suits you because it suits me.' She opened the door he had closed and walked across the passage to the hall entrance, almost bumping into Edmund who was just arriving. 'Hello, Ed, how is the new hawk? She's a beautiful bird,' she said with a smile.

Edmund opened the hall door and let her precede him into dinner. 'You've seen her then, Alice? Yes, she is gorgeous but still in moult. It'll be a week or so before I can start training her.' He had purposely bought the young sparrowhawk while she was in moult so she could settle down while it confined her to the mews.

'I couldn't resist a quick look yesterday evening. I'd love to see her fly.' She had stopped to let him join her and they walked to the table together. John followed; his brow furrowed.

'I don't think I'll have her trained for a few weeks. But

you're welcome to watch when she's settled.' Edmund caught sight of John just behind him. 'Oh, hello, John, you're back. I didn't see you.'

'And I didn't know you'd bought a hawk,' John muttered. 'Where are you going to fly it?'

'In the forest of course. Sparrowhawks are sensational hunters among the trees.'

'Well, make sure you tell the Woodwards when you'll be hawking and where. Otherwise, you'll find her with an arrow in her breast.' John took the head of the table, sat down and threw his napkin over his shoulder. 'Who's missing? Ah, Annie and Nan, and where is Jess? Don't tell me they're all eating with Isabel?' he grumbled. 'Dammit, I want them at my table! Sit down, you two, and I'll say grace.'

47

Wolf Hall

Mid-April 1428

'I GATHER JOHN IS back. Do you know where he's been, Jess?'

Isabel was sitting on the floor and playing with her cup and ball to amuse three-year-old Johnnie, who took no notice of the puckered red scar on her face. Two-year-old Margaret was replete and asleep in her cot and underneath the table Star the sheepdog lay on a mat. Nan and Annie had removed the remnants of the meal and left.

'Somewhere in Somerset or perhaps Devon. Alice didn't know.' Jess was also sitting on the floor. 'She seemed rather annoyed that she didn't.'

'Do you like Alice, Jess? Sometimes I think I don't but I don't know why I shouldn't. Oh look, Johnnie, I got the ball in the cup!' Her satisfied smile was returned by her son.

'Perhaps it's because she spends a lot of time with your husband, but you say you don't mind.' Jess held out her hand. 'May I have a turn now?'

'I really *don't* mind.' Isabel handed the toy to Jess and grinned as she watched her fail consistently to land the ball in the cup. 'In fact, I'm sure they're sharing a bed but that's good because it's better than him visiting bawdyhouses.'

'Whoops! This game is awful,' Jess complained, missing the target again. 'He wouldn't surely! Not after what you've been through.'

'He hasn't the first idea what I've been through! He's not a very nice man, Jess. I'm sure you know that.' She looked up, watching her son crawl swiftly across the floor to where Star was hiding. 'Johnnie, don't worry the doggie!' she called, then she added, 'Has John ever bothered you, Jess?'

The younger girl blushed. 'No, but I'm very careful and I try not to go near him. I don't like the way he looks at me. That's why I'm happy to share your bedroom. We protect each other. No Star, don't growl at Johnnie. He doesn't mean you any harm.'

Jess abandoned her attempts at landing the ball in the cup and offered the game to the little boy. 'Here, Johnnie, you try.'

In the silence that followed she drew a deep breath and broached what she feared might be a tricky subject. 'I need to ask you something, ma'am. Would you be upset if I left you for a while? It's been nearly three years since I came here and I really feel the need to visit my parents. I have sent them messages so they know where I am but they aren't getting any younger and I am their only child.'

Isabel's reply came instantly. 'Of course you must go, Jess. They will be missing you terribly. But I hope you will come back as soon as you feel you can. Do you think the Avebury villagers might now have forgotten their suspicions about your friend Addy being taken by the Devil? Do you know you still talk about him in your sleep? I hear you when I can't sleep myself. You were obviously very fond of him.'

Jess felt her face flush. 'Oh, I hope I don't keep you awake! I do often dream of Addy, it is true, and he always seems to be involved in some battle. I fear he may be in France and in constant danger and I pray so much he will come back! Even if he is injured. He was always practising with his longbow and boasted that he could fire an arrow further than anyone else!'

'I don't know how many times you've told me that, Jess.' Isabel smiled sympathetically. 'Your dreams tell me you miss him very much.'

'Well, I suppose I do, yes.' She frowned, as if she had not meant to admit that. 'But I also get very angry when I think about him because he left without telling me. And he has got me into terrible trouble.'

'Yes, he has, hasn't he? And don't you think walking the Downs alone might get you into even more?'

'I don't believe so,' Jess said. 'There's a big moon and I should get to the farm before dawn. My parents won't let me come to any harm once I'm back in the farmhouse. And I'll take Star with me, of course.'

'Will that really be safe?' Isabel looked troubled. 'I mean, a young woman with a black dog is like a red rag to a bull in some twisted minds. You are safe here at Wolf Hall.'

'Yes, and I'm very grateful for it but I'll wear my shepherd's smock and boots and carry my crook. And the moon is bright for the rest of the week so I hope the journey will be quick. You mustn't worry about me. I'll be fine. I will leave tomorrow evening if that's all right.'

Isabel nodded but with an anxious frown. 'But are you sure you want to go alone? I could get Sparrow to take you on a pillion and you would get there quicker and in daylight.'

Jess's shake of the head was emphatic. 'No; thank you for the offer but I'd rather go alone and anyway Sparrow is needed here. He's doing a good job training up some of the young men in the village as guards for the manor. Master John decided to form a small platoon in case of any incidents such as what happened to you.'

'Goodness!' Isabel looked amazed. 'I did not know that.'

'Actually, I think it was Sparrow's idea. He's mostly teaching the huntsmen how to use their bows and knives as general defence weapons, as well as out in the hunting field. But he's also teaching some of the younger and brighter lads that there is more than one use for scythes and pitchforks.'

'Hmm. I'm not sure I like the idea of that. Nat's father was able to find an alternative and violent use for his hot poker. Surely John hasn't overlooked that!'

'Actually, I believe he is thinking that Col would have been stopped before he used the poker on you if there had been someone less dozy among the duke's guards left in the garden. They were there to guard the little king and someone should have detained a drunken man wielding a hot poker. And that would have prevented the terrible thing that happened to you.'

'Well, there is that viewpoint I suppose,' said Isabel grudgingly. 'But I'm not sure that is what will be fuelling John's encouragement of Sparrow's platoon. It's much more likely to be the fact that he wants to impress royalty with his bodyguard when Duke Humphrey comes to hunt. What drives John Seymour is not his wife's safety but his own desire to win himself a knighthood.'

48

Moonlight on the Downs

April 1428

JESS AND STAR SET out under bright moonlight, taking the most direct route by the pathways on the edge of Savernake Forest and following the few signs there were. Her reading had improved with Isabel's encouragement but handwriting still evaded her. Keeping away from habitations, they bypassed Easton and kept heading west for a village called Ore. Not for the first time, Jess wondered why one signpost spelled it Ore while the next spelled it Oare. 'But we won't quibble, Star,' she remarked to her canine companion, 'because spelling is not anyone's strong point! After all, we're heading for the Downs but soon much of it will be Ups!'

And it wasn't long before the ground beneath their feet began to rise, as undulating hills rose from the flat green meadows of the Avon valley. And where there were hills there were sheep, even at night. When Jess sat down on a welcome stone for a rest, Star's nose began to twitch and she showed every sign of making off.

'Stay, Star!' Jess ordered. 'These are the moonlit Downs. There's no business for you here at night, except to keep me heading for home. Unless the Devil shows himself, when I hope you will protect me.'

Star sat looking up at her mistress, her dark eyes wide and her head nodding. 'You understand me, don't you girl,' Jess told her, leaning forward to ruffle the dog's sleek black coat. 'You're about the only one who does.' Her expression grew wistful. 'Addy did – but he's gone and I so wish he would come back!'

After a few minutes she stood up and shook out her damp clothes. 'It's cold, Star. Let's get going and see if we can find the big barrow where Addy disappeared. If he ever does come back, that must be where I'll find him.'

Having voiced her feelings about Addy, Jess kept an eagle eye out for some remembered landmark that would steer her towards the milestones she knew so well from shepherding her flock – the barrow on the hill above the River Kennet and the ford beyond it that gave access to the great circle of stones and her farmhouse home. She knew that she must keep up the pace if she was to reach safety before sunrise. Otherwise, she'd be in danger of being recognised by shepherds herding their flocks back to their summer grazing and she had no idea if they still called her a witch. So, she kept a wary eye on the big moon, still beaming high in the sky, and headed for the mighty earthwork called the Wansdyke.

At a certain point it was crossed by the Ridge Way, the ancient path known as Britain's oldest road, and Jess recognised it as a vital landmark, for when the Ridge Way met a brake of trees and shrubs, she would know that she had found the ford over the River Kennet, which she needed to cross and then follow the river bank north, to take her up the avenue of ancient stones that led to the mysterious circle that housed Henge Farm. But an irresistible urge was pulling her away from the ford and back up the hill instead, to the site of the long barrow, where, nearly three years before, she and Addy and her flock had taken shelter from a storm.

To Jess's surprise the grass on this part of the hill was growing thick and high, indicating that shepherds were no longer bringing their flocks to graze there. Did they avoid the barrow because of Addy's disappearance, she wondered? As soon as Star caught a shadowy glimpse of the entrance, she stopped dead and the hackles rose on her neck. 'What is it, girl?' she asked in a whisper. 'Is something wrong?'

Jess could see nothing at the barrow except the dark shadow that it made, silhouetted against the horizon, but obviously something had disturbed the dog. The entrance faced them but fearing there might be someone there, Jess decided to make a detour around the southern side, which would keep her hidden from anything – or anyone – making an exit.

Having never actually seen this side of the barrow before, she was surprised to spot what appeared to be an indentation three-quarters of the way down its length. The moonlight intensified the illumination of a dip in the structure. Could it perhaps be another entrance, which might have given access to the rear part of the long barrow? Then another thought occurred which hit her like a thunderbolt. If it was an entrance, could it also be an exit?

'But Addy, if you got out of the barrow here, where did you go?' It wasn't until after the words had entered her head that she actually realised she had said them out loud.

All the way up the hill Star had stuck quietly to Jess's side but now she suddenly let out a loud and eerie yowl. The sound brought Jess out of her own reverie in time to see the dog leave her and run back towards the front of the barrow, too fast and too suddenly to be stopped.

'Star! Come back!' Jess set off in pursuit but she should have run the shorter distance around the back of the barrow rather than heading for the front, because then she might have had an earlier view of the figure in black running at top speed down the hill towards the river. Not that she could have seen the face, even in the bright light of the moon, but she was at least certain that it was a man, judging by the black hose and boots covering the fleeing legs and the black tunic with its flying hood attached. But what such a person could have been doing at night, near or even inside a long barrow, was a spine-chilling mystery.

'Well, you certainly saw him off, Star! It's a pity because I'd like to know who it was.' When the dog gave a vigorous shake of her head Jess was surprised to see a ragged scrap of black cloth fly off her teeth and bent down to pick it up. 'What's this? Have you ruined the man's apparel?' She couldn't see much about it even in the moonlight so she tucked the rag into the pack she wore. 'We must get going now! The moon's becoming pale.'

She took one last look at the main entrance to the barrow, noting that it now sported a wooden gate, and jogged off down the hill to the ford which spanned the River Kennet and led to the chalk highway running further up the Downs to Avebury and the extraordinary stone circle that had been her childhood home. The sky was turning pink as she raced over the causeway nearest to Henge Farmhouse and rapped on the studded oak door.

Nell almost dropped the lantern she carried to answer the knock and Jess had to grab it from her before it fell. 'Careful, Mother, it's only me!' she cried as tears rose in her eyes. 'I knew you'd be up at sunrise.' Turning to close the door, she nearly caught Star's tail as it shut but the black dog ran straight to the hearth where Farmer Matt's new young sheepdog was lying. The two had not met before and there had to be some introductory snarling before they could settle down together.

Meanwhile, with the lantern safely placed on the kitchen shelf, Nell and Jess were locked in a long and fervent embrace and it was minutes before Jess could loosen the straps of her pack and gratefully let it fall to the floor. She gave a happy sigh and planted another long kiss on her mother's damp cheek.

'I thought we'd lost you for good, Jess!' Nell said, wiping her eyes on her apron.

Jess looked shocked. 'But I sent messages with everyone who I thought might be going past Avebury. Did you not get any?'

Nell's cheeks coloured. 'No. Few people talk to us these days.'

'Then I shouldn't have bothered,' she said sadly. 'I'm so sorry, Ma. How is Pa?'

'I'm older but no wiser.' Matthew's voice came down from the ladder stair that led up to the attic sleeping quarters. 'And I'm no shepherd. I've had to hire a useless boy!' He lurched across the floor, revealing a limp from a gammy leg. 'I hope you're here for good, daughter!'

Hugs were not Farmer Matt's style but Jess ran across and gave him one anyway, and a kiss on his forehead. 'I don't know, Father. It depends whether I'm still considered a heathen in the village. What have you done to your leg?'

'One of the sheep kicked me. Ask your mother about the situation in the village.' He paused. 'But not until she's given me my breakfast. I need to get out on the farm. And if you're back you might take a look at the sheep. They're in the fold because the stupid boy can't get them back if they're let out.'

'Well, of course he can't if he hasn't got a trained dog! What does this new one do?' She gestured to the fireplace where Star and the young one had now settled down.

Matt gave her a sideways look. 'I couldn't manage the sheep so I bought some bull calves. They're in one of the river meadows getting fat. He's good with them.'

'You said you would never have calves! Who is going to butcher them? There isn't a slaughterhouse anywhere near.'

'I'll get some neighbours to help come the autumn. The meat will sell well in the village.'

'You hope!' Jess made a worried gesture. 'Ma says people don't speak to you. And killing a sheep is one thing, slaughtering a bullock is quite another. Butchering it is an art; young men are apprenticed for years to learn how!' She had learned a lot from Ham at Wolf Hall.

Her father grew angry. 'Have you only come home to shout at me? Because if so, you might as well go back to where you came from!' He stomped off to his armchair at the end of the trestle table, sat down and looked expectantly at Nell. 'Don't tell me it's pea soup again, wife! I need meat – even if it's just bacon!'

The long-suffering Nell made the position clear. 'You should have bought pigs then, husband, because bread and peas are all there is. Unless I go down to the village and take a fish from the lord's pond. Then you'll have to be buying me out of the stocks.'

'Oh, just give me the pea soup, then. One day I'll turn green. Now tell Jess what's what in the village and whether she dare show her face on the Downs.'

There was silence as Nell ladled soup from the big cauldron at the fireside and carried the bowl with half a loaf of bread to the table. Then she turned back, took her daughter's hand and led her to the hearth. 'I'll give you some in a minute, Jess, you must be hungry. But just let me tell you first that the only way you could go anywhere in daylight here is if you have Addy walking beside you. Even though they barely knew him, he has become a saintly figure to the villagers, who believe that St Michael saved him from the Devil and his acolyte – which is you by the way – and took him off to heaven. At Michaelmas last year some of them even made an image of him and carried it to the church. I hope no one saw you arrive, Jess, because if they did there'll be a crowd at the door calling for the witch of Avebury.'

Even though she had feared this, Jess had not imagined that the story would have evolved to include St Michael and a figure of Addy. Suddenly she felt faint, her knees wobbled and she had to pull up a stool and sit down.

'Oh, Ma! I went to the barrow on the way here and I had the strongest feeling that Addy was alive somewhere. I even dream of him sometimes, fighting in the French wars. But I never imagined him becoming a saint! In fact, I'm certain he isn't. If anything, he's a soldier – an archer and a good one. But sometimes I feel in my bones that he'll be coming home!'

'Well until he does, daughter, I think it would be wise of you to go back to safety at Wolf Hall Manor.' It was Matt who spoke but all Jess could see were the tears that oozed down her mother's face as she nodded agreement.

PART FOUR

49

The Siege of Orléans, France

4th May 1429

JANKIN SQUIRMED ON HIS rank bed, not because lice were feasting on his blood as he lay on the damp straw but because of the pictures that haunted his dream. When he had marched away with the new recruits in Marlborough four years before he had been jubilant, certain that he would flourish as an archer in the Earl of Salisbury's crack troop of Wiltshire bowmen. And the first stage of his training had been good; while others struggled with fitness and skill with the unwieldy longbow, he had garnered praise from his Welsh instructors. But once he was enlisted into the earl's brigade the first thing that happened was a sickeningly rough sea journey in a crowded ship across the Channel to Honfleur and then a long march across English-ruled France fighting all the way, to the crucial city of Orléans, and the glory of further extending the territory King Henry the Fifth had vowed to acquire at the battle of Agincourt.

Jankin had seen it all – skirmish, bloodshed, mounted combat, gunfire and siege warfare. He had seen comrades carried away covered in gore and bowmen made headless by cannon shots but so far, he had survived with only minor injuries and become a member of an elite squad of archers who operated under cover; staying hidden until, when convinced no bowmen were engaged, the enemy might make a charge, only to find themselves showered by arrows shot from bows that appeared from nowhere.

After years of this, the shine had well and truly rubbed off Jankin's armour and he was beginning to long for the quiet slopes of the Wiltshire Downs. Hence the disturbed dreams that had him squirming in his uncomfortable bivouacs. And it was always Jess he saw in these unbidden nightmares; Jess birthing a lamb, Jess counting ewes, Jess scolding his archery practice, Jess frightening him with stories of the Devil's imps. He began to pray that something – anything – might bring an end to the constant bombardment of the walls of Orléans.

As the walls began to tumble and the city looked about to surrender, some of the French troops who had chosen to fight with the English started to swap jokes about a mysterious girl from a place called Domremy. She had managed to acquire a suit of armour and claimed she had been told by angels to help the French drive the English back across the Channel. This unlikely boast provoked mockery and laughter around the English campfires. 'Question: What would happen if a female led an army?' 'She'd fall off her horse!' 'Or drop her sword!' 'Who would follow a strumpet who talks to angels?' 'She might be worth a ride!' 'If you want the pox!'

Jankin spurned this chorus, not because he admired an armour-bearing female but because it made him think of Jess; she was just the kind of female who would fight for her friends if she thought it necessary. And if she put herself in the firing-line, would she be mocked and threatened, like the girl from Domremy? He didn't like to think so but if it could happen in France, he knew it could happen in the villages of England, just as it did around the campfires outside Orléans.

And then, to French disbelief and Jankin's utter amazement, just when the starving citizens of Orléans were eating rats and horses under the barrage of the guns and crying desperately for food, a girl in armour, flourishing a flag bearing an image of Christ, led a column of wagons filled with supplies unscathed through the open gates, to the astonished gaze of the unprepared English and the relief of the cheering French.

Next day the French were buoyant – nourished by the bread and meat and encouraged by the sight of the girl with the Jesu banner. They poured out of the city as the sun rose in the east and caught the English guns all facing west and lacking the troops to turn them. Caught with half their horses unprepared, a small contingent of mounted knights formed a brigade and headed recklessly into the fray. Unable to fire their longbows for fear of killing their own men, the under-cover squad of archers held their fire and watched, appalled, from their hideout as the advancing French troops overwhelmed the English cavalry. Horses and riders fell like a game of ninepins; knights and their mounts lay slaughtered in a heap of bloody destruction as the bulk of the French multitude thundered on towards its objective – the camp, where a quarter of the English army were still scrambling for their arms.

When the wave of warfare petered out, the scene that lay before the under-cover archers was a dreadful spectacle of dead and wounded horses and dazed or lifeless knights. Jankin wandered hesitantly out of his hideout to assess the situation and caught sight of a battered shield bearing a sickle, a heraldic crest he recognised, protruding from under the twisted neck of a fallen horse. Beside the front leg, the booted and spurred foot of the unfortunate rider was visible, his body clearly pinned down by the carcass. As he frowned over the sight, wondering if either horse or rider was alive, the booted foot moved.

Shouting for any of his colleagues within earshot, he managed to gather two more and convince them that the figure under the dead horse's withers was alive. 'The sickle crest on his shield belongs to the Hungerford family and Lord Hungerford is the Lord Treasurer of England. We can't leave one of them to the Frogs, can we?' he insisted. But the extraction of the injured man proved to be more complicated than expected because the pinned-down leg was impossible to pull from under the horse without lifting the carcass and even three muscular longbow men proved unable to perform that task.

After several attempts, the other two archers conspired to agree that there was no point in pursuing the matter as the unfortunate knight under the horse was showing no sign of consciousness. Almost as soon as they left, however, the apparent corpse came to life and shouted for help. Jankin hastened to ask him if he thought he could move his leg.

'We tried to lift the horse off you but it was too heavy but if your leg isn't injured, I could probably manage to lift the horse's head and neck and perhaps you could pull your leg free yourself.'

'I have no idea if it is injured because I can't feel it at all but my armour may be causing that,' the knight said. 'I have my arms free. If you can remove my helmet and gauntlets I'll give it a try.'

Impressed with the man's bravery, Jankin obliged and prepared to tackle the task of raising the horse's weighty head. The knight screamed out loud when he pulled at his own apparently dead leg, but to Jankin's amazement he still did not stop pulling and therefore out of pride he, Jankin, could not drop the horse's head and neck, telling himself sternly and silently that he had the strength of two men in the arm that pulled the longbow string.

When the leg came free its owner fainted again, but not for long. 'What is your name?' he asked Jankin, rubbing life-blood into his thirsty limb. 'Mine is Robert Hungerford and I think I owe you my life.'

50

Hungerford Manor and Wolf Hall

June and July 1429

NOTHING HAD GONE RIGHT for the English in France since the extraordinary girl from Domremy had arrived in Orléans. Now known as Jeanne, she had rallied the French army to such an extent that they had driven the English to abandon their siege and subsequently chased them back north, the way they had come, until in late June news spread that the English army in France had suffered a terrible defeat at a town called Patay. Many archers had been killed or injured and most of the English commanders had been captured for ransom. This disaster had enabled the Dauphin of France and his extraordinary female supporter, now known as 'the Maid of Orléans', to turn and make their way to the cathedral in Rheims, where French kings were traditionally crowned. After a hasty coronation, as far as the French were concerned the Dauphin was now King Charles the Seventh of France.

Meanwhile injured soldiers from the battle at Patay began to arrive back in England to recover from their wounds and among them was the much-reduced detachment from Lord Hungerford's contingent, which included the baron's son and heir, Robert. By early July he had made a swift recovery at the family's main seat, partly because his elderly father had arranged for him to marry the sole heiress of the Botreaux family, who was sixteen and beautiful, with considerable financial prospects.

Among other injured soldiers brought to Hungerford Manor to recuperate was Jankin. At the battle of Patay he had sustained a deep slash wound to his bow arm and although he had escaped capture and it had healed cleanly, it had weakened the strength of his pull and he was having to face the fact that he would not be able to continue life as a champion of the longbow. His rescue of Robert Hungerford from under his dead horse and the resulting friendship had led to Robert offering him the use of a horse in order to ride off to visit his family and assure them of his survival.

'You've not talked much about your family, Jank,' Robert said as they shared a jug of ale in a local tavern. 'Do you have brothers and sisters? Any sweethearts? You're a very secretive fellow.'

Jankin grinned. 'I'm not able to look forward to living off my future wife's substantial inheritance, like one man I know. I had to run away in order to earn my daily groat.'

'Well, you must have a tidy hoard of groats tucked away by now. What are you planning to do with it?'

'Much the same as you, I imagine. Use it to find a wife, acquire some land and have some children. Only my holding might be on a smaller scale than yours.'

'What do you call a smaller scale? A few hides of land and a moated manor house?'

Jankin gave a grunt of laughter. 'I might have to start a

bit smaller than that, but you never know. Where and how extensive are these holdings of your intended?'

'Only a dozen manors down in the West Country, I'm told. Her father is still alive though, and while at present she is his only surviving child, there's no telling whether he'll marry again and father a son and the whole financial plan will collapse. I might end up farming a couple of hides and with a stack of children I can't afford, just like you!'

'I doubt it somehow.' Jankin laughed and changed the subject. 'I think if you are still willing to lend me a horse, I might set off on my travels tomorrow. Would that suit you?'

'Whenever you like, my friend. Are you going far?'

'First of all, to Wolf Hall Manor. Do you know it?'

'I've not been there but I believe we have made an investment in some business of the owners. It's a new hunting tower for the Warden of Savernake Forest. A man called Seymour. Do you know him?'

'No, but I know his wife. She's quite a lively lady and helped me greatly when I wanted to join the army. Before I go home, I thought I'd let her know how I got on.'

Jankin rode into Wolf Hall along the new entrance road and admired the progress of the building work, remembering that Robert had called it a hunting tower and wondering what kind of game merited such a splendid edifice in such a wild location. Despite his departure from the army, he still carried his longbow slung over his shoulder and had been tempted to try his luck on the way through Savernake Forest but remembered Robert's warning of the consequences of hunting in the king's parks without permission.

He was intrigued to find there was now a permanent

armed guard at the entrance to the Wolf Hall manor house, who confiscated his bow and quiver of arrows, agreeing to return them on his departure. A hovering groom took his horse at the stables, while a liveried servant showed him into the newly extended hall. Jankin asked if Mistress Seymour was available and received a guarded response. 'I don't know sir. I'll alert the steward that you're here.'

Alice smiled inwardly when she saw the surprised look on the visitor's face as she walked in. 'Yes, I am Steward Alice. May I know your name?' When Jankin told her she looked puzzled. 'Just Jankin? Nothing else?'

He nodded. 'One name is enough for any man, I think. I am hoping to speak with the lady of the house, Mistress Seymour. Is she at home?'

'Not at present, although she will be back soon. May I know if this is a business matter or a social visit?'

Jankin grinned. 'The latter, I think. Is Annie the maid still here perhaps? She might vouch for me.'

By pure coincidence Annie entered the hall with the clean cloth for the dinner table and paused to stare at the visitor. 'It's Jankin, isn't it? The boy who wanted to be an archer.'

The concerned frown fell from Alice's face. 'You know him, do you, Annie?'

'Oh yes, but he's changed. When he left here last, he was a beardless boy. Now he's a man, with a magnificent beard and a fine pair of shoulders! It's amazing what a longbow can do!'

Jankin sent her his broadest smile. 'You haven't changed at all, Annie. Do you still keep everything clean and tidy here?'

'I do my best. I suppose you're looking for the mistress, but she went to Mass at Easton this morning. She'll be back for dinner though and as the master's away I expect she'll ask you to stay.'

Jankin smiled. 'As you can imagine, I wouldn't turn such an invitation down!'

'I will go and inform the cook.' Alice indicated a window seat. 'Make yourself comfortable here or take a turn in the garden if you prefer. It is the mistress's pride and joy.'

When she rode into the stable yard Isabel noticed the strange horse tethered to one of the hitching rings and wondered who it might belong to. They rarely had visitors when John was away. Her curiosity peaked when she spotted a man in the garden as she passed by and, not wishing to meet a stranger, she upped her pace towards the manor house's rear entrance. She was intensely surprised when she heard him hail her and begin to run in her direction.

'Mistress Seymour! Wait!' he called. 'It's Jankin.'

Torn between wanting to talk to him and not wanting him to look at her, she gradually slowed her pace and let him catch up. Her smile when they met was nervous, almost timid. 'Jankin! I swear you are a foot taller!'

He could not disguise his shock at her nun-like appearance but managed to return the smile. 'Mistress Seymour! How good to see you.'

'Is it good, Jankin? I am hardly the woman who waved you off to war with a sinking heart. But you are back and apparently all in one piece. I am so glad!'

'Have you joined a religious house, or do you just wear this to hear Mass?' He indicated the headdress.

She put one hand to her coif. 'You have been in numerous battles I expect, and you have seen many scars, so you will understand why I prefer to hide this one.'

When she pulled back the left side of her wimple, he caught his breath in shock and tears sprang unstoppably to his eyes. 'How did this happen?' he asked.

'It is a long story, which I will tell you but not until we've had dinner and can return to the garden and sit in private.' She tucked her hand under his elbow and urged him towards the door. 'I hope Alice has told our cook there's one more mouth to feed. Ham joined our household on the day you left and now he is Wolf Hall's treasure!'

51

The Henge Barn and the Barrow, Avebury

July 1429

THE HENGE BARN ALWAYS reminded Jess of Addy, carrying vivid memories of his first 'drowned rat' appearance at the wicket gate. After returning to Wolf Hall for safety as her parents had insisted and staying for a year, she had returned to visit Avebury, partly because she still believed that was where she would find Addy and partly because she still hoped to be able to make her life at her family home when the Godfearers stopped accusing her of witchcraft. But sadly, they still held fast to their belief in her consort with the Devil and the dunking stool still hovered over the River Kennet. So, because she found her mother's frequently reproachful looks in the farmhouse kitchen hard to bear and still did not dare to go out onto the Downs in daylight, she chose to hide away much of the time with Star in the barn's comforting atmosphere of hay sheaves and sheep fleeces.

Just to remind herself of her own shepherding skills, she sometimes took the sheep back out onto the dark slopes of the Downs at night, wearing a hooded tunic over her smock and boots and steering them to places where she did not expect to disturb any Avebury flocks or encounter strangers walking in the night. She knew it was risky but she greatly needed to feel the freedom of the grassy slopes. When her mother discovered what she was doing she was furious.

'You are asking to be discovered if you go on doing that, Jessica! There is nothing to stop the Godfearers dragging you straight to the dunking chair and leaving you to drown! I beg you to give up any idea of living as a shepherd! It is ruining your chance of any kind of normal life. You are nineteen. One day you will inherit this farm and you will need a husband to help you run it. But no man in Avebury wants a wife who pretends to be a man and wants to avoid the confessional. It simply is not acceptable. If you are not drowned, you will be ostracised and driven out of the village and this farm, which has been in our family for years, will be taken over by strangers. He will not tell you but the very thought is killing your father!'

Nell's tirade shocked Jess to the core and for some days she had hidden in the barn and refused to talk to her mother. Mulling over her words, she concluded that she would either have to do what she had told her to do, or ignore it and return to Wolf Hall and her job as maid and friend to Isabel Seymour. Then, as the days went by, she realised that her mother's bleak picture of what would happen if she went on being a shepherd had ignored the possibility that Addy might one day come back to Henge Farm, an event that she still believed would kill all the Godfearers' lust for believing her to be a Devil worshipper. She couldn't get the idea of the long barrow out of her mind, certain that it would be where Addy would go first when he returned, drawn by the guilt she believed he must feel at not having told her he was leaving. So eventually, unable to resist its call, one night she and Star left the sheep in the fold and climbed the Silbury Down together to visit the ancient tomb. 'We'll just go and see whether there is any activity,' she told the dog. 'Let's see if any devilish acolytes come out to play up there.'

There were none that night, nor the next, and Jess even began to think she was imagining the figure she had seen racing down the hill to the bridge over the River Kennet on the night of her first return. However, becoming braver on the third night, she brought candle, flint and spade with her and set about removing some of the wild growth in the dip where she suspected there might be a second entrance. After working away for some time, she suddenly realised that the candle she had stuck on a bare stone had fallen over and set fire to the long grass around the barrow.

Since the resulting flames would surely suggest to anyone on the hill that there was infernal activity there, Jess hastily picked up the hooded jacket she had discarded and began to use it to extinguish the blaze. She had more or less succeeded when she suddenly heard a voice in the night that made her blood run cold. At first, she thought it must be the Devil himself who came in the guise of The Shepherd: the man who supervised the Avebury wool tithes and who had taught her the intricacies of caring for sheep. But he had also expected something in return; something she was not prepared to give then, and certainly wasn't now.

His rasping tone was sneering and hate-filled. 'Well, well! Father Giles is going to be very interested in this activity. There is a dunking stool waiting for you at the village pond, Jessica. Unless of course you choose to share your favours now, which you have doubtless already done with the Devil – ahhh! – damn your evil black hide!'

There was a sudden yelp from Star, who had crept up behind the shadowy figure of The Shepherd and sunk her teeth in his thigh. The yelp came as he kicked back and shook her off but she dodged the slash with his long crook. Taking advantage of this hiatus, Jess made a run for the end of the barrow. But instead of going around it, she crawled up through the dense growth of greenery on the roof and flattened herself among it, hoping the darkness and the foliage would hide her. As she closed her eyes, praying that Star would not give her hideout away by following her up to her barrow-top sanctuary, she could hear The Shepherd swearing and cursing as he made his fruitless search for her. However, through his thrashing about, she thought she could also hear the jangle of harness, indicating the approach of iron-shod hooves. Was it possible that some unfortunate nightrider was about to find himself face to face with the Devil and the black dog of the Downs? And if he did, would he turn and flee or would he stop to investigate? And could that not be just what Addy might do?

By the time Jess had crawled back along the barrow and slid down to the ground, she was covered in dirt and uprooted foliage but she didn't care. From up on her rooftop hideaway, in the light of the moon she had seen a shadowy figure walk down the south side of the mound and find her backpack, pick up the fallen candle and stare at the smouldering patch of grass and wildflowers. But in the darkness, he had not spotted her. With her heart beating as if it might burst through her chest, she decided to wait a little longer, just to see if he tried to find the exit that she was almost certain

Addy had used. If he did, she would know for sure that it was him. As she waited, Star rushed up to her from the north side and she gave her the signal for silence, which the dog obeyed but only after a few excited whines. So, as she patted her quiet, she heard Addy's unmistakeable voice. 'Jess? Jess, is that you?'

Taking a deep breath, she walked towards the voice, her heart pounding so loud that she thought he must hear it. 'Yes, Addy, it's me. Where on earth have you been?'

52

The Long Barrow, Silbury Down

July 1429

Addy moved swiftly over the blackened grass towards Jess and his facial features became clear but the first thing she noticed was his height and the breadth of his shoulders. 'Is it really you, or have I done what I'm accused of doing and raised the Devil?'

There was a white flash from his face as he smiled broadly and his teeth gleamed. 'Star doesn't seem to think so.' He slapped his thigh as he had been wont to do when they were out with the sheep and the sheepdog trotted towards him, her tail wagging. 'At least she is pleased to see me.' He patted her head. 'Good girl.'

Jess felt a surge of anger swell uncontrollably. 'What are you doing here, Addy?'

'Looking for you, of course. Aren't you pleased to see me?'

'Yes, I am, but have you any idea why I am here?'

He spread his hands. 'Because we're friends?'

'No! Why would I be friends with someone who just disappeared without a word, seemingly into thin air, and left me alone to face accusations of witchcraft and threats of the dunking stool, to say nothing of consorting with the Devil and his acolytes? Even poor Star was nearly stabbed to death for being the black dog of the Downs! Why did you leave, Addy, and where in God's name have you been?' The fury in her voice was almost manic but she calmed it for the final declaration. 'I am pleased to see you, because now there is proof that you are alive! That I didn't raise the Devil to call his acolytes to whisk you off to purgatory and you will no longer be considered worthy of sainthood by the misguided priest and congregation of Avebury's Church of St James.'

There was a pause as she stopped to draw breath and Addy strode forward to take her scratched and muddy hands in a tight grip. 'Oh, dear Lord, Jess! I never thought . . . I had no idea such things could happen! I'm a stupid, selfish fool. I found the other exit from the barrow – which I see you have found now too – and when I realised that the rain had stopped and the moon was high, I heard the sound of a military band and soldiers singing a marching song and I just grabbed my bow and raced towards the noise. You knew I'd always wanted to be an archer and fight the French and I just wanted to join them. But when I finally got out it had started to rain again and they'd passed by and stopped singing. I couldn't catch them.'

'Then you could at least have come back!' Jess was in no mood to forgive and wrenched her hands free of his. 'But you didn't, Addy! You did not!'

'I know, I should have done, but I'd left the barrow and lost my sense of direction. The rain was sheeting down and there was no moon. I just carried on walking until I ended up in a forest and I was frightened and decided to take shelter under some tree roots.' He shook his head. 'I'll tell you the rest later. Why don't we go to your barn where we first met and get some sleep. I know it's not far from here and my horse will take two of us for that distance.' His smile flashed again. 'You might be able to find a stream on the way and wash your face. Your mother wouldn't recognise you!'

Jess made no response but walked around him to where her pack and singed jacket were lying, picked them up and stuffed the jacket into the pack, along with the half-burned candle. Then she stood, staring at the attempt she had made to clear the way to the exit. 'It can't have been easy to make your way out,' she said flatly. 'How did you do it?'

'I always had a knife in my pack if you remember, but it took a while. That's why I lost the singing troopers. They'd gone out of earshot and I couldn't tell which way.'

'Oh. What a pity.' Her tone was sarcastic and she immediately set off for the other end of the barrow.

Addy had hitched his borrowed horse carefully over the wooden gate, which had been installed at the demand of the village priest. 'I wondered why this was here,' he said when he retrieved the reins. 'Now I know.'

'To keep out the Devil's disciples,' said Jess with further irony. 'I suppose that was me.'

'Fools!' said Addy, taking her pack and slinging its straps over one of his saddlebags. 'I'll mount up and you can put your foot in the stirrup and swing up in front.'

Jess complied with comparative ease but made a proviso. 'If you break out of a walk I'll probably fall off.'

'Don't worry, I'll catch you. Call Star and we'll be gone.'

Jess had grown used to sleeping in the daytime and working through the night but Addy was tired after his long ride from Hungerford and found it hard to keep his eyes open after he had untacked the horse while Jess washed her cheeks in the bucket of water she kept there. They sat down on haystacks and she began to relate the story of her escape from Avebury but she had only reached her arrival at Easton Priory when she noticed Addy's eyes closing and decided to take her jacket as a pillow and lead him to a pile of hay, where he happily dropped off into a deep sleep. With a smile that unmistakeably held a hint of revenge, she left him and his horse to it and, while it was still dark, took herself and Star off to the Henge farmhouse where her mother was up before sunrise as usual.

'What is there about you today, Jess?' Nell asked as she fried her daughter some bacon on the fire. 'You've been morose lately but right now you look quite serene. Has something happened?'

'Yes, Ma, I've found someone to help Pa with the bullocks.' Jess cut herself a chunk of bread at the kitchen table and took it across to the hearth. 'I think you'll like him.'

'Good. Do I know him?' Nell flicked two rashers of bacon onto the bread and stepped back.

'Yes – it's Addy.' Jess waited for the exclamation, but not for long.

'Addy!' Nell's eyes grew wide and staring. 'Is he back?'

'Yes, Ma, he's back but he's been riding all night and at the moment he's sleeping in the barn with his horse. I'll go and wake him up after I've eaten this.' She moved back to the table and sank her teeth into the bread and bacon. 'Oh, this is great! Whose pig is it from? We should buy one like it.'

'Do you think Addy will stay this time? It's no good if he disappears again.' Nell cut herself a trencher for her rashers and sat down beside Jess.

'Well, I suppose he'll have to go and see his parents at Castle Combe – but yes.' She gave her mother a coy smile. 'If I ask him, I think he'll stay. After all, he owes me a parade down the village street.'

53

Wolf Hall and the Village

July 1429

ISABEL WAS NERVOUS ABOUT making a visit to the tenants' village, especially as she might be seen as the reason carpenter Col was in the lock-up at Marlborough Castle. She feared that his abandoned wife might blame her for his absence and the rest of the cottars might resent the fact that they had lost their carpenter, the man who should be building their houses, mending their carts and making their furniture. But she felt it was time to let them know that she was not to blame for Col's attack; after all, she was the victim. She also wanted to help Col's family, who would presumably be suffering without his wages.

Their cot was at the centre of the street of fourteen houses and she remembered it by the pile of wood planks and half-completed furniture that were stored in the securely fenced toft at the front of the cot, along with a few chickens and geese.

It pleased Isabel to note that there was little sign of the family being on the breadline and then she remembered that as well as Nat, who was now earning money in the manor kitchen, there was his older brother who was able to supplement the family income by making small items of wooden kitchenware and stools. A trio of young girls made up the rest of the family and it was the eldest of the girls that Isabel was hoping might join her household and take the place of the absent Jess. Nat had told her that his sister was twelve and her name was Evie and she found a girl who looked that age sitting on a stool in front of the house, peeling onions and weeping. She did not appear unsettled by the visitor's wimple and nun-like appearance.

'Is your ma at home?' Isabel asked, not wishing to mention her intention before she had consulted the girl's mother.

Evie sniffed and wiped her nose on her sleeve, swiftly abandoning the onions and standing up. 'She's out the back. I'll fetch her for you.'

Isabel could tell she was grateful to abandon the uncomfortable task at hand and nodded. 'Thank you.' She smiled, pleased to see her straight back and confident walk. Clearly onions did not defeat her. Perhaps two young children might not do so either.

Col's wife had not yet entirely lost her looks. Only the worn lines on her brow, chafed hands and grey streaks in her hair revealed a hard-working life. 'I thought it must be Mistress Seymour, ma'am,' she said, making a bob of a curtsy and wiping her hands on her apron, her eyes fixed on the wimple headdress. 'I'm sorry you wear that nun's veil because of my husband.'

'And I'm sorry you have to look at your son's scar because of mine,' Isabel replied. 'Forgive me but I don't remember your name.'

'It's Elizabeth but everyone calls me Liz. Have you come about Col coming out of gaol?'

'I'm afraid not. I didn't know he was.'

She shook her head. 'No, he isn't yet but he should be soon, thank the Lord. It's been hard without him. I had a visit from the master who told me he needed him to make finishings for the new tower, so he's getting him out. But he must have told you that.'

'No, he didn't,' Isabel said flatly.

'Oh!' Liz's face suffused, suddenly contrite. 'I didn't mean he doesn't deserve his punishment. He did a terrible thing to you!'

'I haven't come about that, Liz. I've come to ask you if you might consider letting Evie work for me in the manor house. I need a willing girl to help me with the children and look after my clothes. And as well as bringing money into your home, I would teach her to read and write. Perhaps you won't need money so much if Col's coming back but do you think you might let her come to me anyway? She wouldn't be far away.'

She could hear Evie whispering behind her, 'Yes, yes, yes!'

Liz did not answer immediately, frowning over clasped hands and taking deep, pensive breaths. Eventually she gave a decisive nod. 'It is a great offer for her, madam, and you can tell she knows it, so I can't get in her way, even though she's only twelve. Are you sure she's what you need?'

Isabel laughed. 'The Church considers a girl to be of age to be married at twelve, Liz, and if she can peel onions without complaining then I have every confidence that she will be just what I need.' She turned to look at Evie, who was suddenly bright-eyed and almost skipping. 'What do you think, Evie? You won't be far from home but I'm only taking you if you want to come.'

Her nod was conclusive. 'I do want to come. When can I start?'

54

Wolf Hall

September 1429

Unexpectedly in September, a courier delivered a letter for Master John Seymour from the Duke of Gloucester. It was obviously penned by his clerk but the contents showed Duke Humphrey throughout.

Seymour,

King Henry is due to travel to France early next year, for a coronation in Notre Dame cathedral, and the Regency Council has decided it is essential that he should first be crowned in the abbey at Westminster. The clergy will handle the service but I am appointed to take responsibility for all other aspects of the proceedings: processions, robes, invitations and a celebration banquet. I have been appointed Steward of England for the purpose and will also be acting as Regent of England during the king's absence. Therefore, I will have little time for leisure and will be unable to hunt in the King's Forest of Savernake. However, I would appreciate it if you were able to meet me as soon as possible at my palace of Bella Court because I am also struggling to preserve the present rules governing the parliamentary election of county members. The Lords are conspiring to change the voting system to the detriment of the lower orders of society. I know that you have been elected to represent them in the past and therefore have inside knowledge. I need your help to fight these proposals while I bear the weight of my new responsibilities regarding the king's coronations. With your experience of county representation, you could supply me with information that might persuade a majority of Lords to reject the Bill.

Come as soon as you can, Seymour. There is not much time to quash this worrying procedure! Gloucester.

John had been hoping that during his stay, as well as getting himself a wolf-skin, the duke would officially open the new hunting tower at Wolf Hall and this change of arrangements would have disappointed him greatly had it not been that another matter had arisen to occupy his mind. Despite their best intentions, Alice was expecting a baby.

At first John had been furious. 'You promised there would be no bastards!' he fumed when she told him. 'You said you knew how to prevent it!'

Alice remained calm. 'I used the jet stone my mother left me because she never conceived again after I was born. But it seems jet is not reliable after all.'

'But surely you don't have to bear the child?' John was persistent. 'There must be a wisewoman somewhere in the forest who can help you.'

'Help us, John, help *us*.' Her tone was emphatic. 'This is your child as well as mine! Anyway, it is too late for that.

I'd hoped it was a false alarm for weeks but now we must acknowledge it. The babe is probably due before Christmas.'

John's eyes grew round. 'Why have I not noticed this? We share a bed and all that entails, yet I have not noticed you growing a belly.'

Alice gave a hollow laugh. 'That is because this baby is very discreet. But it is starting to show now, which is why I am telling you. We do not need to announce it just yet but I think one of us should advise Isabel of the situation.'

John grimaced. 'Well, she never speaks to me, so it will have to be you. She'll probably want to throw you out but I can't afford that, so don't let her.'

'Actually, I doubt she will. Very well, I will tell her soon and ask her not to spread the news until we decide it's necessary.' She took a deep breath. 'Now, what shall I reply to the letter from the Lord Protector? Will you go to his aid?'

He looked at her askance, as if she must be mad to imply otherwise. 'Well of course I will! I'll leave tomorrow. You sort Isabel out. And the duke is no longer the Lord Protector, Henry will soon be the crowned king and Duke Humphrey has been designated Regent. A summons from the Regent of England cannot be denied!'

Ever since her arrival Alice had made it her habit to wear the French-style houppelande dresses, the high-waisted and copiously skirted garments that had successfully hidden the first six months of her pregnancy. Even so, when she visited John's wife in her chamber later that day, she was somewhat nervous. However, the news she imparted was of no surprise to the lady of the manor.

Isabel had been writing at a table by the window but

moved around to respond to Alice's confession. 'I have been waiting to be told this,' she admitted, gesturing to a chair beside the unlit hearth. 'How far are you into your pregnancy? Oh, please take a seat.'

She gestured again to the chair and this time Alice took it. 'Thank you. About six months, I think. I'm hoping you might agree to let me give birth at Wolf Hall. I do want to carry on with my work here. The manor needs someone who can keep things under control.'

Isabel gave an ironic chuckle. 'By that you mean that John can't. Well, don't let me stop you. I'm perfectly happy to keep things as they are and when the baby is born, I hope you will let it live alongside its half-brother and -sister. If you want to continue your steward's role, I am happy to run the nursery but we may need to hire another nurse. Nan is getting on in years and could do with assistance. I thought Jess would be returning from her second visit to her parents but there's been no sign of her yet and although I've taken on Evie, there's still the matter of Nan's retirement. She's not getting any younger, even if she insists that she can manage.'

Alice smiled. 'Well, I can organise another nurse. Please don't worry about that.'

'If that's what you want. I'd need to vet her before making it a permanent appointment.'

'If you wish.' There was an awkward silence before Alice changed the subject. 'Another thing I wanted to raise with you is Master Edmund's coming of age,' she said. 'John tries very hard to forget that it is due just before Christmas but I think we should plan something to celebrate the event.'

Isabel pulled her wimple more firmly over her livid scar. 'You'll have to count me out of that,' she said. 'I am very fond of Edmund and I'll support any gift-giving you devise on John's behalf but I won't attend any banquets or celebrations.'

'Well, I cannot blame you for that but of course I will continue to keep you up to date with what is going on in Wolf Hall. After all you are still the lady of the manor.'

Isabel's expression hardened. 'Oh yes, Mistress Alice, I am very definitely still that.'

55

Wolf Hall

September 1429

The manor coffers were almost empty and before he left for Duke Humphrey's palace of Bella Court, John gave orders to Edmund to make a tour of the Seymour manors, starting at Michaelmas when the rents would be due.

'And make sure they pay in coin and not in poultry or rabbits, Ed. The tower is being furnished and decorated and I can't pay carpenters and painters in livestock, alive or dead.'

'I'll take Alice with me again, then,' Edmund replied. 'I'm not nearly as quick as she is at counting the value of coins.'

'No, Alice stays here,' John replied hurriedly. 'She will keep the manor in order.'

Edmund made a face. 'It should be Isabel doing that. She's the lady of the manor.'

'Don't be difficult, Ed,' said his cousin impatiently. 'The women will be protected by the new guardsmen. I don't know how long I'll be away but you can take Sparrow as protection on the road and don't loiter in too many seedy taverns.'

Edmund sighed, resigned. 'Well, just bear in mind that

this will be my last rent-round for you. It's my birthday in December and you promised me the manor of Hatch on my coming of age.'

John stroked his beard. 'There were some provisos to that offer. Such as you beginning a horse-stud there and providing a tun of cider per annum to Wolf Hall. I'll get a contract drawn up.'

By this time the new red-brick tower had reached its crenelated top floor and only the chapel and the viewing platform remained to be installed by the masons. The piles of bricks had dwindled to be replaced with heaps of wood planks and the carpenters had moved in to make doors and window shutters, and a shed had been erected for them to work in during inclement weather. Among them was Col, fresh out of the Marlborough goal. To avoid any unfortunate encounters with her attacker, Isabel now kept her outdoor excursions to a new garden she had designed and which was coming to fruition at the back of the manor house, a refuge she had come to call her Retreat.

'That is typical of John,' she said as she and Edmund walked there with the two children. 'Are there apple trees already growing in the Hatch messuage? Or do you have to start from scratch?'

'From scratch I'm afraid, because the trees in the present orchard are not the right kind – which means I would have to buy in the cider until the orchard I plant has grown enough to supply the amount his high and mighty-ness demands. Which could take years.'

'And reduce your income of course.' Isabel blew out air in an expression of distaste. 'Why don't you just refuse to supply any cider, until you've got an orchard providing the juice?'

'Yes, I might,' Edmund began, 'but not until after I've got the entail. I don't want him thinking he can take the manor away, do I?'

'He's only giving you the loan of it, you know. There will be a closing date on the entail. Surely your Welsh family will provide for you as well.'

'I will certainly make a point of visiting them after my rent-round in Somerset.' Edmund pulled a wooden ball out of his belt purse and changed the subject. 'Did you know that John's been summoned by the Duke of Gloucester to do some kind of parliamentary sleuthing for him? Who knows where that will lead. Here, young Johnnie – catch! Oh, bad luck!'

56

Wallingford Castle

September 1429

A FEW DAYS AFTER John left for Greenwich, Isabel received a summons from Prioress Editha. Although she often attended Mass at the Church of St Mary she didn't always meet with the Prioress, but she made sure to be quick to respond to this note, riding off on Snowflake that afternoon.

Editha looked elated when she greeted her friend. 'I have received another letter from Queen Catherine's lady-in-waiting. It has taken some time to reach me so I wonder if perhaps there has been some interference on the way, but the contents are very exciting. Take a look.' She thrust the parchment at Isabel, who scanned it swiftly.

Greetings, Editha.

Another opportunity has arisen for a visit with Queen Catherine. At present I am still with her at Hertford but the household will soon be moving temporarily to Wallingford Castle, while some repair work is done here. This will bring us much nearer to you and Isabel. Master Tudor is even now making final arrangements for our move and so I would estimate that we will be settled in at Wallingford within a week.

I hope to receive your reply when we get there.

With anticipation,

Joanna Belknap.

'It sounds as if Lady Belknap is quite anxious to get us there as soon as possible,' Isabel remarked. 'Could that have something to do with the young king's coronation, do you think?'

'It is quite likely. I'm hoping we might be able to leave very soon, Isabel,' the Prioress said as she took the letter back. 'When could you be ready?'

'Well, it so happens that John has left for a meeting with the Duke of Gloucester in Greenwich, so as soon as it is convenient for you, Editha.'

They left two days later, their saddlebags packed with court apparel and a parcel of Ham's famous sweetmeats. Edmund was not happy, protesting that he was planning to depart later in the week on his rent-collecting round of the Seymour manors.

'I will only be a few days,' Isabel assured him. 'We're not going as far as Windsor this time. Surely Alice can take charge for a few days.'

'Nevertheless, I don't think John would approve, Izzy,' Edmund persisted.

Isabel gave him a stern look. 'Do not imagine for one minute that I will lose any sleep over that, Ed.'

Wallingford Castle was not as imposing as Windsor but its grey stone walls were high and ancient, dating back to the days of the Conqueror. The outer walls lined the west bank of the upper reaches of the River Thames, where the water ran shallow enough to be forded – hence the name. Along with Windsor Castle, it was where King Henry had mostly lived out his early years with his widowed mother, Queen Catherine, in apartments managed by Owen Tudor, the Welshman who had now risen in rank from child-minder and housekeeper to the queen's steward and receiver.

When the Prioress and Isabel arrived, the queen and her household were already installed, minus King Henry of course, who was now entirely under the care and education of the Earl of Warwick and currently living at Westminster, preparing for his first coronation. The chamber the two visitors were to share was set in a turret off the keep tower and fitted with two truckle beds and a curtained alcove offering private washing facilities. It was basic but clean and not too far from a privy, which was situated on an outer wall of the keep.

Joanna Belknap showed them to their accommodation.

'Well, we may have had a four-poster bed to share at Windsor Castle but it was not so clean and fresh as this,' the Prioress commented with a satisfied sniff.

'I'm glad it meets with your approval, Editha!' Joanna said with a smile. 'It was a little musty when we arrived but Master Tudor ordered an airing. Her grace is waiting to receive you, so if you're ready I think we should make our way to dinner.'

Isabel pulled a basket from her saddlebag. 'I brought some sweetmeats made by our excellent cook at Wolf Hall. Might I give them to the queen herself or should a taster try one first?' Isabel remembered the careful tests Owen Tudor had made before serving food to the little king on the day of her unfortunate injury.

'Her grace has delayed dinner for you, so you may hand them to her yourself and one of the servers will taste them. That is a kind thought, Isabel, thank you.' Thus far the lady-in-waiting had tactfully made no mention of Isabel's change of headdress style but decided to do so now in order to clear the air. 'We learned from the king about your appalling experience during his visit to Wolf Hall, Mistress Seymour. It must have been a dreadful moment and a painful and difficult recovery.'

'Well, it has changed my life somewhat,' Isabel admitted, 'but it has not changed my admiration for the work done by the Trinitarians, so I hope the queen has not changed hers?'

'As far as that is concerned, I'll leave you both to find out for yourselves. Now I expect you are ready for dinner. You must have left Wantage early to get here in time?'

The main part of the Great Hall was busy with staff and visitors being allocated places at the long trestles and the Dowager Queen waited until the diners had settled before making her way onto the dais from the royal entrance and greeting the Prioress and Isabel, who were surprised to be placed alongside her on the high table.

'It is so good to see you both again,' she said in her slightly pinched English, acknowledging their curtsies. 'I fear our last meeting was rudely interrupted and am so happy to be able to settle the matter we broached then. But first . . .' She beckoned to the steward. 'We need to adjust the seating, so that you can both easily hear our conversation. Would you mind, Owen? I would like to have Mistress Seymour on my left and the Prioress on my right with the chaplain beside her.'

There was something in the timbre of the queen's voice when she spoke to the Welshman that piqued Isabel's interest. 'I am sure my chaplain will not mind sitting beside the Prioress so that I can have Mistress Seymour on my other side,' the queen suggested to him. 'Would you agree to being swapped, Isabel?' The exchange was smoothly made and apart from being intrigued by the warmth with which Queen Catherine addressed her steward, Isabel realised that she had also contrived to seat her at her left hand, placing the undamaged ear closest to her. It was a generous gesture made without any mention of Isabel's handicap. After she had arranged herself in her new place, she offered the parcel of sweetmeats to the queen, who took it with delight.

'I detect a slight smell of honey,' she said, setting it down beside her trencher. 'I am afraid it will have to be tasted before we enjoy it but I hope I will find something sweet and delicious that we can share at the end of the meal. Thank you so much for such a thoughtful gift, Isabel. I hope I may call you that?'

'I would be honoured, your grace,' Isabel replied, feeling the blood rush to her wound.

While the butler was pouring the wine the queen broached the subject that was understandably uppermost in her mind. 'Have you heard that my son is to be crowned twice?' she asked, arranging her napkin over her shoulder. 'Once in Westminster Abbey, then again in the Cathedral of Notre Dame in Paris. I am so proud of him but I hope he will not find the ceremonies too taxing. After all he is still only seven years old. It is so young to be always serious and solemn, is it not? The Earl of Warwick is a such stern tutor. I do hope he remembers to let him play sometimes.'

'Will you attend both the coronations, your grace?' Editha asked.

'Of course I will be there in Westminster Abbey but the Royal Council will not let me go to France. I am not sure if it's because they think I might defect to my brother's side!' She laughed at this thought. 'They cannot know what terrible words the Dauphin wrote to me when I married the king's father! I think I would lose my head if I knocked at the door of his castle!' At this point a bell was rung and the hall fell silent. The queen's chaplain stood up to say the grace.

Once the dishes had been served the noise of the diners' conversations justified the queen's rearrangement of the high table placings and Isabel was grateful to be able to hear clearly what she had to say to Editha regarding her support of the Trinitarian missions.

'From a young age I was always impressed with the braveness of those knights who joined the crusades, but I never realised that a number of them who were listed as casualties were actually taken prisoner and used as slaves by their captors. So, I was grateful to you, Prioress, for sending those letters to Lady Belknap, outlining the remarkable work done by your nuns in raising funds to send brave monks to rescue them. It seemed only right that those of us who were safe in England should support such a cause and send our prayers to the relevant saints to ensure their success. My steward and receiver, Master Tudor, has undertaken to send regular donations from my allowances to the Trinitarian Mother House in France, via the Royal Treasury coffers.'

The Prioress responded enthusiastically. 'It is very kind of you to invite us to hear this from you personally, your grace. Our purpose at Easton Priory is not only to provide rest and nourishment to pilgrims on their way to seek help from St James of Compostela but also to collect their donations for the Trinitarian cause, and your contributions will greatly boost our input.'

'Well, I'm delighted to hear that, Editha – may I call you that? It is a much prettier name than "Prioress", I think.'

Editha's response was effusive. 'Your grace, I am honoured to hear my baptism name on your lips.'

The queen gave her a beaming smile and turned her attention to her trencher. 'I'm still not sure about the cooking here at Wallingford. I hope this is a good day! If it is not, at least we have Isabel's parcel to sweeten our palates.'

In the afternoon it rained and the three women walked together in the cloister leading to the castle chapel. 'I feel happier walking and talking here, where there aren't any corners or crannies for eavesdroppers,' Catherine confided. 'When I lived at Wallingford with my son, when he was a baby, there were armed archers everywhere, on the walls, in the passages and on the stairs. Even our beds were searched every day for poisoned pillows. The Royal Council was convinced that there were evil people wanting to capture the young king, and use him to rule in their stead. I believe they were most worried by the Duke of Gloucester. He wanted to take Henry away from me and bring him up himself, even when he was only two years old! Now that they have finally succeeded in separating me completely from my son, I cannot wait to find somewhere to live that does not belong to the crown. Somewhere where my son and I might be able to retreat together, even if only for short spells.'

When she turned her head and noticed her companions' shocked expressions, she looked apologetic. 'Oh, I don't mean I want to go into hiding with him or anything! Just spend some time with him when we could talk together, laugh together, and pray together. And I think I may have found just the place.'

'How have you managed that, your grace, when you seem to have your life completely controlled by others?' asked Editha.

The queen nodded. 'You are right, I am far too restricted. It is my penance for being of royal blood. But recently I received a surprising communication from the Bishop of London, offering me the use of his country palace at a place called Hadham. He wrote that he rarely used it but when he did, he found it a place of great relaxation and calm. But the best thing about it is its location, which is in a village only about ten miles from Hertford. It means I could stay there for extended periods but still be able to ride swiftly to Hertford Castle, should there be any visits from members of the Royal Council, with particular stress on Cardinal Beaufort and the Duke of Gloucester!' She gave her companions a meaningful look. 'I have had copious problems with both of those characters, so I request you to keep all of this a secret between us, even from your families and especially from your husband, Isabel, who I am well informed is closely involved with Duke Humphrey.'

The Prioress responded swiftly. 'There is no problem about that as far as I am concerned, your grace. We are a discreet community at Easton Priory, concentrating on helping pilgrims with completion of their solemn vows. As Isabel will certify, there is little opportunity for idle gossip.'

Isabel nodded. 'Yes, and Editha will reassure you that I have very little society now with my husband John, whom I hold entirely responsible for my dreadful impediment. We have much in common, your grace, in that I, too, feel physically restricted through no fault of my own but intend to make the best of it. I very much hope you are able to find peace and contentment in the bishop's palace.'

57

Avebury and Castle Combe

September 1429

After spending a long day sorting bullocks, Addy had eaten a good meal and slept until early morning, when he mounted up and rode out of Avebury before the village was awake. He had asked Matt for a few days to go and visit his own family and give them what he considered their share of his wartime earnings. Matt, with his pain-inspired grumpy attitude, had failed to inform Nell and Jess of this departure before he left for the fields and Addy's sudden absence distressed Jess, stirring memories of his last disappearance without farewell.

To add to her disappointment, he had not so far shown himself to the villagers, and therefore she was not released from the necessity of hiding herself away from their frightening animosity. 'May Addy come back soon!' she muttered in her regular morning prayers. 'Do not leave me in this constant limbo.'

In Castle Combe Addy met a far from warm welcome, especially from his father. Even the prospect of fifty silver groats did not bring a smile to the face of the miller, who had long ago written his eldest son off the family tree. His younger son had now satisfactorily filled the position of apprentice fuller and the miller had recovered his status in the cloth trade. Only Addy's mother, Maggie, welcomed him back with much relief but warned when they were alone together that he should not linger long in the bustling village of Castle Combe, where the cloth trade was king and the French wars were fiercely disliked, causing as they had, complete closure of their trade with France.

'Too many sons have been lost and no honour is offered to returning soldiers,' she told him. 'And your silver groats are chicken feed compared to the gold nobles to be earned from weaving and fulling and selling cloth to the Low Countries. But I thank you for them and I will add them to my widow's dower, which I fear I may need soon, the way your father is downing tankards of ale. If Matthew will take you in, offer him the rest of your groats, marry his girl and get into the wool trade at the sharp end! That is my advice!'

Addy gave her a hug. 'I have had that in mind but I'm not sure she will accept me since I caused her so much grief by vanishing from the ancient barrow, and the Church and her parents don't like the fact that we're cousins, even if only second cousins. She has had to leave her home and still remains in hiding until I reveal myself publicly in Avebury because, believe it or not, some locals there wish to punish her as a witch for getting the Devil's imps to whisk me off to purgatory.'

His mother became doubly anxious. 'I do believe it and for similar reasons it's time for you to leave Castle Combe, Addy. Thank you for coming but it's not safe for you here.

Will your horse be rested now? I'll pack you some food and you can mount up and head straight back to Avebury.'

As he followed the busy road between the market towns of Chippenham and Calne, traffic kept Addy at a slow pace but once he left this behind, he was able to take to the clear grass slopes of the Downs and let his horse choose his own pace, while he enjoyed the freedom of the open views and the refreshing breeze as the sun began to sink in the west. All thoughts of unpleasant encounters with evil-minded people had left his mind as he turned towards the big Henge Farm barn on the edge of the main Avebury stone circle.

'Time for food and water and a good rest,' he told his horse as he dismounted and tied it to a ring on the side of the barn. Then as he approached he noticed that the small wicket door was ajar and a faint waft of smoke was creeping through the slit.

In an instant his army training surged to the fore and he had drawn his bow from its sheath on the horse's withers, grabbed a couple of arrows from the quiver in his saddlebag and loaded one, ready to pull. Then he kicked the wicket door open.

'Hands in the air or I shoot!' he shouted as a man sprang back from a pile of hay that he was in the process of setting alight. 'And stamp that flame out!' Addy's arrow was pointed threateningly at the chest of the intruder, a tallish man in a brown jacket whose eyes were flickering everywhere with fear. 'Do it!' There was no mistaking the threat in Addy's voice.

'Don't shoot, don't shoot!' the arsonist yelled, stamping

wildly on the flames he had just lit. They still managed to escape however and showed every chance of spreading.

'Come out here!' Addy ordered. 'I still have the arrow on you but there is a water skin in my saddlebag. Come and fetch it and hurry!'

The man hesitated, his eyes roaming for a possible escape route.

'Which would you rather be?' Addy screamed at him. 'Dead or alive? Open the bag and get out the water skin. I'll count to ten.'

By number nine the fearful man had it out and open and ran back into the barn. The fire had spread but not greatly and the water soon staunched it but Addy did not lower his bow. 'Why are you doing this and who are you?' he demanded.

'Sim.' His voice trembled. 'My name is Sim.'

'Do you know who this barn belongs to?'

'Yes. It belongs to the witch's family. The man said I'd be pleasing God if I burned it. I didn't want to, really!' The man was wringing his hands. 'Can I go now?' The arrow still pointed at his chest.

Addy kept it on him for a few more seconds while he said, 'You can, but just remember – there are no witches at Henge Farm. Tell your neighbours! Do you understand?'

The moment the bow was lowered Sim nodded violently as he ran for the open wicket, while Addy suddenly wondered how he'd managed to get in. Then he noticed there was no key in the lock on the wicket door and he swore. 'Damn! He's got away with the key!'

58

Henge Farm

September 1429

IT WAS DARK BY the time Addy had checked there was no more evidence of arson, settled the horse in a stall with food and water and made his way over the causeway onto the Great Circle. Despite his experience of the blood and thunder of war, he still felt a shiver of dread as he walked past the silent megaliths. Although the Henge family considered them benign, to him they seemed malicious; even more threatening as shadows in the moonlight than when they stood as solid slabs of stone in bright daylight. He understood why they were believed by many to be the Devil's disciples.

Approaching the farmhouse he frowned, curious as to why the flock of sheep were folded at the back of the house, because Jess had been taking them out onto the Downs at night to avoid encountering other shepherds. Propped between the fold and the house there was a shed used for treating sick animals and a light was shining from its open door. He made his way between the crowd of sheep to find Jess in there with a ewe lying on the battered table they used for giving treatments.

He put his arm around her shoulders. 'Is there a problem, Jess?' he asked.

Jess shrugged off his arm and stroked the sheep's head. 'This is Curly, the sheep that had two lambs. Perhaps that is why her womb has dropped, but it means she will have to be killed. As you know, she is one of my favourites. Where have you been?'

He gave her a guilty look. 'To Castle Combe. I should have told you but I left before daylight and you were still out on the Downs. Didn't Matt tell you?'

'No, you can't rely on him for that sort of thing. Nor does he have any time for sheep with dropped wombs.' She paused and turned to ask, 'To Castle Combe and back today? That's quite a ride.'

Addy made a grim face and nodded. 'I couldn't stay there. My father had no time for me and my mother warned me that the villagers of Castle Combe have the same attitude to my disappearance as the locals here in Avebury. Both of us are believed to have had truck with the Devil. It seems that unless we show ourselves alive and together there will be no mercy, for either of us.'

'Then that is what we must do. As Ma said, the only way I will escape the ducking stool is to walk down the village street with you, alive and well. I was going to suggest it today but once again you left without saying goodbye.'

'Is that what upset you? Not the poor sick ewe?'

'Both, but I didn't know about her until Jack brought the flock home. Of course he hadn't noticed she was suffering. He seemed very fussed about something else and left in a hurry. But don't ask me what worried him, because I noticed Curly's plight immediately and began to try and help her.'

Addy did not remind her that she should not have had any conversation with Jack, who could tell his friends and family and raise the village with the news of her return. Instead, he told her about the incident with the arsonist. 'He told me his name was Sim, although I'm sure it's not. But in the heat of the moment, I never asked him how he got into the barn and I only noticed that the key was missing after he had fled. Do you think he might have got it from Jack?'

'Well, there is only one key so we must ask him tomorrow and if he looks guilty, he'll have to go. And personally, I won't cry about it. He's useless anyway. But how lucky that you arrived there when you did, Addy! If you hadn't, it sounds as if the barn would be no more.' She turned back to the treatment table. 'And now I really must attend to this poor ewe.'

'What are you going to do about her?' Addy asked.

'There's nothing I can do, except cut her throat. It's a case of using the sharp kitchen carving knife, which is something I hate. But at least we'll have a good supply of sheep meat, which Pa will be delighted about.'

'Would you like me to do it, Jess? Blood is something you see a lot of in war and I'd rather it was from a sheep than a soldier.'

'I'll fetch the knife,' she said gratefully.

She left Addy holding down the ewe and wasn't back for a few long minutes, carrying a bucket and a large cloth over one arm and the swiftly sharpened butcher's knife in the other hand.

Jess put down the bucket near the ewe's head. 'You'll need to move her over a bit so we don't have blood everywhere,' she suggested. 'I told Ma and Pa you were back and Ma is plucking another pigeon for the stew pot. She said supper would be later than usual as a result. So, you can take your time, but I would rather you didn't.'

Addy followed her suggestion. 'Better to get it done quickly now. Just hand me the weapon.'

Jess stood at one end of the treatment table, wrapped the ewe's head with the cloth and kept her gaze averted as Addy skilfully wielded the knife. 'Thank you, Addy. No struggles or loud bleats; that was well done.'

Mutely they both watched the ewe's body twitch its last, then Addy wiped the knife on the poor sheep's fleece and laid it down.

'I have something to ask you before we go inside, Jess.' He took her hand in his only slightly grubby one. 'When we have satisfied Avebury of our innocence and walked down the village street together, if you will have me I would like us to plight our troth. What do you think?'

Jess's shoulders began to shake and this time tears of laughter filled her eyes. 'I'm sorry, Addy, but I have to laugh, because if you are proposing marriage I can't think of a less romantic setting! But it doesn't matter because my answer would be yes, wherever you asked me.'

He joined in the laughter, then kissed her passionately. Drawing reluctantly back with her hand still in his, he added, 'This will be the best thing that has ever happened to me, Jess!'

She nodded and shyly kissed him back. 'Yes, me too. Just one thing though, Addy. You have to promise never to disappear again without telling me.'

The following morning Addy and Jess collared Jack in the sheepfold and asked him where the key was for the barn wicket. With eyes averted, the lad declared that he had not seen it at all the previous day.

'I think the master must have used it and not put it back,' he said, his face colouring to scarlet.

'Not possible, Jack,' Addy told him, 'Because I used it to get my horse ready for the road early and left it on the inside so that the master could get in after he'd broken his fast. But when he went to the barn it wasn't there. He was blaming me for forgetting to leave it for him, but it was you who took it, wasn't it? Did you get it back from Sim last night?' He dived at the lad and felt in the pocket of his smock, triumphantly removing a familiar key. 'Why would you need this out on the Downs, Jack? Or did you just pick it up to lend it to someone else? Someone who paid you to leave it with him. What's his name, Jack? And did you ask him what he wanted it for?'

Jack shook his head, tongue-tied.

Addy continued. 'Shall I tell you what he did with the key, Jack? He set fire to the barn. Luckily, I had just ridden up when he set the flame and I made him put it out. But if I hadn't been there the whole barn would have gone up. When you collected the key from the man you gave it to, did he tell you why he needed it?'

Another shake of the head.

'So, you just let someone have the key to the farmer's barn without asking why he needed it?'

'I just thought he was going to steal some hay to feed his oxen. That's what he told me!'

'And instead, he set fire to the hay and you have lost your job! Because we can't trust you now, can we, Jack?' It was Jess who almost shouted this and shoved the lad towards the fold gate. 'Get out! Some friend he was!'

Jack slammed the gate behind him and shouted back. 'It wasn't a friend; it was The Shepherd!'

Jess swung round to bury her head in Addy's shoulder. 'Oh, dear God, Addy!' she whispered. 'That's the man who was hunting me at the barrow and who molested me when I was his student. He must still be abusing other youths. You should have shot him when you had him in your sight!'

'Shhh!' Addy wrapped his arms around her. 'I'm glad I didn't, Jess, because then I would be in the Marlborough lock-up and we wouldn't be getting married!'

Matt gave reluctant permission for the two young people to marry. 'I like the idea of keeping it in the family but we must not reveal the fact that I have a cousin in Castle Combe because I fear the Church might declare you too closely related. So, I'll give you my blessing but I won't join in the village amazement at you being alive, Addy. I admit I found your disappearance shocking and I hope you will never repeat it. However, I'll be glad to have you join us here on the farm.'

Instantly Addy surprised Matt by going down on one knee and taking his rough farmer's hand in his own worn archer's mitt. 'I have sworn to Jess that I will never disappear without leaving word again, sir,' he said fervently and spat on the matting. The farmer cast an expression of surprise at Nell, who returned wide eyes. The pact was made.

That afternoon Jess put on her church-going dress and walked proudly down the hill with Addy on one side and Nell on the other. But she could not bring herself to wear her church shoes and kept on her shepherding boots instead, remembering vividly her past encounter with Avebury's

Godfearers. At first there were only one or two women at their doors, using their spindles to turn fleece into yarn and watching their children chasing chickens in the road. However, in the nature of village life, it was not long before word had spread that the missing shepherd had returned and something extraordinary was taking place.

As the men and boys left the cornfields and tenterfields, the street filled with the dubious and curious. Addy had not been seen around for several years and much devilish rumour had spread about the nature of his disappearance, so that the story had become a hot topic in both church and village. Father Giles had stirred rumours further by preaching of other strange tales, when careless people had been lured into barrows by black magic and lost God's protection.

Fear of losing the chance of a heavenly afterlife had driven people to name-calling and threats, causing Jess to cease attending church and her ma to dread the comments she had received every time she appeared in the nave. The presence of Addy at their side, the man Father Giles had declared to have been lured into purgatory by the Henge Farm witch, had at last muffled the mudslingers and, to Jess's great relief, removed the threat of the ducking stool.

PART FIVE

59

Bella Court Palace

September 1429

'Great heaven, Seymour! I thought you were never coming!' The Duke of Gloucester's welcome was hardly enthusiastic. 'What kept you so long?'

The travails of the last few days on the road flashed through John's mind as he straightened his bent knee, struggling to swallow the indignant reaction he felt. 'My apologies, my lord,' he managed to utter. 'My horse threw a shoe on the way to Putney and when I got there the blacksmith was drunk. So near and yet so far!'

'Good God, sir, could you not have hired another mount?'

John had a flash image of his much-loved stallion Atlas being left for days in a strange drunk's stable with filthy straw, while he rode away on some knock-kneed gelding to greet the Regent, and shook his head regretfully. 'Not one to be had within a country mile, sir.'

'Huh. Well, you're here now and perhaps you've been mulling over my dilemma on the way? It's a sticky problem we're facing, John, and I'm up against a company of Council bandits, including my uncle Beaufort in his wretched cardinal's hat! He and his followers on the Royal Council seem to think most of England does not deserve to have any say in the way the country is run! They want to restrict the franchise to none but those who possess a freehold worth forty shillings a year. It is ridiculous! Does your county have a great number of men who own such wealth of land?'

'I think it possibly does, my lord, but at the moment I would guess that most of them vote for their own trusted tenants to represent them in Parliament, if they did not wish to perform the task themselves.'

'Yes, well, that is my whole point. We need to drum up a decent number of landowners who will vote this restriction a nonsense.' The duke stood up from his cushioned chair. 'But you must be hungry, Seymour. A man can't think on an empty stomach and I detect a smell of something meaty! Come on – to dinner!'

Even at the Duke of Gloucester's holiday retreat, dinner was a formal affair, served in a beautiful dining hall hung with painted views of the River Thames, which flowed past the palace and, in clement weather, could be seen in all its glorious splendour when the shuttered windows were thrown open. On this occasion however they were closed, due to the wind and rain which John Seymour had just escaped as he outrode it on the last mile of his journey. To his surprise he was led by the steward to a place at the high table which, when the duke and duchess made their entrance, turned out to be next to Duchess Eleanor.

'Do not look so surprised, John Seymour,' the lady murmured before the grace was intoned by Magister Bolingbroke, seated next to him on his other side. 'I specifically asked for you to be my dinner companion.'

It was not until the hot dishes were served and the wine

was poured that John was further enlightened. 'I know you are here to assist my lord to oppose this franchise bill when the Parliament reopens but I hope you will also let me show you the splendid rooms he has provided to house his remarkable library of books.' Eleanor turned to Magister Bolingbroke, who was helping himself to copious slices of some form of poultry floating in a rich brown sauce. 'You have already made considerable use of it, Roger, have you not?'

'Yes, your grace.' The scholar ceased spooning more gravy onto the beautiful silver platter that was restricted to diners on the high table. 'I am completely in awe of his grace's collection of scholarly manuscripts.'

'And I assure you Roger, his grace is anxiously waiting for you to reveal what wonders you have managed to acquire to add to your interpretation of royal horoscopes.'

Having delivered this warning shot, Eleanor turned to John. 'And I know the duke likes to think that your experience of the Parliamentary House of Commons will have given you valuable insight into its secrets. You and Roger are both vital to him securing a successful future for England and a fruitful reign for the next in line to the throne – *whoever* that may be.'

After the meal ended, just as keen to show off his new library as his wife was, the duke joined Eleanor and Magister Bolingbroke and the four made their way along a cloister to the palace's new wing. John was duly impressed by the shelves of books bound with gold-stamped covers and fitted with heavily padlocked chains but, being only educated enough to read a tombstone, could not appreciate the contents or, in some cases, even the gleaming titles.

He made sure to please his host however. 'This is a magnificent sight, your grace, but I fear it would be more thoroughly appreciated by my cousin Edmund. He was destined to be a lawyer and educated accordingly but I am trained more for the battlefield or the tiltyard.'

Fortified by the wine at his recent meal, Duke Humphrey clapped him heartily on the shoulder. 'That is just the training needed for the job I am asking of you, John. Parliament is a battleground and we need to fight for our commoner supporters! They are the men who live and work for their living and who should have their say in how the country is run.'

John was utterly confused by this declaration. How did Duke Humphrey claim to be a man for the people and yet constantly demand enormous sums from the exchequer just for being a duke, draining its coffers that were filled with the taxes paid by the lower classes? In this he mimicked the Lancastrian lords of the Upper House, who were set on voting for a Bill that would deny the common people their franchise but not their tax obligations. To John that seemed two-faced, but he was bound by that sly pledge of three years ago to be the duke's faithful liegeman.

As he stared around the gold-embossed library he realised that above all he had to find a way to keep his host eager to hunt in Savernake. That was his main ambition, and in all faith he didn't think he, or anyone else, would be able to produce evidence that would kill the Franchise Bill, if the majority of the Royal Council wanted it passed.

It was when they had descended a stair leading from the

library into a cellar-like basement where a brazier gave off faint wafts of smoke smelling of something medicinal, that a message was produced which gave him the answer. And it came via the voice of Duchess Eleanor.

'Roger, these flames remind me of a wisewoman I know, who supplies potions to people in need of cures. She lives in woods near Westminster and goes by the name of Margery Jourdemayne. Do you know her?'

The magister's face screwed into an alarmed mask, his eyes rolling around to see who may have heard her. 'N-no, your grace, I cannot recall anyone of that name,' he said in a shaky voice. 'There are many women of skill with herbs who earn a living that way, are there not? Are there none in your Forest of Savernake, Master Seymour?' He sounded relieved to hand the subject over to John.

'None that I'm aware of, no. But perhaps women have more need for such skills and therefore keep to their own sex for treatment.' As he spoke, John tucked the name and place the duchess had mentioned into his mind for future reference. 'And they might charge less for their services than trained doctors, might they not?'

'No doubt.' The magister nodded brief agreement and then turned to cross the room to where the duke was peering at a pile of manuscripts on a table. 'As you see here, my lord, there was much to find of use in my search for the movement of the relevant stars, but I have yet to complete my studies.'

'It all looks like nonsense to me, Roger, but Greek was never my strong point. Just get on with it as fast as you can.' The duke turned to address John and Eleanor, who were still examining the jars and powders lined up near the brazier.

'Anyway, it's time to make some plan how to attack our other business, John, and this smoke is going to my head. Let us leave it and find some fresh air.'

John strode across the room. 'I am right behind you, my lord!'

60

Ludgershall and Wolf Hall

September and November 1429

AFTER TWO DAYS OF intense discussion of parliamentary rules and regulations, John thankfully escaped from Bella Court and Duke Humphrey's probing of his experience in the commoners' chamber, a period he had found difficult to recall. Ten years earlier, when he was a youth of nineteen, his courtier grandfather, Sir William Esturmy, had put him up for election to the Commons, representing the County Court of Ludgershall, a town about ten miles south of Wolf Hall. It was a bustling market town on the eastern border of Wiltshire, attached to a somewhat rundown royal castle, which had been used as a stop-over for courtiers for several hundred years but had received little improvement or repair. Meanwhile the town had thrived, with travellers using its busy taverns and royalty regularly hunting in an arm of the Savernake Forest, which spread out for several miles from the back of the castle. It should have been an excellent place for a youth to learn how to handle himself among a variety of people, young and old, rich and poor, as well as representing them in Parliament when it was in session.

However, young John Seymour had settled down in the castle and done little but make use of the hunting and acquaint himself with the local dignitaries which, as he had deduced, was enough to gain their vote and ensure possession of his parliamentary seat. He had found subsequent attendance at the sessions mostly tedious and soon restricted himself to attending only when there was a debate that happened to coincide with a bear-baiting on the banks of the Thames at Southwark. Hence, he had gained little knowledge of how parliamentary Bills were selected for debate and therefore struggled to offer advice to Duke Humphrey about rigging the subsequent results. His offer to consult with present members of the Ludgershall County Court had been a last resort to remain in the duke's good books and keep him on side for the Savernake wolf hunt – so essential for obtaining future royal visits to the Wolf Hall hunting tower and for attaining his own knighthood.

Meanwhile at Wolf Hall, Isabel returned from Wallingford Castle, Edmund and Sparrow completed their rent-round and Alice was finally obliged to announce her pregnancy to the household and bear the brunt of their various reactions, which fortunately were less judgemental than she had feared, most of them having guessed already. However, after this the news filtered out to the men working on the hunting tower and whenever she ventured out of the house loud and coarse remarks were hurled at her from the woodworkers' shed, mostly coming from Col the carpenter, who clearly hadn't learned his lesson in prison. But his daughter Evie, now well installed in the manor nursery and somewhat in awe of Alice, made the mistake of telling her mother, who remonstrated with Col and received a black eye for her pains.

Isabel decided it was time she called a meeting of the household to make her position regarding the expected child publicly clear. Usually, it was John Seymour who called the manorial courts, but his absence in Ludgershall prevented this, leaving his wife free to call her own gathering, choosing the last Sunday in September, when the outside staff came in to collect their wages and pay their rent. When Alice finished taking in the coin and whatever poultry or livestock some villeins had chosen to use to fulfil their quarterly obligations, and they had accepted the fresh bread loaf, the traditional thank-you gift for the rent paid, it was the Seymour custom to tick off the last entry in the manor ledger and then pour the ale. But before that, Isabel stepped forward to address the crowded hall.

'I'm sorry to keep you all a little longer but want to take this opportunity to clear the air here at Wolf Hall Manor,' she began, putting her hand to her headdress to ensure it covered her scar. 'There can be few of you who are not aware that Master John and I have been living separate lives since I was attacked and left to bear the scars of the red-hot burn made on my cheek and ear which, as you may imagine, caused me much pain and grief. Actually, I can say now that I bear my attacker no ill will, because the experience has taught me patience and brought me closer to God. However, it did not bring me closer to John Seymour, who found it impossible to gaze upon the ugly mess it had made on the face of the wife he once considered beautiful.

'Most of you will be aware that nowadays I spend a good deal of time visiting the Priory at Easton, where Prioress Editha has been of enormous help in aiding my recovery and showing me the satisfaction to be had in placing my sorrows at the feet of Jesus. I have also learned a great deal from the pilgrims who use the hostel there, on their way to Spain to seek indulgence and pray for forgiveness of their sins at the tomb of St James. In due course I hope to make my own pilgrimage but meanwhile I intend to remain here at Wolf Hall as the lady of the manor, where I wish to raise our children.

'Which brings me to the next child due to be born under the Wolf Hall roof, the one that our steward, Alice Weaver, is expecting, and which I'm sure you all realise is also the child of your lord of the manor. Whatever the Church and the crown rule about the sin of illegitimacy, this child will be raised as a son or daughter of the manor and be treated exactly the same as Johnnie and Margaret, the legitimate offspring of their father. In other words, the sins of the father will not be visited on their innocence, not while I am lady of this manor, which I intend to remain, for as long as the Lord God allows me active life.

'So, I pray that the steward's expectation will not alter the smooth running of our household and the peaceful continuation of all your lives. We have plenty to be grateful for and no reason to alter the way we each choose to live, especially as there is much to look forward to. However, there is also a departure to mark and one that I will find particularly sad, while also congratulating the man who is leaving us. Master John's cousin, Edmund Seymour, will achieve the age of twenty-one on the twenty-first of December and at Christmas there will be a feast to celebrate, which I am told will be the first event to be held in the new hunting tower. Master Edmund will then leave Wolf Hall Manor to take residence at, and as receiver for,

Hatch Beauchamp Manor, the head of all the Seymour's Somerset manors.'

There were murmurs when Isabel announced this and she paused to scan the room but could not detect the source. 'I hope those were sounds of approval, because Master Edmund well deserves the position, which he has long been waiting for. But young Johnnie will miss him particularly and we hope he will make frequent visits back to Wolf Hall.'

Here there was a ripple of applause, which caused Edmund to wave and nod his agreement and Isabel to send him a slightly lopsided smile, bringing a sudden flash of her former beauty back to her face.

'Shame he isn't our lord!' This time the voice was more audible and clearly came from Col Carpenter, lurking nearest the door as if ready to make a dash for it. 'Then my son wouldn't be damaged and nor would you, milady!'

Jude the Reeve began to push his way through the crowd to reach Col's side but Isabel waved him to stop and shook her head at Col. 'But your son Nat has found his calling in Ham's kitchen, Col. He is on the way to making a splendid cook and I have learned that happiness does not necessarily live in a beautiful face. So, what began with agony has been the path to contentment for both of us and I hope you, as a craftsman, might find satisfaction in the good work you have been doing here in the hunting tower. I will pray that you do.'

She turned to address the rest of the room again. 'Now it is time to drink your ale and take your bread to share with your families. Have a restful Sunday and thank you for listening. May God bless you all.' And with that, she swept off to the staircase which would take her up to the three chambers she and her children now occupied on the floor above.

Meanwhile in London, despite Duke Humphrey's vocal opposition, Parliament voted in the new rules of entry into the lower house and was then immediately dissolved in order to set about making arrangements for the little king's coronation, due to take place at the beginning of November. Although furious at losing the vote, the duke had agreed to arrange the separate marches and celebrations that were to follow the crowning at the abbey, and he co-opted John Seymour into his management team. So once more John was an absent father when Alice gave birth to his third child, a little girl, who he was disappointed to learn later had been baptised Bridget, after Alice's mother. Hers had been a straightforward birth, supervised by a midwife called in from the nearby village of Burbage and assisted by Nan the nursery nurse and young Evie, the carpenter's daughter, who at age thirteen was proving to be another of Isabel's successful employments.

Isabel herself had purposely stayed away from Alice's labour and only took interest when the baby was swaddled and brought to her apartment on the following day. When she carried her back, settling the child in her mother's arms, she felt a twinge of envy when Alice attached the baby to her breast, as if she had been doing it all her life. 'I'm going to arrange a wet-nurse soon,' Alice said. 'I don't intend to go to work with a baby attached.'

'How was the birth?' Isabel asked, remembering her own desperate deliveries.

'Painful, but surprisingly quick. The midwife said I was lucky.'

Isabel made a small snort, blowing air. 'Oh, you definitely were!' She turned to leave.

Alice called after her. 'I wonder if you might agree to be her godmother?'

Isabel paused, her good cheek blushing. 'Does John know you are asking me?'

Alice laughed. 'Of course not! I am not sure he knows what a godparent is.'

'And where and when will she be baptised?'

'All Saints Church, Burbage, closest to Wolf Hall. Tomorrow if you are free?'

'Very well, I will do it. Someone needs to tell her about the Lord Jesus.'

61

Henge Farm

December 1429

THERE WAS A SENSE of unease around the kitchen table at Henge Farm. Now that winter was setting in and the sheep were kept close to home, Jess and Addy had begun to consider their marriage. They had agreed that marriage was impossible at the Church of St James in Avebury because Father Giles had declared Jess to be a witch and more or less sentenced her to death in the dunking pool. Instead, she suggested that they ask Father Michael at Easton to marry them. 'He's a kind person, Addy, and an honest priest. I trust him.'

However, the couple waited until mid-December to broach the matter with Matt and Nell. 'We think it is time we took our marriage vows,' Jess declared when supper was over. 'I am nineteen and Addy now admits to twenty-one. He even says he still wants to marry me, so we plan to jump the broomstick at Christmas.'

Nell's brow furrowed into deep lines. 'What do you mean, "jump the broomstick"? Surely, you're going to have a proper church wedding? Or are you not able to go to him a virgin, daughter?'

Jess's cheeks flared. 'Having suffered some foul treatment from witch-hunting males, Ma, I have good reason to doubt my intact status, but although we have slept beside each other, here in the attic straw and on the Downs, Addy and I have waited to become one, if that is what you mean! So that bit about jumping the broomstick was just a little joke, Ma. We want to have a proper church wedding first, but definitely not one conducted by Father Giles. Surely you must understand that.'

Her mother nodded, yet her frown remained. 'But he does not allow other priests to officiate in his church, did you know that?'

Addy broke in at this point. 'No, Nell, we didn't, but Jess doesn't ever want to darken Father Giles's door anyway – not after what she has suffered of his diabolical beliefs and hatred of women. She wants to go back to Easton Priory.'

'To Father Michael, Ma!' Jess broke in. 'He is kind and friendly and taught me how to say my prayers. Also, he let Star into his church. I know he will agree to marry us.'

It was Farmer Matt's turn to speak. 'Your mother and I would like to be at your wedding though, Jess.'

'We could all go to Easton, Pa! If you break out the big cart and hire a horse, you and Ma could drive there. We've got it all worked out. You could go via Marlborough, stay a night in an inn and Ma could even do some shopping – she'd love that, wouldn't you, Ma? It would be a bit of a holiday for you. Addy and I can ride to Wolf Hall where I hope Mistress Isabel might lend me one of her beautiful dresses, which she no longer wears. We can probably stay a night there and meet you at Easton for the wedding. What do you think?'

Matt did not speak for several moments, while his brows

knitted and he sighed deeply several times. Nell stared at him; eyes wide with hope. It was clear what her response would be but she waited patiently to voice it. She had not left Avebury once since she arrived from the village of her birth as a young bride.

But Matt shook his head. 'We can't leave the sheep that long. They'll need to be folded at night and the heifers and milk cows need attention twice a day. You'll have to go without me. Addy can drive the cart if Jess can't and the borrowed horse can be hitched on the back.'

Jess watched her mother's excitement vanish from her face and stamped her foot under the trestle. 'No! I want both my parents at my wedding and we can manage it somehow. Why can't we pay one of the other shepherds to mind the stock?' She gave her father one of her most appealing smiles. 'It's only for a couple of days and it would do you both good to get away from the farm for a while. It's your only daughter's wedding and it won't happen again.'

'And I'll hire the stockman and the carthorse,' Addy announced unexpectedly. 'I have the rest of my archer's pay and there should still be plenty to buy myself a horse.'

'Oh, good!' Jess pushed back her stool and stood up. 'And after you've taught me to ride you should have earned enough here on the farm to buy me one as well! I think that is all settled, Father, don't you? And when you have sat in a cart for a couple of days instead of marching around the farm, you might find you don't limp quite so much!'

Matt leaned back in his chair and took a swig from his ale mug. 'I don't know when you learned to be so bossy, Jess,' he said then. 'You must get it from your mother. Are you sure you want to marry her, Adhelm?'

Addy grinned at the use of his full name and clinked his mug with Matt's. 'If it means I can be a farmer rather than a miller – yes, I do.'

'When are you thinking of us making this wedding trip then?'

'Well, as Nell no doubt knows, the Church does not encourage weddings during Advent, so we thought we could make it to Marlborough Christmas Eve because that is when everyone will be decorating and preparing for the Christmas holiday. Jess thinks that if we ride to Easton tomorrow and ask him, Father Michael will agree to marry us on Christmas Eve when Advent ends. Then we hope Mistress Isabel will let us stay for Christmas at the manor.'

Matt and Nell exchanged glances and Matt spoke for both. 'We will stay overnight in Marlborough; see you wed on the morn of Christmas Eve and drive back to the Henge afterwards. If you can arrange that we will be content and the sheep will be safe.'

Nell nodded earnest agreement. 'We are not used to being with strangers, Jess,' she said. 'And don't forget that on Christmas Day in Avebury we receive a gift from the lord of the manor. We don't want to risk someone walking off with our Noel purse. So, you go to Wolf Hall and celebrate your marriage and we will come home to the Henge.'

62

Wolf Hall and Easton

Mid-December 1429

STAR WAS NOT HAPPY to be left behind when Jess and Addy rode to Easton to meet Father Michael but they intended to ride there and back in a day and Jess thought it would be too much for her. So, the sheepdog was shut in the farmhouse kitchen where Nell tried to pacify her with scraps of meat and soothing words. But when Star finally stopped barking, she took to whining miserably. Poor Nell was soon cursing the black dog.

Meanwhile the soon-to-be-wed pair were relishing the freedom of riding the Downs in crisp early morning light, Jess wearing a new woollen jacket and kirtle and holding tight to Addy's belt, yelling with delight when he urged the horse into a canter. When they reached Easton, the bell was ringing for Sext and all the nuns were in the hostel chapel singing a psalm. There was no sign of a groom, so they stabled the horse in the Prioress's yard and wandered into the church across the road. Being unwilling to enter the church at Avebury, it was a good opportunity for them to kneel and pray at the chancel steps and that was how the priest found them.

Father Michael coughed before speaking. 'Jess, my child! How good to see you. And who is this young man you have brought to my church?'

Jess crossed herself and rose and Addy followed suit. 'We have come to ask you a favour, Father. This is my betrothed, Adhelm Miller, and we wish to get married. We are hoping you might be kind enough to perform the marriage Mass.'

'Welcome to St Mary's, Adhelm,' the priest said solemnly. 'What a fine name you were given at your baptism. Adhelm is a saint I much admire, who is said to have preached the word of God in many a churchyard in this shire. But I'm sure you are both aware that the church forbids weddings in Advent.'

'Advent ends on Christmas Eve I believe, Father,' Jess reminded him. 'Would you be able to bless us with a Mass on that day?'

Father Michael smiled. 'That is a blessed day indeed, being so close to the birth of Jesus. But there are various things to clear up before we can settle the matter, so let us sit down together and discuss it. First, though, I would like to offer you both confessions. I think that if you cannot bring yourselves to attend church in your own village you must have been omitting your duty to God.'

After their duty was done with the priest Addy and Jess left the church and sighed guiltily. 'I felt bad not telling him your mother is my father's cousin,' she confessed. 'But I don't believe God would mind, although I feel guilty that we can't invite your parents to the wedding. Are you sure you don't mind?'

'I don't think they would come anyway. There is no love lost between your father and mine. And I don't know about you but I'm starving,' said Addy. 'Is there a chance of getting some dinner here?'

Jess shrugged. 'I think it's too late. But if we ride to Wolf Hall I'm sure Ham will feed us something, even if it's only leftovers. Also, I really want to see Isabel.'

'We should invite her to the wedding,' Addy suggested. 'And I might get to meet John Seymour at last. But first I need to find some oats for the horse or it will never get us back to Avebury.'

But when they went to the stable the Prioress was there, having been called by the groom, who was wondering whose horse it was in the spare stall. Editha was delighted to see Jess and to meet Addy and the groom quickly supplied some fodder for the horse.

'If you have ridden from Avebury, you must be hungry too,' the Prioress said. 'Have you eaten anything today?'

Jess explained that they were going to Wolf Hall to visit Isabel before they turned for home. 'I want her to come to our wedding. It would not be the same without her. Do you think she will come, ma'am?'

Editha frowned. 'She is rather a hermit these days. But she does come here for Mass and she has mentioned both of you. I think she might be pleased that two of her protégées are to marry.'

'But she might be upset that I won't be returning as her maid of the chamber.'

The Prioress shook her head. 'No, she doesn't bear grudges. Anyway, you should go to Wolf Hall now and eat some of that cook's great food! But don't stay too long. It gets dark early on these December days.'

Wolf Hall was busy with workmen making the finishing touches to the hunting tower when Jess and Addy rode down the new road, remarking on the changes. 'John Seymour must have come into some money. I wonder if he is at home?'

'We should know when we get to the stables,' said Jess. 'If Atlas is there then Master John is at home.'

Atlas was absent but Snowflake was in her stable, indicating that Isabel was at home – and as they approached the rear door of the manor house, the lady herself came walking up from the new garden holding the hand of a little girl with a noticeable limp and frowning at the young couple approaching her. But her frown was quickly replaced by a call. 'Jess! And Jankin! It is you, is it not?'

Jess ran up to make a brief curtsy. 'Yes, ma'am, but he is really called Addy! And is this Margaret, walking like a princess?' She squatted down to the girl's level. 'I don't suppose you remember me, do you, Meg? But I remember you very well!'

Isabel raised her eyebrows at the man she called Jankin. 'Addy? Where did that name come from?'

He grinned. 'It's short for Adhelm – a local saint. Father Michael was very impressed with the name. I didn't think it would go with my soldiering so I chose something tougher when I enlisted.'

'And what were you doing down here with Father Michael? No – don't answer that, let us ask Ham if there are any leftovers and take them to the fire in the hall. How long can you stay?'

Little Margaret had shyly allowed Jess to take her other hand and they all walked towards the kitchen door, which as usual was firmly closed, but a good cloud of smoke rose from the chimney. Ham made his usual bellow as the door was opened but he soon changed his tune when he saw who was there.

'We have starving guests coming to the hall, Ham,' Isabel said. 'What can we offer them? Something warm, I think.'

'Mulled wine, milady, and some pasties maybe. Nat will bring them through. I don't dare to leave these cakes.' He waved a ladle at Addy. 'You are the soldier my lady watched marching down the Marlborough marketplace, aren't you? I never forget a face.'

'Remarkable,' Addy nodded. 'And that was when I had no beard.'

'Where is your big brother, Margaret?' Jess asked when they were settled around the fire. 'And your father?'

'They are off in the forest somewhere,' Isabel said. 'Johnnie loves to ride on John's pommel. He wants to be a knight. I hope he doesn't beat his father to it. There would be a terrible fuss.' She smothered a laugh.

Jess cast a sideways glance at Addy with a raised eyebrow. When he nodded, she broached the subject of the wedding with Isabel. 'We went to see Father Michael because Addy and I are getting married and he has agreed to perform the wedding Mass.'

A burst of clapping came from Isabel. 'Oh! Congratulations! How lovely! I am very happy for you.'

Jess smiled and nodded. 'Thank you.' She took a deep

breath. 'We are rather hoping that you might come to the wedding, ma'am. We both owe you so much and we would love you to be there. It will be on the morning of Christmas Eve.'

Isabel seemed to shrink into herself and pulled her wimple over her scar. 'Oh, I don't think so. Forgive me but I don't like to be among strangers. Father Michael lets me hear Mass from the church clerestory and take communion after everyone else has gone.'

'Oh.' Jess felt her heart shift in her chest. 'I'm afraid we have to say our wedding vows outside on the church porch but there will be the wedding Mass in the chancel afterwards. Perhaps you could share that? Only my parents are coming so there won't be a crowd. It won't be the same if you aren't there.'

Nat entered the hall wearing a fresh apron and carrying a tray of delicious-smelling pasties and a jug of fragrant wine. He wore a white cook's cap and surprisingly his scar stood out with distinction on his left cheek. 'Shall I put this on a stool by the fire, milady?' he asked.

'I'll fetch a stool,' Addy offered and Isabel nodded with a distracted frown, obviously still pondering the invitation. 'We could come to Wolf Hall for your blessing if you prefer,' he said as he positioned the stool.

Isabel shook her head. 'There is to be a celebration for Master Edmund's coming of age on Christmas Eve,' she revealed. 'It will mark the opening of the tower too if it is ready and all the household will be coming to inspect it and tour its rooms and facilities. There will also be a bonfire outside and Sherish wine for the village folk to raise a toast. Why do you not come to Wolf Hall after your wedding and stay the night here? Or are you inviting other people after the Mass?'

Jess thanked Nat quietly as he placed the tray down and bowed his way out of the room. Then she asked Isabel, 'Will you be at the party, ma'am?'

'No, it is being arranged by Master John and the steward. But you could visit me beforehand and settle yourselves in one of the guest chambers ready for your wedding night. How does that sound?'

Addy looked at Jess enquiringly and she nodded with enthusiasm before helping herself to a pasty. 'As long as you think Edmund would not mind us invading his party,' she said.

Isabel waved away any doubt. 'I'm sure Edmund will think "the more the merrier". You will be very welcome; I shall see to that. Now you must eat up those pasties and be getting on your way. The winter light is short and the nights are ghostly on the Downs.'

63

Wolf Hall

22nd December 1429

'I HAVE HEARD NOTHING from the Duke of Gloucester since that wretched Bill went through in the Parliament and I fear I am well out of favour. Just when we need his hunting patronage to start so that we can pay the men for their great work on the tower!' John Seymour banged his clenched fists down on the office desk, making Alice jump.

'Steady, John!' she warned. 'We haven't hit the bottom line yet. And the wine business is keeping us in funds. You might think about paying a visit to your father-in-law in Bristol. He has sent you Sherish wine for Edmund's party and writes that the vintners are making excellent profits from the Gascon trade these days. Shipping is much quicker and cheaper from there than from the Spanish Mediterranean.'

John frowned across at her, standing as she did in front of her high writing desk, where she preferred to do the accounts. 'You are ever the businesswoman, aren't you? Does Mark Williams know he is doing deals with a woman?'

'Of course not! It is all done in your name. But his advice is a good idea, do you not think?'

'Yes, but we can't go into the Gascon trade because the

duke says England is about to lose control of Gascony and its wines will be restricted to French consumption. So, we'll stick to the Sherish trade for now, I think.'

'If you believe what the duke says.'

'I have to, Alice, if I'm going to get his hunting trade. That's what the tower is for, after all.'

She gave him a reluctant nod and remarked, 'Don't lose faith in Mark Williams though, will you? He's pulling in coin that his daughter Isabel will inherit.'

John cast her a knowing glance. 'That is too true, mistress, only too true.'

At this moment there was a knock on the door and Edmund Seymour entered without waiting for permission. 'Congratulations, cousin! The hunting tower is a masterpiece, inside and out! And the women are making a great job of the decorations. This party will be a triumph! Is Isabel coming?'

'I have no idea,' his cousin replied. 'Is she, Alice?'

'I don't think so. Her shepherdess chamber girl is getting married on Christmas Eve and she's invited them to stay the night here, so they will also be coming to your party, Master Ed. I couldn't really stop them.'

Edmund waved an untroubled hand. 'Why should you, Alice? I like the shepherdess but I haven't met her intended. What is he like?'

'None of us have met him, except Annie and Nat,' said John. 'Apparently Isabel found him in the forest during a downpour while I was away and brought him to Wolf Hall to dry off. He turned out to be a very skilful archer and she took him to a recruiting sergeant at Marlborough Castle, who scooped him up and marched him off to fight the French. Isabel always likes to favour the underdog.'

'What is his name? Do we know?' Edmund's gaze swept from John to Alice but both shook their heads. 'Right – well, I'll go and ask Isabel.'

As he turned to leave Alice said, 'Was there something else you wanted from us, Ed?'

'No, not really. I just wanted to say how much I admired the tower. I've had a good look round and it really is a fine building. Congratulations, John.'

John nodded. 'Thank you, Ed. And is all well at Hatch Beauchamp?'

'Yes, fine. Oh – and I nearly forgot!' Edmund pulled a bulging purse out of the dagged sleeve of his short houppelande. 'Hatch pulled in an unusually healthy sum for its sheep fleeces this year. I thought some of it should be used for my party. You might consider buying some sheep next year, John.' With a wide grin he dropped the purse onto John's desk and left the room.

John picked it up and opened the neck. Out of it poured an impressive pile of silver groats. 'Who would have thought?' he asked Alice. 'This should keep the carpenters quiet for a while!'

Isabel greeted Edmund with open arms. 'It's been weeks! We've all missed you, Ed!' she exclaimed. 'Have we not, Johnnie?'

The four-year-old Seymour heir had run from his toy horse and tugged at Edmund's sleeve. 'Where have you been, Uncle Edmund? Pa says I'm to get my own pony!'

Edmund eased away from Isabel's embrace and shook the boy's rather grubby hand off his smart fur-trimmed houppelande jacket. 'That is very good news, Johnnie! And how is little Meg?' He swung the other child up onto his hip. 'Have you been looking after your mother?'

Little Margaret looked at him shyly. 'No, Uncle, she looks after me.'

'Evie, could you take the children to the other room, please?' Isabel said to the young minder who had been playing dolls with Margaret. 'They can play there until dinnertime.'

Despite Johnnie's protests, Evie managed to collect up their toys and usher the two children out of Isabel's chamber with foodie promises. 'It is the last day of fasting and if you eat your blancmange first there are honey cakes for you at dinner. I saw them in the kitchen earlier!'

Isabel smiled. 'Evie is such a blessing, Ed! I can't think how I ever did without her! Now, how are your party arrangements going?'

'Very well. The tower is beginning to look like Savernake Forest under Annie's instructions. But why are you not coming to my celebration? You broke your hermitage for the king's mother, why can you not break it for me?'

'Because meeting with Queen Catherine was a fund-raising effort for a great humanitarian cause and a great charity.'

'Well, my party is a great celebration for one of your favourite people and it won't be the same without you.'

'Are you one of my favourite people, Ed? I never knew that!' Her smile persisted.

He slapped his own cheek. 'I meant you are one of my favourite people, Izzy! Call it a slip of the tongue.'

'Well, I'm still not coming. I don't like being among a lot of people, you know that, and anyway Jess the shepherd is marrying her sweetheart and I am entertaining them.'

'Yes, so I heard, but they are also coming to my party, so why do you not come with them? Everyone there will know all about your injury and no one will mention it. I really want you to be the lady of the manor, Izzy!'

'I am still lady of the manor, Ed, and I intend to remain so. Even John cannot deny that and his mistress does not even try to. So, you should come up to my chamber when Jess and Addy arrive and we can drink to their health and happiness together before the party begins. I would like it very much if you did that.'

64

Avebury to Marlborough, Easton and Wolf Hall

23rd December 1429

ONE OF MATTHEW'S FELLOW farmers had made an agreement to lend him his sturdy skewbald carthorse over Christmas. 'It's a three-day holiday, Matt,' he said cheerfully, 'and I'll get paid for it! Make sure you get my bobbish horse back by Holy Innocents' Day though, because I'll need him for sowing if the ground doesn't freeze.'

So, Nell and Jess sat up beside Matthew on the high driving seat of the old farm cart and Addy followed on his borrowed horse as they set off at first light from the Avebury Henge with Star tucked up in the back.

The road was surprisingly clear and they made good progress across the wild and windy landscape of the Marlborough Downs. At the entrance to the town, the royal castle stood proudly beside an ancient and abandoned motte and bailey. As they drove along the defensive wall and past the crenelated gatehouse, Addy gave a military salute to the place where he had lied about his name and age and joined the latest recruits to the army of English archers, who were swiftly marched off to defend the territory that the present little king's father had so valiantly conquered and died to increase.

Matt steered the cart under the Christmas-ribboned green bush that hung over the arch, which signified the entrance to the adjoining Castle Inn, where Jess's parents intended to stay the night. After stabling the horses and the cart, Star and the packs and bags were removed and safely installed under a trestle table in the taproom, before they ordered a substantial dinner and mulled wine to warm them.

Matt seemed to be spending money like he was a landowner rather than a tenant but when Jess questioned it, he just shook his head and said, 'I have been saving for my daughter's wedding and I am happy to be spending what I've saved.'

When they had enjoyed a large and tender leg of a spring-born lamb and consumed the contents of two jugs of fragrant wine, Nell was keen to wander around the market before it closed for the Christmas holiday and Addy and Jess went to the stables to load their saddlebags onto his horse. They were to ride to Wolf Hall, where they would stay the night and Isabel Seymour had promised to lend Jess the dress she wore for her own wedding five years before.

Nell had not stemmed her tears when she kissed Jess an early goodnight. 'It must be the wine,' she gulped, with her arms around her daughter. 'I'll have to buy a kerchief in the market because I know I will be weeping a fountain tomorrow!'

'You cry all you like, Ma. I know it's because you love me. But I'm not going anywhere and we'll be back at Henge after Christmas, as soon as we've returned the borrowed horse and bought Addy another. Then life will return to normal.'

Nell smiled through her tears. 'It will not be normal for you, Jessie. And I'll be hoping to be a grandmama within the year!'

During the afternoon in the hall of the hunting tower at Wolf Hall there was a rush of activity; branches of holly, bright with red berries, were picked in the forest and brought in on ox-drawn sledges, balls of green and white mistletoe had been removed from the bare fruit trees and slung from the ceiling and all the pewter wine cups and spoons were polished to a blinding shine as they decked the two trestles that would seat the guests at Edmund Seymour's coming of age. All the household servants, including the senior grooms, falconers and kennelmen, who had ever served Edmund during his years at Wolf Hall, would be present and, with the exception of the baby Bridget, the Seymour children would be allowed to attend at the start of the party when the toasts would be drunk and the speeches made. By the time the daylight began to fade and the lamps were lit, everything was ready for Christmas Eve. All that remained to complete a magical atmosphere was music and a band of minstrels had been booked to arrive from Marlborough the following day.

Jess and Addy rode into the stable yard to find that the grooms and lads had been let off and so before the light died, they had to see to their mount's oats and fill a hay-bag to see him through the night. It was almost dark by the time they carried the saddlebags along to the new manor house staircase.

'I hope Isabel is here after all this,' Jess said, dumping her saddlebag down beside the lady's door and still feeling the effects of the early start and the mulled wine.

The door opened with a flourish and Isabel's arms were wide with welcome. 'Here you are at last!' she cried. 'The bride and groom in all their glory!'

Jess tripped over the saddlebag and almost tumbled into the lady's arms. 'Not very glorious, I'm afraid, but looking forward to becoming that way! I'm so sorry if we're late.'

'Come in, come in!' Isabel exclaimed. 'No time of arrival was ever fixed but there is one problem. You have to try on my wedding dress, Jess, and it cannot be in front of the bridegroom. So Addy, Evie here will show you your chamber and after we have tried the dress and decided whether or not it suits the bride I will send Jess back to you and you can go down to supper with the rest of the family. They are all keen to see you and I have agreed to let them have you for a while – I hope you don't mind?'

Addy and Evie disappeared down the passage, while Jess stepped carefully over the offending saddlebag. 'I don't know why but I had a dream that the dress was red.'

Isabel took her arm and drew her over to a dressing pole, draped with a white sheet. 'Your dream was right, Jess. It is red. Have a look.' She pulled the sheet off the pole to reveal a full-skirted gown of red satin, trimmed with cream lace. 'There is just one problem though. I was married in the summer and satin is not really a winter fabric. We can't have you dying of cold so I thought you could borrow John's mother's rather old-fashioned cote-hardie, which is lined with fur.'

Jess took one look at the beautifully embroidered and fur-trimmed garment and then eyed the long woollen smock she was wearing and suddenly felt way out of her station. 'Oh no, I couldn't wear that, my lady. I wouldn't feel right. And the dress is too good for me too really, but I can't wait to try on! Red is my favourite colour.'

'Nonsense! You are going to be the bride, a woman on the most important day of her life, and red is definitely the colour to wear!'

Jess and Addy rode out at dawn the next morning, in order to give themselves time to change and prepare for their wedding, which was scheduled for the Terce bell at the ninth hour. Unbeknown to Jess and Addy, Isabel had sent a stable lad to Easton with a message to ask the Prioress if her friends could leave their horse and dog in her stable and use somewhere in her house to change from their riding clothes and Prioress Editha had kindly agreed. Also, they were told that the church had been opened well before the due time so that early arrivals might wait out of the chilly December wind. Jess had carefully packed the red wedding dress and hoped any creases would iron out in the two hours before the Terce bell.

Curiously word had spread around the town that there was to be a Christmas Eve wedding and a number of the local women and girls had come to the churchyard to watch the ceremony, so when Jess's parents arrived in their cart and all dressed up in their best clothes, to their surprise a few voices shouted best wishes. But the best chorus of cheers arose from a group of pilgrim men gathering for the next part of their journey – a long walk to Salisbury, on their way to Southampton and a ship to France. Addy, who had seen many such sights in French villages during his years as a soldier, sent blown kisses and waves of thanks to these hardy souls.

So that Addy should not see his bride in her finery before the wedding, the Prioress was kind enough to help Jess into the beautiful red dress and tie the laces at the back, and when she told the bride that she looked beautiful, the shepherdess appreciated her keen enthusiasm. 'Thank you, my lady, you are very kind. And my mother has made me a beautiful circlet of white linen roses, which I hope I have managed to avoid squashing in my saddlebag. Could you kindly arrange them on my head when I have brushed my hair?'

'Yes, of course. This is beautiful!' Prioress Editha was admiring the circlet. 'But what will you wear to keep warm? There is a cold wind outside, you know, and satin is not a warm fabric.'

Jess shrugged. 'My lady Isabel offered me the use of a cote-hardie that belonged to her mother-in-law but I could not imagine wearing it. I think I will just have to shiver. I am used to cold weather, being a shepherd.'

'Would you consider wrapping a white chasuble around your shoulders? Just for the outside ceremony. You could remove it for the wedding Mass.' A chasuble was a part of the nun's habit and Editha lifted a white shawl-like wrap off a nearby peg and offered it to Jess. 'We could try it before I put the circlet on. I think they would look good together.'

When the Terce bell began to ring and Jess walked out of the Prioress's house she was more than grateful for the protection of the chasuble and did not care that she looked rather like one of the nuns that were hurrying to answer the call to Terce. Addy, however, waiting at the porch, raised his eyebrows when she arrived and murmured, 'Have you taken the veil?'

Jess lifted her head to give him a look of reproach and muttered her retort. 'Just wait until the nun strips off!'

As the only person within hearing distance, Father Michael's lips twitched briefly before beginning the wedding ceremony.

When the bride and groom returned to Wolf Hall as man and wife a cheer rose up from the stable lads, who would not let them attend to their horse but ordered them off to the new tower where the house servants were preparing a special spread in the beautifully decorated ground-floor hall. But Jess was determined to visit Isabel first, to thank her for the dress and tell her all about the wedding.

However, Isabel had a surprise for the two newlyweds. 'I was there!' she crowed when they began their account. 'While you were making your vows outside, I was riding into the Prioress's yard and slipping around to the vestry door to climb the stairs to the clerestory, as I do regularly for morning Mass. And there you were at the chancel steps with Father Michael. You both looked very serious as he intoned all that Latin! And even your lovely dog was allowed to attend! She was so quiet and interested, sitting beside you like a bride's maid. I blessed the priest for allowing her to be there.'

'Poor Star,' said Jess. 'She has gone back to Avebury now, in the cart with my parents, and we are not apart very often so she will be sad. But it's only for a day and a night.'

'Of course we didn't understand a word of the Mass. Do you, ma'am?' Addy enquired.

Isabel sighed. 'I appreciate the language but I confess I don't completely follow it. The priests who do are clever though, aren't they? And you looked marvellous in my red dress, Jess! Perhaps you should keep it.'

Jess looked aghast. 'Oh no, milady! I could never do that. It was wonderful just to wear it for a few hours.'

'Shall I be able to untie the laces this time? Am I allowed to do that now that we are married?'

Addy's question had come with an eager grin and was answered with a knowing smile by Isabel. 'Now that you are married you may do whatever pleases you both, and I am sure you will enjoy a happy and fruitful life together.'

Jess exchanged a meaningful glance with her new husband and smothered a giggle.

The newlyweds returned their saddlebags to the chamber they had slept in chastely the night before and lustily agreed to begin that 'fruitful and happy life together' before they went off to the party, which they knew was being prepared not for them but for Edmund Seymour's coming of age.

65

Wolf Hall

January and February 1430

At Westminster the royal Council, and the Duke of Gloucester in particular, had organised a pared-down coronation ceremony and banquet for the little king, which had taken place at the start of November in the previous year, and shortly before the following Easter Henry the Sixth was to set sail for France to prepare for his crowning in Paris. As a result, the duke had lost his title of Royal Protector and become officially Regent of England for the duration of the king's absence. So, it was a letter from the office of the Regent which finally gave John Seymour the news he had been hoping for. The Duke and Duchess of Gloucester wished to spend time in February hunting in Savernake Forest, along with several members of the royal household. So, it was a happy Seymour who immediately sent for the Head Forester in order to get a briefing on the status of the Savernake wolves, knowing that they would be the Regent's principal reason for coming.

Jem Freeman chewed his lip, considering his answer. 'March would be better, Master,' he said, 'but of course that would mean hunting in Lent, which perhaps his grace would not want to do. So, February I suppose it must be. Last time we spoke, the duke had a particular interest in the alpha male, did he not?'

'The alpha male is a must, Jem. How much would his death disturb the rest of the den? And is there an obvious alpha heir?' John mentally crossed his fingers, hoping for a positive answer.

Jem frowned. 'There is an heir, if you remember the pup with the black stripe on his nose that gave the duke the glaring look when we last visited. He's been harrying his father lately and I think there might have been some scraps between them.'

John interrupted with an anxious question. 'I hope they haven't scarred that lovely sand-coloured pelt. That would throw a hammer on the hunt!'

The Head Forester made a face. 'I'll go and take a look if you like. I haven't checked on them for a while.'

John responded anxiously. 'Yes, Jem – good idea. Keep me informed.'

Compared to his arrival with the little king five years before, the duke travelled with a smaller entourage, aiming not to attract too much attention. Nevertheless, as well as the royal couple's squire and lady of the chamber, Humphrey's friend and astrologer Roger Bolingbroke and Eleanor's chaplain, John Home, there were also two grooms and a four-man escort. And as the grooms and escorts could be housed in the stable accommodation, that meant the royal entourage had the run of the new apartments.

'Well, this is a considerable improvement on the rather rundown manor I recall from my last visit, John,' the duke commented as they enjoyed a comfortable supper in the tower hall. 'But I am so sorry to hear that your wife does not entertain visitors.'

'It is indeed a great pity, your grace, but she does not like to expose her unfortunate facial scars to anyone save her servants and her confessor. Nevertheless, she is a happy mother to her children and enjoys their company. So, she is not lonely.'

'How many children are there, John?' the duchess asked.

'There are three in the nursery at the moment but it won't be long before young Johnnie Seymour will need to come out into society and get an education.'

'How fortunate you are to have an heir. How old is he now?' There was an unmistakeable note of envy in Eleanor's voice.

John knew the duchess to be still childless following her marriage to the duke and was careful to word a tactful reply. 'He is five, going on six, your grace. Thinks he knows everything but cannot yet read well enough to discover he does not.'

'Well, may he live long and profit from the process of learning. Would your wife enjoy the visit of a sympathetic woman, I wonder?'

'I will enquire of course, but she is very adamant.'

Duke Humphrey grew impatient. 'Now, let us discuss the matter of the hunt. Is it possible for Eleanor to do any hawking while we are here, John? She is much enamoured of the sport.'

'My brother Edmund will be here tomorrow, your grace, and I think he will bring his sparrowhawk with him. He would be very willing to accompany you and your lady-in-waiting, madame. Sadly, moulting time has begun for many types of hawks and falcons but our Master of the Mews would be able to find you one that has not started yet.'

'Thank you, John. I would enjoy that.' The duchess turned to include her husband. 'But I would also enjoy following the wolf hunt.'

John's frown indicated that he did not approve of her suggestion. 'Hunting wolves is not really a spectator sport, my lady,' he said. 'I would rather you didn't.'

At this outright refusal Eleanor sent a glare at her husband for support but received none. 'And I would also rather you didn't,' the duke confirmed. 'Wolves are dangerous and unpredictable and on this occasion I do not want any extra followers, not even my lovely wife.'

66

The Wolf Hunt, Savernake Forest

February 1430

'WOLVES HUNT AT NIGHT and so we must take to the forest with torches in order to reach their territory before sunrise.' Jem Freeman had come to the tower hall to brief the duke, his squire and John Seymour. 'Be ready to depart an hour before Prime. If you wish I will come to the tower earlier to rouse you?'

'I am usually up before Prime but an earlier call would be helpful, just in case,' the duke said.

'Certainly, your grace.' Jem made a mental note. 'Then we will take an hour at the trot to reach wolf territory but there might be contact with the pack before that. However, we won't release the dogs if the alpha male is not among them. If he is, then the hunt is on! If not, we ride on to the den, where the dogs will get to work because the wolves will try to defend their young and we will need to cut the alpha out of the pack and put him on the run.'

'Obviously that would be preferable,' said John. 'But what if he takes backup with him?'

'Again, that's where the hunt dogs come in. Some of them will cut them out and the handlers will deal with them;

hopefully send them back to the den. Any that persist in cutting back to their leader will have to be dealt with first. That is the most difficult and exciting part of the chase. We need to get the alpha male isolated so that he has to turn at bay. That is where you come in, your grace. You will be carrying the spear and the first thrust is yours. Preferably through the chest or under the front leg so as not to spoil the pelt.'

'I have done this many times on boar and deer hunts, but this is my first wolf,' the duke admitted. 'I will do my best.'

'Well, the second thrust will be Master Seymour's and he will also carry a spear.' Jem gave John an enquiring glance and he nodded agreement. 'But of course you will both want to take care not to spoil the beautiful coat.' He doffed his cap. 'Very well then, sirs. I will see you in the early morning.'

Heedless of breaking the slumber of the rest of the Wolf Hall household, a huntsman sounded his horn in the torchlight outside the tower. John appeared from the manor house within minutes and was closely followed from the tower by the duke and his squire, who had arrived from the stables. Their horses waited, tacked up and ready, and the grooms handed them their spears, which they pushed into one of the sheaths on their belts. A jewelled sword hilt showed above the top of the duke's second sheath, whereas John's sheltered a shorter and plainer poniard blade. Both men wore plain, dark hunting gear but the duke's was highlighted with gold braid and a white swan badge. In a tight two-by-two formation, with torches lit before and behind, the cavalcade trotted off towards the road that led down to the bridge over the Bedwyn Brook.

'Where are the dogs, Forester?' Duke Humphrey called over his shoulder to Jem.

'They went on ahead, your grace. We'll catch them up, as it's quicker on horseback.'

'What breed of dogs are you using?'

'Six wolfhounds and ten greyhounds. The greyhounds sniff them out and sort them out and the wolfhounds hunt the game into bay. We're bringing no mastiffs so the endgame is yours, your grace. Nice and clean to preserve the pelt.'

'Very good,' nodded the duke. 'Just as I like it.' He turned to his host. 'Where did the wolfhounds come from, John? Ireland?'

'No, sir, from Wales. They still hunt wolves regularly on the Welsh border but they're becoming sparse. They continue to breed the hounds though, mainly for the French market. Wolves remain a big nuisance to farmers over the Sleeve.'

'But not here?'

'No, because wolves like deer meat and at present we have too many deer in Savernake, so we regularly push them over into wolf territory to keep the packs well fed and stop them harrying farm stock. We call it "The Game Game", sir.'

'Ha! Very amusing, Master Seymour!' The duke's teeth gleamed in the torchlight as they crossed the Bedwyn bridge.

In less than an hour the greyhounds were beginning to bay and the huntsmen released them from their leashes. The cavalcade halted in order to see if any wolves broke cover but there was no sign of them. As the dogs crashed through the dry leaves of a glade, several deer went leaping off into the thick undergrowth and after a few minutes the huntsmen blew their horns to bring the dogs back onto their leads.

'No wolves here then,' said John. 'Let's ride on.'

It had been a moonless night but as they set off again there was just the hint of dawn light creeping through the spring green of the forest canopy and with it at last came the tantalising sound of a wolf howl.

'It sounds like the night's hunting is over, sir – for the wolves anyway,' said Jem, easing back to address the duke. 'I was going to suggest a pause for refreshment as I have cakes and ale in my pack but that howling means the pack is gathering to return to the den and unless some of them have made a kill, they'll all be off. So, I think we should ride at speed to see if we can intercept them.'

'By all means!' Duke Humphrey was clearly keen. 'We'll follow your lead.'

Riding at speed in the dim forest was not without dangers and Jem sensibly took it at a steady canter, leading the way down a rough track in the direction of the howling sound. As it grew louder, he stopped and held up his hand, dropping his voice. 'I think they're nearly within earshot. Keep the dogs quiet men. One of you lads should go forward without dogs and see if he can get a view of the pack, then report back.'

They waited on tenterhooks until the boy reappeared and ran up to Jem. 'There are six wolves and they're demolishing a deer fawn. I think they're too busy to listen for anything.'

'Any sign of one with a sandy-coloured coat? He should stand out among the grey ones.' When the lad nodded, Jem gave a thumbs-up sign to the duke and John. 'Right, wolfhounds go in with the dogs and cut him out of the pack. Don't let him follow the rest. We want him running on his own.'

For some minutes the hunters struggled through thick undergrowth, jumping fallen tree branches and sometimes scattering smaller woodland creatures such as squirrels and weasels. They did not catch sight of the alpha wolf until they hit open ground, when his sandy coat suddenly caught the rising sun, which penetrated the bare canopy as he raced along with the wolfhounds close behind.

'Tally-ho! There he is!' cried the duke triumphantly. 'What a beauty!'

'He's not in the bag yet though, your grace,' warned Jem. 'Not until they get him at bay!'

As if his warning had been heard, at the top of the rise the trees suddenly gave way to a thick coppice of thorny brambles, where the wolf was forced to flounder and turn as the thorns caught in his fur. The duke began to mutter about damage to the pelt and brought his horse to a halt. 'This will do for a baying, I am going in,' he declared, dismounting and beckoning his squire to take his horse.

Jem and John exchanged glances but John's frowning shake of the head kept the Forester silent as Duke Humphrey unsheathed his spear and began to make a slow and steady approach to the wolf, waving his weapon to threaten the hounds that were growling for the kill. Their handlers hurried up to grab them and attach the leashes. Meanwhile the amber eyes of the sandy-coated wolf were fixed balefully on his approaching nemesis, who trod carefully on ground still slippery from a recent shower.

Behind him John made silent preparations to take over if necessary, experiencing sudden memories of the boar hunt nearly five years before, when he had made the second and fatal thrust of the spear. That successful lunge had won him a vital interview with the powerful duke but somehow he suspected that same man would not wish for him to do it again. Nor did he think he would have the heart to do it, reading as he did such a desperate desire for life in those wide, flaming wolf's eyes.

There was really no need for concern. Humphrey's lust for his golden wolf-skin was driving his aim; the spearhead that left his hand buried itself without falter in the heart of the beast. Those golden flames gradually flickered out and the legs which had supported that rare and desirable pelt lowered it gently to the ground.

67

Wolf Hall

February 1430

THE ROYAL PARTY STAYED three more days and gathered a dozen deer carcasses to swell the larders of the royal palaces. There were also several visits to the forest by Duchess Eleanor and her small entourage to fly the hawks and falcons available for ground and flying game. Edmund had arrived with his newly trained sparrowhawk, which excelled itself from Eleanor's wrist, much to her delight.

'What have you called her, Edmund?' she asked when they first met and the bird sat patiently hooded on her glove in apparent contentment. 'She is beautiful with her barred chest feathers!'

'I named her Duchess, your grace. To celebrate a certain meeting years ago between a callow youth and a glamorous lady.' Eleanor gave an appreciative laugh and brushed the compliment away. Edmund glanced around before lowering his voice to change the subject. 'Incidentally, have you met the Wolf Hall steward?'

For a short time the duchess appeared a little puzzled by the sudden change of subject. 'Oh! Yes, she is very efficient.

The household appears well run and our accommodation is very nicely served. It is unusual though, to meet a female steward.'

'Yes, I suppose it is. But then John is an unusual lord of the manor.'

'Wolf Hall is an unusual manor altogether, being tucked away in such extensive forest as it is. It houses several unusual people and John is one of them. Has the duke told you that he intends to knight him, following their successful wolf hunt?'

Edmund made a loud exclamation. 'No! He hasn't. Is knighting not the prerogative of the king?'

'Yes, unless it is done by another knight on the battlefield. But then as Regent in the king's absence I suppose the duke considers himself eligible.' Eleanor laughed with Edmund and continued, 'He is going to do it here at Wolf Hall, just before we leave. I wonder if Isabel knows? She is his wife, even if she's a kind of hermit.'

'An eremite, I think she calls it,' Edmund said.

Eleanor showed a puzzled expression before replying. 'A sort of female cross between a hermit and an anchorite, I suppose. I wonder if she will attend the knighting?'

'Have you met her then?' Edmund showed his utter surprise. 'Isabel doesn't usually allow visitors – well, strangers anyway.'

The duchess looked a little guilty. 'Yes, I know, and I'm afraid I rather pulled rank. I followed the little maid up to the lady's chamber and just pushed in. I felt we might have something in common, since I am, like her, considered damaged goods too.'

'Why would you, of all people, be damaged goods, your

grace?' Edmund managed to look surprised, although he knew very well why.

'Princes don't marry their lemen, do they? I am considered a pariah by most of the court. And I thought I might be able to encourage Isabel to consider putting on a brave face, as I do myself.' She shrugged. 'I'm afraid I failed. But she did tell me that her husband was perfectly content with his steward-mistress and so she didn't feel any guilt at closing herself off. It was an interesting conversation – short, but interesting.'

'Does Master John know about it?' Edmund asked.

Eleanor shook her head. 'No, and I'd like it to be a secret between us if you wouldn't mind, Edmund. John just might tell the duke and I'd rather he didn't know. He likes me to do as I'm told and doesn't know, or doesn't notice, that I rarely do.' She gave him an enigmatic smile. 'It may be the death of me one day.'

Isabel said she would not attend the knighting, but she insisted that little Johnnie should go and asked Edmund to make sure the bumptious five-year-old behaved himself.

Standing in the hall of the hunting tower in a white tunic and brown belt with an empty sheath, John Seymour was utterly amazed that the duke intended to keep his promise. Words spoken at their private meeting at Clarendon Palace echoed in his head. 'When you have organised me a wolf hunt and I have acquired a wolf-skin, I might make you a knight.' Words to that effect had been the duke's cold comment, at his first interview spoken with a distinct sneer and a tone tinged with doubt. When John had moved to seal the deal with a solemn kiss of the royal hand, Duke Humphrey's closing words had sent a shiver down his spine.

'That makes you my liegeman, John Seymour, and believe me, I will hold you to all aspects of allegiance and loyalty.'

Now here was the Duke of Gloucester, Regent of England, in his gold-trimmed hunting attire, moving forward, sword in hand, to be true to his word. 'Now, I ask you to kneel, John Seymour,' he ordered in a commanding tone.

John bowed his head. Someone had put a crimson cushion on the floor and he dropped one knee into its forgiving welcome. The sword glittered above his head and for a moment John wondered if it might be used in an ugly slash. Then the duke spoke again. 'John Seymour, in recognition of your loyal service to King Henry the Sixth and to me, his Regent, I hereby dub you a Knight of the Realm.' The flat of the jewelled sword struck each shoulder and the duke stood back. 'Arise, Sir John!'

There was a ripple of applause from the few assembled onlookers and John rose to his feet. 'Thank you, your grace,' he said, his mind racing so that he hardly heard the duke's next words. This had been his aim from youth and he could hardly believe he had achieved it shortly before his thirtieth birthday and without putting himself in military danger.

'Here are your knight's spurs, which confirm your status.' The duke handed the pair of silver spurs to his squire, who knelt to attach them to John's boots. 'And your name and title will soon become known throughout the county, as I hereby appoint you, Sir John Seymour, as the next High Sheriff of Wiltshire, serving for a year from the beginning of March 1431.'

John grew wide-eyed. This was an unexpected honour, which would place the Seymour name on the list of candidates for the Royal Council and among the high society of England. It would also involve a certain amount of unpaid work of a judicial nature. The unpaid side of it disturbed him a little but he made a deep bow and a huge smile lit his face. 'I thank you with a full heart, my lord. It will be an honour to serve my county.'

The Regent's mouth echoed the smile of his new knight. 'Well, Sir John, I said I would hold you to all aspects of allegiance and loyalty, did I not?'

A child's voice piped up from among the onlookers. 'I want to be a knight!' It was young Johnnie Seymour. 'Can I be a knight one day?'

The Duke of Gloucester laughed. 'Ha! Young man, you may have your father's name, but it doesn't follow that you will gain your father's title. You have many years to go before you might qualify for your spurs, young man. But you never know!'

At the door of the tower, hidden from onlookers, Isabel stood well back and watched the formalities take place as her husband received the status he so coveted. There were tears in her eyes as she heard the Duke of Gloucester announce his appointment as a future High Sheriff of Wiltshire.

'Don't these people know that you are a godless creature, John Seymour? If not, they soon will,' she whispered. 'Time will tell.'

GLOSSARY

ague: a common malady – e.g., a cold or cough
barbe: a pleated linen collar worn by nuns and widows
barrow: a long or circular prehistoric earthwork, often containing bones
Bella Court: a palace on the Thames at Greenwich
clerestory: the top story of a cathedral or church, intended to let in light
daub: dried earth, especially clay, used for building (see 'Wattle')
fulling: a process used to 'finish' loom-woven cloth
fulling mill: a machine powered by water for the fulling process
haunch: leg and loin of an animal, especially a term for cooked deer meat
Kalendaries: a community of Bristol monks and scholars who ran a library
kirtle: a dress with tight sleeves, often worn under a sleeveless robe
longhouse: a home built for a farming family and their stock
lymer: a dog run on a leash to scent out prey for hunters
magister: title granted to a university teacher of grammar
manchet: the best 'white-flour' bread served in wealthy homes

manumission: the fee a villein had to pay the lord to leave the manor

matins: the 'hours' of the Catholic church. Bells are rung and psalms are sung to mark Lauds, Prime, Terse, Sext, None, Vespers and Compline. Used by churches and convents but also marked secular time

messuage: a plot of land with a house and extra land and buildings

pottage: basic meal stewed beside the fire in most minor houses

Sherish: wine from southern Spain; basis of modern sherry

tester: four-poster bed, usually with a canopy and curtains

tithes: a form of tax based on ten per cent of a yearly profit

trencher: a thick slice of bread used as a 'plate'; also applies to a platter

Trinitarians: a community of monks and nuns who worship the Holy Trinity

vair: heraldic name for fur, usually shown white on crests

wattle: twigs or stalks mixed with clay to form 'bricks' (see 'Daub')

wyvern: a stone-carved dragon, often found in or on churches

AUTHOR'S NOTES

As I live in Wiltshire, I have plenty of opportunities to visit most of the places mentioned in *The House of Seymour*. Although there is still an inhabited Wolf Hall, it no longer resembles the house of Seymour that features in this book, although there are a few places in the 'messuage' (see Glossary!) where occasional evidence of the fifteenth century pops up in today's house or garden. I am very grateful to Orlando Binny, a descendant of the Seymours, who lives at today's Wolf Hall with other members of his family. He was kind enough to show me around and give me a good description of the surroundings as they might have been in times gone by. Savernake Forest still lies very close to Wolf Hall and can be seen stretching away into the northern distance, as if ready for the galloping hooves of the hunters of the past – easy to get lost in.

There are some interesting exhibits displayed in the Wiltshire Museum in Devizes. I bought a mug with a fascinating selection of the local vernacular printed on the side. Some of the words are now to be found in this book, mostly spoken and translated by Ham, the Wolf Hall cook. I notice that J.K. Rowling also selected a few for use in her Harry Potter books; for instance, 'dumbledore', which is Wiltshire dialect for a bumblebee, but in 'muggle' language was the name of the headmaster of Hogwarts School for Wizards!

The village of Avebury is a place I'd advise any of my readers to visit. The present-day circle, listed as a Henge in the Domesday Book, is where Jess the shepherdess lives on her father's farm and often keeps her flock when not out on the Downs. It is still an amazing feature where sheep safely graze among huge standing stones and is frequently compared to Stonehenge, but I think Avebury's stones give more rewarding glimpses of the lives of the early neolithic residents of Britain. Walking down the avenue of stones leading from the circle to Silbury Hill provokes vivid images of extraordinary events, lived long ago. They also lead the eye to the East Kennet Long Barrow, which dominates the hill beyond the River Kennet and becomes the cause of all young Jess's tribulations. With its domineering entrance stones and the strange entrance hall behind them, it is still a magnet for visitors today.

The final port of call goes to Clarendon Palace – now almost completely destroyed but, in the days of the Seymours, a favourite and expansive royal hunting lodge. Dominating a steep ridge to the east of Salisbury, it was once surrounded by a high fence known as a 'pale' and overlooked the recently completed cathedral with its remarkable spire, which still stands today. But the cathedral rarely welcomed royalty then, because Clarendon was a place where they and their chosen favourites went to 'let their hair down'.

ACKNOWLEDGEMENTS

When I began writing historical novels, my intention was to start at the beginning of the fifteenth century and see where my research took me. And I soon knew exactly how I would start, because in the first year of that century a French princess called Catherine de Valois, who was destined to become both the wife of Henry V and the mother of the Tudor dynasty, was born. So, it was Catherine's extraordinary life story, told in the pages of two books and through the eyes of her fictional maidservant and confidante called Mette, which formed my first historical effort.

My faithful readers might know that I wrote six novels before I completed the fifteenth century and nudged my seventh Tudor novel briefly into the sixteenth century. I took a young Henry Tudor through the prolonged death of his father, Henry VII, and then the happy early years of his reign and first marriage to Katherine of Aragon.

At this stage I decided to avoid the murkier years of Henry VIII's reign, with his five more wives and religious upheaval, and fulfil my original intention, to turn back to the fifteenth century's beginning. So, here we are back in the fourteen hundreds, with a remarkable young woman from Bristol called Isabel, who marries into the House of Seymour and discovers that all is not riches and roses when the partner your father chooses for you is a young landowner, hell-bent on using his lucky inheritances to raise himself into royal circles.

By now you have possibly read John and Isabel's story and may be wondering where I will venture next. Well, it will be set once again in the fifteenth century and as I write this, I do have ideas, but I'm not sure who will feature or where they will be . . . But stay with me, please!

Meanwhile, I'd like to take this opportunity to thank the hard-working experts who have used their various skills to bring this book to life.

Firstly Emily Langford, who brought *The House of Seymour* to life in beautiful blue and gold on the cover and Terence Caven, another designer, whose work made a faded map of old Wiltshire provide a useful guide to the towns and villages mentioned in the Seymour story.

Susan Opie handled the copy editing once more, Rhian McKay took on the early proofreading, marketing was in the hands of Jo Kite and PR was handled by Susanna Peden.

Katelyn Wood was the patient editorial assistant, and for the eighth time, Kate Bradley has been my editorial heroine, encouraging my good ideas and calmly rejecting the rubbish.

Finally, from her Edinburgh office and with frequent and much appreciated trips to London, my great friend and agent Jenny Brown continues to guide my literary efforts with wise words, hugs and humour.